Ogaman: The Birth of a New King

Dami Edun

The Garden of Edun Publishing

Ogaman: The Birth of a New King

Book Cover by Amani Brooker

Edited by Eleonora Kouneni

1st Edition 2024

What Readers Say

"I couldn't put the book down. The emotional depth and character development were so well done that I felt every twist and turn!"

— **Mojo Obadina**

"An epic journey that left me speechless and emotionally invested, with characters that truly resonate—an unforgettable experience!"

— **Tumi Edun**

"The vivid imagery fully immersed me in the story. I can't wait to see where the plot takes Tundé next. This deserves to be adapted for the screen."

— **Darius Johnson**

"Ogaman is a refreshing dive into London life, brilliantly blending humour and cultural elements while keeping the pacing smooth and engaging."

— **Roy Mugera**

To my mum, for always supporting my dreams and inspiring me to write a story I was very passionate about. I hope this novel makes you proud of the son you have raised.

Ẹ ṣé gan. Mo dúpé lọwọ Ọlọhun.

To all my brothers and sisters in the African diaspora, I hope this story inspires you to reconnect with the heritage embedded in your DNA.

If it feels right for your soul.

Acknowledgements

While my name is plastered all over this book, I have to acknowledge the people who helped me over the nearly 7 years it took to transform this project from an idea into the published work you see today. Without them, this would not have been possible.

Firstly, I want to thank my mum. She has been a huge inspiration and guiding figure on this journey. From helping with the publishing process, proofreading the manuscript and editing my Yorùbá translations. In fact, she sparked the entire novel's journey when she suggested I should write a story "for all you London youth to understand." Haha. Love you, Mum!

Big thanks to my sister, Tumi, for her emotional support—particularly during my 2023 spiritual awakening—and for proofreading the entire manuscript. As always, I appreciate your continued support. Love you too.

I would also like to thank Anna Robinson, my writing mentor under the Pen to Print Challenge. Her knowledge and experience helped me bring my ideas to life while structuring my book properly. Thank you to Eleonora Kouneni for her invaluable copyediting and for going above & beyond with her developmental recommendations. Her efforts ensured my novel became a body of work that I'm proud of and excited to release.

Thank you to Darius Johnson and Roy Mugera for offering their valuable time as beta readers for the final manuscript. Blessings to you both, and I hope you enjoy the finished product!

Another shoutout to my friend and old Stratford flatmate, Odain Clarke, for our discussions about writing and storytelling principles. Quickly turning into the good ol' days! Look forward to reading your novel series when it's finished too.

Big ups to London's Black British culture for providing me with a foundation to lean upon, in a country with which we all share a complex relationship. Despite its challenges, I'm proud of the unique, distinct blend of cultures we have created here. Shout out to all the mandem and gyaldem.

Special thanks also go out to Amani Brooker for designing the book cover, Noureen Sultangani-Duch for her positive encouragement after reading the preliminary version, Garry Russell for his guidance and wisdom in helping me reconcile with my experience growing up as an African in the UK, the partnership between London Borough of Barking & Dagenham and the Arts Council for funding my mentorship, Tolani Agoro for affirming me during my Yorùbá identity crisis while finishing this book. I'm grateful to all my friends and family who have influenced or supported me on the journey to writing my first novel.

Blessings to the Yorùbá ancestors for their strength and courage over the last few centuries. It is no small feat to maintain a cultural connection throughout our dark ages, whether that be in Nigeria, Togo, Brazil, Cuba or the United States of America.

Finally, I give thanks to Olodumare for my existence and the necessary wake-up call in June 2023. It gave me the drive required to finish this book and allowed me to answer a deeper calling.

Preface

Ever since my 5-year-old self was introduced to the world of storytelling through titles like The Famous Five and Animorphs, I've wanted to write a book. I also fell in love with the superhero genre as my weekends became consumed by the cartoon adventures of Spiderman, Static Shock and Samurai Jack. Despite my early passion for books, my adolescence eventually got in the way, as well as my desire to become a professional footballer. It didn't quite work out, but I digress!

After graduating from the University of Nottingham with a Master's in engineering, I still felt a deep restlessness about my true calling in life. That was until November 2016, when during a spring clean, I stumbled upon an old notebook filled with dozens of stories I wrote as a kid.

The heartbreaking realisation though? None were ever finished. I vowed to myself from that day on to bring my childhood dream of publishing a novel to life. Soon after, I created the Garden of Edun blog to sharpen my writing sword.

Fast forward to 2018. I was living in Edinburgh and began writing a story about a detective to kick off my author career. But I struggled to get past the first chapter. The passion just wasn't there. A few weeks later, I watched a Hollywood superhero blockbuster that inspired me. Seeing an authentic, nuanced expression of different black communities on screen was monumental. Speaking to my mum on the phone about it, she said something which would change the trajectory of my life forever.

"Maybe you'd enjoy writing a superhero story that you London kids would understand."

Her intuitive words struck an instant chord. Why not create a hero for the London that I know?

A few days later, I put pen to pad—or finger to keyboard—and just wrote whatever came to mind. No planning, just word-vomiting on Evernote. Within an hour, I had what became the foundation for the first chapter of ***Ogaman***. Over time, I added small details to the story piece by piece and fell in love with the process. I was hooked.

While being a childhood superhero lover, I also wanted to explore the complex humanity of those gifted individuals. Can you imagine what your life would be like if you had superpowers? Do you think you would help everyone? Would your selfishness creep in? Would the power corrupt you? Who is worthy to be the moral judge? All these nuances and intricacies regarding the concept of good and evil fascinate me.

What's been even more magical during this process was the rediscovery of my Yorùbá culture. As a British-born Nigerian, a huge chunk of my ancestry has been robbed from me, in a lot of ways, due to many tragedies. But after spending 7 years working on this book, I've reconnected with my heritage in unimaginable ways. Now, I feel much more grounded in the world with that knowledge of Self. Maybe Tundé's story is more similar to mine than I'd like to admit!

Regardless, I hope you enjoy my interpretation of a Black British teenager with superpowers in a dystopian London. Like all great stories, a moment in history sparked the birth of this book, which has changed my life. The rest is history. But for you, the journey is about to begin. I wish you a thoroughly enjoyable read. Bless up!

Chapter ZERO

Before embarking on your journey through the story, it's important to note that many of the characters speak **Multicultural London English**.

As a general guide, *Urban Dictionary* is your friend if you get really confused with any of the slang terms!

Several Yorùbá Orishas are also mentioned throughout the story. Their pronunciations are provided below for clarity:

Olodumare = Oh-low-doo-mah-ray
Shango = Shorn-go
Ọṣun = Oh-shoon
Obàtálá = Oh-bah-tah-lah
Èṣù = Ay-shoo

Happy reading.

Chapter 1

"...AND THAT'S WHY WE need to know the difference between mammals and reptiles."

"Miss Stevens, all this animal stuff isn't gonna help man stack bread, is it?"

The classroom murmured with giggles. Miss Stevens' patience had been wearing thin for the entire lesson. Now, she was on the verge of losing her temper, evident from the vein on her forehead visibly pulsating.

"Well Ton-dee, you may want to become a zoologist or veterinarian one day. Both are very well-paid jobs. So, my biology lessons would be extremely useful in that case."

"How many times, Miss? It's pronounced *toon-day*!" Tundé corrected her.

"Haha, what? Tundé Adeyemi? Working with animals?" called out a hoarse voice. "My man's scared of common cats and dogs you know, Miss."

The classroom gradually erupted into a mixture of taunting laughs and provocative jeers, stirring up tension between Tundé and the boy with the hoarse voice.

"Oi, shut up, Lorenzo! Just cos you don't know how to get gyal, you dickhead," Tundé retorted ironically, since he was clueless about women himself.

A complete loss of control in the classroom followed. Miss Stevens' pupils were so loud that the caretaker mopping in the school corridor came to an abrupt halt. While Tundé and Lorenzo found themselves engrossed in an intense stare-down, Miss Stevens was waving her hands around aggressively to grab the attention of her pupils.

"Okay, silence now class! Boys, you've had your fun," she said sternly. "I expect much better from Year 11s. We are continuing with our lesson RIGHT THIS SECOND!"

I can't believe this wasteman Lorenzo tried to disrespect me again, Tundé thought as he kissed his teeth. *He thinks having that spicy name means he can just par me. Nah, I'm not having it.*

The boys exchanged hostile glares. Lorenzo mouthed the word 'watch' to Tundé, then turned back towards Miss Stevens, who had resumed teaching. Tundé knew it was on. Oh, it was so on!

"Right, now that I have everybody's focus again, let's turn to page 269. We'll be reading about the common animal species found inhabiting the West African coastal region. Interestingly, there's a large dolphin population in the Gulf of Guinea..."

Once the biology lesson ended, Tundé strode out of the classroom with an air of bitterness. At a height just shy of six feet, he possessed a towering figure for his age. His skin bore a warm, rich hue reminiscent of brown cocoa; accompanied by broad shoulders and a slender frame. Tundé was also blessed with a warm, disarming smile, which was nowhere to be seen after his tense encounter with Lorenzo. As he headed for the school exit, Tundé felt a stinging slap across the side of his head. Quick to rage, he turned around with the hunger of a predator in his eyes. However, the feeling soon dissolved into petty annoyance when he realised who it was.

"That's 1-0 to me, bro!" laughed the slapper, who ran towards the school's main entrance.

The school hallway was full of deteriorating wallpaper, damaged furniture and the decaying memorabilia of their minimal past achievements. A distinct smell of must and damp hung in the air. The environment didn't appear to provide its pupils with the best foundation for success.

"I'm getting you back, bruv!" Tundé yelled back in jest, chasing his friend down the corridor.

The boys were running at full speed, so consumed by their little slapping game that they barely noticed the school bell for the end of the day, or the countless pupils that filled the corridor as a result. They weaved their way in and out of them like obstacles on an assault course. Tunde had his eyes firmly set on his target, and just as he was about to catch him...

A loud crash boomed through the hallway, and the noise of chatter that usually drowned out the space quickly turned into a collection of inflammatory taunts and heckles.

"Nah, I wouldn't have that!"

"Rah, you see how my man got floored?"

"Man's taking liberties you know. You should bang him for that!"

The catalyst for all this commotion? An outstretched leg that brought Tundé to an almighty fall, forcing him to hit the floor hard and roll over like a sack of potatoes. Incensed and embarrassed, Tundé hurriedly got to his feet and fixed his ruffled uniform—consisting of a pair of black trousers, a white shirt and a maroon-red blazer with the same coloured tie. Amongst the crowd of onlooking pupils, he noticed that a particular group were enjoying themselves. A little too much. Tundé walked boldly towards them.

"If you wanna step to me, Lorenzo, do it to my face. You pussy!" Tundé shouted at the group. Loudly enough that the headteacher, Mr Bull, heard it from his office on the other side of the building.

Meanwhile, Tundé stood defiantly before the group of three boys. Two were of similar height to himself, while Lorenzo, despite being of shorter stature, was clearly the leader among them. A girl was also present. But not just any girl. One that jolted Tundé to a standstill. Her presence sparked his hormones and caused nausea to swirl around in his belly. The smell of her vanilla-scented perfume filled his nose with delight. Her long, silky black hair complemented her athletic figure.

With a face that peng, any mum in the world would want Laura Thompson as their daughter-in-law, Tundé pondered while lost in his romantic fantasy. Quickly though, the teenager's anger resurfaced.

"Chat to me now then, you wasteman," Tundé boomed as he pushed Lorenzo in the chest. He believed the only way to resolve this type of disrespect was physically.

"Are you dumb?" retorted one of Lorenzo's boys, grabbing Tundé by the scruff of the neck. Then, the other tall boy smacked the side of Tundé's head with a solid fist. He wasn't prepared for this to escalate so fast!

Now, Tundé was dazed. Like a flash bomb had just detonated in his face. Another blow struck him on the chin, sending him tumbling to the ground. He scraped against the uneven corridor floor as he fell, disorientating him further. Instantly, a blizzard of kicks, punches and stomps from Lorenzo and his boys rained in on Tundé. The sounds of bone-to-bone contact were resounding as the pain mounted, to the extent that his mind was disconnecting from his body. Amongst all the gasps and cheers from his peers, Tundé heard distinct voices filter through as he took the beatings.

"Come on, bruv, get up! Don't let him win."

"Bang him! Bang him!"

"What are *you* saying now? *You* wasteman!" shouted Lorenzo.

"Yo get off him, fam. There's bare of you man. Allow it."

Even though Tundé's mind was disassociating, the physical pain had reached an unbearable threshold and a state of panic had set in. He couldn't bear it for much longer.

"THAT'S ENOUGH! GET OFF HIM NOW!" bellowed Mr Bull, breaking through the crowd of pupils. Tundé felt the threatening presence around him slowly disperse as the attacks ceased.

Yo, I really needed that break.

"Bro, you alright?" said the boy who playfully slapped him earlier. Tundé squinted open his rapidly swelling left eye.

"Yeah Remi, I'm good. Why didn't you back me up, fam?"

"Fam, I came back quick time init," Remi pleaded.

"But you know what the M.O. is bro. You're supposed to back your boys whenever there's beef."

Not willing to accept that he may have broken their brotherhood code, Remi continued pleading.

"I ran out the doors, but you didn't come through for *time*. Then I saw people running back into school with bare excitement. I knew suttin' was gwarnin', still."

Remi then pulled up Tundé by the arms and brought him to his feet.

"When I came back in, I saw a big crowd of people with you nowhere to be seen. Then I clocked it was you in there. So boom, now man's here, init."

"Nah, I bet you were shook. You think I would've been too shook to defend you?"

"Come on Tunds, don't move like that. I did what I could," Remi dug in his heels. Just as their falling out was spicing up, there was a timely interjection.

"Tundé Adeyemi. Come with me to my office—now!" signalled Mr Bull, as two large, brawny teachers manhandled Lorenzo and his gang down and escorted them towards the exclusion room.

"Don't worry, Lorenzo and his merry men have gone with Mr Hellier and Mr Roberts. So, that won't be kicking off again. Not under my watch."

As he made his way through the crowd with Mr Bull, Tundé noticed his fellow pupils' responses. A few had sorrowful glances, some were in discomfort. But most were giggling, smiling or taking some form of joy in his defeat, with a select few recording the moment on their smartphones. He hated this treatment. How could they laugh at him? How could they make fun of *him* like this?

Noticing Tundé's unease, Mr Bull intervened. "Everyone: put your phones away and go home, now! School is over."

Feelings of inadequacy and self-doubt filled Tundé's mind. How could he be worthy when he allowed himself to be shamed in front of so many of his peers? As they walked down the hall, Tundé took a peek at Mr Bull. His skin was bright red, the veins on his neck were pulsating and he was breathing heavily.

Oh shit, my man seems vexed. I could get in bare trouble for this, Tundé thought, momentarily breaking away from his superficial worries. As he was in Year 11, he could face serious consequences for fighting on school premises. *For fuck's sake, mum's gonna kill me!*

His mum, Mrs Adeyemi—or 'Fola' as his British teachers frequently called her during parent's evening or whenever they reported Tundé's nuisances—was a typical Nigerian parent. She disciplined him with a mixture of strictness, tough love and religious dogma. Not to mention, of course, the harsh beatings he would get for anything she deemed as unacceptable misbehaviour.

"You must behave as if you're serving Jesos at *all* times, sha!" she would say whenever setting Tundé straight. He dreaded what she had lined up if he got in trouble today.

I'm going straight to the worn-out slipper if she asks me what I wanna get beats with!

Anxious about his fate, Tundé was directed through Mr Bull's intimidating office door. The headteacher helped Tundé into a squishy leather chair, encouraging him to relax into the seat. He then sat down on the other side of his desk, donning a calm but firm facial expression as he faced Tundé.

Ahh, he's about to do an absolute madness init, Tundé thought while tensing up again. The leather material of the chair awkwardly creaked in response. A knock on the door broke the tension steadily building in the office.

"Ah, that should be the nurse," said Mr Bull expectantly. "Please, do come in."

Tundé was confused. He didn't think it was that serious.

A big man like me don't need all of that.

As he turned around to see her walk in, Tundé caught a glimpse of himself in the mirror across the office. He almost sprained his neck having a double-take. As he examined himself in the mirror, shock spread across his face. Tundé's bottom lip was bust. His left eye was dark purple and cut open. His nose had swollen up. He'd been roughed up a lot more than he realised.

How didn't I feel it? Tundé questioned himself, as the pain became even more apparent. A drop of blood fell from his nose and splashed onto the office desk.

"Your adrenaline masked the pain," said Mr Bull, sensing Tundé's concern. He got an approving nod from the nurse, who began to arrange her kit. "I got one of the pupils to call over Nurse Joyce as soon as I saw you come out of that scrap."

"'Old still, luv, it's gunna sting," she said in her thick Cockney accent, as she started to dab and douse Tundé's injuries. It felt like sharp, rusty nails were scraping across his face as Nurse Joyce wiped down his wounds with antiseptic liquid. His body was incredibly tense.

"Let the pain out, son. There's no harm in expressing it," said Mr Bull caringly, noticing Tundé's uncomfortable posture.

"Nah, sir. I... I'm fine," he said, as he struggled in the chair. Mr Bull raised a quizzical eyebrow.

"Sir, I can't afford to be weak out here, you know. If everyone thinks I'm weak, then I'm gonna be pissed."

"Ahem. No swearing here, Tundé."

"Sorry, sir. What I meant is that it's a dog-eat-dog world. The streets are dangerous and anyone can get it. Man has to look tough so nobody thinks they can try me."

Mr Bull nodded his head with understanding. As he paused in thought for a moment, Nurse Joyce continued cleaning Tundé's cuts up, making him writhe in his seat while the leather continued to creak.

"Sorry, it's gunna sting," Nurse Joyce said quietly. "But I'm almost done."

"Tundé, as tough as life out there can be," Mr Bull finally said, "you're only human. It's perfectly fine for you to receive help and express your feelings. Especially pain."

But Tundé was reluctant to show any signs of weakness and maintained his unsettled demeanour—even though tears had forced their way out of his eyes and were streaming down his cheeks. Sensing the teenager's resistance, Mr Bull chose not to probe.

"There you go, love. Hopefully, it gets better over the next coupla days," Nurse Joyce concluded as she packed up her medical kit and headed for the office door. "Take care now."

"Thanks..." said Tundé meekly.

"Thanks, Joyce. See you tomorrow," Mr Bull smiled as she left. When the door clicked shut, however, he swivelled back to face Tundé with the same seriousness with which he started this conversation.

"Now, I'm aware that Lorenzo and his sidekicks went well over the top today. I've decided that they will all be excluded until the start of the GCSE exam period so that this doesn't kick off again. Those boys are too much trouble."

Rah, that's like almost two months! Damn, Mr Bull ain't ramping. But at least I won't have to be around those pricks again.

Tundé anxiously gazed at the headteacher. He seemed in a ruthless mood.

"However," Mr Bull said so gravely that Tundé's insides were filled with butterflies. "You were involved here too. Listen, I know your situation at home is difficult, what with strict parenting and all."

"Strict *Nigerian* parenting, sir."

"Yes, I get that. But from what I've gathered, this whole incident was started by you."

Tundé's drawn-out silence confirmed Mr Bull's accusations. The teenager feared the worst. This was going to create some unnecessary drama in his household. And his mum was already stressed out enough as it was.

"I see potential in you, Tundé. But I'm unsure. From what the teachers tell me, you're not very attentive in class. You're overly boisterous. And you don't seem to demonstrate a passion in anything specific unless it involves an element of destruction."

Tundé's school persona sat somewhere between class clown and playground aggressor. He was a naturally disruptive presence. But he had an incredible knack for not landing into too much trouble for his actions. That was all about to change, though.

"Frankly, I've had doubts about your potential during your time here at Stebon High School. And, because of that, and in addition to what's happened today, I will be excluding you from school for one day. Go home tonight and think about how you want to move forward with school and life. Come back on Friday, and maybe you can start proving me wrong."

Tundé's face dropped and his entire forehead flared up.

I've never been excluded from secondary school before. Mum's gonna kill me, revive me, then kill me again bruv!

"Sir, you know how important this whole school thing is for my mum," pleaded Tundé, who understood the potential ramifications. "I'll do bare detentions to avoid getting kicked out for a day. Allow me!"

"Unfortunately for you, Tundé," Mr Bull responded after a few seconds of deliberation. "I'm going to stick to my decision. One day of exclusion should be sufficient for you to learn from this incident."

Tundé's despair turned into a blind rage. From his point of view, Mr Bull had just screwed him over.

My man's a fucking dickhead you know, Tundé began thinking angrily.

He leapt off his seat and stormed out of the office, without so much as a side-eye at Mr Bull as he slammed the door behind him. Mr Bull wondered whether that would be another young boy from Stebon High who miserably failed to live up to their promise.

Tundé, righteous as ever, walked through the now deserted corridor and towards the bus stop near the school exit. Lingering under his annoyance, though, was a deep sense of worry and regret. He was feeling good before the biology lesson too. As he pushed through the double doors bearing the institution's name, he had a moment of reflection.

This is so peak. Can't get any worse than this, surely?

Chapter 2

"Honestly, I can't believe it's so hot today."

"My phone says it's 27 degrees Celsius. In March! That's mental!"

Tundé couldn't help but eavesdrop on a random conversation happening between a pair of older women. They walked ahead of him as he made his way to the bus stop. It was located on Wharf Way, a busy high road with dozens of corner shops, ethnic grocery stores, beauty salons, takeaway restaurants and other commercial outlets just a few streets away from the main school gates. The bus stop itself sat in front of a patch of grass between two buildings, with a large advertising board hanging over the space.

Rah, those creps are peng, not gonna lie!

Tundé was impressed by the billboard's display of the latest pairs of London x Heritage trainers inspired by the authentic street culture of the city, designed by world-renowned German apparel and footwear brand Ralisad.

Alongside the sting of his injuries, Tundé was irritated by his school shirt sticking stubbornly to his skin. He was sweating profusely due to the unexpected scorching hot March weather. The intensity of the sunrays reached an unbearable point, forcing him to remove his blazer and stuff it in his school bag so he could cool off.

Various scents wafted through the air along Wharf Way, stemming from the diverse establishments that lined the high road. The unmistakable, oily aroma of fried food coming from the nearby Horley's takeaway shop mingled with the earthy scent of fresh vegetables from the market stalls. Meanwhile, the car garage on the other side of the road provided hints of tyre fumes and wisps of smoke from its overheated machinery.

Most of his school peers had gone home or to the local park, meaning that the bus stop was mostly filled with adults. Amidst the background noise of vehicles buzzing down the road and children playing in the nearby park, Tundé could pick up distinct languages being spoken by the older commuters, such was the diversity of this particular area of London.

"Hello, kemon acho? Ami bhalo achi"

"Ẹ kasan, mo wa dada. Ṣé alaafia ni?"

"Can't believe the CCA got us living back 'ere, Shannon. It's awful."

A droning noise grew closer and closer until the bright red D7 bus appeared and parked up at the stop, prompting all the passengers to clamour to the door and jostle to get on first. Tundé strategically positioned himself by the timetable, ensuring he was close enough that he could just squeeze on. Stepping onto the D7, he pressed his London Transit Network (LTN) Pulsecard onto its card reader. It responded with a series of loud beeps and a flashing green light, indicating his status as a schoolboy eligible for free bus rides. Tundé ran up the stairs onto the top deck and dived into his right-hand side pocket to fetch his miCell 6 smartphone. As he navigated around its cracked screen, he clicked on a contact listed in his favourites.

"Hey... wassup, neph," a seasoned but youthful-sounding voice picked up the call.

"Ayy, Auntie Abi!" replied Tundé with a sprinkle of happiness lifting his flat mood. "My g!"

"I told you to call me 'big big g'—remember?" Auntie Abi sounded deadly serious.

"You know you're gassed, init!" Tundé joked heartily.

Abiola Ọṣun had a more casual relationship with her nephew since she was the youngest of his maternal grandparents' children and only had a twelve-year age gap. Because she was mostly raised in the UK, Abiola had a very different perspective on life compared to her older sister, Fola Adeyemi.

"Alright, calm down bro! Anyway, how you doing, Tunds?"

Tundé had a lump in his throat. He knew that sooner or later, he'd have to confess to what happened at school.

"Well, I'm not gonna lie, Auntie. I'm in a bit of a sticky one, still."

"It's okay, I've got a little bit of time. What's happening?"

"Well, basically, erm... remember that guy from my school that I hate bares?"

"Yeah, Larry or something right? Go on."

"Yeah, Lorenzo. Well, him and his wasteman crew, came for me today. So, we kinda got into a little bit of a scrap..."

"Oh, Tundé? Are you okay, sha? What did I say about fighting at school in your last year? Especially with our melanin."

"I know, Abs. I know. I should've allowed the beef."

"Yeah, you should have. But I guess shit happens. What did the teachers decide to do then?"

"Well, the headmaster excluded them pricks for pretty much the rest of the school year. But... they've excluded me for one day. Just for tomorrow, init."

"Oh dear."

"What should I do, Abs?" Tundé said worriedly. "I can't lie, I dunno how to handle this one with Mum."

"To be honest, it's not the *worst* thing in the world. But you defo have to tell her. You shouldn't lie about it, otherwise karma could come back to bite you."

"Please, allow all that mystical stuff, Abs. I just don't wanna stress her out bares. Can you help me?"

"Well, that's my two cents. I'm not gonna get involved, Tunds. It's not my ting. I trust you to handle it and deal with the consequences."

"Okay," Tundé grunted back, disappointed by the lack of support.

"Anyway, I hope you're okay and not too hurt. Take some time to rest tonight and just be honest. It's the best way. Keep your head down too. More trouble will bring more stress."

"Yeah, I'm ite. Thanks."

"Alright, take care, Tunds. I'll speak to you later. Got some things to sort out."

"Cool, in a bit, Abs."

When Tundé hung up the phone, he couldn't help but feel a bitter taste in his mouth. Auntie Abi usually took his side and actively guided him through the worst of times whenever he messed up. But now, she was forcing him to take sole responsibility for his actions. After mulling over all the potential ramifications of telling his mum, Tundé searched for another contact on his phone. Moving fragments of broken screen glass out of the way, he dialled the number.

"What's cracking, bro?"

"Yo, man. My bad about what happened earlier. These things are part of the game though."

Tundé snarled, but since he felt down, he decided to bite his tongue and accept the attempted apology.

"Okay, safe for that, Remi. It's peak though. Bull excluded me from school for tomorrow."

"Ah shit, your mum's gonna kick off, init?"

"Yeah, safe for the reminder, bruv."

"Haha, it's calm, man. I'm sure you'll live!"

"We'll see, bro. We'll see."

"Well, now that you have the day off tomorrow, I may have a likkle opportunity for you, Tunds. Think of it as my way of making up for earlier."

"I'm listening..."

"Basically, you remember that older don from North?"

"Campbell?"

"Nah the other don—Rishi."

"Oh yeah. I remember him, still. What's he saying?"

"Ite boom, there's this new ting that's just started to hit the roads called *bairaff*."

"Bairaff? What the fuck's that, bro?"

A few people on the bus gazed suspiciously at Tundé after his loud retort.

"Yo, let's speak in person," Tundé suggested in a hushed tone. "Man's on the bus right now, and I don't know who could be listening."

"Yeah, you're right you know. I'll buck you at your yard in like an hour?"

"Ite, cool, you just gotta dip before Mum gets back at seven."

"Yeah, that's calm, we got bare time."

"Alright, safe."

"Catch you later bro."

A short while later, Tundé stepped off the D7 at the Crossharbour bus stop along Manchester Road—a vital artery coursing through the Isle of

Dogs in East London, linking every cul-de-sac on the island. He paused for a moment to mindfully observe his surroundings. When he glanced towards the north side of this island, Tundé's attention was captured by the glitz, glamour and riches of Canary Wharf, as its skyline was filled with tall, shiny corporate buildings and countless plush apartment blocks.

Looking in the opposite direction at Cubitt Town, in the southern part of the island, Tundé observed a strikingly different atmosphere of bleakness and underdevelopment. The skyline was marked by ageing council estates, with dilapidated storefronts and weathered community centres lining the streets further. It was devoid of the opulence seen in Canary Wharf.

Over the years, Tundé became accustomed to calling this place home. But whenever he paid close attention to his circumstances, the severe contrast between the different sides of the island caused waves of anger and envy to engulf him.

Why is my family struggling bares, when all them rich dons are living cushty down the road? Fucking pisses me off man.

After turning away from Manchester Road and walking through the backstreets, he entered one of the residential estates, which had a large signpost planted by the entrance that read:

> ***The Samuda Estate – owned & operated by the London Borough of Tower Hamlets, C.C.A. division***

Sections of the pavements here were stacked with endless amounts of garbage, and accompanied by a pungent stench of expired food forced its way into Tundé's nose—amplified by the hot weather. Just a few feet ahead of him, a junkie appeared from a nearby alleyway and began rummaging through the various bags and boxes of rubbish. He soon pulled out a shiny item that glimmered like a valuable piece of jewellery. Perhaps it was a gold chain. With a slurred tone of voice, the junkie yelled out seemingly to no one.

"John, John! Look 'ere mate. I might've found sumfin to pay for that new purple stuff!"

Tundé was no stranger to seeing drug addicts in his neighbourhood, or other areas like it. From time to time, he would see one scouring through bins in the hope of finding either their next meal or their next high. As he strode past this junkie, the roughness of his skin, the marks where injections had left their trace, and the tattered state of his clothes became glaringly evident. Logos were worn away and frayed, and the overpowering smell of body odour and cigarettes emanated from him.

I wonder what made my man become a nitty and mash up his whole life, Tundé thought judgmentally.

Continuing through the estate, he reached a fork in the road with a park nestled in between. The road split around the park gates and then reconnected thereafter. Beyond the park, the road was directed toward a series of council estate blocks, accompanied by a corner shop, laundrette, kebab house, and a local hairdresser. The sun blanketed the park in bright light, as its rays elegantly reflected off the leaves, creating a summery green tinge.

The joyful sounds of children playing in the grassy area grew louder as Tundé walked by the park's railings. The cheerful scenes were coming from a group of young kids he recognised from his estate. They were deeply engrossed—some kicking around a worn-down football, others on rusty bikes, and a few playfully scrapping in the mud. In their world of play, nothing else seemed to matter. Some of them spotted Tundé and paused their activities to acknowledge him.

"Man like Tunds!" shrieked one of the boys with a high-pitched tone.

Tundé hailed them with a wave and smile, "Wagwan, my young g's!"

Quickly, the group of kids resumed their playtime.

As he arrived at the main set of estate tower blocks, the car park came into view. Some of the older boys from the area were occupying it. They were gathered around one of the latest WMB releases—a state-of-the-art metallic blue car with blacked-out windows for an extra touch of luxury and privacy—with some seated inside and others standing around the car. Tundé recognised the model, having seen it in a car showroom in central London a few weeks ago.

Rah, I swear that car is worth like 50 bags.

Tundé wasn't completely surprised, though. He knew the boys, while not officially working as a gang, were deeply involved in shady activities like fraud, robbery and the sale of stolen goods; the proceeds of which were sustaining their lavish lifestyles. These extravagant possessions stood in stark contrast to Tundé's circumstances, and a twinge of jealousy couldn't help but creep into his heart.

Ah, I dunno if I can be like these man. But I wish I just had it like they do.

Passing by the car park en route home, Tundé noticed the boys were draped head-to-toe in designer brands like Legani, Stabiliaga, and Streetelite London. The visuals of red cups and shimmering lighters enlivened the scene, accompanied by a potent blend of alcohol, cigarettes and weed aromas in the air. The car reverberated with local music blasting from its speakers. While the sonics of grime played in the background, Tundé could hear the echoes of a heated argument.

"Bro, Diggs is the king of our music ting. Can't tell me no different!"

"Listen, I fully rate what he's has done for the UK scene. Man buss open bare closed doors and that. But I'm telling you *now* fam, Ray Hus is the GOAT!"

Tundé signalled to them with a half-hearted thumbs up. "Safe you man."

They responded jovially.

"My younger!" said Sinker.

"What's good, my YG!" said AJ.

"What you sayin', lil brooo!" said Steven Whiteman, who was three years above him at Stebon High. "School been alright since I got kicked out, yeah?"

"Yeah, it's calm bro. Man's ducking yard now anyway, so catch you man later."

"Ite, in a bit, Tunds."

Tundé was about to reach the entrance to his block when two random junkies chasing after each other barged over Mrs Peterson—an 82-year-old woman who had moved into the block a few years prior—along with her walking stick and shopping bags.

"They're trying to kill us!" they both laughed hysterically as they continued to run away.

"Dickheads!" Tundé shouted at them with irritation. He jogged over to help the elderly lady from the floor.

"I'm sorry about that, Mrs Peterson, they can be bare ann—they can be *really* annoying sometimes," he said code-switching.

"It's okay. Thank you so much, Tundie," Mrs Peterson said, mispronouncing his name. He let it slide since he rarely ever bumped into her anyway.

"Let me help you back in," Tundé said, helping to carry the shopping as he handed Mrs Peterson her walking stick.

"You know, I'm still not used to this whole thing. This area has changed so much since I last lived here."

"Oh, you used to live here before?" Tundé asked as he opened the main door of the block, where the name 'Equiano House' was displayed on the wall.

"Yes, I was born and raised in the Isle of Dogs until the late '80s. I got a council house in the countryside, but they forced me back here because of that bloody Council Care Act. I'm too old for this city life!"

"Rah, I had no idea."

"Oh, and life was much better before that bloody Mary Catcher became Prime Minister. She made the country go downhill. And the TP were supposed to make up for that with this CCA. They didn't half botch that up!"

The Council Care Act 2015 was a policy introduced by the TP—otherwise known as the Traditionalist Party—which mandated working-class families and government benefit receivers under a certain income threshold to be rehoused into inner-city London properties, pledging more employment opportunities. However, the reality was far from the vision.

"Yeah, my mum told me they promised all these jobs for CCA people, but now everyone's broke. That doesn't sound great."

"No, it isn't. Those two drugged-up lads are the effect. But what can we do, eh? We're at their mercy."

"I hear you, Mrs Peterson. I hear you."

Chapter 3

After helping Mrs Peterson into her ground-floor flat, Tundé walked through the corridor to call the lift for the building. His nostrils picked up a strong smell of urine as if it came directly from the entire city's sewage system. The stench was so dominant that most visitors would gag instantly, but over the years, like his fellow residents, Tundé had become begrudgingly accustomed to it. Once he entered the lift, he pressed the weathered fifteenth-floor button on the panel. The lift started shaking vigorously, triggering his claustrophobia.

I pray I never get trapped in here.

As the lift slowly climbed up the building, Tundé was in a state of frustration.

There's so much shit wrong in this place. All the crazy junkies, the olders flossin' on me and these fucking pissy lifts!

The lift made a whirring noise halfway up, whilst Tundé stared into the grimy mirror, still absorbed in his thoughts. Even though things were far from perfect, it was still home at the end of the day.

Probably that Swedish syndrome ting.

Tundé bumped into a familiar face waiting in the lobby when the doors creaked open on the fifteenth floor.

"Yo, Kwame! Long time big bro, what you been saying?"

"Yes, Tunds. Good to see you. I'm blessed man. How's life treating you?"

As Tundé stepped out of the lift, they fist-bumped in acknowledgement before catching up in the corridor lobby.

"I'm good bro, just getting ready for GCSEs soon init," Tundé wasn't keen to delve into his fight earlier that day. "I swear you just finished uni recently, right?"

Kwame Agyekum shared similar life circumstances similar to Tundé. He was born in the nearby Tower Hamlets General Hospital to Ghanaian parents, five years before the teenager's birth in August 2011.

"Yeah bro, I finished at Warwick last summer. First time I've ever lived away from these ends you know! It was bare fun, but I've just been in full-on grind mode since coming back, not gonna lie."

"I was gonna say, bro, I haven't seen you in time! At least a couple summers. Would you recommend me going to uni as well?"

The lift's doors shut abruptly, followed by loud rattling sounds as it moved erratically down the levels.

"So, uni," Kwame resumed. "It was a sick experience being away from home. It did get really hard though, especially in a place like that with all them posh yutes. But you move with it, init. Obviously, bare buff gyal there too..."

Incessant laughter from the two Samuda Estate boys followed, as they laughed and playfully grappled each other.

"Of course man was on tings while he was up there! Nah, but for real though, you'd say it's a good thing?"

"Bro, I'm mad grateful for going Warwick. My degree fully buss me for this banking job I'm in now. Dunno if you know this too, but my dad's been pretty unwell for the last few months."

"Oh swear down? Sorry to hear that, Kay Dot. If you don't mind me asking, what happened?"

"Safe bro. He's got something called MS. It's quite serious, but thankfully it's not immediately life-threatening. Just a lot of changes, you get me?"

"Yeah, I fully hear you man."

"And if I didn't have this banking ting right now, we might all be fucked. It pays pretty good money, so I can take care of the fam while we work out what to do next."

"It's sick you can do that for your fam," Tundé tried to mask any undertones of envy. "Hopefully, Uncle Alidu gets better soon too."

"Amen. But yeah, I just came home to grab a box of mumsy's jollof and plantain. I'm lucky I live bare close to the office. Some of my colleagues live all the way out in Reading, bruv."

"Rah, that's next ends. Must be long for them man!"

"Well, I don't feel too sorry for them. A few dons used to own flats in CCA areas like here and Bethnal Green. When the government forced them to sell up, they got almost twice the value of their properties. So they're balling now!"

"Swear down? That's crazy."

"Believe. They got lucky, bro! Imagine these man will still say the wildest shit about CCA people being lazy and druggies too. These times, bare sniff sniff happening in the toilets."

"Ironic, init."

"Trust. Anyway, man's gotta go back to the office now. Probably gonna be there for another six or seven hours."

"Rah boy! So, you're finishing work at like midnight? Is that even allowed?"

"Welcome to the real world, my yute! I gotta work hard like this to earn these kinda P's. Especially people like us. It's not easy, but I have to take care of the fam. Anyway, I need to dip."

"Alright, bro. Enjoy your jollof. Even though it won't be as good as ours!"

"Ah, allow it. You know using basmati is the one! In a bit, Tunds."

"Bless bro."

I wish I could find a way to support my mum and Abs like what Kwame's doing for his family, Tundé pondered as he walked down the fifteenth-floor corridor of Equiano House.

The place had an old-fashioned, concrete feel. The carpets were well-used, the wallpaper was peeling and the lights flickered eerily. He eventually reached a red-coloured front door with the number 243 plastered on it. Turning the key to open it, Tundé entered a narrow hallway, which was laminated with wooden flooring, and veered off to the right leading to other rooms in the home.

When he entered his bedroom—the second door on the left-hand side—he thrust himself onto the bed and killed time by scrolling through his miCell. It supported the new holographic view feature that was now standard in most smartphones, allowing him to scroll through multiple social media platforms simultaneously as they projected out from his screen into mid-air. Tundé got so lost in the comedy skits on ClikClok, that by the time Remi arrived, it felt like only fleeting seconds had passed by in his digital daydream. It had actually been 45 minutes.

"Damn, I didn't know you got hurt that bad!" said Remi as Tundé opened the door for him.

"Bro, you're bare late. Mumsy's gonna be home soon, you know."

"African timing bro, you know this! Anyway, it takes longer when I'm on the lookout for anything booky. I know I've got my cousin, but this is still Samuda Estate after all."

After initially screwing his face up, Tundé's demeanour softened. "Yeah, I know my area's had a reputation from day dot."

The Samuda Estate was prominently known for being one of the most dangerous estates in East London, dating back to the late 1980s.

"Didn't Steven's older brother Billy get sent down for murder a few months ago?" Remi asked. "Heard he cheffed up two Irish dons from Greenwich just for chilling in these ends."

"You mean Billy Whiteman? Nah, I heard it's cos they tried chirpsing his girl and she wasn't having it. One of them tried to grab her arm."

"Bruv, Janet from school posted on Chirp saying Billy attacked them cos they were from Greenwich and acted like they owned this estate."

"False news, bro. The young bucks living *here* told me that they saw the Greenwich dons touch his gyal."

"Fair enough, fam. It's peak for Billy, though. He got 25 years minimum sentence! But yeah, I gotta be careful here."

Tundé kissed his teeth with annoyance. "Bruv, you're just making excuses for being late! You know it's calm for you here since you're like my family."

As Tundé walked Remi through to the living room, he was reminded that, while his mum tried her best to make their flat as homely as possible, he felt uncomfortable inviting guests. The flat was worn and jaded, matching the energy several locals felt about their own lives. Even Tundé himself. The living room was barely furnished, mainly featuring a small, faded three-seater sofa and a TV in the corner. The bareness added to the dreary feel. But his mum's insistence on keeping it tidy meant it was somewhat accommodating.

"Trust me, bro. When you start moving bairaff, you're gonna have this place looking like a C-Dubs apartment," Remi said while pointing out through the living room window at the Canary Wharf skyline.

Outside the window, the majestic City Lofts of Canary Wharf rose in the distance, their reflective glass façades glistening in the dusk of sunset. The main building bore the name 'City Lofts' emblazoned on a brilliantly illuminated sign, visible from afar. Each block of luxurious flats boasted a modern design, with distinct rooftop gardens that resembled a lush oasis amid the urban landscape.

"Don't try and gas me up, bruv," Tundé said as he sat on the sofa while Remi continued staring out of the window. "I don't wanna get involved in any of that drug shit. But what's this stuff about, anyway?"

"Ite boom. My cousin's boy, Rishi, has connections to big batches of this new ting called bairaff. Apparently, you can use it to get some insane high. It makes you feel stronger and smarter. I've heard it's crazy, bruv."

Tundé listened intently as Remi, who was usually quite nonchalant, described this new street drug to him with the animation of a toddler seeing their favourite TV show start.

"As sick as that sounds, I can't get involved in that madness. If Mumsy and Auntie Abs ever found out, I could get kicked out of the yard for good. Or shipped straight back to Naija!"

Remi took a long scan of the flat, then looked Tundé square in the eyes.

"Fam, I fully hear you. But if you do nothing to get your fam out of these bummy ends, your mumsy's just gonna toil away forever. That might be an even bigger risk as things get worse with this CCA shit, still."

"What do you mean bummy bruv? Are you dumb?"

But, without uttering a word, Remi eyeballed Tundé with intense sincerity. The reality of his situation sank in. His mum had laboured as an NHS nurse for as long as he could remember. Yet, their living situation had barely improved, despite *The Council Care Act 2015* coming into legislation to supposedly lessen the burden.

"I'll be real," Tundé eventually said. "Even though you pissed me off, it's the truth. Mum's been wanting to leave the ends for time and buy a yard for retirement. But she can't afford to cos she doesn't earn enough bread."

"So, what are you gonna do about that, Tunds? Just sit there letting her suffer?"

Maybe this is my chance to be like Kwame and help my mum out with some extra P's...

"Fuck it, maybe I could try working with you guys once. And once ONLY. Tell me more about your cousin's movements."

"Just think of it this way: it will be like carrying a box of Jupiter chocolate bars from Wiley's to the playground," Remi gleefully persuaded his best friend, "then someone else will sell it. It's not *allowed* at school, but it's not that deep. Light work, init."

"Surely it's not that simple?"

"Fam, trust me it's calm. The bairaff ting is patterned. Rishi's uncle has direct access to the purp. He used to be a big man around East Ham a few years ago. But he did the uni ting, and now he works for the government. Anyway, he said they've been testing this drug to learn what it does, but so far, it's very low priority for the feds."

"Wait, so they know about this new ting in proper detail, yeah? And they aren't gonna stomp people's headtops?"

"Yeah man, I think they're treating it like weed right now. Class C and dem tings dere. So it's not being monitored as seriously as other things."

"And Rishi's uncle has confirmed this, yeah?"

Remi nodded firmly. "Yes man, and all you have to do is move it from A to B."

"Alright cool. I guess I can work on this bourraff ting a couple times and see wagwan."

"BAIR-aff my g!" Remi corrected him, trying to contain his excitement. "So, you know my big cousin Jerry who owns the restaurant in South?"

"Yeah, I remember him."

"So, for one, he's managing this whole operation and will make sure things move *correctly*. And two, his restaurant gives you a certified cover to tell your mumsy if you ever give her any P's."

"Okay, I guess I could roll with that story."

"Yes, man like Tunds!"

They instinctively fist-bumped.

"Jheeze, I'm gassed I'm not gonna lie!" Remi said, letting his emotions spill over. "Jerry planned to start moving his first packs from tomorrow. So, I'll tell him you're available for the day. Be ready, bro."

"Last question bro..." Tundé said, not yet matching Remi's level of enthusiasm.

"What's up?"

"Am I gonna need muscle from Jerry? Should I be expecting any beef? Cos we've all heard the stories about how things can go left real quick."

"Bruv, don't stress. It's calm. The people we're working with are Jerry's certified affiliates. And no one tries to fuck with them too tough. Besides, he just wants us to focus on deliveries so we can all get paid, rather than getting into unnecessary beef."

"Are you sure bro?"

"Bro, 100%."

"Alright, that's calm then," Tundé said, feeling reassured. He had a glimmer of optimism. Despite being excluded from school, Remi may have presented him with a pathway to contribute to his family's situation.

"Never know, bruddah. One day, that could be us..." Remi said while peering out at the City Lofts again. "Dream!"

Tundé followed Remi's lead, envisioning a better future for himself, his mum and Auntie Abi. Then, his miCell pinged, breaking the pair from their trance. It was a text from his mum which read:

'Dear son, I have a night shift at the hospital. Your uncle Blessing arrives from Lagos tonight. Please don't forget to take the jollof out of the freezer. God bless you.'

"Oh shit, I forgot all about that!" Tundé burst out while he typed out a response.

After reading the text, Remi gave him a wry smile. "At least you won't have to tell her you got excluded before you earn some P's!"

"I know, but this random uncle is around. That's not calm at all!"

"Don't worry, I got you" Remi said as he fetched a pen and paper from his backpack. "Tomorrow, go to Jerry's restaurant at this address. He told me to write it down by hand, so it doesn't bait things up or leave a trace."

"Sounds like he's thought things through."

"Yeah, he's bare strategic like that. But, trust me, Tunds. You'll make more P's with him than you ever did hustling in those dead part-time jobs. Not many humans work in shops now, anyway. Just bare self-checkouts and auto-scanning."

"For real, it feels weird... wait a second. How are *you* making money from this?"

"Man's referred you to Jerry, init! After you've done a couple moves, I'll jump in on more jobs too. Everyone gets to eat fam. Unless there's a problem?"

"I guess not. But bro, you need to duck. I need to get the yard ready before my uncle gets here."

"Alright cool, I'll shout you again tomorrow," Remi said as he walked towards the front door. "In a bit, bro."

They fist-bumped, and then Remi left. After cleaning up, Tundé turned on the TV to pass some time before Uncle Blessing's arrival. The London Living News channel popped up first, most likely because that's what his mum usually watched.

I wonder what this Uncle Blessing is like. He could be cool. He could be jarring. We'll see.

"...that concludes our recap of the PMQs here at the Houses of Parliament. The Strive Party leader, Glen Bowen, announced his desire to constitutionally challenge the TP's ongoing stance that they provide CCA residents with the basic human needs from Maslow's hierarchy. Further broadcasts will update you as this develops. Back to you in the studio."

These politicians really love chatting the most hot air.

A few moments later, Tundé's ears were perked by another announcement.

"This is Misty Rainford, reporting the weather live at seven o'clock from the LLN weather studio. I need to tell you about the exciting African Ascent hitting the capital and other parts of the country over the next week or so!"

Where are they going with this?

"This phenomenon was aptly named by our meteorologists, who recently observed a cluster of abnormal clouds forming above the coast of West Africa. At the border between Nigeria and Cameroon. Extreme winds from Togo's coastal capital, Lomé, have pushed these heat-infused water droplets towards the UK and Ireland."

Interesting...

"So, what does that mean for you at home?" Misty asked with a beaming smile. "Well, we're expecting soaring temperatures to continue over the coming week, with current estimations predicting record highs for March of 30 degrees Celsius, with clear blue skies and little to no wind or rain. Get your sunnies dusted off and your Factor 50 at the ready! That's it for the weather report—back to you in the newsroom, Gloria."

Tundé was enthusiastic, but not without some scepticism. He knew far too well how sporadic British weather was, and that it would likely disappoint. Nevertheless, he still typed into the status box of his Chirp social media profile:

'Rah, the weather this week could bang, still!'

A huge gust of wind sharply came through the window, blowing the curtain firmly into the air. Tundé was taken by surprise, then he rolled his eyes.

What happened to all that heat and no wind? Typical weather forecast, always gassing it.

Suddenly, a massive lightning strike crashed down near the Samuda Estate, its light so fierce that it lit up the whole flat and temporarily blinded Tundé. He rubbed his eyes vigorously and peered outside the window. The rain had started pouring down. Even though he was familiar with inaccurate weather forecasts, they were really off the mark this time. Not giving it too much thought, he jumped back onto the sofa, picking up his miCell to write on Chirp about the schizophrenic nature of British weather.

Bruv, what the f-, Tundé thought with confusion.

His phone wasn't working. A blank screen stared back at him regardless of which buttons he pressed. He was baffled. Having just charged it before Remi's visit, it didn't make sense to be dead now. He tried to charge his phone again, but it was no use.

"You've got to be taking the piss, man!" he yelled, throwing his phone against the sofa in frustration. "Thank you, World. You've completely fucked things up for me today!"

While that helped release some tension, Tundé was still reeling. He decided to rush to the local takeaway shop to get some comfort food before the family guest arrived.

Maybe I can stretch for 3 wings and chips with my last 3 pounds. I swear I could get 6 wings for that last year!

The teenager was then caught off guard by the flat buzzer ringing unexpectedly.

That can't be Uncle already, surely?

"Hello?" Tundé answered the intercom system.

"Hello, is that Babatundé?" responded a deep voice with a strong, Nigerian accent. "It's your uncle Blessing. By the grace of God, please let me in, sha. It's raining outside!"

Tundé winced. He hated when people used his full name, as he usually heard it when he was in trouble with his mum.

"Sure. I'll come down and help you with your stuff, Uncle."

After buzzing him into the building and heading down to the ground floor, Tundé was met by a soaked man. He was a few inches shorter than him, stocky in stature and donned a red Yorùbá fila hat paired with Western-style jeans and a jacket. He had a patchy grey beard and faded

Egba marks on both cheeks. At his feet laid a small travel bag made almost entirely out of an Aso Oke design that Tundé recognised. The yellow and burgundy material had a mix of warm colours and lively patterns, blending tradition with a modern touch. It was also symbolically tied to the Adeyemi's for nearly two centuries. Many generations of the family used it to create clothing for specific cultural events or sentimental items.

Why does he only have that small bag though? Nigerian relatives usually bring bare stuff when they travel to England.

Tundé observed Yorùbá custom and bent down to greet Uncle Blessing, arching over his back and touching the ground to show respect to his elder. He never really enjoyed this part of their tradition, but he preferred to oblige rather than face the wrath of his mum for being disrespectful. However, he was shocked when his uncle responded with a similar, highly respectful greeting—bringing his hands together whilst bowing his head downwards at Tundé.

"Ẹ kaale, Tundé," Uncle Blessing said. "It is great to finally meet you, as you are."

"Same, Uncle," Tundé said, sensing an unusual vibe. "Same."

"So, my friend, where is your house? Or are we sleeping out here?"

Now that was a tone more familiar to Tundé.

Chapter 4

UNCLE BLESSING MADE HIMSELF comfortable in the living room and unpacked some of the contents of his small bag. He brought out a bag of ugu leaves, a large packet of amala flour and a tin of Rilo chocolate-flavoured malt drink powder.

"Please, put these in the kitchen," Uncle Blessing said, handing the items to Tundé one by one. "I brought these from Naija at your mother's request."

Tundé put the items on the counter, and after a quick detour to his mum's room, he returned to the living room with bedding to set up on the sofa for Uncle Blessing.

"Mum said she's sorry. She would normally let you stay in my room, but–"

"I know, you will be facing your exams soon. And of course, she wants you to succeed! I hope school is going well for you, sha?"

"Yes, Uncle. It is, and I have a lot of studying to do."

"And what happened to your face? Have you been fighting?"

"No, Uncle. I just had a really bad fall in the playground," Tundé lied, keen to change the subject. "Please could you tell Mum that you're here now? My phone broke earlier, so I can't do it myself."

"Sure, son, I will let her know. How is she doing anyway?"

"Fine, sir, fine."

"And what is it that your mum's baby sister is called? Abiola, abi?"

"Yeah. She's fine too, sir."

"Okay. But kilonṣele now? What's going on with the family? I can sense a lot of tension here."

Tundé was apprehensive. Uncle Blessing gave him a strange vibe from the moment he'd arrived. His other older relatives never cared enough to take an interest and ask him personal questions as a child in the family.

"It's hard here you know. London's a tough city, especially nowadays."

"See, I know that finances are very challenging here. But what for the relationship between you and your mother?"

"Well, it can be tricky sometimes. But it's blessed for the most part."

"I just hope you care about her enough to take responsibility for your actions," Uncle Blessing said thoughtfully. But Tundé was concerned.

There's no way this don knows what I did at school today, surely? He only just got here!

"Any actions that could put her in unnecessary danger, anyway," Uncle Blessing continued.

"If anyone I care about is in danger, I'll always ride for them," Tundé blurted out, his words charged with an instinctive truth.

Is this uncle tryna say I'd put my fam at risk? He doesn't have a scooby, bruv!

"That's good, Tundé. Because who knows what could happen in this crazy world, abi!" Uncle Blessing checked his watch as he yawned and stretched his arms out. "Time for bed. I'll eat in the morning. It's been a long day, and tomorrow I have a lot to do. So, I need to be well-rested."

"Okay, goodnight, Uncle. I'll see you in the morning," Tundé said as he walked towards his bedroom.

"You're going to school tomorrow, yes?"

Tundé gulped. But a little, white lie to his uncle wouldn't hurt. "Yeah, that's right. And I should be back around five or six in the evening."

"By Olodumare's grace, you will have a wonderfully productive day tomorrow, Babatundé."

"Yes, Uncle. Good night."

The next morning, Tundé followed his usual routine—use the toilet, shower, eat bran flakes in his towel and change into his uniform in under 45 minutes—which was a lot easier without the distraction of social media now that his phone was broken. Due to his mum's night shift, she wouldn't be back home before he left the flat. She was an expert at sussing out his lies, so Tundé was thankful. However, he still had the small matter of their guest to deal with. Fortunately, Uncle Blessing had woken up earlier and was ready to leave the flat before Tundé had eaten his breakfast.

"Goodbye son, I'll see you soon, sha," said Uncle Blessing in a jovial voice. "Have a blessed day!"

"Bye, Uncle. See you later," Tundé waved, as Uncle Blessing left the flat holding the small Aso Oke bag.

Later that morning, just before Tundé left, he remembered that his mum kept a spare, old-school brick phone in the kitchen drawer. He decided to use it for the day while his miCell was broken. After switching the brick phone on and inserting his sim, he texted Remi:

'Yo, it's Tunds. My miCell is fully mash up. Using mumsy's now. What time for the meet?'

Seconds later, he got a response:

'That's peak fam, back to old skool texts and green bubbles lol. Meet @ 11.'

Tundé chuckled, then responded:

'Loool fuck you, bruv. That's calm tho. In a bit.'

Tundé grabbed the piece of paper given to him by Remi last night and read the address:

'JERRY'S JAM, 29 ACRE LANE, BRIXTON, SW2 5SP'

It only just dawned on Tundé how long the journey to Jerry's restaurant was going to take him.

Man's gotta trek all the way to South. That's a mission!

Turning the paper over, he noticed that Remi had written some additional information:

'From Brixton station: turn left and then take your second right on Acre Lane. Can't miss it.'

To get around the city, Tundé used his under-16 Pulsecard, which gave him free LTN bus journeys. But to get to Brixton on time, he would need to get the Tube. The only issue was that he didn't have enough money to pay the £5 fare.

It's so expensive these days. I'm gonna have to bump it, still.

He deleted the text exchange with Remi, picked up his backpack and headed towards Crossharbour, the closest station to his estate. As Tundé approached the station's entrance with a heavy feeling of apprehension about the day ahead, various distinct sounds bombarded his senses: the beeping of numerous Pulsecards tapping in to start and end their journeys at the designated touch points. The screech of the rails as trains pulled into the station. The treading of people's feet running up and down the stairs to the elevated platform. Because Crossharbour was on the Docklands Light Railway (DLR) line, there were no physical barriers at the station.

Okay, Tunds. Just walk past the touchpoints and act like you've got everything under control...

What the East Londoner enjoyed most about using the DLR was the train's route through elevated tracks that weaved in and out of the magnificent Canary Wharf and Tower Hamlets skyline, providing a scenic view to an otherwise boring trip. As they entered the underground tunnel to arrive at Bank station, where Tundé needed to change for a London Underground train to Brixton, there was an announcement from the PA system.

"Unfortunately, LTN has announced minor delays on most London Underground lines this morning due to staff shortages. We apologise for any inconvenience this may cause to your journey."

A chorus of groans could be heard throughout the train, as Tundé himself joined in. "Fucking typical!"

Eventually, he reached Brixton station, and after trailing behind a commuter through the barriers to avoid paying the fare, Tundé walked out scot-free. The main high street was very similar to the one near his school in Poplar. However, there was more of a Caribbean essence influencing the retail outlets due to the demographic living in the area. Checking the time on the station's board sparked Tundé into a rush.

Shit, it's almost ten o'clock. Gotta get moving!

When he finally arrived at Jerry's restaurant, Tundé was nine minutes late. The entrance was warmly lit with flickering lanterns, and a subtle, Afrobeat melody resonated through the windows. A modest sign welcomed customers to a cosy space where the aroma of exotic spices encouraged visitors to experience a taste of Africa and its diaspora. Standing outside the door was a burly, well-groomed bodyguard. He was dressed in a tailored shirt with well-fitted trousers and dress shoes. While he appeared fairly relaxed, his imposing presence served as a clear warning not to cause trouble.

"You're the yute here to see the boss, right?" he asked the teenager.

"Erm, yeah."

"Okay. I was expecting you earlier, but you can go inside."

As Tundé hesitantly entered the restaurant, a big, powerful figure oozing with authority came walking towards the door, working his muscles as he dried a glass with a kitchen towel.

"It's 10:09. You're late," the man said with a booming voice. "So, you're doing chores this morning, fam."

Tundé was confused. "Wait, Jerry, is that you?"

"Yeah, it's Jerry. Been hitting gym since you last saw me!"

Tundé nodded slowly in agreement. There was no arguing with that.

"What happened to your face?" Jerry asked.

"Ah, long story man. But I'm cool."

"Alright, say less. Anyway, if you wanna make money with me, then you'll get going with the dishes."

Tundé stared back at him blankly. He didn't sign up to clean plates! "But Jerry, I just got lost and—"

"Enough with the excuses! If this was a white man's business, you wouldn't be late, would you?"

Tundé gave it some thought. Maybe Jerry had a point.

"More importantly, if this was one of my big boy deals, best know, you can't be late for them. We'll talk proper business soon. But before all that..."

Jerry went to the cupboard behind the counter and retrieved a pair of rubber gloves, a bottle of washing-up liquid and a fresh sponge. Handing the cleaning equipment to a bemused Tundé, he said, "You need to learn discipline, my yute."

"But, but... ah, okay."

After an hour of washing up what seemed like the aftermath of a royal feast, Jerry called Tundé into a dark, discreet room hidden at the back of the restaurant. The perfect place to talk shop, Tundé presumed. Jerry signalled the teenager to sit down in the chair on the other side of his desk.

"Rah, this chair's mad uncomfortable, you know," mumbled Tundé.

"Wagwan, Tunds?"

"Oh, don't watch, bro," Tundé chose not to raise the issue in case he received another lecture.

Jerry shrugged his shoulders, then swivelled around and unlocked the safe behind his seat. He pulled out a plain, thin folder, which contained two sheets of paper that he placed on the desk.

"Alright, this is some intel I got from Rishi's uncle, Tamwar, init."

"Oh, you know Rishi's uncle?"

"Yeah, Tamwar used to run a few moves with me back in the day. He works with them government man now. But he still tries to bless the mandem with special access every now and then."

Jerry pulled out the first document from the folder.

"Especially with stuff like this," he said, waving the paper towards Tundé's face. "Stuff that will hopefully change your life too, bro."

He had Tundé's full attention now.

“Anyway, let me explain the operation. All you and Remz need to do is move my stash from one location to another. You only need to interact with people that I’ve set the pick-ups and drop-offs with. You pass over the goods, they give you the P’s, you bring the P’s back to me, I take my chunk, and then you and Remz split the rest. Seen?”

Tundé nodded affirmatively as a surge of enthusiasm swept over him.

“In terms of P’s,” Jerry continued, “the price bairaff moves at right now is nuts, fam. I’m talking almost five times what cocaine sells for. People are ready to pay BIG to escape from their lives.”

“Rah, I’ve heard that coke’s supposed to be mad expensive as well. Is that right?”

“Let me put it this way. You and Remz are gonna get paid better than any of dem crummy CCA yutes you see running about on road. Trust me.”

Tundé couldn’t help but dream about a financially prosperous future. Maybe soon, he could buy a luxury coat for his Auntie Abi, like the older boys on his estate had. Or he could help his mum take care of household bills like Kwame did for his family. Or he could buy himself the latest Lemon miCell with all the latest AI and AR features.

“But we gotta establish our place in the market quickly before the bairaff availability increases. It’s powerful, but it’s expensive mainly because of limited supply through exclusive, trusted channels. Tamwar told us that supply is expected to triple over the next few months.”

“Swear down? Why are the government and dem man allowing it in?”

“Best believe they’ll be making bread too. They always are. And it’s probably cos moderate purp usage enhances your physical and mental abilities for a short time. So, if you don’t do too much, then it’s calm.”

“And what would happen if people *did* start doing too much?”

"You ask too many questions, my yute! Don't worry about the nitty dem. They fucked their lives up time ago. You just need to do your job and get paid, so you won't ever have to rely on empty promises from the system or become a drug fiend like them."

Tundé bit his tongue. Jerry clearly didn't want to explore the topic any further.

"Anyway, for your first job today, you're gonna pick up a batch of our highest quality from our spot in East. Then, you'll transport that pack to one of my business associates. Have you clocked why I'm bringing you and Remz in for this operation?"

Tundé shook his head. "Not exactly, why?"

"Even though the rules are lax, I'd rather have two young bucks move the goods so there's less heat on the experienced workers. You man look youthful, can wear school uniform and don't even drive cars like they do. So, use that to your advantage, yuh understand?"

"Yeah, that's calm."

"Cos you man are what, like 16 or 17, init?"

"I'm 15, still."

"Rah, even younger then! That's very calm," Jerry said while fetching a pen from his desk drawer. He scribbled down more notes on one of the sheets and slid it across the desk to Tundé. "You gotta go to this address first, fam."

"Ah, what? Man has to go back up to Plaistow?" Tundé said, visibly worried. "Jerry, that could be a bit of a sticky one, still."

"Wagwan?"

"Basically, about a year ago, one older from our school had beef with the PMD lot. He punched up one of their members, but bare people from our school went to back him. Bare youngers like me and Remi were there to watch it too. I'm a bit shook that I might get recognised. I haven't gone back there since."

The PMD—also known as the Plaistow Man Dem—were a gang named after that specific area of East London. They had a notorious reputation for being violent, disorderly and ruthless.

"I hear you, but you know they're under investigation now, right? So they shouldn't be moving mad. But just in case..."

Jerry rummaged through the desk drawer and handed Tundé a New Evo cap. "You can wear this to disguise yourself, especially since its bare hot right now. All you need to do is pick up the pack and bounce quick time."

"Alright, safe."

"And the meeting place for the drop-off is..." Jerry said as he scribbled down on another piece of paper. "Here. Follow the route on the map and walk through the back roads to the exchange spot. It's Stratford Cemetery in Maryland. Stay off the main high streets for as long as possible to avoid getting captured on CCTV. Just in case feds wanna change up their approach."

Jerry handed over the second piece of paper to Tundé. He stuffed it in his back pocket along with the first sheet.

"Alright, Tunds. You're meeting our chemist, Mad Medy, at one this afternoon in Plaistow. Then, you're gonna deliver the package to my long-time client, Biskit, in Maryland at two o'clock on the dot. Make sure Bis gives you the five bags before you give him any stash."

A wave of ecstatic disbelief washed over Tundé.

Rah, did a man say £5,000? Five thousand pounds sterling? I must be dreaming!

"Yeah, I see you getting gassed! Best make sure all that bread gets back to me first, though," Jerry advised humorously, with a hint of threat. He proceeded to hand Tundé a vintage lighter. "Make sure you burn dem pieces of paper once you're done. It's got too much traceable info to end up in a next man's hands."

"Yeah, Jerry, I got this," Tundé said confidently, trying to prove he was ready for the task.

"Okay, calm. You ain't got too long. You should probably dip now. Remi will send you the number to hit me up on if you've got any problems."

"Alright. Catch, you in a bit, bro."

Tundé gave Jerry a thumbs-up before leaving his office and the restaurant. As he walked to the bus stop, Tundé pulled out an old-school MP3 player from his backpack. It was Auntie Abi's, but he'd forgotten to give it back to her when they met last.

Jheeze, I'm so lucky! No boredom for me, he thought joyously.

He loaded up one of her rap playlists to hype himself up for extra motivation. The striking sounds of the South London artist Steve's chart-topping song "Thrilling Thursday" bounced off his eardrums, as Tundé bopped onto the 133 bus from Brixton Hill with boisterous energy.

Chapter 5

After an hour of sitting on the bus as it droned through the streets of London, the high spirits that Tundé started the journey with had somewhat dampened. The reality of what he was getting himself into had slowly sunk in.

What would Mum think if she found out? What would Auntie Abs do if she knew I was moving like this?

Glancing up at the bus's digital display, it read 'Next Stop: Greengate Street'. Tundé was due to arrive at his intended destination. He pressed multiple stop buttons while rushing frantically through the top deck aisle and down the stairs. As Tundé stepped off the bus and placed his foot on the Plaistow pavement, he began contemplating more deeply.

But what if Mum keeps struggling and things get worse? What if we can't afford to leave Samuda Estate? What if we have to live in this miserable routine forever? Fuck that!

Despite his serious concerns about affiliating with Jerry, the teenager felt more compelled to acquire some joy for himself and the people he cared about.

Besides, all I'm doing is taking something from one place and moving it to another. It's harmless. I just need to keep my head down, get my bread and keep it stepping.

Paying more attention to his surroundings, he noticed that Plaistow itself hadn't changed much over the years. It had always been fairly run-down and dreary even before *The Council Care Act 2015* came into effect.

As he tried to memorise Jerry's handwritten instructions, Tundé instantly grew alert. He couldn't shake off the anxiety stirring inside him. This job wasn't just an idea in his head anymore. With every step he took towards the pick-up spot, he was manifesting this illicit underworld into his reality. A reality where he had to be mindful of any danger presented by his enemies or authorities lurking to thwart his plans. Or worse.

His main concern, though, was the notorious Plaistow Man Dem crew. The PMD mainly operated in the Plaistow and West Ham areas of East London. The gang were notorious for their involvement in the activities of drug dealing, kidnapping and murder. London Living News had recently reported on a ground-breaking police investigation into their operation, including claims that the PMD was handling millions of pounds worth of cocaine and heroin every year by supplying most of the East and Southeast London areas. Worryingly, their business dealings were tied to a string of killings, as a direct result of the competitive drug trade since *The Council Care Act 2015* was enforced. One thing was for sure; the PMD crew were to be feared.

Jerry didn't seem too bothered about them, so hopefully that means he's got shit on lock and I don't need to be shook.

Tundé recalled the fight last year between Alex—a rowdy boy in the year above him at Stebon High School—and a young PMD member called Bengal Bil. Tundé was present among many of his schoolmates that day. Some were there for the entertainment value, while others were there to back Alex if necessary. After a lengthy verbal exchange, the two youngsters got embroiled in a short but brutal altercation where punches and kicks were thrown incessantly. Towards the end, numerous boys from both sides were drawn into the brawl. All the Stebon boys ran off before an instant retaliation from the PMD crew could be made. But, news quickly spread that Bengal Bil was badly hurt and subsequently hospitalised—so much so that his father flew in from Dhaka to visit him. Bengal Bil was eventually diagnosed with a spinal cord injury that would affect his ability to walk for the rest of his life. Overwhelmed by fear, Alex's family decided to leave London abruptly, worried that the notorious gang would bring insurmountable revenge to their doorstep. Indeed, PMD members visited Stebon High School numerous times in the following weeks after the fight in search of Alex or anyone recognisable from the incident. But it was to no avail.

It's a Thursday, though. Surely most of these Plaistow man are in school today.

Walking towards the pick-up spot, Tundé noticed the area's ageing council estate blocks towering high in the sky, the bustling energy from the various market stalls and corner shops, and the large numbers of senior women wearing traditional clothing of West African or South Asian heritage as they strolled through the streets. While these settings were a common theme in other CCA-governed areas, Plaistow still had its unique blend of old-school architecture with modern inhabitants.

What soon caught Tundé's eye was a small group of boys loitering outside Wiley's Supermarket—a large, multinational grocery store with its headquarters based down the road in Bow. His heart was pumping faster and faster as he got closer, but Tundé tried to remain calm and undeterred. Anything less could make him an easy target and compromise his job. Putting on a mask of resilience, the teenager held his head up high while avoiding eye contact with the boys. He could feel the burning sensation as one of them examined him sharply as he walked by. Tundé gulped.

Uh oh...

But nothing came of it, and he kept walking onward, breathing a sigh of relief.

Phew!

Tundé soon turned right, heading towards the first meeting point through the Plaistow backstreets as Jerry instructed. Eventually, he came across the faint, red brick house with a tainted, beige door. Cross-referencing Jerry's notes, it matched the description he was told to watch out for.

"Alright, this is the one," Tundé mumbled as he read Jerry's note. "So, I need to knock on the door with a certain rhythm. One-two, one-two, then one-two-three."

He was met with a drawn-out silence, heightening his nerves.

"Hello!" a voice responded in an unfamiliar accent, throwing Tundé off-guard. "Who sent you?"

"Erm... Jerry sent me. I'm here to meet Mad Medy."

Another few seconds went by, and then what sounded like hundreds of latches began rattling. The door opened slowly, and to Tundé's surprise stood a short, stubby man with a tanned olive skin tone.

"You have meeting location, yes?" he asked the teenager.

"Mmhmm, it's somewhere close to Stratford. Guessing you're Mad Medy?"

"Yes," he answered bluntly, as he shuffled Tundé into the house and slammed the door closed while applying the latches.

"You wait here," Mad Medy directed the youngster as he walked into another room.

Tundé's nose was inundated with a god-awful smell. It was a cocktail of various chemicals and substances. Taking a glance around, he was shocked at how filthy the place was. Alcohol bottles, moulding plates, takeaway boxes and haggard clothing were piled up around the house. The carpet was completely worn away in patches, and there were yellow-stained mattresses and sofas with ash-covered throws over them. Graffiti tags and unidentified stains covered the walls too.

This is the most disgusting house I've ever seen in my life!

Mad Medy soon returned, carrying a large, black carrier bag containing several cubes wrapped in foil. "This very high quality and important stuff. Cannot afford to lose."

The words were said calmly, but laced with the threat of severe consequences if something were to go wrong. Tundé felt the weight of responsibility energetically shift to him as Mad Medy handed him the carrier bag.

"I hear you," Tundé said anxiously as he stuffed it into his backpack.

Absolutely no turning back now. I'm fully locked in.

"Make sure you see money before you show bag."

"Yeah, sure. In a bit, man."

As Tundé departed, Mad Medy wasted no time shutting the door as the aggressive sound of the endless latches being locked quickly followed.

Rah, my man wasn't tryna waste any time.

Tundé headed back to Greengate Street, slowly transitioning from the quiet lull of the backstreets into the frenzy of Plaistow's main road. Checking the time on his mum's spare brick phone, he was startled.

Shit, it's almost half one already! I need to get moving.

He was keen to walk the whole way through the backstreets to keep a low profile. But Tundé wouldn't make it to Maryland on time unless he jogged. Since he would be crossing three busy main roads on his way, Tundé would catch his breath at those intervals to avoid drawing unwanted attention. After crossing over the busy Greengate Street, he started his jog to the meeting spot. Very quickly, his lack of fitness became apparent. This journey was going to be a challenge. But he had no other choice than to keep going.

Why does getting good shit always have to be so hard?

Meanwhile, Tundé was unaware of the developments happening outside Wiley's Supermarket.

"Yo, Bullet!" the young affiliate exclaimed as he fist-bumped his elder. "I saw that yute walking back this way after ten minutes. Looked bare sus."

"Man like Brootz," Bullet responded. "Did you keep following him like I told you?"

"Of course, bro. And look what I found for my troubles," Brootz waved around a note in his hands. "This dropped out of my man's pocket when he left GG Street. It's got an address on it too."

"Okay, good job, my young g," Bullet said as he read the note with glee. "So, you defo saw him come out from one of the yards?"

"Wallahi. Honest to God, fam," replied Brootz. "I just didn't clock which one. But he had a backpack on him and all sorts. He must be moving suttin' for someone."

"He's probably gone to deliver in Maryland. I'm certain he was one of the Poplar yutes there when Bilal got badded up last year."

"Swear down?" asked another one of the boys.

"100, bro," said Bullet firmly. "And he thinks he can come and move shit on our ends too? Without even paying tax? He must be mad!"

"What should we tell the boss though?" asked another of the boys to Bullet. "Remember, he told us that some President advised us to keep things quiet right now."

"Fuck Zaid for now, man. We can tell him wagwan later. Right now, we're gonna do our own ting and teach that Poplar yute that the PMD ain't dead yet."

Bullet was met with a chorus of affirmative noises from the other boys, including Brootz.

"For real."

"Let them know!"

"Ite boom, you lot. Get the dingers round the corner so we can all drive there," Bullet signalled to two boys who then rushed onto a side road. "That little Poplar yute's gonna get dealt with properly!"

Chapter 6

"Oh fuck!" Tundé said aloud with concern. He was struggling to get to the second meeting spot on time.

I'm lucky Abs used to live around here. Otherwise, I'd be so lost!

Since he had memorised the address to save himself some time, Tundé stopped briefly to unzip his backpack and pull out a half-drunken plastic bottle of water. The humid conditions had made him extremely thirsty in his rush to Maryland. Much to his surprise, the previous evening's weather forecast was coming to fruition.

Tundé shuffled his hand into his backpack for his faux Rhythms headphones, which he bought for a discount at the Isle of Dogs Sunday market a few months prior. He mounted them over his ears and continued his journey. The playlist's mood switched from the standard, high-tempo music to a slower, more reflective song. Tundé found himself resonating deeply with the music and its lyrics:

"And it might seem sick right now; but would your mum back what you do for the pounds?

That could be a question of life or death; but it's your power within that keeps you blessed..."

The words spawned doubts in the teenager's mind and forced him to question his choices. His brain was flooded with imagery of his mum breaking down if she found out about his dubious actions. But Tundé tried to suppress it, reasoning that he was ultimately trying to provide for his family. Despite the motivation, he couldn't shake the feeling that trouble lingered if he followed through.

Jerry and Remz would have my back if shit hits the fan, though. Surely?

Tundé eventually reached Crownfield Lane, the final main road he had to cross before the meet-up point at Stratford Cemetery. As he crossed the road, he detected a tall dark figure out of the corner of his eye. He spun around to get a clearer view, but the mysterious figure had vanished.

Strange. Bare strange, Tundé thought fearfully, hoping he wasn't being followed. He soon entered the backstreets where he checked the time on his phone.

Jheeze, it's 1:51 p.m. Man's still got bare time.

He was nervous, but the potential rewards were too enticing to concede now. The radiant sun beaming down made him feel even more buoyant. Everything felt better under the sun. When he was a couple of minutes away from the cemetery, Tundé sensed the dark figure flash by his periphery again, raising his anxiety levels.

Bro, what the fuck? Is someone following me?

Tundé decided to take a small detour, walking onto a side road close to Stratford Cemetery. Here, he could work out if his suspicions were true.

Oh rah, I forgot this is Greenfeel Road.

The pavement was overgrown with shrubs and weeds, and the few houses around were boarded up and clearly unattended. Further down the road, in the distance, stood a charred and gutted structure with its exterior marked by the visible damage. This is where the now remnant Greenfeel Tower stood—the location of an infamous housing estate that was destroyed by a politically controversial fire a decade prior, killing hundreds of people. The residents knew the building was a huge fire risk and made numerous official complaints for years, but the government didn't intervene until it was too late.

And no one went to jail for that shit. Maybe I shouldn't feel that guilty for working with Jerry after all. At least I'm not killing anyone.

Halfway down, Tundé was alarmed to see a car parked up sideways, blocking the passage completely. Sensing danger, he turned around to walk back towards the cemetery. Out of nowhere, a second car came speeding down Greenfeel Road and broke sharply before him. Three men, all wearing balaclavas, dark grey hoodies and black gloves, jumped out of the vehicle and stormed towards Tundé. Grey clouds began forming, gradually blocking the sunlight as they imposed an added sense of gloom onto the abandoned street. The breeze that followed sent a chill down Tundé's spine as the ambushers encircled him.

"Don't try run you likkle pussio," Brootz said excitably. It was his first time on a manhunt with the PMD crew, and he wanted to make a good impression on the more experienced members.

"Tryna make P's on the PMD's turf yeah?" Bullet barked menacingly. "You're a brave yute."

Tundé was struck with fear and confusion. His intuition told him that this was the same group he saw outside Wiley's. But he couldn't work out how they found him so easily. Meanwhile, more boys could be heard getting out of the first car blocking the road behind him.

They must've been the ones following me.

"Shoulda known better not to get caught slipping, fam," laughed another of the PMD boys, holding up a scrunched-up piece of paper for all to see.

Tundé froze. He couldn't believe he'd made such a vital mistake.

How... how could I be so careless?

Tundé quickly broke out of his self-pity and searched for a way out, as the eight-strong gang surrounded him. They had blocked all the practical exits. There was no way out. He was trapped. Some of the PMD boys chuckled wickedly, enjoying Tundé's helplessness.

"Run us your bag before it gets peak, fam," Bullet said while stepping up to him aggressively.

Tundé didn't know what to do. There were consequences either way. If he handed over the bairaff freely, Jerry would be livid at the very least. But if he didn't comply, the PMD crew could cause some serious damage.

"Too late!"

Bullet got frustrated and whacked Tundé flush on his chin with the blunt force of his fist. Tundé crashed to the floor. Thinking on his feet, he tried to roll onto his bag to protect the valuable stash. But it was futile. He was met with a flurry of shoes and fists as the PMD boys unleashed violence on him. From a distance, it looked like a ferociously grey cloud had descended upon Tundé. Blow after blow, he slowly started losing grip of his bag. Then, a thunderous punch connected with Tundé's eye socket, cracking the skull beneath his skin.

"Agggh!" He screamed in despair.

Tundé always thought of himself as a warrior who could manage the classrooms, the playgrounds and the streets. But the last couple of days made him seriously reconsider his self-image.

My life is fucked... maybe I was never that guy after all... maybe I'm always meant to be at the bottom...

"That's ours now, cuz," Brootz grabbed the bag from Tundé's weak grasp. He unzipped it and inspected its contents, pulling out the black plastic bag.

"You know what?" Bullet said, snatching it from Brootz's hands and looking inside. "I think it's that new food the druggies are mouthin' off about. Bairaff or purp or whatever."

Suddenly, a lightning bolt struck the earth a few hundred yards away, prompting thunder to roll loudly across the sky and rain to start violently hitting the tarmac. Tundé watched on helplessly, but the murky vision from his blood-soaked eye made things hard to see. Bullet opened one of the cube-shaped foil pieces to reveal the bairaff. It was a powdery, shiny purple substance made up of fine granules that were a little thicker than sugar in texture.

"Oh, that's defo the purp ting, you know," said another member of the PMD crew. "Banging quality stuff from what I hear."

"Should we take the rest of his stuff, Bullet?" Brootz asked, still eager to please the rest of his crew.

"Yeah, take all his shit," said Bullet, passing the black plastic bag to one of the other PMD members. "This yute needs to learn that he can't be tryna make P's in our ends."

Tundé, still struggling from his wounds, watched his aggressors empty his backpack. He saw his keys, jumper, coins, water bottle, schoolbooks and other random items tipped onto the soaked icky floor.

"All this stuff's shit, man," said one PMD boy as he kissed his teeth. "Wait, what's this? Some dead material ting. Rah, you really are a broke yute, init?"

The PMD boy had picked up a handkerchief woven from the Adeyemi family's Aso Oke fabric. The yellow and burgundy patterned material was mucky after being dropped in a grimy puddle. It meant nothing to the PMD boys, but for Tundé, it carried a sentimental value close to his heart. His mum had recited the origin story to him numerous times when he was growing up:

> *"Your great-great-grandfather, Mr Adeniyi Balogun Adeyemi, was a high-ranking Yorùbá warrior within the Kingdom of Abeokuta in the late 1800s. He had also learnt how to become a very skilled tailor in his teenage years before joining the military forces. During this time, there was increasing pressure from British colonial powers to create free, unregulated trade within the Kingdom, as Abeokuta was seen as a key region within Yorùbáland. However, the Aláké[1] of Abeokuta was extremely reluctant to their wishes. British officials arranged to send representatives to the Aláké to discuss a possible agreement.*

> *"Secretly though, the British were plotting to send an army of their commanders and traitorous Yorùbá porters to invade Abeokuta, overthrow the Aláké and extract the resources within the Kingdom for their own gain. Fortunately, Adeniyi was on an unplanned visit to a friend who lived in the porters' village in Ilaro, when he overheard a conversation about Britain's plan for an invasion rather than a trade discussion.*

> *"He returned to Abeokuta to report his findings to*

the Aláké, who thanked him and held an emergency meeting with the Kingdom's military personnel. The Aláké believed the best course of action would be to send officials out to the British to find out their true intentions. As commander-in-chief, Adeniyi disagreed. It was very risky in his opinion. But, out of respect, he said he would follow the Aláké's plan.

"The village elders say that in the build-up to the British officials' arrival, Adeniyi sat on Olumo Rock and prayed to Olodumare, seeking guidance from the Yorùbá deities and our ancestors. They say that Adeniyi received a powerful impulse, urging him to go against the Aláké's wishes and attack the British representatives on sight.

"While your great-great-grandfather prepared for the arrival of the colonisers, he wove together a fine handkerchief out of the distinct yellow and burgundy Aso Oke fabric that has become our family's legacy pattern. Along its edge, Adeniyi stitched in small print the phrase 'Mo máa gbé pẹ̀lú yin lailai' which means 'I will live with you forever'. Fearing an impending war, Adeniyi sent his wife and five children to stay with distant family in Ketu and handed his eldest son the handkerchief as a parting gift to remember him by should he not return from the battlefield.

"Adeniyi's decision to fight turned out to be a masterstroke, as the British representatives were carrying enough

weaponry to initiate a full-scale invasion. Because he had prepared the Abeokuta Army for battle, they massacred all but three of the British soldiers, who were taken in as prisoners. Unfortunately, this event sparked the Abeokuta War between the Kingdom and the British, which ultimately led to Adeniyi being killed in battle while leading the front line.

"From then onwards, the legacy of his strength and bravery is remembered through this bespoke garment, which has been passed down to the eldest male of each Adeyemi generation ever since. Now that you are becoming a man, Babatundé, it's your turn to honour the tradition."

When the PMD dashed this cherished piece of family history back into the puddle, Tundé's body charged up with rage. It was one thing robbing him of the bairaff, but his spirit couldn't just lie there and accept the disrespect to his heritage.

"Get off my stuff, you fucking dickheads!" Tundé shouted with all the energy he could muster. He stumbled to his feet and sucker-punched one of the PMD boys to the ground. Then, he took a few steps back as the rest of the crew reacted with surprise.

"WHAT FAM? You think you can move to us man like THAT?" Bullet raged, slamming Tundé's backpack to the ground as he matched his aggression.

Bullet turned to Brootz with violent intent. "My young g, show this yute why he should never fuck with us!"

"You want me to back out the ting?" Brootz replied frantically.

"Back it out now, bruv!"

Brootz slowly lifted his jacket, dug his hand into his tracksuit bottoms and pulled out a long, sharp object with a slight curve in its centre.

Oh shit, thought Tundé, whose fighting spirit diminished with every breath he took.

That's a samurai sword!

Chapter 7

BROOTZ'S ERRATIC WIELDING OF the samurai sword painted a canvas of worry across Tundé's face. He had entered survival mode. He became acutely aware of the rain pattering against the concrete, the rumble of the thunder and the PMD boys' provocative chants.

I can't take my eyes off this yute or that weapon...

But Tundé sensed that Brootz was a little fearful and jittery too. Despite being frozen to the spot, Tundé felt a glimmer of hope. Maybe the young PMD member's tentativeness would give him a small window to escape.

"Bro, why are you moving shook? I thought you were ready!" Bullet shouted at Brootz. "You want the mandem to keep you safe from all the fuckery, right?"

Despite the peer pressure, Brootz remained hesitant. While it was an opportunity to prove that he was capable of handling violent confrontations, he too was concerned about the consequences of harming Tundé. That conflicted with his knowledge that inaction could jeopardise his place in the PMD crew. And losing their protection from local rivals and other threats could be precarious.

"Do it, bruv," Bullet said darkly. "Show us why you belong here."

Tundé noticed an energetic shift, as Brootz snapped out of his cloud of uncertainty and his eyes lowered with sinister intent. The moment was intensified by the rolling clap of thunder in the distance as the heavy rainfall continued. Brootz lifted the sword and moved threateningly towards Tundé. He tried to flee but stumbled helplessly to the cold, wet ground. With his reputation on the line, Brootz couldn't let Tundé slip away now.

"You can't run from me, y-you pussy'ole," shouted Brootz with a nervous quiver. He raised the sword high above his intended victim. Tundé struggled to get up. The razor-sharp blade swept down with unrelenting force.

"AAGH! AAGH! HELP ME!" Tundé screamed in excruciating pain.

Brootz was stunned by the horror. The other PMD gang members were unfazed. The sword had pierced through Tundé's school shirt, taking a chunk of flesh from the right-hand side of his chest and instantly dyed the shirt crimson red. Brootz was visibly panicked as Tundé lay flat out on the ground. However, the gang was not satisfied.

"Jook him again, fam!" one of the PMD boys commanded.

But Brootz was apprehensive. He had never seen so much blood spurting out of a human. It began to stain his dark grey tracksuit. He could barely process the gruesome sight of Tundé's cut-up flesh.

"Are you deaf bro?" Bullet intervened, keen to continue the massacre.

"NO, PLEASE! ALLOW ME MAN!" pleaded Tundé, as Brootz held the sword up menacingly, despite his clear reservations.

"AAGGHH! AAGGHH!" Tundé repeatedly screamed as Brootz hacked away at his torso multiple times.

The abandoned street resembled a slaughterhouse in a butcher's shop. As the rain continued pouring heavily, it dispersed Tundé's blood across the tarmac.

"Take the rest of his shit too, Brootz," laughed Bullet coldly, "including that cloth ting. Seems like he really wanted it back."

Tundé was wheezing for air. His lungs had been cut open and were steadily filling up with blood, forcing him to cough it up desperately. His heart pumped aggressively to keep him alive, while a pool of blood formed underneath him. He was panic-stricken.

Oh shit. I'm actually gonna die. What was I thinking? I should have listened to Auntie Abi and stayed out of trouble. I'm scared to die.

Suddenly, loud noises came booming through from the sky. The blasts were so intense that the PMD boys looked upward with terror. The sky directly above them had rapidly changed from the overcast grey to a distinct, magnificent black, covering the quiet side road in a veil of darkness. The deafening noise also compelled Tundé to squint up too. It seemed like he was experiencing the expedition of his imminent death. The paranormal scenes continued to unravel in the rainfall. The lightning from the dark, black cloud concentrated itself into a large, bright red fiery ball, leaving the PMD boys bewildered. Before they could react, blinding thunderbolts shot out from the ball progressively—striking down the old lampposts, slicing trees in half and carving up sizeable craters on Greenfeel Road. The apocalyptic scenes stunned the PMD gang to a standstill. Even their seemingly fearless leader, Bullet, was gobsmacked by what he was seeing. Then, a powerful, swirling wind erupted from the storm. The noise was ear-splitting.

"Bruv, what the fuck?" cried one of the PMD boys, whose voice cracked because he was so petrified.

"Inshallah, we make it out of this alive!" cried out another.

"Oh my fucking days! Are you mad?" Brootz hollered with dread.

More ferocious lightning bolts fired down and struck both the PMD's vehicles. One car flipped upside-down onto the other side of the road, while the other instantly caught fire, leaving the crew mystified and looking to Bullet for guidance. Despite these frightening moments,

Tundé felt a warm and comforting aura around him that was too inviting to resist, as he was quickly fading away.

Maybe this is what death is supposed to feel like.

Meanwhile, Bullet was trying to work out how to lead his boys through the supernatural storm. He glanced at the car burning a few yards away from them, then over at what he thought was Tundé's dead body.

"Yo!" Bullet howled, cupping his hands around his mouth so he could be heard over the blistering racket. "Dash his body and the sword onto that burning car so there's less evidence. Then we'll bounce!"

"What about all this?" Brootz strained to speak above the storm as he pointed to his blood-soaked clothes.

"Wallahi, we'll burn all our garms when we get out of here. Let's not dilly dally, mandem!"

Brootz and another PMD boy treaded anxiously towards Tundé, fighting the wind and rain that was pushing them back. Tundé was still breathing—just about—and could sense the PMD members approaching. He was too hurt and debilitated to fight back, even if he wanted to. His body had almost entirely given up.

Without warning, a sequence of lightning strikes hit the ground one by one, bringing Brootz and his associate to a halt. Each bolt of lightning stayed fixed in its position and created a circular shield around Tundé's body.

"There's no way, bruv! What the actual fuck?" Brootz screamed while running backwards with his accomplice, as more lightning bolts began striking down towards each of them. "I'm not on it AT ALL, fam!"

As they scurried back to the rest of the crew, Bullet made signals for them to get out.

"For fuck's sake! He's probably dead already. Dash the sword in the fire and let's get outta here before this madness kills us too!"

Bullet took off his jacket and barked amidst the deafening chaos. "Brootz, put this on to cover the blood on your clothes! Everyone split up and go different ways back to ends."

The PMD crew vacated the scene, and soon after, the howling wind slowed down, the heavy rainfall ended, and the thunder strikes ceased. All that remained now was a dark cloud lingering over Greenfeel Road, the thick smog from the burning vehicle and a dying teenager lying on the street. Resigned to his demise, Tundé's senses were dwindling. But his ears still functioned enough to detect movement nearby. Someone was walking down the street hurriedly.

Is that the police? Or a paramedic? I can't hear any sirens though. Maybe it's a passer-by?

The footsteps came closer and closer.

Maybe it's a junkie who wants to try a ting...

The footsteps were dangerously close.

Maybe it's one of the PMD boys coming back to finish me off?

"Babatundé! Praise be to Shango that I found you!"

Tundé stirred slightly, trying to open his eyes as he recognised the man's voice.

"Don't worry, now. It's me," Uncle Blessing said as he came to terms with his nephew's predicament. "My goodness, I must hurry!"

Chapter 8

Uncle Blessing gently pressed his index and middle finger against Tundé's neck. As the teenager lay unconsciously in his pool of blood, his pulse grew weaker with each passing second. His pupils had rolled into the back of his head, with only the white of his eyes visible through his eyelids.

"I know you're wondering how I found you here," Uncle Blessing said aloud while hastily opening his Aso Oke fabric bag. "Maybe you sensed that I was here with you all along. You almost saw me watching you a few times. But when those area boys arrived, I had to go and hide sha!"

As the toxic smell of smoke continued entering his lungs, Uncle Blessing took a deep breath while he laid out a tiny, brown mat on the wet tarmac beside Tundé. He placed a range of items from his bag onto it—specifically, a hand-sized wooden mixing bowl, three bronze spice tins, a small wooden spoon and a water flask. And, Uncle Blessing's favourite beverage, a glass bottle of Wuimmess. He used his molars to pop open the cap and chugged the beverage down like a man who had been trapped in the desert for 30 days and 30 nights. Within seconds, the drink was finished.

"Ahhh, I needed that. Babatundé, do you know what your name means? Ṣé o mọ?"[1]

Uncle Blessing laughed to himself. He knew that even if Tundé were conscious, his lack of Yorùbá knowledge would have rendered him silent anyway.

"I told your parents they should have spoken Yorùbá to you when you were a child! Don't worry, son, all will be well soon."

Uncle Blessing held the wooden bowl up to the dark cloud above them. He could feel the gentle breeze blow against the tiny hairs of his hands and wrists. Looking down at Tundé's limp body, Uncle Blessing took a deep breath and began chanting. "Ejòó, Olodumare, ẹ mu orisha yin wa sibi bayii. Shango, ṣí ọ̀run ki o fi omi aye kun igbá mi."[2]

The wind howled back at Uncle Blessing in response and quickly gathered speed. The dark clouds started expanding while they descended closer to the pair, eclipsing the abandoned Maryland street even further. Uncle Blessing remained calm and focused. He then called out to the sky again.

"Fun mi ni àrá! Give me lightning!"

The dark cloud immediately acknowledged the request, as it flashed with a distinct brightness before shooting a bolt of lightning directly onto the bowl and Uncle Blessing's body. The force was so powerful that it rumbled the ground tremendously and created a dust fog. As that settled, a formidable ball of light was left in its wake, with Uncle Blessing's silhouette visible in its centre. The brightness was so intense that people from neighbouring streets rushed to their windows to

1. *Do you know?*

2. *Almighty Creator, please bring your orishas here now. Shango (orisha of thunder and lightning) open the sky and fill my bowl with the water of life.*

witness it. The ball of light slowly dissipated, reintroducing the gloomy setting, but a small glimmer was left in its place. The wooden bowl was now glowing scarlet red. Uncle Blessing immediately began to recite Yorùbá passages aloud.

"Mo pè Obàtálá. Ẹlẹda ti awọn ara eniyan. Fun Babatundé awọn ibukun ti ilẹ, ọ̀run ati okùn[3]. Give him the light to handle the darkness."

Uncle Blessing was seemingly possessed, as his eyes became rich, deep crimson while he sat down cross-legged on the mat with the bowl and three spice tins laid out in front of him.

"Imú ẹja abanișere! Nose of the dolphin!" Uncle Blessing chanted, as he added a grey, rubbery substance to the bowl.

"Ẹjẹ alangba! Blood of the lizard!" a dark, red liquid was poured into the bowl.

"Awọn iyẹ idì! Wings of the eagle!" he dropped a brownish-grey bundle in the bowl and began mixing the concoction with extreme focus, whilst humming Yorùbá passages.

Shortly afterwards, he raised the bowl to the sky again and demanded, "Mo pè Ọṣun. I call upon Ọṣun. Fun wa l'òjò! Give us rain!"

That triggered the hovering cloud above to gush heavy rainfall that soaked Uncle Blessing and Tundé as if a colossal showerhead had just been switched on. Deep within his trance, Uncle Blessing retrieved a small, tin container from his pocket and opened it. It contained crushed leaves, but these were no ordinary greenery. Despite the darkness, they shone bright like LED bulbs. A thick cloud of purple smoke arose from the leaves, giving them a mystical quality. Uncle Blessing poured the leaves into the bowl whilst chanting and humming rhythmically.

---

3. *I call Ọbàtálá. The creator of human bodies. Give Babatundé the blessings of the land, the sky and the sea.*

"Mo dupẹ Olodumare ati awọn egún wa[4] . Shango, use the Kogi seaweed to infuse the three elements. Jẹ ki ó ṣe nisin!"[5]

As Uncle Blessing released those words into the atmosphere, the wind lifted the bowl out of his hands and into the storm. A thunderbolt struck at its core as it shook violently in mid-air. The resultant force whizzed it down back into Uncle Blessing's grateful hands. His eyes were gradually returning to their natural, hazelnut colour as he smiled at the contents of the bowl. The liquid concoction was bubbling frantically as it emitted a strong green and purple light.

"Just as I expected, it's ready! Babatundé, you need to drink th—"

Uncle Blessing froze. Tundé was gone. Absent. Departed. His body lay motionless.

"If I pour into his body, it should work. I pray."

Uncle Blessing had no other choice. He lifted Tundé's heavy head up and forcibly opened his lips to pour a considerable amount of the concoction down his throat. He ripped open Tundé's clothing to douse his extensive wounds with the remainder of the mixture.

A few seconds ticked by. Nothing happened. There was only silence. The tension could be sliced by a needlepoint. Uncle Blessing was conscious of his heavy breathing as he observed Tundé diligently. Still, there was no response. The faint sound of the pores on Uncle Blessing's forehead could be heard cracking open as they unleashed large drops of sweat. He was becoming increasingly worried.

"Maybe... maybe I was too late. Olodumare, please forgive me if I made any errors, but we nee–"

"HUHH!" Tundé gasped deeply like a beached whale.

---

4. *Thank you to the Supreme Creator and our ancestors.*

5. *Let it be done now!*

The unpleasant sounds of his body squirming relentlessly against the tarmac followed. His limbs were spasming out of control while his eyeballs rolled around incessantly. Uncle Blessing watched on with agitation.

"I pray that my first attempt at this ritual is successful. It hasn't been performed for almost two centuries. Olodumare, I pray it will be done. For us all our sakes."

Chapter 9

WHILE UNCLE BLESSING WAS praying for his nephew's wellbeing, Tundé had entered his own trance. He felt himself gravitating away from the Earth and into the cosmos. What was most striking, though, was that he was being stripped from his human body. Now, he was interacting with the Universe in a wholly transcendent form.

Tundé soon reached a point where a cluster of seemingly random stars met him. He cautiously analysed the environment. He made out the vast emptiness of space itself, the spots of brightness coming from planets and suns lightyears away, and the cluster of stars close by. Tundé noticed that three stars, in particular, shone bolder and brighter than the rest. Suddenly, the cluster dissipated into thin air, leaving only the three standout stars. They swished through the dark space to surround and close in on Tundé.

Fearful of what he was witnessing, Tundé tried to wriggle himself away. But it was in vain. He couldn't move; he forgot that he had no tangible body! Vulnerable to the circumstances, Tundé let go of struggling and observed as the three stars swirled around his spirit in several directions, until they collided before him. There was an intense explosion of dispersed light. In the aftermath, a celestial, dark-skinned man faced him, radiating powerfully throughout the cosmos. Tundé was in awe at the powerful essence emanating from this entity. While the celestial man's mouth remained closed, his thunderous voice rumbled through the East Londoner's consciousness.

"Babatundé, mo ń bù kún fun ẹ o.[1] "

A pang of terror hit Tundé as the mysterious figure hovered closer to him. But he knew there was nothing he could do. The man placed his hands over the teenager and transmitted shock waves throughout his entire spirit. Tundé was sent hurtling downwards into total darkness as he gradually reassembled back into his human form. Images were projected onto the pitch-black space around him. He observed a sequence of visuals depicting birth, death, life, lifelessness, nature, the planets and the stars. Then, a burst of light erupted spontaneously, accelerating Tundé's downfall within this unknown plane of reality.

The ethereal projections now showcased a scene of a large human migration via land and river to establish a new settlement. The speed at which these pictures flickered indicated the passage of time over centuries. Tundé witnessed the group experience periods of community building, patriotism, war and famine. He saw a nation growing, developing, becoming corrupted and repeating the cycle numerous times until the visuals slowed to a real-time pace. The focus was on a settlement of people somewhere in Yorùbáland, showing each other love and solidarity, which exuded a sense of warmth within Tundé. Without understanding why, he somehow recognised those people. Before he could figure it out, Tundé was abruptly swallowed up by the pure darkness again and his descent accelerated.

Is this ever gonna stop?

Eventually, a projection was cast into Tundé's line of vision once more. It was a scene of three unidentifiable animals running in formation

---

1. *"Babatundé, I shall bless you now."*

alongside a human. As the view became clearer, Tundé could just about discern the features of the man leading the way. What startled him the most wasn't the man's battle scars, his bulging muscles or the controlled authority that he radiated. Instead, Tundé felt a pure, spiritual connection with him.

Hold up. why does that guy seem bare familiar?

As Tundé continued watching, he was struck with a realisation. He recognised the man. He knew everything about him, from his deepest desires to his darkest fears. Was he an honourable mentor? A close relative? A best friend?

That's... that's me!

Suddenly, Tundé was thrust forcefully against the ground with a reverberating impact.

"HUH, PHOO! HUFF, PHOO! UGH, PHOO!" Tundé shot upright, gasping for air.

"Fantastic! It worked! Thank you!" Uncle Blessing's voice boomed gratefully to the sky. "Thank you to our ancestors and the Orishas! Ẹ ṣé gan!"

The dark clouds and stormy weather that hung over them seamlessly vanished, restoring the blue sky and scorching hot sun that graced East London before Tundé's run-in with the PMD crew. Uncle Blessing halted his celebrations when he noticed Tundé's severe state of shock. He didn't know exactly what his nephew experienced during the ritual, but he was aware of its harrowing nature.

"Ah, pẹlẹ," he said comfortingly while patting Tundé on the back. "You're going to be okay. Just keep still and breathe deeply."

Tundé, still perplexed by the unfolding of events, obeyed his uncle. He inhaled and exhaled as deeply as possible. He soon remembered that he'd been stabbed numerous times. As his memory slowly returned, so did the pain. But not quite as he imagined.

It fucking hurts, but it feels like it's going away.

"Uncle, do I need to go hospital?" Tundé asked as he removed his ripped clothing to show his uncle the wounds. After a few seconds of inspection, Uncle Blessing had a wry smile.

"Incredible! Don't worry, Babatundé. You will be fine, I'm sure of it. Besides, we *cannot* let the authorities know about this. There will be too many questions. Questions we'd rather not answer."

"To be fair, *I've* got bare questions myself," Tundé half-joked. "For real though, will I be okay?"

"I promise you, you'll be fine, sha. You and your 'bare questions' will all be answered in good time. First, we need to make sure you get home safely."

Tundé had only rested for a few minutes, but he felt energised enough to attempt standing up.

"Oya, here," Uncle Blessing offered Tundé his hand. "Let me help you up."

Uncle Blessing hunched his nephew's arm over his shoulder to support most of his body weight. As they walked past the abandoned houses of Greenfeel Road, Tundé pondered over the abnormalities of London's weather and the scenes he had just witnessed.

"Uncle, are you some magician or juju man or suttin'? Cos some weird things have been happening the last couple days."

Uncle Blessing chuckled. "Babatundé, what did you tell me your name meant?"

"Errr... return... return of the father, init?" replied Tundé, uncertainly. "Why do you like talking in riddles so much, Uncle? It's a bit long."

"Ehen, you are right! What else do you–"

Uncle Blessing stopped walking and pricked up his ears. A distinct, distant sound threw them both off. It was sirens.

"Oh dear. That must be the police, the ambulance and whoever else!" Uncle Blessing said worriedly, examining the destruction left behind them. "Okay, let's walk through that alleyway. We'll move as quickly as possible. Getting caught here will give us a lot of wahala, o!"

With Tundé still using him as a crutch, Uncle Blessing stumbled over to the alleyway as the sirens grew closer and closer. As they struggled out onto the other side, the first police car arrived at the scene. They were extremely wary since several calls had put the fear of God into the telephone operators.

"You 'ear what the guvna said?" one policeman asked another in his strong Cockney accent.

"Sumfin' about a distress call for an apocalypse."

"Yeah. Apparently, the person on the phone lives local. Called about eight times before they was put through to the Met. The Ops team thought it was a hoax!"

"Doesn't look like a hoax now, does it mate?"

A few minutes later, police cars, ambulances and fire brigades piled up onto the abandoned road. There was an air of trepidation among the emergency services staff. Two burning cars, scythed trees, a destroyed landscape and blood splattered on the floor, after being told to expect a doomsday-like scene. Hesitantly, they began to leave their vehicles one by one. Greenfeel Road was soon filled with dozens of people. The firemen prepared their hoses to deal with the burning cars, the paramedics looked for anybody in need of medical assistance and the police officers scoured the area for clues.

Except one officer, who remained in his car. Watching the investigations unfold through his windscreen, the lone officer had a moment of realisation. He nervously checked to see if any colleagues were around, and proceeded to pull out an old phone from a discreet jacket pocket. He texted an anonymous contact.

'Mate, work just sent me to a bizarre incident in Stratford. I think they're here.'

Chapter 10

"Come on, Tundé. We're almost there now."

Uncle Blessing and his nephew were walking through the dark Isle of Dogs streets on their way back to the Samuda Estate. The deep indigo shade of the night sky loomed over them as Uncle Blessing took up the challenging task of carrying the injured teenager back to safety. Fortunately, they had escaped from the chaotic scene at Greenfeel Road unnoticed. Spotting a clothing donation box on their way back, Uncle Blessing picked a few items for disguises just in case. Tundé donned a black puffer jacket and a woolly hat, while Uncle Blessing had a grey scarf wrapped around his neck with a brown breast jacket. Their outfits were a little unusual considering the record-high temperatures, but that wasn't their biggest concern. They just wanted to get back home unscathed as soon as possible. They felt a huge sense of relief once they entered the Samuda Estate grounds.

"Seriously, Uncle. What was all that?" Tundé asked Uncle Blessing as they approached the block entrance for Equiano House.

"Don't you worry, son. I will explain everything in due time. Just focus on your rest for now."

"Uncle, tell me *something*. This whole thing is so weird!"

"Okay, okay. All I will say for now is that I did something an uneducated mumu might call juju."

Tundé was stunned. He almost wished he hadn't gotten an answer now.

"And you wanted to live, abi?" Uncle Blessing asked.

"Yeah, of course. Thanks for that, I guess."

"And as I said, if you are still suffering tomorrow, I will take you straight to the hospital. I promise you that."

They soon boarded the Equiano House lift to the fifteenth floor. Tundé worried about what his mum would think if she saw him in this condition. But peering at Uncle Blessing through the mirror, he seemed rather unconcerned. So he thought it best to follow his elder's lead. Upon entering the flat, they could hear his mum engrossed in a phone call from the corridor. Much to Tundé's relief.

"Make sure you cover your face up and go straight to bed," Uncle Blessing whispered, letting Tunde go so he could walk alone. "I'll distract her when we go in. We don't want Sister Fola asking too many questions, abi?"

Tundé nodded in agreement. Keeping his mum out of the loop was definitely in his best interests.

"Ṣé kosi pẹlu ọmọbirin yẹn?[1] What for her parents now?" Tundé's mum could be heard saying loudly down the phone as they walked into the living room. She acknowledged their presence with a wave.

"Ehen. Ehen. Listen, my son and his uncle are here now. Let's talk later, sha. Tomorrow? Okay, o dàbọ̀![2] Yeah, bye, bye..."

Mrs Adeyemi turned her attention to the recent arrivals.

"Good evening, Sister Fola," Uncle Blessing said as she slowly got to her feet.

---

1. *So, what is wrong with that girl?*

2. *Goodbye!*

"Ẹ kààlẹ[3] , Brodah Blessing! We thank God you arrived safely in London."

"Good evening, Mum," Tundé said, following Yorùbá custom by bowing down to greet her. But he could only reach halfway because he was too hurt.

"Ah ah, can't you greet properly in front of our guest, Tundé?" Mrs Adeyemi asked.

"Sister, now, now. Please, be easy on him," Uncle Blessing interjected. "You should go to bed, Tundé. You've been telling me it's been a long day."

Tundé didn't waste any time and plodded straight to his bedroom. Mrs Adeyemi kissed her teeth.

"But he's going to help me make rice and stew for you, Brodah. It's the least he can do to show he hasn't forgotten his manners!"

"Don't worry, he's fine. Let him be, jor!" Uncle Blessing boomed with a light-hearted tone.

"Night, Mum," said Tundé hastily, "And goodnight, Uncks. Thanks."

Tundé rushed into his room, with the indistinct chatter of the adults catching up about Nigeria and life in the background.

"Fola, we are missing your presence in Naija, now. It's been a long time since you came to visit."

"By God's grace, I will find a way to come soon, o. But my bills have become wahala!"

Good thing they haven't seen each other for a long while. That should keep them busy while I get some rest.

---

3. *Good evening*

Tundé was so drained that he didn't bother getting undressed, only removing the puffer jacket. He slid under his tattered covers and stared at the ceiling. He reflected on the craziness that ensued over the last couple of days, and how grateful he was that, in the end, Uncle Blessing was there to save him. He still had a lot of questions, though.

Tundé turned over in his bed to look out of the window. He could just about see the bright rays of light from Canary Wharf filtering through his flimsy blinds. Fantasising about the dream of moving his whole family there, the obvious soon dawned on him.

Fuck! I lost Jerry's stash and the family heirloom!

Tundé's mind switched gears and went into overdrive. It was filled with a myriad of worries. Money, death, loved ones, friends, girls, school, bairaff, his status, the city and magic. Consumed by agony, he hid under the duvet and desperately tried to switch his brain off...

After some time, Tundé was subtly awoken by an unfamiliar noise. Listening closer, he identified the harmonies of crickets singing and birds chirping. Confused by its clarity, Tundé stirred and opened his eyes. His body, surprisingly, was completely re-energised after the day's heavy events. As he rose to his feet and took in his surroundings, he was alarmed. Tundé was in a shadowy grassland, covered by large trees with considerably long branches. The atmosphere was strikingly humid as the sweat dripped from his forehead. His ears picked up echoes from indistinct animals in the distance. This place felt sparse.

Man's not in the ends no more...

Looking down at where he'd been sleeping, Tundé saw a bed of leaves and other plant debris, which had crumbled when he stood to his feet. He soon felt a slight breeze blowing around his nether regions.

Bruv, why am I naked?

The only item on his body was an ancient Yorùbá loincloth, covering a few inches down from his hip. It was made from the Adeyemi family Aso Oke fabric. Without warning, the bushes around Tundé started rustling. It unnerved him. Cautious to avoid danger, he quickly stepped onto a trodden path between the trees, illuminated by spots of sunlight penetrating through the greenery. Just as Tundé joined the pathway, an army of giant lizards burst out of the bushes and darted straight for him.

"Uh oh!"

In a panic, he ran at full speed down the pathway. He had no idea where it was taking him, but he had no choice but to follow it with the large creatures hot on his tail.

"SKREEAGHH! SKREEAGHH!"

As Tundé peered over his shoulder to know where those menacing cries came from, he saw a mob of eagles flying above the giant lizards. They were also in close pursuit.

For fuck's sake! Why are they chasing ME?

As he sprinted towards the sunset on the horizon, Tundé realised he was approaching a river shore. The backdrop of the fiery red sun gave him a sense of hope, but fatigue was catching up with him too. Weighing up his options, he wasn't sure that he could trust the river. But staying on the land would be difficult with both the eagles and lizards chasing him relentlessly.

Swimming isn't my forte, but I'm gonna have to firm it and jump in.

"Tundé!" boomed a high-spirited voice that filled the entire space.

The teenager was rattled. Not just by the nature of the voice, but because he recognised it too. And he hadn't heard it for a very long time.

"Tundé!" the voice called again.

Now only a few yards away from the river shore, Tundé lifted his head and took a full view of the horizon ahead. The face of a dark-skinned, fresh-faced man with a defined jawline was projected onto the sun. He recognised him.

"You must allow it to happen, Babatundé. You cannot run. You cannot hide. You must embrace it."

Tears raced down Tundé's cheek. He fiercely shook his head from side to side in disbelief.

"No, I can't! I can't do this!" Tundé cried back at the man on the sun, as he took a few steps into the shallow edge of the river.

"Of course, you can! You are a Yorùbá man. You are an Adeyemi. The power is within you."

Out of the blue, a formation of dolphins launched themselves out of the river like missiles, aiming straight for Tundé. It brought him to a horrifying standstill. The lizards and eagles quickly closed in on him too. There was nowhere to run. So, he braced himself and surrendered.

"ARGGGH!" Tundé bellowed as the lizards, eagles and dolphins simultaneously fused into his torso as if his spirit was absorbing them all.

His body shuddered with intensity as the animals continued to amass into his being. Unexpectedly, Tundé burst into thousands of tiny pieces scattered along the riverbed, onto the land and floating in midair. Then, the pieces began to pulsate and gradually roll back together, reassembling into one entity. Tundé had returned to his normal state.

"Woah."

The landscape, however, was now pitch black. The only source of light was coming from an enlarged moon. The ethereal man reappeared before him, levitating down from the moon and towards Tundé, who was speechless.

"It is your destiny, Babatundé," the man said, placing his hand over Tundé's eyes, blinding him to everything. "You must embrace the darkness that comes with the light!"

"No! I'm not ready for it, Dad! I can't do this!" shouted Tundé, as he shot up, sweating profusely. It was still pitch black.

Where am I? What's going on?

A flash of light hit his eyes.

"Ah ah, is everything okay? You've been making noises all night. Are you having those nightmares again?"

Tundé was panting heavily. But he was relieved to hear his mum's voice as he slowly recognised his bedroom. Glancing at the time, he realised why she was so concerned. It was four o'clock in the morning!

"I'm okay, Mum," he said as he composed himself, trying to put her mind at ease. "I'm okay."

"Let us pray that God will cover you in holiness and protect you from evil."

"Thanks, Mum. I might need that."

Chapter 11

"Coo! Coo!"

Tundé was awoken by the sounds of birds outside his window. Despite his concerns, he soon realised that it was a normal flock of pigeons on this occasion. As he sat up in bed, he looked over at the wall clock.

Shit! I'm gonna be late for school.

It was already quarter to eight in the morning. While he stretched his arms out and yawned loudly, something became clear to him.

I feel... really fucking good, considering.

Flashbacks from the last 24 hours came flooding back to his mind. The apocalyptic weather. Uncle Blessing's ritual. The nightmare starring his dad.

Hold on. I got stabbed too!

Tundé threw off his bed covers and undressed hurriedly in front of the bedroom mirror to inspect himself. He was flabbergasted by what he saw.

Rah, am I going crazy? I'm... I'm completely cured!

His bruised eye from the fight with Lorenzo had cleared up. The swelling and pain had vanished. All his wounds had fully healed. His torso was entirely rejuvenated, with no scars or tissue damage anywhere. Not even a scratch. His body was in perfect condition. Tundé was amazed. He questioned whether the last couple of days were even real. Glancing back at the clock, it was now almost eight o'clock. Tundé had barely any wiggle room to make it to school on time now. He scrambled chaotically around the room to get ready. Just as he was about to leave the flat, his mum appeared in the hallway.

"Morning, Mum," Tundé greeted his mum hesitantly, remembering that she checked up on him during the night.

"Good morning, dear," his mum said with obvious unease. "Are you okay?"

Tundé wanted to squash this conversation as soon as possible. He didn't want to add fuel to his mum's worries and make life more stressful.

"It's okay, Mum. I'm fine."

"Are you sure? I heard you calling out for your father again."

She didn't want her son to suffer. Not if she could help it.

"Honestly, Mum, I'm fine! It's not a ting, so let's not worry," Tundé blurted out, fighting hard to hold back his tears. "Anyway, I need to leave. Otherwise, I'm gonna be late for school."

"Okay, son. As long as you're sure. Have a blessed day."

Tundé moved briskly through the streets to get to the bus stop on time. When the D7 arrived, he sat himself at the back of the top deck. He was especially anxious about being late after his recent exclusion. It wouldn't put him in Mr Bull's good books, that's for sure. But he accepted there was little he could do now. He was at the mercy of his environment, just as he had been in his surreal dream.

Peering outside the window, Tundé noticed a young child at a crowded bus stop who was holding his father's hand. Tundé's attention was then drawn to the ladybird sitting on this young boy's shoulder. The vibrant red hue of the outer shell and the minuscule detail on the wing shields captivated Tundé, as the ladybird moved steadily across the boy's school jumper, busy chasing another small green insect. Based on his memory of Miss Stevens' biology lessons, he was sure it was an aphid.

"Wait, wait, hold up!" he hissed aloud, suddenly grasping the profound nature of what he was experiencing.

Did I really just see those insects up close like that? Or am I bugging?

Tundé shook his head, rubbed his eyes and redirected his focus to the front of the bus, taking a few deep breaths to calm himself down. When the bus stopped at a red light, Tundé peeped out of the window again. On his left was a schoolgirl his age who was texting on her miCell while waiting to cross the road. Lured in by her attractiveness, his eyes stayed glued to her until he noticed something quite unusual.

'Yh, she's such a dickhead. She won't even reply to my msgs now xxx'

From 20 yards away, Tundé could easily read—word for word, pixel by pixel—exactly what this girl was texting her friend 'Shanice' on the internet messaging platform, HowRU. Trying to process this mind-blowing experience, Tundé's eyes fixated on her fingers as she typed. Disturbingly, the various marks and cracks on her fingertips were vivid. As though he was viewing all this through a telescopic lens. She had probably been biting her nails. When the girl noticed Tundé watching her, he ducked away from the window.

Fam, why are my eyes bugging? I must be in another dream.

He rubbed his eyes again. Surely, he wasn't going insane? Once the traffic light turned green and the D7 started moving again, Tundé slapped his head a few times and faced the bus's windscreen. He didn't want to spook himself out any further.

A few moments later, a man got on the bus and sat a few rows ahead of Tundé. Then it happened again. His eyes swiftly zoomed in to the back of this random man's head, revealing the finer details. A few small strands of his hair were turning grey, while one of every twenty hair strands was a different shade of brown, subtly indicating the use of hair dye. Tundé was grossed out by the clear sight of lice crawling across the man's dry, crackled scalp, as the parasites went to work.

"Ahhh!" gasped Tundé, as he rubbed his eyes again and shook his head. "Just make it stop!"

A few people on the bus, including the man with lice, stared back at him with bemusement.

"You alright, mate?" the man asked hesitantly.

"Yeah, I'm good, bro. We're cool," Tundé replied, still disgusted by the man's poor hygiene.

"Alright then, fella," said the man as he turned around scratching away at the back of his head. Tundé cringed.

"Next stop: Mile End Park North," came from the bus's speakers. He'd missed his stop!

Tundé banged the stop button several times as he ran downstairs from the top deck. The disgruntled bus driver let him off, and Tundé ran desperately to Stebon High. He was sure that he'd messed everything up at this point, reminding him about his lost belongings.

First the bairaff ting, then all those dreams, and now my eyes moving mad? How am I meant to handle all these damn problems?

Unfortunately for Tundé, he got to the registration class a few minutes after the school bell rang. Thus, he decided to use all his charm to reason with his form tutor, Miss Schmidt.

"Miss, I promise you, I love your registration session so much. And I hate being late to them. This is the last time until exams, I promise. You can bell my yard and badmouth me to Mumsy if it ever happens again."

The classroom murmured with laughter.

"Hmmm, okay," Miss Schmidt said reluctantly. "It better not, otherwise I'll be talking to your mother about more than just your lateness."

"Deal," Tundé said as he sat down at his desk. He was relieved to escape the punishment of an after-school detention or Mr Bull's judging eye. He soon caught a glimpse of Remi's face in the classroom. He seemed frustrated and distressed, which was no surprise given the circumstances.

Tundé mouthed over to Remi, "Talk later, yeah?"

Still visibly annoyed, Remi nodded his head to acknowledge the message. Once registration finished, Tundé headed to the school's science department for his first lesson of the day. He avoided Remi, whose eyes he could feel burning into the back of his head en route to Physics. When they entered the classroom, the boys sat at opposite ends of the room. Their teacher, Mr Panther, had separated the two a few weeks prior for constant chatting.

"Like I said, we'll talk at break, init," Tundé said while taking his seat. Remi gave Tundé a displeased nod.

"Do I need to separate you two lovebirds from the entire *class* now?" Mr Panther joked at their expense, prompting a chorus of giggles from the class as everybody took their seats.

"I beg you get on with the lesson, then," Remi retorted with an uncharacteristically blunt tone.

Startled by his assertiveness, Mr Panther took a second to pause.

"Okay, class. Remi seems extra eager for Physics today, so let's get started! Please turn to page 118 so we can revisit Newton's Laws of Motion for your upcoming exams."

As the lesson continued, to Tundé's surprise, he became increasingly engaged with the material. Every individual word, each guiding principle, and every final equation uttered by Mr Panther captivated him in a way that had not happened before. He usually found the topic of physics quite mundane.

Mr Panther drew an example of a ball dropping from 30 metres high on the whiteboard, explaining the theory the students needed to use to figure out the required answers for their exam.

"All these components are important to remember for your upcoming paper. By multiplying the mass of the object by acceleration, we can calculate the resultant force of the ball dropping in the air."

In a strange development of circumstances, Tundé's mind projected a vivid schematic overlay onto Mr Panther's simple illustration. The projection included several related variables and complex equations placed at different points in Mr Panther's example.

Bruv, what the fuck! Can anyone else see this too?

Tundé took a glance around the classroom. None of the other students seemed to be fazed. He turned back to the whiteboard, and in a flash, his mind began projecting the schematic onto the example again. Realising that only he was privy to this extraordinary view, Tundé studied the various elements. With a deeper level of understanding, he was urged to intervene.

"Sir, there's so much missing from this calculation."

Mr Panther, who was adding arrows to the diagram, halted in surprise. He thought it was the beginning of an elaborate joke.

"Now, Mr Adeyemi, don't start your comedy career during my cl–"

"Firstly, you need to account for the air resistance the ball is experiencing," Tundé interrupted again, "and to calculate that, you would need the drag coefficient and the variable density of the air. Then you need to find the friction contribution from the material on the surface of the ball. And there's the heat coefficient of the ball to consider, as the temperature in the air at that altitude also impacts the resultant downward force of the ball."

Without a second thought, Tundé started scribbling out the schematic he was seeing in his mind onto a piece of paper. He was completely astonishing himself. But he persisted. It felt like a specific part of his brain had taken over. Mr Panther and his classmates watched on with bewilderment. This was entirely out of character.

"Then," continued Tundé, "we can also account for the wind movement in the air that would affect how fast the ball travels."

Seemingly possessed, he took his piece of paper up to the whiteboard, barely acknowledging Mr Panther's presence while he picked up the marker from the stand and began transferring his notes onto the board. He unashamedly corrected and changed most of the equations that his teacher had neatly drawn on the board.

"And who qualified you to be a teacher, then, Mr Adeyemi?" Mr Panther uttered, feeling undermined by his pupil's unexpected takeover.

But Tundé was undeterred by Mr Panther's latent insecurities. He was too focused on the powerful connections his brain was making, employing all his scientific knowledge and real-life experiences for the sole purpose of solving this GCSE Physics question.

"If we assume the drag coefficient for the ball is 0.13, and an air composition of 79% nitrogen and 21% oxygen, then the resultant force acting downwards on the ball would *actually* be 7,384 Newtons. Rounded to the nearest whole number, still."

There was a brief moment of silence, as Mr Panther and the class stared blankly at the whiteboard, baffled—but impressed—by the masterpiece Tundé had just produced.

"Rah, when did you become such a neek, Tunds?" one boy in the class said, breaking the silence. The comment was met with a burst of collective laughter from everyone in the room. All except Remi, Mr Panther and Tundé himself.

"Okay class, that's enough," Mr Panther ordered, still assessing Tundé's work. "I have to say, this would be quite impressive for a Physics Master's student, let alone a kid in set two at Stebon High School."

Tundé, however, wasn't focused on Mr Panther's remarks or the jokes at his expense. He was trying to comprehend what was happening to his body. Looking at his textbook, Tundé's mind was projecting endless equations and schematics onto its images. He couldn't control it. It was a repeat of the bizarre experience he had on the bus in the morning.

Big man ting, what is actually going on?

"Uncle's magic!" Tundé accidentally said aloud.

"Oh, so it's Nigerian juju making you smart?" said the same outspoken boy, making the classroom giggle again. "I swear that's cheating, sir?"

"I beg you shut up, Eddie," Tundé said, turning to the boy. His eyes spontaneously zoomed in on Eddie's face, spotting a familiar cluster of crisps scattered around his mouth. "Just cos you can't clean them Moritoes off your face properly, you dusty yute."

Eddie was stunned. He couldn't believe Tundé knew what he'd been eating on his way to school that morning.

"You're... you're gassing, fam," Eddie faltered, as he started wiping his mouth unconsciously.

"So, why you cleaning your face then, big man?" a girl in the class chimed in. Tundé knew that voice. It belonged to Laura. The class laughed raucously at Eddie, and Laura gave Tundé a big smile.

Rah, I didn't think she'd have my back like that!

Tundé was in good spirits. Since he'd become the butt of jokes in this class recently, he was hyped that he could turn the tide. Especially with his crush noticing.

"Right, right! Settle down, class. Let Eddie finish cleaning himself up while we continue with our lesson," Mr Panther said cheekily, picking up the textbook. "Okay, now turn to page 148 and get started on exercise 11.8."

At the end of the lesson, Tundé left for the playground, needing some definite answers to more than just Mr Panther's physics questions.

I need to work out wagwan before something bad happens.

"Yo bro, we need to talk."

"Yo, Remi," responded Tundé meekly. "Yeah, let's talk bro. It's been a mad ting, I'm not gonna lie."

Tundé and Remi walked over to a secluded area of the school playground, usually reserved for Lorenzo and his crew. But since they weren't around anymore, the two best friends could use it for their important conversation.

"So, what you saying, fam?" asked Tundé.

"What do you mean what am *I* saying? *You're* the one who's in debt, fam!"

"Bruv, abeg you keep it down," Tundé hushed, glimpsing around to ensure no one was in earshot. "I seriously could have died, bro!"

Remi's expression changed from impatience to intrigue. Tundé spent the next few minutes explaining to Remi everything he could remember from his meeting with Jerry, right up to the point where he escaped from the storm. He left out the part where he got stabbed, Uncle Blessing's arrival and the magic ritual, of course.

"Rahtid! That sounds mad, bro," Remi sympathised with Tundé's woes. "I'm not sure Jerry's gonna buy that though. He tried to call you bare times last night as well."

Tundé remembered that he switched his brick phone off. He was too scared to face up to the music now.

"Bro I fully hear that, but why would man lie? I know Jerry's not the guy to fuck with, so I wouldn't steal his stash. Plus, you're my bruddah."

"Yeah man, I know. I thought it would be very wild of you to bump him. Jerry's still fucking mad though, and he wants answers by tonight. I don't know what he's gonna do cos you lost big P's for him."

Tundé was distraught. He didn't have a clue how he was going to resolve this situation now.

"Jerry said that Biskit—the buyer—told him about the weather doing an absolute madness. Then bare feds turned up. So what you're telling me checks out. But when Jerry's still vexed..."

"Yeah, yeah, I hear you. He's probably on demon time."

Tundé wished he hadn't got himself involved now. If he did nothing, Jerry would hunt him down. If Jerry retaliated against the PMD crew on his behalf, it could spark a street war that would put his safety at risk anyway. It was quite a dilemma.

"Let's talk after school, bro. Give me some time to work out what I'm gonna tell Jerry."

"Alright, Tunds. Make sure you shout me straight after. Like I said, Jerry isn't usually shy to get shit cracking."

"Yeah, I will do. Don't watch."

"Say nothing."

Remi fist-bumped Tundé just as the bell signalling the end of the break time rang. They headed back to the main premises for the next block of classes. The final lesson of the day was one that Tundé generally enjoyed, but wasn't particularly good at.

"Alright lads. Since we're so close to exam season, we're gonna play 7-a-side football for our PE lesson today," Mr Athlima said, savouring the power he wielded over his class as they lined up on the weathered, synthetic grass pitch. "Be thankful I ain't making you lot do laps!"

"Whichever team I'm on, I'll go in goal!" Tundé declared.

He was keen to use the extra time away from the action to think of his options to get Jerry's bairaff and his heirloom back. As expected, his classmates clamoured to add him to their team so they could play outfield for longer. Once the match started, instead of Tundé to focus on his plan of action, he got progressively immersed in the football. His reaction time to shots at his goal was tenfold better than he was ever capable of before. Not a single goal was scored past him. Even the most powerful of strikes he saved with minimal effort.

"Where did this come from, Tunds? You're playing like me in my goalkeeping heyday," Mr Athlima said jokingly. "Might have to test you for enhancement drugs, son!"

"Only sugar and H2O, sir," laughed Tundé.

If only he knew. If only I knew!

Halfway through the match, James—a slightly overweight pupil—got too tired to keep playing outfield.

"Beg you... let me... go in bro..." he struggled to catch his breath. Tundé hadn't gained much traction with his plotting while in goal. He might find more inspiration if he got into the thick of things.

"Fuck it, you can swap with me, mate," Tundé said as he handed the gloves to the exhausted James.

"Put a shift in, bro," said another classmate encouraged. Tundé put his thumbs up.

As the match progressed, the Isle of Dogs teenager excelled. He felt stronger, moved quicker and passed the ball more precisely than his fellow pupils. He even outclassed the two boys who represented the London County under-16s team. One of the larger players on the opposite team, Yannick—who the Stebon pupils referred to casually as 'The Beast'—tried to barge him off the ball. But he bounced off Tundé like a stone from a catapult. It was to the shock of all those in attendance.

"Maybe we do need to test you," Mr Athlima said with a hint of suspicion.

Towards the end of the lesson, Tundé tripped over a little divot on the pitch, slid over and scraped his leg along the surface. He inspected the damage. His leg had a massive burn with a patch of skin hanging off it.

Fuck me, that hurts!

But then...

"Rahhh!" Tundé gasped, watching the wound on his leg start to heal instantly. Fresh, healthy skin was growing gradually over the exposed flesh.

"You okay there, mate?" asked Mr Athlima, walking over to attend to him. Tundé pulled his football socks over his leg. He couldn't let anyone spot this strange phenomenon.

"Yeah. I'm blessed, sir."

"Alright. Get back up quickly then, your team needs you! Last 5 minutes, lads. Let's see which team comes out on top!"

After the lesson, once all his classmates had left the changing room, Tundé loitered behind. He wanted to inspect himself more thoroughly. Having stripped down to his vest, boxers and football socks, the teenager stood in front of the mirrors to assess himself.

Rassclart, man's getting proper hench you know. Damn!

Tundé marvelled as he took in the astounding transformation his body had undergone. Every muscle appeared chiselled and defined. The mirror reflected a physique that had toned up exponentially in just a few short hours. When he sat down to take his socks off, the burn had vanished. His leg was fully healed without a single trace of injury left behind. At this point, Tundé was beginning to accept how peculiar his life was becoming. Out of the blue, an idea came to him.

Maybe I can use these changes to my body to get the bairaff back myself. Maybe.

He packed up his backpack and headed for the school exit. Despite his reservations, Tundé felt some relief that he had a potential route to get his stuff back from the PMD that was in his hands. Before he could plan any further though, his thoughts were interrupted.

"Yo, I've been waiting for you," Remi said bluntly as he leaned against the school gates. "Wagwan?"

"My bad. Man's just a bit drained after the last couple of days, init. A lot's happened."

"I hear that. But obviously, Jerry needs to kno–"

"Listen, bro," Tundé interrupted. "Don't worry, I'll handle it. Tell Jerry to give me the weekend to get everything sorted with the PMD. If not, tell him he can deal with it however he wants to from Monday morning."

"Have you lost your mind, bruv? Why do you sound bare confident you can sort this out now?"

"I don't really have another choice, bro," Tundé looked boldly into Remi's eyes while suppressing the doubts arising in his mind.

"Okay, do what you need to. I just beg you don't do anything too stupid. This is big boy territory, you know."

“Fam, don’t worry. I might be able to get something done.”

“Just remember, you’re not Superman, fam,” Remi warned Tundé. “These man are killers. It’s not like when we were likkle yutes back in primary school.”

Chapter 12

Tundé sprinted across the playground at breakneck speed. He was desperate to make it to the other side as fast as possible. Everything was on the line.

"Tunds, you cheater! Come back, not everyone was ready yet!" a high-pitched voice wailed at him from a distance.

"Oh, Lorenzo! That's not fair, it's my turn to say 'go'," Tundé shrieked, turning back to see a sea of his peers setting themselves across a faded white line next to the main entrance of Tophall Primary School.

"I was going to catch you anyway!" declared a shrill voice.

"Nuh-uh! Not even if I gave you a head start, Remi," Tundé said as he stuck his tongue out. "I'm going to win today, just like I did two weeks ago."

"Poku created this race first," Remi suggested. "So he should do the countdown this week. He's never done it since!"

"Nooo, I just want to race this time!" Poku declared.

"I'm going to be 10 in five months," said another of the kids. "Because I'm the oldest here, I should do it."

"Alright James, the September baby. I know you really don't want to run because you ate too much for breakfast!" Lorenzo taunted the overweight child.

"I'm telling Miss Webb on you!" James started to sob.

"Stop being mean and leave him alone, Lorenzo," Tundé said defensively. "Are we going to start soon or what?"

The Year 4 pupils were gearing themselves up for their weekly race. Their lenient teacher, Miss Webb, allowed them to leave the classroom five minutes before the lunch bell every Wednesday. For the 2020 Spring Term, this set of schoolchildren used their precious extra lunchtime to race across the empty playground—from the west wing to the east wing—which spanned roughly 90 metres. The finish line was represented by an old Victorian wall on the east side, its appearance seeming out of place amongst the sleek, modern buildings installed since the school's inception in 1897.

The prize for winning? An opportunity to gloat that you were the fastest pupil in the class until the next race occurred seven days later. However, given the circumstances, this week's edition was even more significant for the kids.

"Last race before Easter holidays!" Remi shouted. "Winner holds the title for three weeks!"

"Orie-me-dee, your feet are over the line," said Rizwan, another of the contenders.

"How many times, Rizzy?" Remi responded. "If you're going to say my full name—Oremidé—it's pronounced 'ohr-reh-mee-day'. But just call me Remi!"

"It doesn't matter who does the count, I just want to race," said a softer voice placed further down the starting line.

"Laura, you're always trying to distract us, when *you're* the one always cheating," Tundé said rolling his eyes.

"Okay, everyone ready..." James announced as he stood along the faded starting line, where all 15 racers had placed their front foot in preparation.

"On your marks... get set... Go! Go! Go!"

A collective, thumping noise echoed through the playground. The soles of their trainers stomped down heavily on the concrete surface as the kids darted towards the Victorian wall. Jovial ranting emerged as they jostled for their race positions. A few seconds into the race, Laura was nudging ahead, with Lorenzo and Tim in close pursuit, while the rest of the kids were a few yards behind. Seconds later, Laura began falling behind, and Remi made his way towards the front, getting ahead of Lorenzo.

"Yes!" Remi exclaimed.

He rarely ever won these races but found himself in the pole position with a third of the way gone. At that moment, Lorenzo outstretched his arm, grabbed Remi by the back of his top, and dragged him back, taking the lead in the race. Tundé, seeing this from behind, instinctively pulled Remi back up to his feet as he was on his way down. He then accelerated and caught up with Lorenzo.

"You're a cheater!" Tundé growled as he stuck out his right foot and swiped Lorenzo's trailing leg. They both tumbled over disjointedly to the ground, as the rest of the running pack zoomed past them.

"Yes, I won!" Rizwan declared as he smacked his palms onto the wall. He was closely followed by Remi in second place, with third place just edged by Laura.

"Laura, you smashed it," said Precious, who came in seventh. "Repping us girls strongly!"

"You know it!" Laura huffed as she caught her breath.

As Tundé hit the finish line, Lorenzo—now the last person to finish—ran as fast as he could to confront him.

"Oi, Tundé. Why did you fucking do that?" he barked furiously, with no care about the punishments for swearing at school.

"I'm teaching you a lesson. You're always picking on people that are smaller than you," Tundé explained with a righteous tone, "and if it's not fair, then it's not right."

"Well fuck you and your fairness," Lorenzo snapped back at Tundé. "Go suck your mum, init."

The other kids gasped in shock. Disparaging people's mothers was a cardinal, inexcusable sin. The bell for lunch then rang, momentarily overshadowing the the playground clash.

"You fresh off the boat Nigerian batty boys go finish your race together," continued Lorenzo, spewing more venom Tundé and Remi's way.

"What did you say, you idiot?" Tundé barked as he walked towards Lorenzo.

Remi watched on worriedly. He didn't want to get involved in any fighting since he was much smaller than the other boys.

"Don't talk about my mum when you were at my house a few days ago!" Tundé said, feeling betrayed.

How could Lorenzo say that in front of everyone like that?

"Lorenzo, please calm down," said Laura worriedly. "I don't want you to get in trouble."

"Stay out of this, Laura!" Lorenzo shouted as he rolled up his burgundy Tophall uniform jumper. "It's none of your business."

As more schoolchildren started filling up the playground, some were drawn towards the building clash between the eight-year-olds.

"I'm gonna knock you out now," Tundé went to punch Lorenzo, met by cries and cheers from the onlooking pupils.

Lorenzo ducked Tundé's fist and then grappled his body with all the strength he could summon. The boys fell to the ground in a scuffle.

Before the fight could escalate though, their deputy headteacher Mrs Sherley stepped in and separated them.

"Break it up now!" she said sternly, towering over Tundé and Lorenzo as she pulled them apart. "I'm very disappointed in both of you for behaving like this on school property!"

Mrs Sherley then grabbed each of the boys by their wrists and forcefully dragged them inside towards the main reception. "I'm going to be calling both your parents about this. You will be punished."

Lorenzo kept his eyes fixed on the ground, visibly upset as the tears began streaming down his face.

"Tell my mum it was HIS fault! I don't want to get in trouble for him starting it."

Tundé was very anxious. Technically, he did start the fight. But he knew it was for a justifiable reason. Lorenzo was a bully who inconsiderately cheated a friend in their sacred race. In Tundé's mind, he deserved to be addressed accordingly. Even so, that reasoning wouldn't be deemed near good enough for his parents.

"I am surprised though. I thought the two of you were friends?" questioned Mrs Sherley, as she instructed them to sit on the vacant seats outside the school's reception.

"No, he ain't my friend for nuffin'!" Lorenzo said angrily.

"Lorenzo will never ever be my friend."

After being held in detention for the remainder of the day, Tundé bumped into Remi outside the main school building.

"So, did you get in trouble with Mrs Sherley?" Remi asked curiously.

Tundé sighed, "yeah, me and Lorenzo have detention all day tomorrow. And she told my parents too. I'm going to be in SO much trouble when they get home!"

"Oh man, I hope they don't give you too many beats! Thanks for backing me up though."

"It's okay. I hate seeing Lorenzo pick on people, so I had to do something. It's just annoying that we got caught fighting. But I'm not friends with him anymore now."

"Oh, okay. Even if you get in big trouble at home, can we still be friends?"

"Yeah, we can," Tundé reached out to shake Remi's hand with a wry smile. Remi returned the gesture.

"Did you know that my mum and your mum are friends too? They met each other at a Nigerian prayer study group a couple of weeks ago."

"No way? That's random," Tundé said with intrigue. Maybe that could work in his favour. "Do you want to come to my house and play Smash Randiscoop? My auntie Abs got me the chipped version on GameVerse for Christmas. And I live three minutes away, in Seacole House."

"Yeah, that would be sick! I know a lot of people from Tophall live there too. I will call my mum to ask her on the way. Would *your* mum mind though?"

"I think it will be okay. If she knows your mum, then it's fine, sha," Tundé imitated his mum's Nigerian accent. "My auntie will be there to take care of us too."

Tundé reckoned that his mum might be more merciful if a church friend's child was visiting their house. It was a gamble worth taking, anyway.

"Hello, Tundé! How was school?" Auntie Abi asked the boys as she opened the flat door for them.

"Good afternoon, Auntie!" Tundé said as he took his shoes off.

"Good afternoon," Remi added shyly.

"Oh, who is your little friend, Tundé?"

"This is Remi. Is it okay if he plays on the GameVerse you got me? His mum said it was okay and she's friends with Mum."

"Erm, okay. But I'll be leaving as soon as your mum gets back. So if she gets angry, you're on your own!"

A couple of hours later, while the boys were still glued to the GamesVerse console, Tundé's mum, Mrs Adeyemi, arrived home from work, prompting Auntie Abi to say her goodbyes. The jubilant mood in the living room flatlined in sync with the aggressive drop of the house keys on the kitchen surface. Mrs Adeyemi was clearly showing how she felt about her son's misdemeanours earlier that day.

"Good evening, mum," Tundé said nervously, as he got up to greet his mum in traditional Yorùbá fashion.

She threw a vexed glance his way. Remi proceeded to stand up and greet Tundé's mum too.

"Good evening, Auntie," Remi said awkwardly, acknowledging the tension in the room.

"Ah ah, Babatundé, can't your friend greet properly?" Mrs Adeyemi asked irritably.

Before Tundé could say anything, Remi quickly bent down and touched the floor. "Oh, sorry I forgot to, Auntie."

A sly grin cracked through Mrs Adeyemi's otherwise frustrated expression.

"Ehen, that's better. How are you doing?"

"I'm fine, Auntie," Remi said shyly, feeling under the pressure.

"Tundé, where do you get this audacity from?" she asked exasperatedly. "Bringing your friends home to play after the phone calls I've been getting from your school? HEEEY!"

Tundé didn't answer. He was too scared to look his mum straight in the face.

"Ohhh, so you want to ignore me now? Maybe my belt will help you find your voice! Or should we wait for your fahda to get home?"

"Auntie, my mum is actually one of your church friends. That's why I thought it would be respectful to come here and see you. We only just started playing games now."

Tundé nervously observed his mum as she wondered whether to believe Remi.

"So, what is your name? And who is your mother?"

"Well, I can't say my mum's first name out loud. But my name is Oremidé Balogun."

"Balogun? I'm not sure that I know of her," Mrs Adeyemi said with growing impatience. She would prefer to use her energy disciplining her son instead of focusing on trivial matters.

"Er... you met her at the prayer study group last Tuesday," continued Remi. "And she's wearing braids at the moment."

"Oh, you mean Yabo? Ah, that woman is very fun, o! And she's a GOD-fearing woman too."

"Yes, she is."

"I like her! And you're her son?"

"Yes, Auntie."

"That's amazing. Please tell her I said hello."

Mrs Adeyemi then turned angrily towards Tundé.

"Anyway, my son! What are you doing fighting at school? Kilonshele? Are you mad? Give me one reason why I shouldn't *slap your face* back to Ikeja right now?"

Tears began streaming down Tundé's face. He just couldn't get the words out, which made his mum increasingly enraged.

"Ehh? So, you don't want to open your mouth? Do you want me to beat it out of you?"

"Erm, Auntie?" Remi interjected awkwardly. As a Nigerian child, he was used to these situations, but that didn't make them any less tense.

"Oya, speak."

"Please, don't give him beats. He was defending me from a school bully. That boy has been picking on me for ages, so Tundé backed me up and it caused a fight."

"Aww, really?" Mrs Adeyemi said softly to Remi. "So, my son wasn't being violent for no reason?"

"Auntie, I promise you. That boy even said something really bad about Africans. So, please don't beat Tundé."

"Well, I can't just ignore his detention or his teasha's phone calls, just because you say I should."

"Auntie, if I'm lying, you can call my mum and tell her to beat me three times harder than you would Tundé."

Tundé was surprised. No one had ever backed him up like this before.

"Okay, I see you are a good friend to my son. If you're lying, then I'll make sure your mother, Yabo, deals with you very harshly. Tundé, is this all true?"

Tundé, still crying, just nodded his head.

"Oya, is this TRUE? Speak up, jare! Before I change my mind."

"Yes, mum..." Tundé sniffled. "It's... it's true."

"Okay, okay," Mrs Adeyemi said as she visibly calmed down. "It's good that you want to defend your friends. But you still shouldn't be fighting, so you will be grounded for your whole Easter holidays."

Tundé was mortified. Two weeks indoors while all his friends were playing out was going to feel like torture!

Maybe I should take the beats instead...

"Just make sure from today, you end all this your fighting nonsense. Because if it happens again, I will let your fahda deal with you. Have I made myself clear?"

"Yes, mum," said Tundé sheepishly as he wiped away the snot and tears dribbling down his upper lip.

"Good. Oremidé, I'm going to make pounded yam and egusi," Mrs Adeyemi continued. "So you will stay and have some before you go home."

"Thank you, Auntie! My big cousin Jeremiah lives nearby and said he'd pick me up in an hour, so I can stay and eat. Thank you again."

"Ah, I love how polite you are! I wish Tundé could be more like you."

Despite that comment annoying him, Tundé knew it was best to bite his tongue.

"I'll start making the food now. Tundé, come and help me in the kitchen while your friend plays the game."

After devouring their tasty Nigerian cuisine, Jeremiah had arrived to take Remi home. While he was enjoying some of Mrs Adeyemi's homemade puff puff, Tundé pulled Remi aside for a quick chat.

"Thanks for helping me with my mum," said Tundé gratefully. "You really had my back there, man. She would have gone crazy tonight if you didn't."

"It's the least I could do," said Remi happily. "You had my back at school earlier."

"Friends?" Tundé said holding up his palm.

"Friends!" Remi replied, high-fiving Tundé with eagerness.

"Come on Remi, we're going now," Jeremiah said hastily. "Thanks again, Auntie. We gotta dip. I've got bare things to do."

Chapter 13

Fam, I've got bare things to do.

Tundé was deep in thought while he sat on the droning D7 bus back home after school. He needed to come to grips with his body's transformation and find out whether he could gain control of it. It was essential for his plan to retrieve Jerry's bairaff and the Adeyemi heirloom back from the PMD crew. He turned his brick phone back on, feeling apprehensive. It revealed dozens of messages and missed calls from Jerry.

Damn, he's probably so pissed. I'm glad we don't live in Seacole House anymore.

It didn't matter too much though, since Remi knew the Adeyemis were relocated to Equiano House during the CCA migration. It was just a few minutes' walk away from his old block. But that still gave Tundé a bit of extra time to sort things out before Jerry kicked his front door in. Tundé reflected over the sequence of events in Plaistow to understand where he should start. Suddenly, as if an eyeglass projector had been activated, a screen was overlaid onto his usual field of vision. He was now playing back the moment when he walked past the PMD boys loitering outside Wiley's Supermarket and the area around Mad Medy's base.

It's still a madness to me that I can even do this!

"Next stop: Crossharbour."

As the D7 parked up, Tundé decided to continue strategising when he got home. When he eventually opened the front door to the flat, his nose was bombarded by the delicious aroma of red stew and meat. Before reaching the kitchen, the brick phone buzzed in his pocket. It was a message from his mum:

'Your uncle and I are visiting Mama Kent and her family, and we will be away until tomorrow evening. Jollof and meat is in the fridge. God bless.'

Tundé was curious about the timing, considering he hadn't heard about their relatives in Kent for years. But he was relieved to get the time and space to recuperate after such a life-altering couple of days. His only concern was Uncle Blessing's absence.

What if I need help while my body keeps changing? I guess I'll have to work it out myself.

He thought it best not to call his uncle in case his mum would eavesdrop. From out of the blue, his belly screamed out to him. Was it another strange phenomenon taking place?

Fam, I'm hungry. I need to eat now!

Scouring through the fridge, Tundé found a Roof's Ice Cream tub filled to the brim with jollof rice, and there was a pot full of red meat and stew on another shelf. As he munched his dinner on the sofa, Tundé turned on the TV. Various panoramic views of London's skyline flashed across the screen as a crisp voice spoke. It sounded like a documentary.

"The city has seen a dramatic shift since the nationwide election of 2015. The Traditionalists were keen to clean their negative image, heavily contributed to by the infamous reign of Mary Catcher as Prime Minister in the 1980s."

With his hands now full of stewed meat, Tundé kept the programme on because he didn't want to get his oily fingers on the remote.

"The supposed effects of her strategy? Crumbs for the people. Profit for the corporations. The 2015 UK Election was all about redemption for The TP, who launched the 'Responsibility Starts at Home' campaign. After a landslide victory, they implemented the Council Care Act in the same year. It was a promise to rehouse the working class people back into the capital for vast economic opportunities."

"That plan worked out perfectly, didn't it?" Tundé mocked with food bits flying out of his mouth. The TV screen then panned over to the city's financial district.

"While the public was generally in support of the new policy, many political commentators were sceptical of its possible success, particularly because it would be funded by a 2% tax hike on the FTSE..."

"God, I hate all this political talk. Reminds me too much of Dad."

Tundé wiped his hands on his trousers and flicked the remote. The TV changed to the channel Toon Stream. *UnicHorn*, a popular Japanese anime show amongst young Londoners, was playing as it had recently been dubbed into English for its Western audience. Whilst having such subscriptions was an expensive luxury, Tundé's home was equipped with a dubiously chipped internet box, installed by Auntie Abi's ex-boyfriend, Dayo, a few years prior. It contained free access to all the movies and series usually protected by copyright licences.

He was brimming with excitement to watch the premiere of the newest episode, which featured a graphic fight scene between a man-like unicorn and a dragon. The moves were influenced by styles from kung fu, wing chun and Brazilian jiu-jitsu. Abruptly, Tundé's mind pulled him back into his Physics lesson where he had the supernatural visual encounter with the dropping ball example.

He experienced a sensation akin to being loaded into a simulation, as he completely relived the moment. Tundé was back in the classroom. He could see the distinct, stunned facial expressions at his exceptional mathematical skill from Mr Panther. He could hear the exact comments made by his peers when he stepped up to solve the problem. He could see every section of the diagrams he had drawn out—number for number, equation for equation—all in real-time. It felt so real. So vivid. So tangible.

"You're no match for me, Equinode!"

In a flash, Tundé was thrust back into the present moment. He was in the living room again, with *UnicHorn* still playing on the TV. The enthralling fight scene between the two characters was ongoing. While he reacquainted himself with his surroundings, Tundé had a brainwave.

If I combine these crazy visualisation powers with my new physique, I could learn some fighting moves to defend myself against those PMD boys.

Tundé thought learning from the basic tutorials could give him an added advantage in one-to-one combat. Fortunately, the chipped TV was an old first-generation smart version with access to WeView, an online video-sharing platform. Tundé searched for wing chun basics. Clicking on the first video displayed on the page, he engrossed himself in an extensive tutorial of the Lap Sau and Luk Sau moves.

Tundé prepared himself to practise executing one of the lengthy fighting sequences, when suddenly, his body froze still. A chaotic inner turmoil ensued. A stream of images and experiences from various points in his life flooded into his consciousness. His tough upbringing in London, countless fights from his youth, the heartbreaking experience of racism and the pain caused by the absence of his father. All these core memories overwhelmed his amygdala. Sweat droplets gathered all over his face. The torment was so intolerable that it forced him to his knees as Tundé shook his head vigorously, trying to break free from the agony.

Am I going crazy?

He was losing control of his mind. And he couldn't stop it. It felt like he was developing psychosis. Or perhaps it was a late reaction to Uncle Blessing's magic? Maybe he was still in a convoluted, unexplainable dream?

Whilst trying to overcome the psychological onslaught, Tundé felt a sharp sensation on his left arm, as though something had bitten into his flesh. He smacked at his arm with his right hand. He turned it over, expecting to see a dead insect. But, instead, Tundé's palm was full of dark brown gunk.

Rah, is that my skin?

Upon further inspection, Tundé realised that his arm was shedding off heaps of tissue. He rushed to the mirror in the lounge to examine the rest of his body. He was in disbelief. The skin on his face was peeling off substantially. He could feel the skin on various parts of his body become tighter while the top layer curled up and flaked off. A wave of violent rage began flowing through Tundé's system, as the struggle to regain control of his mind and body continued. He could feel the skin gunk collecting under his clothing, creating an unpleasant, clammy sensation. He angrily ripped the clothes off his body, tearing them into pieces. Breathing heavily, he stood bare-chested in the living room, fury pulsating through his veins.

SKREEAGHH! SKREEAGHH!

The screeching sounds of the eagle were blaring away in his head. He couldn't bear it anymore.

"ARGGHH!"

Tundé stormed around, knocking over furniture and ornaments all over the living room to dissolve his frustration. The TV, the sofa and the lamp, a few pots and an armchair had been tossed around. At the climax of his anger, Tundé bent down low, using only his thumb and index finger to lift the sofa and the dented TV in each hand with ease. As the surges of anger continued to propel him, Tundé teetered the household items closer to the window, with a strong, destructive urge to throw them straight through the glass. Until...

"The power is within you!"

The resonance of his father's words from the dream brought him to a sharp halt. Tundé snapped out of his troubled state and carefully placed the sofa and TV down. Standing still, he focused on those words and allowed his anger to flow freely, breathing deeply to prevent it from rising to the surface. The emotion steadily died down, like a water hose had doused the fire within. The flickering images, sounds and thoughts in Tundé's head slowly faded away.

I'm a lot stronger than I thought if I only needed two fingers to lift these. Mad ting!

Glancing at himself in the mirror, Tundé marvelled at the sight of his fully replenished skin. His superhuman eyesight kicked in, allowing him to zoom in and inspect the finer details. His skin cells had been reinforced with an intricate network of additional layers, creating a dense barrier that made it both tougher and stronger. Despite these remarkable changes, he was relieved that his skin retained its normal appearance.

"Shit," Tundé said aloud when he became aware of the state of the living room. "Mum would go nuts if she saw this!"

The sofa was bent out of shape and the TV had a notable dent on the side. Fortunately, the TV screen was still intact, bar a minor section of discolouring in the bottom left corner. But interestingly, while his mind fixated on his mum's likely reaction, Tundé found himself recalling the Lap Sau and Luk Sau sequences he was watching before his outburst.

Once he tidied up the mess, he reloaded WeView and dedicated the rest of the evening to studying, practising and perfecting the basics of wing chun and kung fu. With his newly enhanced superhuman memory, he discovered that each repetition of a move or sequence brought about a smoother flow. His muscle memory was highly adaptive, allowing him to seamlessly integrate various strikes and manoeuvres with increasing ease over just a few minutes. Tundé trained arduously until the early hours of Saturday morning, then passed out on the sofa. It had been a hectic and exhausting day.

Chapter 14

Meanwhile, a stone's throw away from Tundé's Samuda Estate, a blacked-out Scheep vehicle pulled up on a quiet, dark street near Canary Wharf. The driver left the engine purring silently and dimmed the headlights. Shortly afterwards, as if by magic, a lean-figured man appeared out of the shadows on the other end of the street. He was wearing a navy jacket, black trousers, a cap and a scarf that protected his face. It looked rather suspicious considering the early March weather had been scorching hot.

The lean figure scanned the street cautiously to ensure he wasn't being watched. Then, he slowly walked to the Scheep. The windows were tinted and because it was so dark, the man couldn't see a thing. He gently tapped on the window of the back door twice. There was a pause. The sound of a click followed, and the driver's seat window gradually rolled down. The lean figure reached out to open the back door.

"Stop right there," ordered a calm, low voice from inside the car.

As the driver's window lowered, the barrel of a pistol soon popped out from it, pointing directly at the lean-figured man. He was stunned into a frozen stance.

"Your badge in five seconds. Or you're fackin' toast, mate," said another cold voice from the car with a thick Cockney accent.

The lean man fretfully searched all over the pockets of his jacket and trousers. He eventually reached into his left-sided pocket to retrieve it, but that action was met with a resounding click of the gun being cocked back. The lean figure agitatedly showed his Metropolitan Police badge to the driver through the window. There was another pause. The lean man was shaking with terror like a leaf in the wind, and the quietness of the night added to the tension.

"Now, now, Steve," the calm voice eventually broke the silence. "Let's show some grace and allow our little mole to join us in the vehicle."

"Alright, boss," said Steve, the Cockney man, who sounded disappointed that he couldn't pull the trigger. "Alice, open the back door behind me, will ya?"

"Certainly, sir," The car's virtual assistant—found in most modern cars—responded.

The back door automatically opened, and the lean figure slid in as it shut behind him. He unwrapped his scarf and took a deep long sigh. He was still very flustered.

"Don't be so frightened, Harry!" joked the calm man in charge, as if it was unreasonable to be shaken up after being held at gunpoint.

"Easy for you to say, Christian," Harry said warily as he adjusted himself. But he couldn't take his eyes off Steve in the driver's seat. He seemed like a loose cannon.

"Ugh, my mother calls me Christian. Please, just Chris will do."

The driver made a notable groan.

"And don't worry about him," Chris continued. "He only takes orders from me. Otherwise, Steve wouldn't harm a fly."

Harry quickly assessed Steve, who was quite the burly, solid figure. He also had a meaty, shaven head. Steve looked back at Harry with a menacing grin.

"I'm sure he's a good lad," Harry said, his eyes narrowing.

"Anyway, since we haven't got much time today," Chris switched the agenda, "let's get down to Project Pareto. Our stakeholders want to know what's been happening on the streets lately as it relates to the wider mission. What have you got for me, my friend?"

Harry was distracted. He couldn't fully focus on Chris's words without being hyper-vigilant of Steve's threatening intentions.

"So?" Chris was getting impatient.

"So," Harry said tentatively, "as you know, I've been patrolling the Stratford and Plaistow areas recently, keeping an eye out for any suspicious activity since the influx of that new bairaff drug. Just like you instructed me to."

Chris nodded while Steve grunted again.

"There was a strange incident the other day, though," Harry continued. "I got a call for a 'very dangerous situation' unfolding on Greenfeel Road between a local gang and two individuals. Usually, in those situations, there are injured persons and obvious clues to what has occurred at the scene. But this mate? This was far from it."

Steve grunted once more while Harry kept his eyes glued to him as he recounted events.

"I was only driving from Plaistow to Maryland. When I got the call, it was a warm summer evening. By the time I got close to the scene, the weather was like doomsday! It seemed like a hurricane had torn the whole place upside down. The buildings were damaged, the roads were dug up and the cars were completely fucked. But there was no evidence of any collisions or powerful weaponry."

"Interesting," Chris said thoughtfully. "Continue."

"Some of the other officers spoke to the locals that called in. They described something you'd expect to see in an apocalypse movie.

Ludicrous or frightening, you choose. After speaking to the paramedics, I learnt that another witness claimed to see two people in the wreckage. An adolescent boy and a middle-aged man. Both of African descent."

Chris held a blank expression, barely responding to the intel Harry had just given him. He nodded at Steve to signal that they had received enough information. Steve used his spare hand to type on his phone, keeping his right hand firmly holding the pistol. Chris turned back towards Harry.

"So," continued Harry, "since you told me to warn you of any potential supernatural activity, I messaged you."

Chris faced away from Harry and stared out of the backseat window, deep in thought. Harry was uneasy. He couldn't read much into Chris, other than his intimidating aura. Chris sighed and turned his gaze back to Harry.

"Thank you, Harry. You did very good work for us yesterday," he said with satisfaction. "This mission is not only key for our organisation, but also the future of humanity's progress too. And just to make sure, none of your colleagues were suspicious about you, were they?"

"No, sir. I know how... *difficult* it can get if the Met discover their officers are working with outside entities. I've been very careful to cover my tracks."

"Good. Because, as you know, if our stakeholders were to have their plans revealed, there would be severe consequences. But since that's not the case... Steve, get the duffel bag under your seat for our pleasant mole."

Steve shuffled around under his seat before producing a small, leather duffel bag. He handed it over to Chris, who unzipped it. Harry tried to contain his elation when he saw the stacks of cash staring back at him from the duffel bag. Chris picked up five bands, each worth £1,000, and handed them to Harry.

"Great work for our mission, Harry. As agreed, here's your latest instalment for our deal. Keep using your position to monitor any other unusual, supernatural occurrences in the area. It's required for our project to succeed. And, of course, more rewards will be coming your way if you do."

Harry couldn't hide his beaming smile any longer as he stuffed the cash into his pockets. "Thanks, Chris. I won't let you down."

"Oh, you wouldn't *dare*," Chris replied with a knowing smile. "I don't have a Cambridge PhD in psychology for nothing!"

Unimpressed by proceedings, Steve butted in as he pointed his gun towards the door.

"Alright mate, sling yer 'ook now."

Harry was caught off guard by Steve's interjection, but he was in no mood to argue. With the five grand comfortably tucked in his pockets now, Harry saluted Chris with a nod, then bolted out of the car. Within a matter of seconds, he disappeared into the same dark alley that he emerged from.

"Not the nicest way to treat our guests, Steve," Chris laughed.

"Can't stand those low-level, rat coppers," Steve was still annoyed that he couldn't get violent tonight.

"Now, Steve. We at the DSU are *essentially* the same thing. But we're playing at a much higher level."

The DSU, aka the Discrete Services Unit, was an organisation within the secret services department of the UK government. It was created just before the start of the Cold War. They were tasked with carrying out a range of different local and national level projects on behalf of the UK establishment which, if known by the wider public, could be perceived as extremely controversial or unethical. As a result, the details of individuals working for the DSU and their specific projects were kept strictly confidential.

"Anyway," Chris resumed, "did you send over the message to our boys in the Docks?"

"Yes, boss."

"Excellent. We need to move forward with Project Pareto quickly. It seems like the Yorùbás have sent reinforcements here a lot sooner than I expected."

"Aren't that lot already all over this place?" Steve expressed with a tinge of disdain.

"Not like these guys, Steve. Not like these guys..."

Chapter 15

"ARGH! UGH!" TUNDÉ GRUMBLED exasperatedly as he rose from a deep sleep.

Something irritating was crawling on his forehead. He raised his hand to his face, only to realise that the culprit was no bug as he expected—it was human fingers!

"Oh my days, that was too funny!"

It took a moment for the expression of surprise to leave Tundé's face.

"Auntie Abi? What... what are you doing here?" he asked worriedly as he scanned the room. He recalled the turbulent events that unfolded the night before.

"Well, I came to check up on you since your mum asked yesterday. And it's the weekend. What on earth has happened here?"

She gestured towards the damaged sofa and messy flat.

"Erm... we're replacing a few things soon, so I just started breaking them apart a little."

"That's odd, cos Big Sis said money was tight right now."

"Abs, don't watch. I've got it all under control. I've started a new job, so I'm gonna use the P's to buy new stuff for the yard."

Tundé jumped off the sofa and gently guided Auntie Abi towards the flat's front door.

"I wish you could chill here today, but I've got bare things I need to do. Duty calls and all that."

"Wow, is this how you're moving? I hope you're not kicking me out to do anything naughty!"

"Oh my days—no! Can't believe you'd even *ask* me about that," Tundé knew his face would be scarlet red if his complexion lacked melanin. "I just need to sort some stuff out. And I can't do it properly if you're around."

"Rah, okay then, big man," Auntie Abi was defensive as Tundé opened the front door. "I just wanted to make sure my supposedly lovely nephew was okay. Are you?"

"Yeah, I'm fine. I'll holla at you later, yeah?"

Auntie Abi was sullen. "Okay, in a bit then."

Tundé shut the door and sank straight to the ground, letting out a heavy sigh. Despite their close relationship, he didn't want his auntie snooping around in case she found out about his superhuman abilities. Not just yet.

"Fuck me! This place looks like a bomb site."

The flat was in much worse condition than he initially thought. Broken plates, granules of mud from the vase and pieces of fluff from the damaged sofa were scattered across the living area and the hallway.

After Tundé cleaned up the flat and tried his best to mask the broken household items, he recommenced his plan to get the stolen items back from the PMD crew. He thought determining the whereabouts of the main PMD lieutenants was paramount, as they were the best route to finding where his stuff was being kept.

I've defo lost my marbles tryna infiltrate these guys on my own!

Tundé laughed nervously to himself as he logged onto the home laptop. He shared it with his mum, but she rarely ever used it. He loaded up a map of the Plaistow area on Guides. He knew that the boys loitered in the area close to Wiley's Supermarket.

It was the youngers who spotted me. They'll be out on the roads more than the lieutenants. How could I use them to get my shit back?

Like a thunderbolt, he was struck by inspiration. He had watched a classic Mafia film recently about El Grande Spreco, a prominent New York drug lord in the 1920s. Although Spreco's ruthless, cold-hearted nature didn't resonate with Tundé, the teenager was impressed by a particular tactic of his.

He was great at using important hostages to trade for what he wanted. I could kidnap one of the key PMD youts, then set up an exchange. My stuff for the hostage.

Tundé sighed deeply, understanding how big of a risk this approach would be. But no other feasible choices popped up in his boyish mind. Other than Jerry instigating an all-out war, which he didn't have the resources or emotional bandwidth for. He kept navigating through Guides to find the most ideal place to hold his hostage. Soon enough, Tundé found an abandoned warehouse that was formerly owned by the Hades delivery company before they went bankrupt. It was walking distance from the likely territory of the young PMD soldiers.

I'll need to knock the hostage out cold completely so it's easier to move them to the warehouse.

Tundé used his fingers to massage his temple and de-stress. The scale of the task was becoming increasingly daunting. But he was compelled to act. It was his responsibility and his alone. He planned to go to Plaistow at noon on Sunday. He would inspect the abandoned warehouse, and then head to the PMD area to capture a hostage for the warehouse trade.

The teenager hoped that his strategy would be enough to get his items back while preventing an escalation of the situation. He intended to wear a disguise to create as much separation from his identity as possible. Tundé spent the remainder of the day studying the area on Guides, mastering its layout with his superhuman memory.

When he woke up the following Sunday morning, the youngster sat up in bed. He was conscious of the relentless anxiety that was flowing through his body. Tundé was extremely aware that he was putting himself at the heart of a life-or-death situation. From hearsay, and his own experience, he knew the PMD crew were a ruthless bunch.

Thank god that I've been blessed with these unbelievable powers.

He was still a novice at controlling them, but he sensed an improvement that would give him a critical advantage against ordinary boys. Considering all the possible outcomes, Tundé wrote a letter for his family should the worst happen:

'Dear Mummy and Auntie Abi,

As much as we may have our disagreements, or that I disappoint you, I want you both to know I'd do anything for you and that you mean the world to me. If you're reading this now, then you probably realise that. I pray that whatever happens, God guides you everything. Love you, Tunds x'

Tundé hid the note in a corner under his bed. Then he opened his wardrobe to prepare for battle. He took out his disguise outfit—an old slim-fit black tracksuit with a hoodie, a black t-shirt, navy gloves and worn-out black trainers. He reached into the far regions of his wardrobe to pick out a black, woolly balaclava. He bought it from the local Isle of Dogs market a while ago.

Only got this for the snowstorm last year. Never thought I'd use it for serious tings!

He stuffed it into the crotch area of his tracksuit. Just before leaving the flat, Tundé stopped by his reflection in the living room mirror. He saw apprehension. He saw trepidation. He saw tension. But it was too late to turn back now. Tundé had convinced himself that he was responsible for dealing with it before anyone else got involved. While he mentioned God in the letter to his family, he didn't embrace the same religious belief. Somewhere deep in his soul, though, there was a strong sense of duty and faith. He couldn't explain it, but it was there. And it propelled him forward.

Coming out of the lift on the ground floor of Equiano House, Tundé met a familiar figure at the main door.

"Babatundé! Good afternoon. Where are you going?"

"Errr, afternoon, Uncks," Tundé was alarmed by his unexpected arrival. "Why are you here so early? Thought you were coming back in the evening?"

"Your mum was called into work for an emergency shift tonight. A lot of drug abuse victims recently. She dropped me off close by, but she's gone to buy garri and pepper before she starts work."

"Okay, fair enough."

"Anyway, where are you going now, Tundé?"

"Erm, just gonna run some errands, Uncle."

"Mm-hmm. Listen, son. We have some important topics that we must discuss."

"Let's talk later, Uncks. I've really gotta go now."

Uncle Blessing inspected Tundé's choice of attire closely. He looked behind the unassuming mask that his nephew wore. He sensed a latent aggression, subtle fear and surging vengeance.

"My son, it's dangerous out there, jor. Especially if you're going to cause trouble. You don't even understand how to control your powe–"

"Uncle, we can chat about all that later. I really need to dip now."

Tundé tried to walk past Uncle Blessing to the main door, but the elder grabbed his arm.

"Babatundé, listen. You better be sure of what you're doing. It is very risky to go and get in any fights right now!"

Tundé instinctively swiped off Uncle Blessing's grip using a martial arts technique he had studied the night before. He was taken aback as his nephew stood resolutely before him.

"By our guiding principles, I'm not allowed to stop you now. But you will land yourself in wahala, o."

"Listen, Uncks. I'll be okay," Tundé said defiantly as he opened the main door. "Just don't follow me this time."

Chapter 16

"I'M STRUGGLING FAM!"

Tundé didn't anticipate how tough of a challenge this would be. He was sweating copiously. The short-term climate change from 'The African Ascent' had brought intense hot weather and humidity. He would normally be appreciative, but Tundé felt differently as he cycled through the gruelling conditions to Plaistow. He used a well-known hack to unlock an LTN Bryson Bike in the Canary Wharf district without paying.

Them man got enough money to allow me a free ride anyway.

Before long, he reached his first destination on Factory Road. This was the location of the abandoned Hades warehouse, where he planned to hold the PMD hostage in exchange for the Adeyemi heirloom and Jerry's bairaff. Flustered from the sweltering heat, he thought it would be a good idea to cool down away from the scorching sun in the privacy of the warehouse. Before walking to its gates, Tundé slipped on the woolly balaclava to conceal his identity.

To his surprise, the balaclava barely impaired his senses as it would with the average human. His peripheral vision was still very clear, as the smell of the overheated tarmac clung stubbornly to his nostrils. Suddenly, Tundé's ears pricked up at a distant noise becoming more distinguishable by the second. Underneath the sonics of an aeroplane flying over his head, he heard distinctly:

"Ladies and gentlemen, please remember our Captain has turned on the Fasten Seat Belt sign as we will soon land at London City Airport. For your safety, please stow your carry-on bags underneath the seat in front of you..."

Tundé was puzzled as he looked upward at the sky.

Rah, how's a man hearing that? Must be another power. I wonder if I can turn it off if I focus hard...

While he tried to calibrate the new ultra-sensitive hearing ability, Tundé was bombarded with a multitude of sensations converging from different directions. Bus stop bells. Car engines revving. Lorry doors opening. Supermarket barcode beeps. His brain was overwhelmed as he became disoriented. He stood completely still, taking several deep breaths to regain control of his body.

I gotta learn how to use this properly. Don't want it to sheg me at the wrong time.

The thought of being vulnerable to sensory overload during combat made him nauseous. Once he managed to recentre himself, Tundé took a few steps to test his state. While he was back to equilibrium, he now had a heightened sense of awareness. The sound of a leaky tap in the warehouse could be heard. He could hear the rustle of a pigeon's feet as it crept along the roof. Everything was clearer.

Tundé arrived at the tall, iron security gates guarding the Hades warehouse. They appeared to be quite sturdy, although he could tell they had seen better days judging from the rustiness. After taking a cursory glance around to ensure he was alone, he wanted to climb over the gates. They were three times his height though, so it would take some effort. And despite the ability of his body to self-heal, Tundé wanted to avoid cutting himself against the dirty, old rails. Only the Universe knew what type of infections he would risk catching. He took a few steps backwards, steadied himself, and then ran towards the gate.

Just as Tundé was about to land his foot on one of the railings, an animalistic instinct took over him. Instead of climbing the gate, he leapt mightily above them, clearing the security spikes entirely. He landed haphazardly on the other side but briskly got to his feet.

That felt bare weird, but I'm in!

The front yard of the warehouse was quite unremarkable. It was overgrown with weeds, littered with old, decaying equipment and had several sand pits scattered across the grassy area. The teenager walked over to the main warehouse building, which had countless smashed and boarded-up windows, weathered bricks in its structure and large, corroded steel doors shielding the entrance. He tested the door's sturdiness by pushing against it, but his right hand stuck to it like super glue. After some struggle, he eventually yanked it away. Rusted fragments of the steel door had stuck to his gloves. He tried to pat them off, but it was no use.

"Ouch!" Tundé yelped as he pulled the glove off his right hand.

Something sharp had pricked at his index finger. Zooming in on the microstructure, Tundé observed tiny, prickly hairs emerging from the palmar skin under his hands.

"Woah," he uttered under his breath.

He placed his right palm onto the clean side of a glove. It firmly stuck to his hand. After pulling the glove off again, Tundé tried to control the movement of the prickly hairs with his mind. Before long, he could make them retract and extend at will.

"Jheeze, that's too sick!"

Returning his attention to the warehouse door, he struggled to push it open. It was firmly lodged in place. Intuitively, Tundé roundhouse kicked it, taking the door off its hinges. He was delighted he could replicate the Muay Thai technique practised the night before. It showed that he was acquiring the knowledge rapidly.

Just before stepping in, he registered that a small building was connected to the right-hand side of the warehouse, and made a mental note to scope it out before he left. Now that the shadows inside masked him, Tundé pulled the balaclava off his face. A huge, sweaty weight dismounted from his head, while the cool breeze of the warehouse soothed his skin.

"Cough! Cough!" he spluttered, as his bliss was interrupted by the undesirable, musty smell.

Tundé could barely see a thing, other than the minimal light that crept in through the warehouse door and a few of the broken windows. He tried to adjust his supernatural eyes, but it didn't work. The warehouse was still extremely dark. He refrained from pressing any random buttons just in case they rang an alarm or attracted unnecessary attention, rather than switched on a light.

While he thought of a solution, out of the blue, a sizzling sensation sparked off from the back of Tundé's skull and spread itself behind his eyes. He dropped to the ground and rubbed his eyes incessantly. He held down his screams as best he could while his eyeballs were being rearranged. When the pain subsided, Tundé wiped his face and got to his feet. He was mesmerised. It was like he had put on night vision goggles. The interior was abundantly clear to him now, without requiring any technology or instruments. He didn't know what to expect from his body next!

There were endless aisles of metal storage shelves. They were stacked high towards the ceiling and arranged with small walkways between each other. A hoard of junk was also scattered around the deserted warehouse. Just a few yards ahead of him, there were some reach trucks and electric carts with faded Hades logos.

They probably got dumped here when that shitty delivery company went bust.

His eyes lit up with excitement. The warehouse set-up would work very much in his favour against the PMD crew. The unpleasant sound of rats scurrying across the floor echoed in the background aṣ Tundé continued investigating. An elevated platform spanned the entire perimeter of the warehouse, and when he peered over to his right, he detected a door in the wall, assuming it was an entry to the adjacent building. Assessing the distance, he reckoned he could easily jump directly to the door above from his ground-level position. Lining himself up, he dashed forward and leapt forcefully into the air.

"Woo!" Tundé soared high above the storage shelves and was headed straight towards the door on the platform. But he was flying much faster than expected, and now he was out of control.

Oh shit...

A loud crash rumbled through the warehouse, as Tundé whacked into the brick wall and slid painfully down onto the platform. It wasn't quite the landing he had in mind. He dusted himself down and walked along the steel platform to the door mounted in the wall. It was cerulean blue with a bronze door handle. A creak pierced through the warehouse as he opened the door. He was presented with a dark, black hole. He stuck his head in and tried to employ his night vision to get a better view. All he could gather was that the hole was connected to a slide or chute.

I wonder wagwan down there.

Tundé spent the next few minutes surveying the property for other access points, hidden spots and the navigation of the walkways. Satisfied with his examination, Tundé put his sweaty balaclava and gloves back on as he left the warehouse. He knew the biggest challenge lay ahead. Taking a hostage from the PMD crew would not be an easy task.

He jumped back over the warehouse gates and made his way to Plaistow. After a lengthy walk under the sun, he was only a few hundred yards away from the crew's terrain. The lack of people on the streets made him feel uneasy. Despite the area's dangerous reputation, it was still a surprise that many of the locals weren't outside enjoying the rare, tropical weather. That filled Tundé with jitters.

He soon arrived on Darcy Road, a few streets down from Mad Medy's base. Wary of getting too close to the trap house, he walked through a nearby alley that would bring him to Seely Road, which was in the heart of the PMD's known territory. He expected that part to be quieter than usual given the increased surveillance on the gang. He thought that could give him a better chance at staging a successful kidnap. Still, the teenager chose to remain suspicious. As Tundé crept through the alley, the sound of good-natured fun and commotion came from the other end. He slowed down guardedly, even though he didn't want to presume it was dangerous.

When he stepped out of the alley, he was dismayed. There were loads of them. The street was packed. Twenty boys congregated on a small section of Seely Road. They were drinking alcohol from red party cups and blaring out music from a large set of speakers. Some of the boys were rapping directly to drone video cameras and posing in their luxury WMB and Machini cars with gang signs.

PMD gang signs. This must be a music video shoot. They must've filmed all over the place. No wonder the roads are empty!

Taking a hostage under this many people's noses would be an impossible task at this point. Tundé was caught in two minds about whether to go home to regroup or hide and take a different course of action.

"Yo," said one of the PMD members. "Who's that ballied up yute?"

They had spotted him now. The rest of the crew heard the call. They paused the music and put their drinks down. Their masked, uninvited guest now had their full attention as the mood swiftly changed from playful to menacing. One of the PMD members stepped forward. Tundé recognised him straight away.

"What you saying fam?" Bullet shouted. "You're on PMD turf, you know. Who are you, rudeboy?"

Uh oh.

Tundé was still speechless as Bullet advanced towards him.

"What are you on?" he shouted while lifting his t-shirt to reveal a bladed weapon held to his waist. "Cos this is what I'm on!"

Chapter 17

Tundé was firmly on the back foot as Bullet edged closer, with the other PMD members mobilising behind him.

"Bruv, you best fucking speak up, ya kna!" Bullet shouted impatiently as he gestured to his weapon.

The metallic glint of the blade reflected brightly from the sunlight. Tundé's adrenaline was surging through his veins. His heart was pounding so fiercely that it reverberated from his stomach up to his throat, each beat echoing in his ears like the bash of a drum. His hands were clammy and his legs rattled like a maraca.

"D-d-don't worry about me, init," Tundé responded shakily, adding significant depth to his voice to prevent being identified.

"Oh, so you think you're that guy, yeah?" Bullet stopped in his tracks. "You man, go check this fool. If he tries anything funny, fuck him up."

Without delay, a few of the PMD boys accosted Tundé. Droplets of sweat gathered under his mask as Tundé's fight-or-flight response kicked in. He took up a kung fu stance. His unfamiliar pose was met with snickers from the PMD crew.

"Oh, you think you're bad, yeah?" said one PMD boy as he withdrew a chrome zombie knife from under his puffer jacket.

"Stuntin' like you're Jackie Chan or suttin'," said another boy, who slipped on a shiny knuckle duster.

"Ching up his eyes so he can look like his idol, init," joked another of the PMD boys at the back.

Tundé quivered nervously as he tried to steady himself.

Come on powers, let's go...

He was reassured by feeling the impulse of the animal DNAs activating within. He assessed the threats in his vicinity using his superhuman vision. In a matter of seconds, Tundé determined that ten boys were advancing at once. The three at the front were the most threatening because they each brandished blades. The three just behind them were carrying baseball bats and knuckle dusters, while the next set of four lurked threateningly in the background.

Oh, boy. I need to strike quickly cos this is gonna be a lot of work!

Suddenly, Tundé was hauled back into the present when a sword was plunged in his direction. Moving his hips briskly to the left, Tundé dodged the blade by millimetres. Tundé reacted instinctively, seizing attacker #1's wrist. His muscles rippled as he twisted attacker #1's fully extended arm, then delivered a devastating blow with his elbow. A sickening crack echoed in the air as attacker #1's arm buckled in half beneath the force.

"Ugh! Ugh! Ugh!" attacker #1 screamed in awe at his deformed arm, before he fainted.

As attacker #1's sword bounced off the tarmac, Tundé effortlessly swung his foot high and kicked attacker #2's wrist with force, releasing the zombie knife from his grip. Tundé proceeded to land a devastating fist to his nose, dropping attacker #2 to the ground.

"Argh!" Tundé exclaimed, having been slashed across the side of his torso by attacker #3.

"Come on then, you prick. Let's go!" attacker #3 declared, lunging at Tundé with his sword again.

As the attacker swung, Tundé's brain spotted an exposed gap and drop-kicked him directly in the testicles. But the sword had gained enough momentum that it cut right into Tundé's quads, causing the teenager to yelp out.

"Argh!"

"Yeah, cut him up, fam!" Bullet cheered from a distance, failing to clock onto the fact that Tundé had the upper hand since attacker #3 was vulnerable.

Sensing his opportunity, Tundé grabbed attacker #3 by the head and plunged it into his blood-soaked knee. The gruesome clap that followed sounded like a pack of meat smacking against a boulder. Attacker #3 now lay unconscious as scarlet drool spilt out of his mouth. Tundé wiped the blood from his leg, safe in the knowledge that he would self-heal.

"Bruv!" Bullet was unsettled. "Why is it taking you man so long to end this guy?"

The other seven attackers approached Tundé, albeit reservedly, after witnessing how swiftly he dispatched the first three boys.

"You man best not pussy out," Bullet barked with annoyance at his troops. "You know what's gonna happen to our ends if we let this dickhead beat us?"

Tundé stood tall, his posture defiant and unwavering. As his nerves subsided, his body language exuded determination. An aura which was undoubtedly sensed by the PMD crew.

"You've got some shit that I need, lads."

"Rah, man thinks he can start making *requests* now?" Bullet was bewildered, kissing his teeth in disgust.

That sparked the next set of attackers to charge at Tundé. The lone teenager threw his forearm above his head to block an incoming swing of a baseball bat. The vibrations oscillated through his skeletal frame as he absorbed the impact. With Tundé preoccupied, a second aggressor cracked his right leg with their baseball bat, forcing Tundé to fall to a half-kneeling stance. Now that Tundé was vulnerable, the knuckle duster holder smashed him squarely on the cheek, launching him a few yards backwards as he painfully scraped against the turf. Cries of encouragement came from the onlooking PMD members—the ones who hadn't been knocked out, anyway.

"Let me take this tapped yute's mask off before you duppy him!" Bullet shouted as he walked over, while the knuckle duster holder cautiously approached Tundé. "He must be MAD thinking he can step onto our turf, like some kinda superhero."

A section of Tundé's mask—and the skin underneath—had been scraped open by that last punch. It left a fleshy, blood-soaked wound. But he was still conscious, and after hearing Bullet's call, he had to keep fighting if he wanted to stay alive. Tundé sprang to his feet, freezing the knuckle duster holder in his tracks. He sensed the self-healing kick in as he wiped the excess blood off his face, revealing clear, rejuvenated skin.

The entire PMD gang was in sheer disbelief. They couldn't fathom how he just brushed away the damage. A lingering silence followed as the tension rose to a grand peak. A gentle gust of wind blew Tundé's hood cinematically in the air. He was deeply in the zone now, feeling in complete control of his powers. While he was propelled by drive and resilience, his enemies were apprehensive.

"What the fuck?" Bullet finally broke the silence after Tundé's self-healing spectacle. "How is he still standing?"

"Rahtid," said another PMD boy.

"Nah, that's a mad ting!"

Confusion grew within the PMD ranks, as they realised a formidable adversary stood before them.

Chapter 18

It was clear to the Plaistow Man Dem that they had to take this lone soldier very seriously. He had *them* firmly on the backfoot now. Despite Bullet's latent worry, he felt somewhat secure in the knowledge that Tundé would need to get through his whole squad before getting to him. In a flash, Tundé was back on the offensive. He punched one boy in the face, elbowed another in the chest and kicked the next PMD crew member in the hips. With further combos of punches, kicks and elbow strikes, Tundé took down six assailants with masterful grace.

"You man aren't chatting shit now!"

His momentum was exponential. He felt untouchable. Tapping into his superhuman vision, Tundé effortlessly dodged the retaliation attempts, anticipating the PMD boys' attacks within milliseconds. Battering his way through the group, Tundé struck down six more gang members—smashing the last boy's head brutally against the curb.

"That's for spitting at me, you disrespectful prick," he said while stepping over the victim's unconscious body.

Bullet hurriedly signalled over to a young PMD member who was fully hooded with a bandana plastered over his face. Only his bright, hazelnut eyes were visible.

"Go get the ting under the backseat. Now!" Bullet demanded coldly.

Without hesitation, the hooded youth ran to the back seat of a Machini SLK parked a few dozen yards away from the conflict. The dimming light of dusk crept over the horizon, as Tundé landed a punch that left yet another PMD member laid out on the pavement. One attacker sliced Tundé's arm with a blade, but it healed within milliseconds, and Tundé threw a left hook with tremendous force that cracked the attacker's ribs.

Weary from combat, Tundé sauntered over to Bullet. The PMD lieutenant was flanked by the last two soldiers. They drew their blades in sync, like guards protecting a royal figure. As he approached, Tundé smelt the burning fear radiating from Bullet, who was gradually stepping backwards. He glared impatiently towards the Machini where he sent the hooded youth.

"Why you man stalling here?" He ordered the last two guards. "Go chef man up!"

The two men reluctantly advanced toward Tundé. The first guard eventually swung his blade at Tundé's neck. He swiftly ducked. In the same instant, the second guard thrust his weapon towards Tundé's midriff. Tundé narrowly evaded the blade by rolling backwards and ended up on his knees as he faced the guards.

Daaamn, that was close! I've gotta be careful.

The PMD boys swung their blades at him in unison. With mere seconds to react, Tundé swiftly jumped onto his back and blocked both swords with his feet.

"Fuck!"

The blades had sliced through his trainers and were pressing up against his heels. Tundé generated the power from his legs to thrust upwards and disarm both the guards of their blades. Meanwhile, Bullet had stepped away from the altercation and peered anxiously at the hooded member still ruffling about in the backseat of the Machini.

"Hurry up, bro!" Bullet hissed, trying to be discreet.

However, Tundé's heightened awareness allowed him to register the PMD lieutenant's words. He didn't know exactly what was coming, but he was expecting something serious. He proceeded to smash the first guard with a lethal uppercut, rendering him unconscious. His jaw crumbled into a thousand pieces. Tundé then roundhouse-kicked the second guard to the ground, then stomped his head into dreamland. Looking over his shoulder for Bullet, Tundé saw the PMD lieutenant holding his knife as his last line of defence.

"Don't think you can fuck with me, fam!" Bullet cried out as he pointed the tip of the knife menacingly.

"Stop playing games, bruv," Tundé closed in on him. "Like I said, you have something that I need."

"I ain't giving you nuttin' but smoke today, rudeboy!"

Bullet's ego couldn't accept that a lone, masked stranger would even contemplate stealing from his gang.

"So, you wanna end up like these man?" Tundé gestured to the unconscious PMD boys scattered across the road.

It was such an extraordinary sight that even Bullet couldn't help but acknowledge it with a grunt of respect.

"What exactly do you want anyway?"

"You have something that... something that I've heard is valuable."

"What fam?"

"Something purple, perhaps."

Bullet was puzzled for a moment. Then, his face lit up like a bulb, prompting a smirk at Tundé.

"Oh, you're here for that likkle yute we jacked the other day?" he laughed. "Is he even still alive? If he is, tell him it won't be for long! That yute is done out 'ere, I swear fam."

Those threats irked Tundé's soul. "Don't swear on it, dickhead."

"Listen, that pussy'ole and anyone he knows best watch out. Cos my team ain't gonna rest until we get even."

In a fit of rage, Tundé charged at Bullet and grabbed him by the throat with an unyielding, vice-like grip. Blinded by his fury, though, Tundé forgot to assess the danger. With a desperate thrust, Bullet plunged his knife deep into Tundé's abdomen. The searing pain ripped through him like fire.

"Arrggh!"

Blood erupted from the wound, adding a wet sheen to his black tracksuit. But Tundé still had enough presence of mind and strength to keep his hands firmly forced around Bullet's neck. He tightened his grip. Bullet was running out of breath, as his attempts to claw and punch his way out from the teenager's grasp were futile. Tundé refused to let go. His prey was there for the taking. All of Tundé's built-up frustration was being unleashed as the life was fading out of Bullet's eyes.

"WHERE... IS... THE... STASH?"

Tundé yanked the knife out of his stomach, causing blood to splatter over them both. He threw the knife to the ground with a resounding clang.

"You think I'm PLAYING?"

Struggling to stay conscious, Bullet tellingly blinked to his right towards the Machini car. Tundé saw the hooded individual rustling in the backseat. In a split second, the PMD lieutenant collapsed to the floor and spluttered for air. Tundé had released him and darted straight for the car. Bullet was begrudgingly thankful that luck had saved him.

But Tundé was spooked. He witnessed the life force draining from Bullet's eyes, and it had made him shudder that he almost lost complete control of himself. Tundé snapped open the left rear door of the Machini. The hooded youth stared back at him with agitation.

"Where's the stash, young buck?"

The silence told him it was there. But Tundé sensed some suspicious movement.

"Take that, pussy!"

Two bullets smashed through the car door's windows, as the hooded youth fired shots from a .22 pistol at Tundé. Now, the masked teenager was nowhere to be seen. The hooded youth kept his gun at the ready.

"Where the fuck are you, fam?"

The gun gave the hooded youth an inflated confidence, as he crept towards the left side of the car. To his surprise, there was nothing but broken glass and aluminium fragments where Tundé had stood.

"Looking for me, pussy'ole?!"

From out of nowhere, Tundé smashed through the right door window, hitting the hooded youth with a flying two-footed kick that sent him hurtling out of the car. As Tundé wiped the broken glass off his clothes, he spotted a bag lying underneath the debris in the backseat. Upon opening it, the purple substance and his precious family heirloom shone brightly back at him.

"Yes, I've got it! I've actually got it!" Tundé murmured excitedly to himself.

He tied the bag securely around his chest, then stepped out of the vehicle and thoroughly assessed the scene. Now that he had what he came for, Tundé was keen to get out. Fast.

Hold on, where's that yute with the gun?

"Yo!"

"Woah!"

More gunshots were fired, forcing Tundé to backflip instinctively onto the roof of the car to evade the bullets. The hooded youth walked menacingly over to Tundé, finger on the trigger ready to discharge any quick shots.

"You tried to take my big bro's life!" he growled.

Glancing over at Bullet, Tundé saw him wheezing desperately into an asthma pump as the gasps for air grew louder. The wrath of the young PMD gun-wielder was unmistakable. His hazelnut eyes were overflowing with tears.

"You think I'm gonna let that shit SLIDE?"

He fired more shots at Tundé, who managed to take cover behind the random car.

"Fuck me!" Tundé shouted as the car's windows were being continually smashed by constant bullets, setting its alarm off.

"I want you to see who bodied you," the hooded youth continued, taking the bandana off his face.

"No, Brootz! You're holding the strap!" Bullet rasped over to his younger brother.

"Oh shit, it's him," Tundé murmured from behind the trunk of the car. "The yute that cut me open in broad daylight."

Woah, I don't feel too good now...

Tundé was suddenly overcome with dizziness and disorientation—like he'd been clubbed on the head multiple times. Brootz's presence ignited a severe trauma response within Tundé's psyche. He lucidly relived the experience of his body being sliced through on Greenfeel Road a few days prior. A full-scale internal chaos ensued. Tundé was on his knees. His fluctuating emotions and hormones were paralysing his body against his will. His eyes were zooming in and out of focus, his reptilian hairs were extending and retracting repeatedly, and his self-healing function was regressing.

"Argh!" Tundé squirmed in agony, as he fought to take control of his tumultuous mind while hiding from the gun.

"Hold that, dickhead," Brootz shouted as he pulled the trigger twice, hitting Tundé's left arm and grazing his torso.

"ARGH!" The pain was excruciating.

Brootz ambled cautiously over to Tundé, who was sprawled out helplessly on the pavement. Brootz was breathing heavily, in anticipation of dishing out the final blow. The Isle of Dogs teenager was crawling away fervently. In the background, some PMD soldiers were regaining their senses like an army of zombies rising from the dead. In a strange twist of events, the tide of the fight had swung back in their favour. Brootz now had the pistol pointed tensely at Tundé from only a few yards away.

Oh shit! Oh, fucking shit!

"Look me dead in the eyes before I dead you, bruv!" Brootz roared, stepping closer and closer to his target. "I've killed before, and I felt nothing after. Nothing. So, I'm ready to do it again."

Tundé was still grappling with his unstable condition as he frantically tried to escape from the line of fire. While he didn't have the answers for why his complications, Tundé knew if he didn't act quickly, Brootz would ensure that he never found out. Out of the blue, a familiar voice entered Tundé's awareness.

"Babatundé, you have the power within!"

The dream with my dad.

Unexpectedly, the message etched a refuge within Tundé's psyche, shielding him from the internal turmoil and granting him a quiet place to observe. Time felt a lot slower here. It was in this brief moment of clarity that he spotted a motorbike parked on the other side of the road.

Could that be a sign? I've never ridden one of those before. Maybe this is the end of the line.

Brootz aimed the barrel of the gun towards Tundé's head, determined to show everyone just how cold of a killer he had become. He cocked the gun back.

"Any last words, you likkle pussy'ole?"

The seconds that followed felt like millennia. The spectating PMD members watched on. Bullet appeared hopeful. A tiny droplet of sweat slowly rolled down Brootz's youthful, sinister face as he pulled the trigger...

"PAP! PAP!"

"No!" Bullet shouted. "How?"

"Seriously?" yelled another PMD member.

"Stop him!" commanded another voice in the crew.

At the very last moment, Tundé used his superhuman strength to pounce on Brootz and redirect the first shot, then smacked the gun far away from Brootz's hands as he fired again. It gave Tundé a few precious seconds, as he darted to the motorbike. Some of the injured PMD soldiers staggered after him in pursuit.

Tundé's enhanced memory recalled a WeView tutorial that he stumbled upon a few months ago on how to hot wire a motorbike in under 60 seconds. Fortunately, he watched it numerous times because the instructor had a similar, funny voice to that of Barry Bill—a comedic TV presenter from his childhood.

Thank God for TV Bloop!

Wary of the oncoming threat, he soon found both cable and wiring and rubbed them together frantically while a few PMD boys were breathing down his neck. The motorbike's engine started abruptly, and Tundé wasted no time kicking away the haggard PMD soldiers as he rode off.

"DON'T LET HIM GO!" Brootz shrieked while firing two shots at the fast-escaping bike, missing Tundé both times.

"Yo, jump in the whips!" ordered Bullet, who had almost regained his breath.

"That was fucking close," Tundé muttered to himself, as he sped through the backstreets of Plaistow. He was still struggling with his injuries, despite the adrenaline rush of riding the two-wheeled vehicle and feeling the constant hum of the engine.

From out of nowhere, a blue Machini appeared from a bystreet and tried to ram through Tundé, forcing him to swerve out of the way and screech his tyres loudly on the tarmac. Considering his minimal experience and the gunshot wounds he carried, he was steering quite steadily. His wing mirror showed a fleet of cars on his tail, though. There was still work to do. Much to his dismay, the petrol gauge on the dashboard started beeping.

"You've got to be fucking with me!" Tundé said aloud, realising the vehicle couldn't get him back to the Isle of Dogs.

But I could go warehouse! It's the only place nearby that I know could give me an advantage. I hope.

He swerved off to the right headed for the abandoned building.

"Ease up bro, lemme get a good shot," Bullet pestered the driver, leaning out of the blue Machini car with a .45 ACP handgun.

"Man's trying, init!" the driver was struggling to keep up with Tundé's unorthodox steering.

Bullet fired more shots at Tundé, who fortunately managed to dodge them while maintaining control of the two-wheeled vehicle. But then, his back tyre burst!

"Wooaahh!" Tundé and the motorbike skidded hazardously along the road.

A yellow Wilwo carrying Brootz—the person responsible for shooting the burst tyre—was not too far behind. Sore from scraping harshly against the tarmac, Tundé was lucky to land a short distance from the warehouse gates. Deep in survival mode, he used all his energy to run over and climb the gates as quickly as possible. While he hobbled into the warehouse, three PMD cars parked outside the gates.

"Guess that prick wants to die in here, yeah?" Brootz said as he stepped out of the car, gun still firmly placed in his hands. "So be it."

"Remember. Fire first, ask questions later," Bullet instructed the gang. His gun audibly clicked as they primed themselves for action.

The PMD crew collectively forced open the gates and burst through the entrance of the warehouse. They were met with the same pitch-black darkness that welcomed Tundé on his first visit. Numerous torches from their miCell phones partially lit the warehouse, but their visibility was still quite low as the sky had darkened.

"Everyone, look out for this prick," Bullet whispered, his tone as tense and dark as the environment.

Slow footsteps, heavy breathing and nervous murmurings were heard in the warehouse as the PMD boys walked through the passages between the storage units, hungry for their victim.

"Yuck!" squealed one of the PMD boys, as a rat ran over his leg.

"Concentrate on the job, Umar," Bullet demanded as the sound of scurrying and squeaking could be heard in the background.

Meanwhile, Tundé was on the elevated platform. He was trying to activate the self-healing process, but he was still struggling with his injuries. In this state, he didn't want to risk fighting with multiple armed people. He was shaking with terror, as he stood by the door in the wall. Tundé reached out and cautiously pushed down the handle, then slowly turned it to open the door—all while hearing the faint footsteps of the PMD crew hunting for him on the ground below.

"He's defo somewhere here, fam," a PMD voice could be heard as Tundé felt a slight wobble from the steel structure of the platform.

"Trust, he can't be that far," echoed Bullet's voice from a different direction. He also sounded like had climbed up to the second level.

Tundé's heart pounded relentlessly in his chest. The looming door into the unknown appeared to be his best option right now. Pressing himself against the door, he eased it shut behind him before taking a few cautious steps forward. Tundé abruptly stumbled into a concealed opening, sliding down what he thought was a dark chute. When he reached the end, Tundé landed in a large container filled with old cardboard boxes, used safety equipment and other random muck.

"Yo, I just heard a sound! I think he's here," said the PMD boy on the raised platform as he flickered his miCell torchlight up and down, pointing towards the nearby door. The stench in the container was horrendous, but Tundé tried his utmost to remain silent and still.

"Let me see what this door's saying."

Just as Bullet stretched his hand out to investigate, the piercing sound of multiple sirens broke the backdrop of silence and engulfed the warehouse. Quickly, the windows of the warehouse lit up bright blue and the rustle of tarmac could be heard as numerous vehicles pulled up outside. The entire PMD crew were brought to a standstill. Before they could properly respond to the situation, dozens of Metropolitan Police and Specialist Firearms Command units came bursting through various entrances of the warehouse.

"Yo," Bullet said worriedly, stepping back from the door in the wall. "We need to duck!"

Bullet and Brootz both threw their guns into the shadows. Vulnerable to the situation, the rest of the PMD crew followed suit as the two brothers put their hands up and surrendered to the officers, who were now pointing torch-mounted guns into their faces.

"Freeze!"

"Hands up!"

"Don't move!"

"Ahhh, didn't think I'd find you and your crew all here together, Bullet," said a police officer, as he shone his blinding light on him aggressively. "You're making this job too easy for me, lads!"

Bullet closed his eyes and refused to respond, kissing his teeth instead.

"Fuck this Harry guy, man," Brootz said petulantly. "Always moving like a prick."

Harry—the man who was unknowingly working as an informant for the Discrete Services Unit—chuckled back.

"I've known your troublesome little self since I joined the Met a few years ago. I thought you'd have learnt your lesson by now, kiddo. Don't fuck with us."

"Boss, we found these," said one of the officers inspecting the property, as he produced the two guns for Harry to see.

"Interesting. Fellas, were you lot planning a fireworks party without inviting us?" Harry asked tauntingly. "You are all under arrest on suspicion of gun possession and for breaking & entering into a private property."

Harry and his team of police officers whipped out their handcuffs and detained all the PMD members.

"You have the right to remain silent. You do not have to say anything, but it may harm your defence..."

While Harry whisked the boys to the police van outside with his fellow officers, he curiously examined the warehouse.

"The operators told us these boys were chasing a man on a motorbike here. Search this place from top to bottom. I have a feeling there's more to find."

Chapter 19

"Oh shit!" Tundé exasperated. "Can't believe it's one in the morning. So gassed to see my bed though!"

After laying in the rubbish pit for what felt like an eternity, Tundé healed enough to attempt a getaway. He stealthily navigated his way through an air vent in the adjacent building and escaped the scene, without being spotted by the swarm of police officers on the premises. Reassured by the snoring of his adult guardians, Tundé charged his brick phone and took off his bag. He gazed happily at its contents—the Adeyemi heirloom and Jerry's bairaff—hoping that no unfortunate consequences were coming his way. He changed clothes and jumped into his bed with a huge sigh of relief.

Gotta wash these bedsheets tomorrow after being in all that shit.

Reflecting on the day, he shuddered when he realised how close he was to death, after his last direct encounter with it only days before. Processing how quickly his life had changed, Tundé slipped into a slumber. His awareness morphed from nothingness into an alternate realm, where he dreamt about the different phases of his battle against the PMD boys.

His mind replayed each jump, each punch and each dodge, while his brain analysed and pinpointed where adjustments in his actions could be made in every movement. It was like a rigorous training simulation.

The vivid playback allowed his cerebral network to rewire its circuitry and craft his timing as he slept through the night.

"Coo, coo! Coo, coo!"

The teenager was awoken by the irritating pigeons that had found a regular resting place on his windowsill. While the sun's rays brightened his room with a golden-yellow tinge, he assumed it was still early in the morning. Checking the time on his phone, Tundé instantly leapt out of his bed in a frenzied panic.

For god's sake, not again. It's ten past eight!

He was late for school, but more importantly, he didn't want to concern Remi and Jerry that he was going AWOL. While getting dressed into his school uniform, he flinched as he noticed his injuries from last night had completely healed. As amazing as the power was, he was still somewhat freaked out. Opening his backpack, Tundé shoved the bairaff package firmly under his schoolbooks and hurried for the front door.

"Ehen," Uncle Blessing called out from the living room. "So, you're not even going to acknowledge me today?"

"Ah, morning Uncle. Sorry, I gotta bounce cos I'm already late. Promise we'll talk later though."

Uncle Blessing yawned. "Hmm okay, son. Get to school. Just know that your mother is worried. She heard you come back late last night."

"Really?" Tundé smacked his palm against his forehead.

He thought he was in the clear! Given how much his mum worried about even the minutiae, he knew he would have to deal with some stress when he returned home.

"I explained to her that you're becoming a young man, so you will do odd things to find your way. She's still concerned though. I promised her that we would talk. But please, reassure her yourself too."

"Thanks, I will. See you later, Uncks."

Luckily for Tundé, his bus arrived on time, meaning he got to the Stebon High School bus stop a couple of minutes before the morning bell. As he walked to the entrance gates, he was met by a distressed Remi.

"Yo, Tunds. We need to leave school for a bit. Now."

"Bruv, what do you mean? What's happened?" Tundé was concerned, sensing Remi's uneasiness. "I managed to get the stuff back, you know."

"Bruv, Jerry's around the corner right now. We need to go link him for a bit, init."

"But school's just about to start and I just got exclu–"

"Fuck school for now, man! This is real-life shit. We need to duck."

Alarmed by how shaken up Remi was, Tundé chose to follow his best friend's lead. They walked around the corner and straight through the small park adjacent to their school's entrance. On the other side, a dark silver, tinted-window WMB 8-series was parked outside the gates. Remi walked up to the driver's side and knocked on the door. Its window lowered a couple of inches.

"Get in," said Jerry with a stern, dead-serious voice. "Alice, open the back doors."

Alice, the virtual car assistant, instantly obeyed, as the mechanised back doors smoothly slid open, revealing the spacious interior. The boys promptly bundled into the car.

"Yo Jerry, you alright?" Tundé asked meekly, before noticing Jerry's less-than-friendly associate in the passenger seat. The teenager gulped.

He's defo on smoke.

Jerry briefly glanced at the boys through the rearview mirror. His eyes were like thunder. The veins on his forehead bulged as the strained silence in the car continued. Their boss was furious. Tundé thought now would be the best time to hand Jerry the bairaff.

"I got this back for your deal with Biskit if that helps."

Jerry was motionless. As if he hadn't been spoken to at all. The boys shared a look of surprise at his reaction. Despite the snugness of the seats, the discomfort in the car was mounting. Then, Jerry readjusted the rearview mirror and leered at the boys through it.

"What. The. FUCK happened yesterday?"

Tundé was feeling the heat. His legs were shaking, and he had a lump stuck in his throat. Remi and Jerry's associate stared at him too, adding to the pressure.

"Someone just went to get my stuff for me, why?" he said, feigning ignorance.

"Because that bastard has almost shegged our whole fucking ting!" Jerry raged. "After Remi told me about the ambush by dem Plaistow pricks, I spoke to my regular plug cos he supplies their top dog too. What's his name again?"

"Fuckin'... bumbaclaat Zaid, init?" Jerry's associate answered.

"Safe, Yusuf. Bumbaclaat Zaid!"

Yusuf then handed a finely rolled joint to Jerry. He pulled out a lighter from his pocket and lit it, taking two drawn-out hits as the cannabis smoke quickly filled the car and assertively invaded the boys' noses.

"I spoke to my plug to arrange a meeting with Zaid. They even sell directly to the consumer, so we're not even competing with each other like that."

Jerry paused, ensuring that the boys were concentrating fully as he spoke.

"So, you know what my issue is now? We were meant to chat today about his youngers jacking you. But last night, the feds wrapped up bare PMD boys. And apparently, the don who took the purp off them didn't get bagged, even though he was in the building with them. You see why this is a problem?"

Tundé looked at Remi for an answer, but he seemed just as puzzled. Jerry took another long drag from the joint and then blew a smoky trail through his nostrils.

"Yo, Alice, beg you do that air suction ting."

"I'm sorry, I don't understand that yet," replied Alice, the WMB car's virtual assistant.

"Oh yeah, I forgot this ọ̀dẹ́ doesn't understand us man like that. Gotta speak to it like them posh, white people do."

Jerry cleared his throat.

"Alice, please turn the ventilation fan on," he said, mimicking a British Home Counties accent. Instantly, the fan buzzed on, gradually sucking the weed smoke out of the car.

"I know you lot can't be smelling of weed in school," Jerry was considerate despite his frustration.

Maybe Jerry isn't gonna kill me...

"The problem now is that the mandem are suspicious of my operation. I've heard a few people are unsure of doing business with me cos they think I'm an informant. So, I need to rebuild my trust. To do that, I've squashed the beef with Zaid by promising to peel off a certain percentage of our earnings for the next few weeks."

Jerry took another hit while the boys waited intently.

"For two reasons. One: I wanna avoid an expensive beef. There's enough bread for everyone to eat, I've just had a daughter and a war right now would be very long. Two: I don't want all the plugs to freeze me out. My business would go tits up, so I need to re-establish my credibility in the ends."

Jerry passed the joint to Yusuf. His eyes were weary and bloodshot, and not only from the cannabis.

"I need people to move this bairaff for me. Rishi warned me that we can't sell it in them uppity establishments or we'll get shut down quick time. Instead, we're going wholesale to the big movers on road. Tunds, since you got us into this bloodclaat debt, you're working back the time for me, understood?"

Tundé wasn't so enthusiastic. Being forced to work for free didn't sit well with him. But he was in a difficult position considering the seriousness of the situation.

"Is it cool if my guy helps me do this job for you?" he suggested.

"Who even is that bruddah? I need to chat to him and make sure he ain't a snitch, still."

"He's like my third cousin, but he grew up in Nigeria mostly. That's why he's fucking crazy and rattled them PMD boys proper! After all, they wouldn't have chased him all over town, especially with the feds on their case. And he still got the package back."

Tundé sensed Jerry's doubt. So, he sat up, projecting an assurance and capability to the senior businessman.

"Okay, Tunds. So be it. But if he fucks up again, we're gonna cut him up and you'll be working for a *long time* to pay off your debt."

"And after the debt, can we start getting paid?" Tundé asked boldly, to Remi's surprise.

"If you want him involved that much, you two can split your percentage."

"Understood," Tundé was pleased. He could still work for Jerry under the identity of his mysterious distant relative. But he knew the stakes were higher now. Any little slip-ups and the consequences could be tragic.

"Here, you and Remi will need these to work for me," Jerry said as he handed the two boys a black brick phone each. "We've managed to hack the phone network, so I can anonymously send one text and both of you will receive it with info about pick-ups and drop-offs. And you'll both be able to keep tabs on each other, so there are no excuses."

The boys pocketed their phones. Tundé was relieved that Jerry had spared him and that his secret was somewhat intact from any suspicions. For now.

"Alright, don't chat about any of this outside with your little mates at school. You've been warned. Alice, open the bumbaclaat back doors!"

Tundé and Remi got out of the car and walked back to school.

"Bruv, how did you do that?" Remi asked Tundé once they were finally out of sight from Jerry's car.

"Do what, bro?"

"Negotiate with Jerry like that. Who you learning from?"

"I dunno, man. I guess it's just Olodumare and the Universe guiding me, init!"

"Whatever you say, fam!"

They shared a laugh and re-entered the school premises. Tundé was buzzing with optimism that he resolved things with Jerry. Throughout the school day, he heard animated gossip from his fellow Stebon High peers about reports of an elusive character dressed in all black riding a stolen motorbike through Plaistow.

"Bro, I've seen a few clips of this don all over LyFilter. It's a madness," Jakub, a Year 11 prefect, told a group of classmates in the playground at break time. "My mum even saw a likkle column in *The Direct Message*. But them man are always chatting shit to get clicks, so who knows."

According to the reports, numerous Plaistow residents had recorded snippets of the incident on their phones as the PMD chase whizzed past their homes. Tundé found it amusing, but it reaffirmed to him that he couldn't afford to screw up and reveal his identity with videos like these being shared around.

During lunchtime, Tundé sat in the canteen with a plate of underseasoned rice and beef that his school sold. While he was eating it apathetically, a girl sat right beside him. He froze. His pupils dilated, his pores opened, and his heart thumped like a drumming band. It was the apple of his eye—the same eye that got thumped by her brother Lorenzo and his boys a few days prior.

"It's you, isn't it?" Laura said to him with a starry-eyed gaze.

Tundé was thrown off. "Errm, what? What do you mean?"

"This guy everyone's talking about is you, isn't it?" she had a sly smirk.

As smitten as he was by her, Tundé didn't want to give anything away.

"That don? Don't be silly, Laura!"

That made me sound like a wasteman. What's she gonna think of me now?

Laura burst out laughing, "Haha, jokes! I know that ain't you."

She pointed to another table in the canteen where her group of girls—or 'witches' as Remi liked to call them—sat during lunchtime.

"Me and the girls were playing this game called Scaredy Cat. You have to talk to the guy you're most scared of, and I needed an excuse!"

"You were scared? To talk to me?"

"I mean, yeah. After what my brother and his little bum boys did to you the other day, I felt *really* bad."

"Yeah, that was peak. But don't worry, things between me and you are blessed."

Laura smiled back and extended her pinky finger out towards Tundé. "Promise we're okay?"

Tundé wrapped his pinky finger around hers. "Promise."

They gazed into each other's eyes as time stood still. They were lost in a moment that felt almost eternal. Then, Laura shyly released her finger and stood up, walking back to her table, too awkward to say bye properly.

"By the way," she blurted while turning back to Tundé, "now that I think about it, your body does look quite similar to this mystery man's. When did you get so hench?"

"Erm, probably just puberty, init," Tundé laughed.

"Anyway, I know it's not you. Tunds ain't on all that badman shit!"

Tundé smiled and let Laura walk back to her table giddily. He was happy to avoid diving deeper into that topic.

Gotta watch out for that one!

***

When Tundé arrived home later that evening, Uncle Blessing was waiting for him in the living room. He signalled Tundé to sit down on the sofa beside him.

"Your mother will be at work until late this evening. The drug overdoses here are really rising! Anyway, I want to know what *the hell* you've been doing for the past few days."

"Uncle, there's no need, I've already got it sor–"

"Don't play with me, Babatundé! Because when I was in the Naija shop earlier, di woman was telling me about a big police chase last night. In that Playstowe."

"*Plaistow*, Uncle."

"Playstowe. Plaistow. I don't care! Anyway, she told me that a gang was chasing a lone man. Apparently, he had been fighting with all of them."

Tundé shrugged his shoulders, trying to play dumb. "I dunno."

"See, I'm not stupid. Do I look like an ọ̀dẹ́ to you? Like a fool?"

Before his nephew could respond, "Don't even answer that one, o!"

"Okay, Uncks."

"As I told you before, it's dangerous for you to be gallivanting outside with a lack of understanding. I'm sure since last week, your body has gone through some... some interesting changes since, abi?"

"Yeah, it's been pretty wild! And I still don't know what I'm capable of and whether I can control it. It's all a bit mad right now."

"You are still very young. You haven't even finished puberty! It is not how I envisioned your destiny, but Olodumare and the ancestors have made it so. I hope you know that I'm not just here in London for h'enjoyment."

"Yeah, I clocked. Please, tell me more."

Tundé sank comfortably into his seat, sensing a long explanation on the way.

"Centuries ago, our Yorùbá ancestors practised spirituality through the Ifá divination system. Through this magical discipline, they discovered an unusual strand of seaweed at the confluence of the Benue and the Niger Rivers in Lokoja, Kogi State. The seaweed contained ingredients that allow a mystical connection between di physical and spiritual realms. Thus, it was used as a source of power. It also had the ability to enhance a human's physical capabilities once consumed. Characteristics such as speed, agility, and intelligence were increased by tenfold!"

Tundé listened attentively, curious to understand how events from the past were influencing his present-day experience.

"Over time, though, there were some devastating side-effects. Many people fell ill, became disabled or suffered brutal deaths from the seaweed's continuous usage. Our ancestors came to understand that it was highly unpredictable while having the potential to wipe out the entire Yorùbá ethnic group if its consumption spread. To prevent this, the highest order of Yorùbá priests, also known as Babalawos, were called in to help."

"Rah, I thought those guys did evil juju. That's what all Nigerian olders have told me, anyway."

"It is because they don't know their history or their culture. We were practising these things for millennia before those barbaric outside forces came into our land."

Uncle Blessing paused to reach into his Aso Oke bag and pull out a bottle of Wuimmess. After taking a sip, he resumed the story.

"Anyway, the Babalawos carried out a ritual with the help of Oduduwa—the orisha of humans. He granted the paternal lineages of the three noblest Yorùbá families with the genetic capability to use the Kogi seaweed to protect its source and thus, the existence of the Yorùbá nation. Oduduwa also declared that the consequence for any other being's usage would be an accelerated death. In the centuries that followed, unfortunately, much of the knowledge, rituals and practices of the Yorùbá people were lost due to the colonisation of our culture and religions. Eventually, the Yorùbá people were integrated into what is now known as Nigeria."

Uncle Blessing looked at Tunde, his eyes betraying the gravity of the situation.

"You see, Babatundé. The Adeyemis are the last known family with the genetic, spiritual connection to the Kogi seaweed."

Tundé fidgeted uncomfortably with the arm of the sofa. It was a lot for him to take on board.

"Ọmọ, you were far from ready for Oduduwa's ritual. But you were dying, so I had no choice! Our tradition also dictates that a warrior created from ritual must be left alone for 48 hours to prove themselves worthy of holding such power. Ideally, I would have prepared you for some weeks beforehand."

Tunde was gobsmacked.

Am I in a fucking movie, fam?

"But what you tried yesterday in that Playstowe was too risky! You could have been killed—again! And this time, there would have been no returning."

"I thought I had to prove myself worthy though, Uncks?"

"Ehen, I did. However, Mr Gallivanter, you do not understand the dark side of your powers. Èṣù, the orisha of mischief, forced Oduduwa to include a sacrifice in exchange for your superhumanness. As a Yorùbá warrior, you must become one with the forces of the Universe to maintain orderliness. Thus, you must confront your internal fears, worries and traumas as your connection with the spiritual realm builds. If you succumb to these, the animal selves within will cripple your mind into self-destructive chaos."

"Animal... *selves*?"

"Yes, the animal psyches. Where do you think your new abilities came from? Chai! Did you not hear me chanting?"

"Well, I knew *something* was happening to me."

Tundé thought back to the point when he lost psychological control after coming face-to-face with Brootz, triggering the traumatic memories of being gouged out on Greenfeel Road.

"Son, I understand that you are concerned. But everything will be explained in good time."

Uncle Blessing walked to the living room window to observe the glowing sunset. Tundé stood beside him, staring outwards. The unpredictable shifts seen in the twilight sky mirrored his own life.

Chapter 20

"PLEASE! PLEASE! I PROMISE I didn't do anything. I swear it!"

"I've always seen you as an honest man, Michael. But my impression of you is now at odds with whatever *the fuck* I'm seeing on my report logs!"

"Chris, I beg you, plea–"

"Shut yer mouth, you silly twat," ordered Steve—Chris's henchman in the Discreet Services Unit—as he pressed his 3D-printed gun firmly onto Michael's temple.

Michael was tied from the shoulders down to his waist in a worn-out leather chair. He was being held captive in a barren, dull room, at the mercy of Chris and Steve.

"Let Chris finish talking, or else," Steve advised as he cocked back the gun. The sound reverberated through the room, striking a chord of fear in Michael. His eyes widened as the pores on his forehead gushed out sweat.

"You see, Michael. I can't quite understand how a classified DSU shipment from Southern Nigeria could have *possibly* been intercepted without insider knowledge."

A deafening silence followed before Chris resumed.

"It was orchestrated with fine precision, yet we're experiencing a lengthy delay due to unexpected turbulent seas and tsunamis appearing mysteriously across the Gulf of Guinea. It's almost like those wizards were tipped off about our important stock. Remember, only a few of us are working on this part of the mission."

Steve pressed the gun harder against Michael's head, making his gulps of despair echo loudly through the room.

"Chris, I promise you. I haven't spoken a word of it since we left Nigeria. I swear!"

"Your wife, Claire? Your children, Tammy and Mark? Your father, Michael Jones Senior? Are you sure you spoke to none of them?"

Chris's words were laced with frustration. Michael was teary-eyed and filled with terror. The terror one would feel if a heartless man recited the names of immediate family members without so much as a stutter.

"You know how important Project Pareto is to the future of our organisation, don't you?" Chris smacked his fist down angrily on the table. "Don't you?"

"I would never because... because I know what you're both capable of!" Michael blabbed through the tears streaming down his face. "I beg you, please don't hurt my family. Or make me disappear like you did to those other agents!"

"Then tell him the truth, you soppy bastard," Steve demanded as he waved the gun.

"Okay... okay... I may have made a mistake somewhere," Michael tried to compose himself in his distressed state.

"I'm listening."

"Erm, recently, I went for a walk in a country park with my dog, Trina."

"Which park, Michael?" Chris grilled him impatiently. "And when?"

"A park just outside Cheltenham, in the Cotswolds. On March 8th. I was really stressed out about executing this operation properly.

I understand how important this is for the DSU and the future of humanity. I needed to send an encrypted update to Connor about the shipment because he was still in Southern Nigeria. As DSU protocol requires, I used my CloudBerry phone. But my connection to the DSU transmitter from the park was weak..."

A few seconds of silence in the interrogation room followed as Michael couldn't get the words out.

"And, Michael? AND?" Chris probed with annoyance. Steve tapped his gun against Michael's head again, reminding him of the consequences if he remained mute.

"And... and because the CloudBerry's signal in the park was weak, I... I used a personal H2O sim network to send the message. I know it was risky, but I couldn't shake my nerves!"

"So, you're telling me *all* you did was use a network you weren't fucking supposed to?" Chris was puzzled.

As a skilled analyser of human behaviour, he observed that Michael was nodding his head positively while explaining himself and that his breathing was fairly steady, given the circumstances. All indicators of truthful communication, even for people under duress. But Chris couldn't see Michael's eyes properly under the tears. It raised an inkling of doubt. He glanced undecidedly at Steve, who wasted no time.

"That's for using a public network, you silly wet wipe," Steve whacked Michael's head with the gun, knocking him down to the ground. Blood trickled from his forehead as he remained tied to the chair.

Steve stepped over to Chris, who was deep in thought as he scanned his phone. He was using DSU tracking software to check Michael's message logs and verify the legitimacy of his explanation. Other than the security alert from the network, his encrypted messages seemed appropriate. But Chris still didn't feel satisfied.

"Can you believe this prick took a risk like that?" Steve lamented. "The way technology is these days?"

Michael's sobbing in the background was a stark contrast to Chris's calculated quietness. He glanced back and forth from Michael to his phone with greater urgency, his suspicion remaining. Steve was oblivious to the underlying tension in the room and continued berating their captive.

"I tell you what, Chris, I bet this lad has talked. I wouldn't dare talk. Not even if a saucy tart was suc–"

"BANG! BANG! BANG!"

In a flash, multiple gunshots went off.

Chris had swiftly drawn a handgun from his blazer and fired multiple bullets that tore through the flesh of Michael's face and chest; leaving a blood-soaked, tied-up corpse on the cold, hard floor. Steve was stunned. He had his back slightly turned away from Michael before the gunshots. Michael's limp right hand slid out through a small gap that had formed between the ropes. It revealed his fingers wrapped around a loaded pistol.

"Ah ha, I knew I couldn't trust that fucker," Chris was seemingly unfazed by the horrifying aftermath of bodily fluids and human meat that had splattered all over the room—some even got onto his and Steve's clothes. "Looks like he was fiddling with the trap to get to his strap."

Retrieving the handkerchief from his blazer pocket, Chris gently wiped the splatter off before stuffing it away with an unsettling calmness. He ran his fingers through Michael's bloody hair while making his assessment.

"He *was* a very skilled liar. He had all the physical signs of somebody being honest. But his crying trick threw me off because I couldn't see his eyes properly. My gut told me not to trust our old boy, though. Always remember, Steve. Never turn your back in this game. No one can truly be trusted."

"Yes boss, I know. It won't happen again," said Steve meekly, still recovering from the shock. He was thankful to Chris for remaining vigilant and saving his life.

"He even covered his tracks with the message logs. But I soon determined that a private server was accessing the CloudBerry messages too, which were linked through Michael's account. That led to an unknown entity gaining temporary access to our shipment information."

Chris whipped out his phone again and dialled one of his contacts.

"Hello...? President B? ...Yes, yes, it's Chris speaking. How are you doing these days? ...Great, lovely. And the family? ...Wonderful. Okay, let's talk business now. We've had a protocol breach for Project Pareto within the last few days, so we need to put some serious contingencies in place. The stakeholders are pressuring me to execute this plan swiftly and thoroughly. That unfortunately means that measures must be taken."

Steve could hear unclear murmurings from the phone.

"Yes, Prez, don't worry. I haven't forgotten about your needs. When I eventually oust that incompetent bastard Russell Bennett and take over as Director-General of the DSU, I will place you in control of the Treasury and ensure that your child has guaranteed admission into one of the colleges at Cambridge, as promised. You just need to do this for me, as my pathway to that position depends on this project's success. Is that understood?"

More inaudible muttering could be heard but judging by the sly smirk that emerged on his manager's face, Steve assumed it was a positive response to Chris's request.

"Perfect. After this call, you will receive the addresses of houses, schools and workplaces. I want you to organise your men for round-the-clock surveillance at each location. If I give you the action text, I want the relevant person associated to be taken hostage. Is that clear?"

There was another slight pause from Chris, as President B's distorted phone voice was the only sound that could be heard in the grimy, blood-stained room.

"Yes, Prez, for the health of the project and our agreement, you must be ready to kill them. So, ensure you can dispose of any leftovers cleanly should that be the case."

While more chatter came from the other end of the line, Chris put the call on speaker and began typing on his phone.

"...and I'll have my hitters on escalated standby by noon tomorrow," Prez's deep voice boomed through the speaker.

"Good. I've just sent through the access instructions for those details. Otherwise, I hope all's well with you, my friend. Speak soon."

"Laters, my guy."

"So, what was that about, boss?" Steve asked once Chris hung up the phone.

"It's suspected that Michael was selling us out to external parties. Why? I haven't worked that out yet. Regardless, we must mitigate the risk of this happening again with the rest of the team. Project Pareto will succeed, even if it means resorting to extreme measures."

After Chris and Steve headed back to the DSU HQ—situated within a highly classified location in the South East of England—they held individual interrogation sessions with each of the eight remaining project team members in the onsite holding cells. Chris approached each conversation with the same rhetoric.

"I have some news to share, both good and bad. Unfortunately, Michael decided to betray the Unit by breaking high-risk protocol, resulting in severe consequences. As his close mentor, I was deeply disappointed by his actions. Regrettably, the senior leadership deemed this breach a serious threat to Project Pareto, and as a result, they have sanctioned his extermination. I must also inform you that, due to the leadership's increased sense of doubt surrounding the project, they have approved 24-hour surveillance to monitor the movements of everyone that you know and love."

As Chris had intended, each DSU agent responded with a sense of dread and anxiety, amplified by the threatening presence of Steve in the interrogation cell.

"Now, the silver lining here is that I've worked tirelessly with our leadership to ensure the surveillance team act harmlessly if our protocol is followed up until the project's completion. Working for the Unit, I'm sure you understand how important it is that we fulfil the mission for our country's future prosperity. All we ask for in return from you is that you refrain from divulging classified information to ANYONE outside the DSU. Failure to adhere to this will assure you the pleasure of being forced to watch footage of your loved ones being tortured and killed. Person by person. Frame by frame. Before exterminating *you*, of course. So, the choice is ultimately yours. Is everything clear?"

Every single agent felt it necessary to declare their overwhelming commitment to the project and emphasise their compliance with DSU protocols. All of which satisfied their domineering project leader. Once the final interrogation was finished, Steve unlocked each agent from their cells and guided them to a conference room in the HQ. Chris was waiting there patiently, standing by a large monitor with a remote control in his hands.

"Welcome, welcome, welcome."

Unsurprisingly, Chris was met with a less than enthusiastic response from his agents. Undeterred, Chris switched his attention to the screen to commence his presentation.

"As all are surely aware, the completion of Project Pareto is of paramount importance to the DSU and our mission of national prosperity. But thanks to the snake in the grass, we've hit a snag. That means now, we must adjust our strategy to ensure a successful shipment of our valuable ingredient from Nigeria."

Chris pressed the remote and a picture of a purple substance appeared on the monitor for the room to see.

"You're all familiar with Odabozite Trioxide. After importing an initial 75 tonnes into the country for our urban rats to play with for a few months, we had a large cargo shipment for a further 3,500 tonnes that was scheduled to arrive on British shores in a fortnight. But things went horribly wrong, as it appears that the Yorùbá wizards were tipped off about our route."

Those words injected more tension into the room. Once Chris took a moment to relish the increasing panic amongst his project team, he resumed, flicking through to the next slide on the screen.

"I'd hazard a guess that these ageing bastards used what's left of their weakening powers to change the weather conditions in the Gulf of Guinea. It's since caused a significant delay to our progress."

"Why would they do that?" one of the team members called out. "I thought we gave them a decent price for the bairaff?"

"Well, yes, Tamwar. If pennies and a few splodges of blood are seen as adequate legal tender," Chris chuckled with a cold, detached demeanour. Tamwar—the supplier for Jerry's bairaff trade—was visibly uncomfortable with the response.

"Furthermore, since you're a Junior Officer here," Chris continued condescendingly, "please leave those issues to the higher-ups and concern yourself solely with your assigned duties as they relate to the mission. Can you manage that?"

Tamwar nodded feebly.

"Wonderful. Anyway, as I was saying, we have now changed our strategy. We've split the next shipment into three batches. They will be transported by land, air and sea respectively."

He clicked over to the next slide, which included a table listing logistical instructions and the names of each agent assigned to individual line items.

"The first batch will be travelling by land from Nigeria up to Morocco, then driven through Europe to the UK. The second batch will be flown via cargo plane from Benin to France, then on a charter plane to Heathrow. The third batch will be split into smaller packs, and transported by multiple cargo ships headed to Portsmouth, Southampton and Dover. Each of you has been assigned a DSU logistician expert on the screen to ensure our shipments arrive at the warehouse accordingly. Once we complete this four-week process, the next stage of the Project Pareto will commence."

Chris paused. Gauging the room, he was pleased to see his fellow project members were engaged—albeit begrudgingly—with the task ahead.

"Are there any questions before we proceed?"

Chapter 21

"BAWONI! HOW ARE YOU doing, Abi?"

"I'm okay, Sister Fola," Auntie Abi said, as she was welcomed through the front door of the Adeyemi home in Equiano House. "Ṣé wà dádá?"[1]

"Ko bad now, ko bad," Fola Adeyemi said while leading her younger sister to the living room. "But I'm working very hard while this country is trying to kill me, o! We thank God that they have not succeeded."

"You're telling me! I'm feeling under a lot of pressure right now myself."

Abi sighed heavily, slumping herself down on the sofa. Fola was concerned as she fetched two glasses of water from the kitchen.

"Ọmọ, what's the matter now? Don't tell me it's a man causing you trouble?"

"Naaa, if it was about my romantic life, you'd have heard about it already!"

Fola gazed at her questioningly as she handed Abi the glass. "Hmm, well, you've been a secretive one ever since you were a child. So, I wouldn't be surprised if you were hiding something."

"No, Sister," Abi said while casually rolling her eyes. "I promise you, it's not a man. Not a specific one, anyway."

1. *Are you okay?*

She took a sip of water from the glass and continued. "Thanks for this. I just feel under pressure. I'm in my late twenties and my life is a mess. My career in marketing looks under threat as technology keeps developing. I have no kids. And I'm still living in that bummy part of East London. E dey pain me, o!"

"Izz okay dear, keep talking to me."

"To be very honest, my career trajectory concerns me the most. Especially because I'm on my own. Something just feels off. And I don't wanna go back on government allowance again. My sanity just about stayed intact when I signed on for a few months after graduation."

"Well, dear. You are a Yorùbá woman. We are strong. Our lineage is resilient. We must be mentally and emotionally tough for everyone, including our own selves, sha."

"I know, I know... but I'm just not feeling all that strength at the moment."

After a short pause, Abi pressed her hand tightly against her chest, as if trying to contain the turmoil within.

"Ah, pẹ̀lẹ́ now, Abiola! I'm sorry. You have to trust that God has the best plan for you. He will never give you something you could not handle."

"Yeah... amen?" Abi said rather meekly. It appeared her level of faith didn't match Fola's.

"Have you been going to that new church in Aldgate? The one that all your young friends are going to?"

"Oh, you mean Mound Psalms? No, I haven't had the chance to yet."

"Ehen, you really should! There, you can grow a closer relationship with God and who knows? Maybe you'll find a nice, Christian husband that will save you from yourself too."

"Ah, Sister? That dig was uncalled for! I don't need a man to make me happy."

"Abi, you're sad about your life while you're currently single. What other suggestions can I make, now? Kil'o fẹ kin sọ?"[2]

"You've done pretty well with Tunds on your own. You don't see me telling you to move on and find a new partner, even though it's been almost eight years since–"

Fola gasped as she locked eyes with Abi in disbelief.

"Ah ah! How dare you? That is a completely different situation! I want you to go to Mound Psalms to grow closer to Christ, who will deliver you from your pain. And I pray that you find a God-fearing husband there. Because this life, o! It is very, very hard as a single woman."

A teardrop slowly trickled down Fola's face as she contemplated the words. "Even with all this my faith."

"Oh no, I'm sorry, Sister. You've always been a strong woman to me. But you still find life this challenging with all your belief in God?"

As the words left Abi's mouth, Fola felt her throat dry up. She struggled to hold back the tears threatening to spill from her eyes. But soon, they were streaming down both her cheeks.

"H'of course! I've struggled more than I may tell you. My miscarriage before Tundé was born still haunts me. We thank God that I survived, but I always ask why I lost my first baby. It certainly tests my faith."

"Wow. That must've been so painful. I guess it's hopeless for me, then."

As Fola rummaged through her bag for some tissues, Abi's dejected demeanour became more apparent. She was far from her warm and

---

2. *What do you want me to say?*

bubbly self. Known for her comforting hugs and reassuring gestures, Abi appeared distant and detached in stark contrast.

"Abiola, please. Don't speak like that. I rebuke it in the name of Jesos! With God, all things are possible. Oya, come here."

Fola held her arms out to warmly invite Abi for a hug. But her younger sister wasn't very receptive. She turned her body away, causing Fola's eyes to widen.

"Abiola, come here jor!" Fola said, forcefully wrapping her arms around Abi's stiff frame. "Where's the girl that loves hugs?"

Abi was tense, barely softening up to her sister's affection.

"She's... she's a different person now."

"Ah, please. Let us rebuke this negativity in the name of Jesos!"

Abi nodded wordlessly in response. Fola thought it best to change the subject.

"Anyway, when was the last time you spoke to ọmọ mi o ni wahala?"[3]

"Sister, don't be too harsh on Tunds. He does try hard to do the right thing, you know. And he's still a teenager at the end of the day."

"Oh, you say he tries hard. Does he finish top of his class? Does he go to work? Does he pay these bills? Does he even wash the dishes when I tell him to?"

"Ah, give him some slack now."

"He's a lazy child! I'm worried about his future. I don't know if he can go to university and study something proper like engineering or computer science. All he seems to care about is playing outside with his friends and that stupid Assna team!"

"Yeah, I hear you," Abi said meekly, retreating into her shell again.

---

3. *My troublesome son*

"I need you to speak to him and make sure he's going in the right direction," Fola asked while scouring through the kitchen for different items. "It feels like he doesn't want to listen to me anymore."

"Yeah, I'll try my best," Abi said wearily as she rose from the sofa. "But I need to get going now, sha. I have some things I need to take care of."

"Okay. Before you go, please, take these."

She handed a plastic bag to Abi. It contained a 12-pack of aspirin, a container filled with jollof rice, a tiny pouch of raw ginger and lemons, and a red pocket-sized bible.

"These will all help you feel better in different ways. Especially the ginger and lemons, as you remember."

"Of course," Abi recalled with a brief, wry smile. "I used to drink that all the time when I got ill after we first moved back here from Nigeria."

"I'm glad you do. Remember that the word of the Lord is with you too."

"E ṣé gan, Sister. I will see you soon. Send my greetings to Tunds and Uncle Blessing."

"Ó dàbọ̀. Safe jonny home and God bless!"

Chapter 22

"TUNDÉ, PLEASE COME TO the living room now!"

"Coming, Uncle!" Tundé stormed out of his bedroom in a hurry. "What's up? You know it's Wednesday night, so Arsenal is playing soon."

"Assna? We have more important matters to deal with than watching grown men kick around that pig's bladder," Uncle Blessing retorted, while Tundé scoffed. "Anyway, how are you doing son?"

"Yeah yeah, I'm good."

Uncle Blessing was sceptical, prompting Tundé to sigh deeply.

"Actually, Uncks, I'm a bit confused. What exactly is happening to me?"

"Ah, great question. Well, your body is still gradually morphing to accommodate the three animal DNA strains added during the ritual."

"Okay, I hear you. And the magical seaweed ting allows that to happen, right?"

"Ehen, you're learning! After consumption, the average human would go through a process of genetic rejection, eventually causing your DNA to collapse and induce death. However, in your case, the mystic composition of the Kogi seaweed is remodifying your entire genetic structure instead."

"Rah, that's actually a madness."

"Indeed, son."

"Why did you pick these animals, Uncks? Why not a lion or a tiger so that no one could fu... mess with me."

"Maybe you know this, but each animal I used is commonly found in Yorùbáland, and they represent the fundamental elements of our planet: earth, water and air. Your powers draw from this principle, giving you an advantage whether you're on land, in the sky or at sea. Just as Oduduwa has ordained it centuries ago."

Tundé eyes widened in fascination at what he had just heard. "Wow, so when I heal mad quickly, that's coming from the lizard init?"

"Ehen, precisely."

"And I'm guessing the eagle genes let me see things in detail from afar, right? And which animal makes my old memories and thoughts pop up in front of me like I'm using those hi-tech AR glasses?"

"Yes, that hyper-vision would appear to be influenced by the eagle. And olphins are known for their vastly superior memory. Because your physical body is still adapting to the DNA restructure, who knows what other abilities you may come to possess with time. We just thank Olodumare that you are learning what you're capable of without getting yourself killed, o!"

Tundé leapt off the sofa excitedly and stood at the living room mirror to inspect different parts of his body.

"So, I could become even more powerful than now yeah?"

Imagine, I could get myself paid and solve all of our family's problems. I'd be my family's version of Kwame the banker, but slyly different!

"Basically, I can do what I want!" The teenager continued, visualising the opulent lifestyle he could create with his growing potential. "Jheeze!"

"No, not quite," Uncle Blessing said abruptly. "We must train. Like every respected Yorùbá warrior before us. My mentor once told me: 'a man is only as powerful as his discipline and integrity allow him to be.' You possess great power, but you must learn to control it wisely."

"Yeah, yeah. I hear you," Tundé muttered absentmindedly, still preoccupied with his reflection.

He thought Uncle Blessing was too far removed to understand why he felt justified using his gifts for his own purposes.

"Babatundé, like I explained before. If you don't manage your temperament properly, the animal psyches will overwhelm your consciousness and you could lose your mind as they take control. The powerful forces of Èṣù control this balance. It could be catastrophic."

"Alright, so what's the plan, Uncks?" Tundé asked, trying his best not to sound condescending.

Despite the elder's warnings, Tundé's ego was in the driver's seat. He dreamed of all the extravagant things he could acquire with his powers.

Maybe I could move the whole fam to the City Lofts in Canary Wharf.

"The extent of your power derives from your level of internal control. This is the most important aspect of your training, sha. Without authority over your thoughts and emotions, it doesn't matter how much potential you have. Acting in a responsible and measured manner will be very difficult."

Maybe I could buy myself a WMB when I turn 17 next summer.

"I spent almost fifteen years in the Omo Forest. I learnt how to sit with myself, how to breathe with the appropriate techniques and how to deal with my mind during physically demanding situations."

Maybe I could get a girlfriend as buff as Laura at the snap of my fingers.

"Ọmọ, do you think I just woke up one day with the ability to manipulate the weather and perform these intense rituals?"

But all these strict lessons Uncks is talking about sound long for man.

"Tundé, ṣé o gbọ́ mi?[1] Are you even listening to what I'm saying right now?"

"Yes, Uncle. We need to do training for my powers and that. I heard you."

Judging from Uncle Blessing's reflection in the mirror, he was anything but happy with Tundé's lack of engagement. The teenager turned to face him.

"Son, everything I'm saying is vital for you to understand. Even with all my years of experience, I still require long breaks because of my age. Your youth is a blessing though, with the potential to become much more formidable than I ever have been. But youth can also be a curse if you're careless. Please do not waste it, o."

Tundé nodded passively as his uncle opened a bottle of water to quench his thirst.

"Anyway, we shall start with the beginner exercises to help you master your newfound powers. With regular practice, you will build a sturdy foundation to become a well-equipped Yorùbá warrior."

Tundé couldn't hide his disinterest as he sighed heavily and avoided eye contact. Noticing this petulant behaviour, Uncle Blessing thought Tundé would disengage completely if he continued lecturing him. He had to make his nephew enthusiastic.

"Tundé, di truth is it's going to be tough. But remember, you are going to find *many* ways to enjoy your powers with my coaching."

---

1. *Can you hear me?*

Like clockwork, Tundé's ears perked up with curiosity. "For example, like?"

"Now that you have entered puberty, you probably want to court the attention of the girls in your school, abi?"

Tundé's mind immediately raced to fantasies about Laura Thompson. His eyes became love-struck, prompting a smirk on Uncle Blessing's face.

"Ehen, I see you've thought of her already! Don't forget, I was once a young man too. I know what kind of desires you have at that age, o!"

Tundé couldn't bear to look his uncle in the eye. He was too embarrassed. "Haha erm, yeah. Suttin' like that."

"What is this your girlfriend's name?"

"Erm, she's not my girlfriend, Uncle. But I'd want her to be. Her name is... is Laura... why?"

"Think about how impressed Miss Laura will be when you start showing the confidence and strength of a true warrior."

"Oh yeah, that would be quite sick actually," Tundé replied gleefully, beaming from ear to ear.

"Well, this disciplined training will turn you into that person, Tundé."

"I mean, if it can help me get Laura, then maybe I can try it out," Tundé said, pleasing Uncle Blessing with his openness and lack of resistance.

"Not to mention the other girls in your class will take interest, too. It's even my fault for assuming you'd know about these things without your dad around."

"Yeah, I guess."

"Ah pẹ̀lẹ́, I shouldn't have mentioned him. I'm sorry. I just wanted you to know that this training will transform you into a desirable man. Is that what you want?"

Tundé couldn't hide his excitement. "I mean, it sounds good to me, Uncks!"

"Ehen! Let's get started then."

They both sat cross-legged on the living room floor, as Uncle Blessing prepared to put Tundé through a series of drills.

"In traditional Yorùbá spirituality, your spiritual power, or àṣẹ, is deeply connected with your mastery of breath. Most of our training will focus on this aspect, due to our faith that Olodumare will empower you, should it be ordained."

"Err okay, Uncks."

"Oya, for our first exercise, I want you to inhale through your nose for five seconds. Make sure the air only fills up in your lungs. Hold it in for three seconds. Then, exhale gently for five seconds. Make sure you don't force it out!"

This seems easy enough, Tundé thought while following the instructions and maintaining his posture. As the evening progressed, Uncle Blessing increased the intensity of the exercises.

"Listen carefully now. You will lie across di floor, and lift yourself using your toes and forearms. You must keep your legs straight too."

"So, what now?" Tundé asked Uncle Blessing with a tone of overconfidence after assuming his position.

"Ehen. You will hold this plank position until I tell you to stop. This will test your stress threshold. Simple."

"Alright, should be calm."

After several one-minute cycles, Tundé was struggling tremendously. Panting like a furry dog on a blistering summer's day, he collapsed to the floor, as the sweat drenched his t-shirt.

"Not as easy as it looks, abi? Just imagine what developing a high pain barrier will do for you?"

"Yeah," Tundé gasped, spreading himself out on the floor in a desperate heap.

"Okay, our next exercise might be something your mum punished you with for misbehaving! It is called the murga position. You will squat down while looping your arms behind your knees and holding your earlobes."

"Uncks, let's just allow this, I beg!" Tundé urged as he got into the required stance.

"My son, I know it's hard. But patience is paramount here. Without it, you will never gain command over your mind and body, o."

"But this is long, Uncks. This ain't doing anything for me."

"With time, you'll feel the difference, sha. Anyway, let us continue."

Tundé couldn't bear it any longer. His muscles ached. His mind struggled to fight off the panic signals from his body. His sweat-laden t-shirt was becoming very bothersome. Caving into the pressure, he broke out from the murga stance and fell to the floor.

"I know it's painful, but you must continue," Uncle Blessing uttered sharply. "We have no choice."

"What do... do you mean... no choice?" Tundé panted. "What am I even... going *this* hard for?"

"For NIGERIA, jor! NIGERIA!"

Tundé was startled. He gazed at his uncle with exasperation and confusion. Uncle Blessing took a deep breath to recompose himself.

"I'm sorry. I shouldn't have exploded like that. But our situation is more substantial than you can even begin to imagine."

"So, why is Nigeria so important? Why does it need to be my problem now?"

"Tundé, your frustration is valid. But you need to understand this. You have a duty and an obligation that runs deep in your bloodline."

"What does that even mean, Uncle?"

Uncle Blessing paused in deliberation for so long that it put Tundé even more on edge. The teenager knew the answer was going to be far from simple.

"You remember when I explained that the Kogi seaweed fuels your powers?"

"Yeah?"

"Well, there is more to that story. While the physical enhancements from ingesting the seaweed were clear, our ancestors identified that there was an active ingredient within it which they called ìṣẹ̀dàbọ̀."

"What's that?"

"Ah, you'll need to ask a chemistry expert for that one, o! But our ancestors realised it could power the agricultural and infrastructural projects of Lokoja, which became a thriving West African village at the time. Imagine towering watermills harnessing the current, irrigation systems quenching the thirsty soil, and mechanisms utilising the sun. All powered the Kogi seaweed."

"That sounds sick. But I guess the main problem was that it was killing people consuming it, right?"

"Yes, the compound would attack the infrastructure of the human body, decaying its host slowly over time."

Tundé gulped loudly as his eyes startled, knowing this substance was flowing through his body. "Rah."

"While the seaweed powered many necessary functions, it was deemed a risk to the community's survival. However, the Lokoja leaders were afraid of the catastrophic consequences if other groups learnt of its power and fought desperately to obtain it for their own use. This is when they sought counsel from the Babalawos."

"Okay, but what's the issue if they did all that?"

"Initially, Oduduwa was asked to bury the entirety of the Kogi seaweed deep below the riverbed of the Benue-Niger River confluence. But during the ancestors' spiritual negotiations, Ẹ̀ṣù was unhappy that nature was being distorted. And he was unconvinced by their desire to relinquish such great power. So, to maintain balance, Ẹ̀ṣù deployed a sinister spiritual demon beneath the riverbed, entrusting it to safeguard the iṣẹ̀dàbọ̀ source and act as a deterrent should humanity ever become greedy."

Tundé remained speechless while nerves jangled frantically throughout his body. He was fixated on every last word his uncle spoke. Each new revelation terrified him.

"When the elders learnt of this, they pleaded with Oduduwa for a defence against any power-obsessed people or the demon itself if it were ever released. This is why Oduduwa restructured the genetic code of the three noblest Yorùbá warriors. He also made a limited amount of the Kogi seaweed accessible for the warriors to tap into its spiritual powers and defend the people from these threats. As I said di other day, much of our ancient knowledge was lost over the centuries. However, there is a reason I am here with you now. We are fearful that a major breach in the riverbed will happen in the coming months."

Tundé was quivering in his seat. His mind was racing. His palms were clammy. He wanted to cry and scream all at the same time. He couldn't comprehend it all.

"Uncle, a sinister spiritual demon? But I'm only 15! Pardon my French, but that's bare fucking responsibility."

"Ah ah! No swearing, abeg!"

"Sorry, Uncks. But that really is bare responsibility."

"No, son. It's *a lot* of responsibility."

"Exactly, that's what I mean. I don't think I can hack it."

"That is why I am here, though. To guide you in fulfilling your destiny!"

"I know," Tundé trembled. "But that sounds like way too much for me to deal with. Even you looked scared just talking about it."

Uncle Blessing rubbed his chin sheepishly, embarrassed that he projected his worries onto his teenage nephew.

"Please understand, I too am fearful. However, I believe that with your power, our preparation and the unwavering support we will feel from the almighty Olodumare, we can overcome any obstacle that comes our way."

"Amen?" Tundé said meekly. Uncle Blessing realised that his nephew was still very overwhelmed.

"Babatundé, forget all those crazy wahala stories I just told you, sha. Just get some rest now and we'll continue this another time."

"Yeah, that sounds good. I'm bare tired anyway. Goodnight Uncks."

Uncle Blessing entered a challenging meditation pose with one foot on the ground and the other foot placed on his knee. He then gave his nephew an approving nod.

"Goodnight, Babatundé. Please, only focus on how blessed you are now. Olodumare is on our side."

Tundé responded with a forced smirk and then sauntered sullenly to his bedroom.

"I really hope that boy will be okay, o. And I pray that all of us will be too."

Tundé planted himself face-down on the bed and the depressing thoughts began whizzing through his mind.

Fam, that whole Naija stuff sounds too mad for me right now. It's not my problem.

Even with his underlying dread, Tundé was drained from what had been a testing day. He subsequently dozed in and out of sleep, entering the fantasy land where he was in complete control of his spiritual energy. In this dream state, Tundé envisioned himself as a powerful man who could command anything the world had to offer. But a looming figure of obligation shadowed him and darkened his dreams. As he tossed and turned in his bed, Tundé woke up feeling spooked. His heart was pounding aggressively. Full of restlessness, he checked the time on his brick phone.

Rah, it's only half 2! I thought it was much later.

Too alert to go back to sleep, Tundé slid out of his bed and shook his body to acclimatise to the chilly air in his room. Weirdly, despite only sleeping for a few hours, he felt energised. But with school in the morning, he wanted to blow off some steam.

If I go for a wander around the block, maybe I can tire myself out and get back to sleep.

He got dressed in the same all-black attire that he wore during his showdown with the PMD crew. The tracksuit had a few rips in it, but he thought it would still do the job. Tundé quietly opened his bedroom door and crept slowly towards the front door of the flat.

"Babatundé, where are you going?" Uncle Blessing asked softly, just as Tundé was passing the living room. "Your mum may be a heavy sleeper. But me, I'm not di same."

"Honestly, I just gotta get outside to sort my head out right now."

"Hmm, okay. I'm not going to fight you. Just remember what I said earlier. Use your breath inwards to control the outwards. And be careful."

"Promise I will do. See you later, Uncks."

Chapter 23

THE LATE SPRING BREEZE whistled through the air as the moon shone brightly on the streets of the Isle of Dogs. Tundé had been wandering around the area for a short while now. Still keen to exhaust himself, he was also coming to grips with the mounting responsibilities. Let alone figure out how to get a full command of his superpowers. It had been quite a confusing past couple of weeks. When he reached the bottom of a ten-storey-high tower block, Tundé stopped to inspect the building. Peering up towards the roof, the view ignited him with an instant spark for adventure.

That parkour binge on WeView a few months ago might actually come in handy.

Earlier that year, Tundé was deep in a rabbit hole of parkour, spending countless hours watching videos about the discipline for entertainment. He never attempted any of the moves at the time, but with several rooftops lacing the local skyline and superhuman tools now at his disposal, he was inspired.

Maybe this is the moment to try it in real life.

After glancing around to ensure the street was empty, Tundé triggered the emergence of the reptilian hairs from his hands and the soles of his feet. He stuck his palms on the cold, rough concrete wall of the building, and steadily began climbing it, using the balls of his feet to propel himself upwards. He became more aware of the chilly conditions as the breeze in the air seeped through the rips in his clothes as he ascended further up the building. Fixated on the roof's overhang ahead, Tundé tried his best not to let the shivers knock him off balance. At a certain point, he looked down to assess his progress, assuming he was still close enough to disembark onto the pavement if needed.

Rahtid! I'm bare high up now.

The street below was a significant distance away, and by his judgment, he was just about to reach the midpoint of the building. Tundé continued to battle against the increasing strength and iciness of the wind as he climbed upwards. Soon enough, he reached the top, using the ledge to pull himself over and onto the roof.

Okay, that was the easy part. Now for the difficult shit.

Tundé looked outwards across the skyline, noticing several buildings of similar height. The closest one was just across the street from where he had climbed. He recalled how effortlessly he soared to great heights to hurdle the warehouse gates and escape from the police during his run-in with the PMD gang. Tundé gauged the distance he would need to jump to reach the building across the road. He estimated that it was roughly fifteen metres away, which seemed reasonable initially. However, as he peered down at the deserted street far below, he was sobered by the fate that awaited him if he didn't stick the landing. As the biting wind persisted, it caused him to shudder.

Oh boy, going out like that would be very peak.

Tundé took a few deep breaths. His legs wobbled like jelly and his heart rate rose dramatically. Still, he staggered backwards in preparation. Tundé then ran briskly towards the edge of the building. But at the last moment, he planted his heel down on the roof and ground himself to an uncomfortable halt.

Fuck man, can I even do this?

He was terrified. He peeked over the edge of the roof again to make sure his initial assessment was right. While the challenge felt harder with each passing second, the distance hadn't changed. Slowly stepping backwards, Tundé slapped his chest multiple times to gear himself up.

"Come on bro!"

But the doubt was crippling him. He still wasn't convinced that he could do it.

"The power is within you," the same voice from his ethereal dream rumbled into his consciousness. It completely threw him off guard. However, it seemed to be precisely the injection of motivation that he needed.

That voice is right. I have to believe I've got this.

Tundé walked purposefully to the opposite side of the roof to gather enough speed. He took one last deep breath.

"Let's fucking go fam!"

As soon as the words left his mouth, Tundé sprinted with sheer determination towards the other side of the roof. Just a few strides before the edge, a seed of doubt dropped into his mind. But his momentum was too much to stop now...

I've just gotta make it!

He thrust himself off the roof and powerfully into the air, soaring through it like an eagle. While airborne, Tundé felt the surreal experience of time dilating, as his surroundings appeared to be in a languid state. His eyes were inundated with the intensity of the wind hitting his face through the balaclava, and he struggled to breathe under its ferocity. Suddenly, a random gust blew in his direction, throwing him off course and decelerating his movement in mid-air.

Oh fucking hell!

Tundé panicked. He glanced down momentarily at the pavement that he would plummet into if he missed the landing. He stretched every muscle fibre in his body to reach his target, feeling the force of gravity start to pull him down. Then, there was a loud crash.

He just about managed to hold onto the eaves of the rooftop! He desperately hung on using his arms and shoulders while the rest of his body dangled.

"Jheeeeze! I made it! I fucking made it!" Tundé declared ecstatically, thankful to avoid being scraped off the ground had he failed. He pulled himself up onto the roof of the new building. The adrenaline was coursing fiercely through his body now.

Fam, I'm gonna try that again!

The next building's rooftop was a similar jumping distance. Feeling a surge of confidence, Tundé dashed rapidly across the rooftop and rose into the air with ferocity and boldness.

"Woooooo!" the teenager was exhilarated as he soared through the sky. The tiny hairs on his body stood up as the icy breeze continued to seep into his clothes. But he didn't care. He felt alive. He felt majestic. He felt supreme. This time, Tundé landed on his feet with ease and then progressed into a smooth forward roll. Under the balaclava, he smiled gleefully to himself.

Man hasn't done one of them since primary school times. This parkour ting is bare fun! I wanna keep practising.

Tundé spent the next half an hour sailing through the skies of the Isle of Dogs as he bounced from building to building. He was improving gradually as time went by, increasing his jumping distance with each attempt. And enjoying himself in the process too.

"I love this shit man!"

Under the whistling sound of the high-altitude winds, Tundé could hear a few late-night wanderers acknowledge his bewildering presence up above.

"Yo, what's that in the sky fam?"

"Oh my god, babe! Did you see that guy jump across from that building up there? He's a madman!"

"I know it's dark on my cam, but something weird is in the sky. Might be one of dem big cats escaping the zoo. Be careful on these streets, bro!"

When Tundé decided it was time to take a break from his newfound hobby, he arrived on a housing estate just outside Millwall Park. Despite the buzz of excitement, he was starting to feel tired. He sat on the edge of the rooftop with his legs swaying off the edge. It was a new building containing units of residential flats. He read at the sign hanging up to his left:

> ***Millwall Park Plaza: Luxury apartments to buy and rent. CCA residents need NOT apply.***

Tundé kissed his teeth. As he cast his gaze on the surrounding area, his attention was captured by the bright lights shining mightily in the distance from Canary Wharf. Close by, the natural darkness of the park was complemented by the shadowy figures of trees and small hills. The sheer quietness of the moment struck him, as it was something he rarely ever experienced during his years living in the inner city. Only the leaves on the trees rustling in the breeze or the occasional owl hoot added faint background noise. Otherwise, it was a calmness that was somewhat new to him. Maybe he was seeing things differently after Uncle Blessing's sessions. That, unfortunately, reminded him about his obligations.

I got bares to think about after this evening... but this midnight stroll BANGED!

Tundé stared hopefully at the few stars that twinkled luminously in the night sky.

Maybe Uncks was right. Maybe Olodumare is really with us.

Out of the blue, Tundé's attention was captured by a faint sound coming from a distance.

"Please, help me! Please!"

The shrieks of terror sent a tingling sensation down his spine. Tundé could hear the distressed woman, but he didn't know where the sounds were coming from. He fine-tuned his superhuman ears like a radio receiver to listen closer.

"Listen, you. Shut up," said a man in a hushed, threatening tone.

It's coming from the park.

"I'm warning you, don't make another noise again," growled another man's voice.

Alarm bells rang off in Tundé's head. It sounded like the woman was in serious danger. He started questioning himself.

Should I get involved? I know Uncle Blessing called me a warrior, but I'm not ready to help other people yet. What if I have another mental breakdown?

"No, please!" the woman shrieked. The utter panic in her voice jolted through Tundé's body like an electric shock, sparking him to his feet and into an aggressive stance.

Fuck it, I'm the one with the powers. If it's not me, who else is gonna make sure that lady is safe?

As if he were riding a skateboard, Tundé slid gracefully down the wall of the Millwall Park Plaza building and landed smoothly on the street level. He rushed towards the entrance gates of the park, which were bolted shut by a heavy chain and sturdy padlock the size of his head. Tundé inhaled a deep breath while focusing his attention on pinpointing where the woman and her aggressors were. At first, he couldn't detect anything. But soon enough, ruffles were heard from the bushes a couple hundred yards away.

"No point fighting us, bitch. Your research should've told you not to fuck with Chris. Don't worry, it will all be over soon..."

Tundé leapt over the gates in a hurry, and readjusted his eyes in the process, activating his night vision. He dashed towards the direction of the sounds. As he advanced, his eyes soon distinguished some silhouettes through the bushes and trees further ahead.

Looks like a few of them are about, still.

"Get off me!" the woman screamed, as the sound of hitting and clothes being ripped came from the area, prompting Tundé to move quickly. Rushing the scene, he inadvertently stepped on a random branch lying on the grass.

"Did you lot hear that?"

"No, mate. Stop being paranoid, there are four of us here. They can't do nuffink."

Tundé's heart pounded like a drum, as he crouched low to the ground and slowly edged forward. Assessing the situation, he saw the terrified woman doing her best to fight off one of the men as she tussled with him in the mud, while the other three men stood around precariously. The sight enraged him.

"You're right, it probably is nothing... for me to deal with you bombaclaat dickheads."

"Who the fuck's that?" said the man tussling with the woman.

"Sounds like one of those mandem people," said another of the aggressors, as he pulled a knife out from his pocket. "Why don't you fuck off before we ship you back to where you came from in pieces?"

"Oooh, you're making me feel proper scared now!" Tundé taunted.

He deliberately circled the group while remaining cloaked by the shadows. The three men standing up were aimlessly trying to spot Tundé in the darkness, while the main culprit, who was tussling with the woman, got to his feet too. The woman wasted no time escaping and crawled desperately away from the situation, occasionally glancing back to make sure she wasn't being followed.

Hopefully, that's her out of harm's way. Now I gotta deal with these pricks.

Just as one of the men turned his smartphone flashlight towards him, Tundé leapt into action. He flew nimbly through the air to dish out a vicious kick to the phone carrier's jaw.

"Woah!" exclaimed another of the men, who caught a glimpse of Tundé's leg emerging from the darkness right before hearing the thud of his accomplice drop to the ground. The smartphone fell on the grass with the flashlight turned upwards. The resulting dim glow gave some faint visibility to the aggressors in the otherwise pitch-black settings.

"You can't hide from us now."

A brief pause followed as a whistle of wind brushed against the grass, adding a layer of suspense to the moment. The three men were searching frantically for Tundé.

"Can't see my melanin in the dark? Hold up, lemme give you a better view!"

Tundé swooped out commandingly from the bushes and knocked out the second man with a devastating punch.

"Where were you sending me back to again? Cos it looks like *I'm* the one sending *you man* to the shadow realm!"

Tundé spotted the woman heading further away towards the park gates. Then, the main man who was tussling with the woman stepped forward.

"You're messing with the wrong people, fella," he said sharply. "We've got most of what we need anyway."

"Oh, you man still want this smoke?" Tundé asked smugly.

Sensing fear in the leader's accomplice, Tundé pounced and hit him square on the nose bridge, narrowly avoiding the knife pointed towards him.

"Because you're messing with the wrong bruddah."

Realising he was alone, the main man started to back off. But Tundé wasted no time and sprinted at him aggressively. The man threw a punch, but Tundé dodged it. He tried to kick Tundé, but the teenager jumped over his leg, then landed a powerful uppercut on the man's jaw that floored him immediately.

"Jheeeze, that was easier than I expected!"

With all the men slumped to the ground, Tundé rounded them up and dragged their limp, unconscious bodies to a nearby children's playing area. There, he used his super strength to bend the steel bars of a jungle gym and tie it around each of the men, one by one.

"That should hold you lot until the pigs come get you. I don't fuck with them man, but I'd rather they deal with you perverted, evil bastards."

The teenager quickly made his way to the park entrance, where the woman was sitting close by outside with her head in her hands. She was dressed in a hooded cardigan, a pair of scruffy jeans and some worn-out white Sky Glide 1's. All her clothes were covered in mud, grass stains and random twigs. The sound of her muffled crying brought a pang to Tundé's stomach.

"Hey madam, I'm so sorry that happened to you," Tundé said sombrely. "I hope you're better now though."

"Th-th-thank you," said the woman, trying to speak over her tears. "L-l-luckily you g-g-got there just as I was c-c-close to giving up."

"Don't worry about it, it's calm. You got somewhere safe to go tonight?"

"I-I-I can g-g-go to m-m-my mum's house," the woman stuttered. "Sh-sh-she lives about f-f-fifteen minutes away."

"Okay, that's good. If you don't mind me asking, who were those guys?"

The woman turned to Tundé, crying less intensely now.

"I d-d-don't know. They must've just been nasty muggers chancing it. B-b-but I don't know."

Tundé knelt and put his arm around her. "Well, they should get locked up for harming you like that. I've tied them up in the play area for you, so you can call the feds to get them if you want, Miss...?"

"P-p-please, call me Anna."

She reminded him of Auntie Abi, just a few years older.

"My name is T– actually, just call me D.D.," he said, correcting himself before he gave his real identity away.

"Okay, nice to meet you, D.D. Don't worry about me. I just want to get home and forget about all this. Someone's coming to pick me up soon, anyway."

"Are you sure? They shouldn't get away with what they tried to do to you."

"No, it's okay," Anna said with finality. "Oh, there's my ride."

Tundé could see that a red 4x4 Wilwo with tinted windows just pulled up on the other side of the road, prompting Anna to gradually rise her feet.

"Thank you so much for saving my dignity, and perhaps my life. You get home safe, D.D."

"No problem. Take care, and same to you," Tundé said, as Anna walked across the road and stepped into the vehicle. He waved as the red Wilwo pulled away. He soon climbed back up to the top of the Millwall Park Plaza.

"I wonder why she didn't wanna call the feds? The main don even mentioned something about getting what they wanted."

Conscious that he had been outside for a while, Tundé checked the time on his brick phone.

"Rah, it's ten past four already! Fuck these guys, I need to bounce!"

Chapter 24

AFTER CREEPING INTO THE flat and his bed at half four in the morning, Tundé woke up a short few hours later.

I feel like shit bruv.

But he imagined what would have happened to Miss Anna if he hadn't been outside that late.

I hope she's doing alright.

"Babatundé!" a loud voice startled him out of his thoughts. "Are you ready for school now?"

"Mum, I'm just getting my bag and stuff ready!" Tundé shouted as he threw himself out of bed and got ready for school in a frenzy.

"But it's late, now. You better hurry up before I have to drag you out of there myself, o!"

Tundé kissed his teeth under his breath. Once he was ready, Tundé rushed to the kitchen, the distinct smell of the blended pepper hitting his nose as his mum was cooking on the stove.

"Oya, make sure you take this for breakfast," his mum said, pointing to two pieces of wrapped foil. "It's moi moi, your favourite."

"Aww, thank you, Mum!"

"I've been very busy with work, so I'm happy that I can cook some good food again this morning. I hope you've been facing your books. Your h'exams are coming soon."

"Don't worry, Mum, I'm studying hard. I'll be fine."

"Amen. As you should. You need to get very good grades so you can go to university to be an engineer or a computer coder, remember?"

"I know, Mum. I know. But I've gotta leave now."

"Okay, I will see you later. Have a good day at school and be safe. May God bless you!"

Just as Tundé closed the front door of the flat, he bumped into Uncle Blessing. "Oh, good morning Uncks. I didn't realise you'd gone out."

"Yes, I just went for a morning walk. How was your gallivanting last night? You weren't behaving like an ọ̀dẹ́ out there, abi?"

Tundé had a momentary flashback where he saw himself climbing up to the top of a ten-storey building with no safety net, developing his parkour skills as he soared from rooftop to rooftop and garnering awe-filled attention from onlookers. And, of course, rescuing Anna from the muggers in Millwall Park.

"Yeah, it was calm. Just went for a walk and came back, init."

Uncle Blessing gave him a doubtful glare. "Okay, if you say so."

"Promise you, Uncks, it was calm!"

"It's okay, you're becoming a big boy now. Oya, don't miss your bus to school!"

***

During his school day, Tundé managed to stay relatively attentive despite the lack of sleep. However, while he sat in his afternoon GCSE Biology lesson, he stared aimlessly out of the window at the bright sun and clear blue skies. He was trying to keep himself awake by daydreaming about all the new tricks he could learn with his powers, and how long it would take before his more mature aura would draw Laura—or the other girls—in.

His fantasy was interrupted by a specific passage that his teacher, Miss Stephens, was delivering to the class.

"...van der Waals is the name of the electric forces that attract neutral molecules in almost all organic liquids and solids. It's this phenomenon that allows reptiles like geckos and lizards to stick to flat surfaces—even when they're upside down!"

As that caught Tundé's attention, his focus immediately switched to Miss Stephens, who noticed the change in his body language.

"Glad to have you back with us, Tundé," she scoffed. "Since you're already so clever that you don't need to engage with the lesson, maybe you can share some of your expert reptile knowledge with the class?"

The classroom murmured with giggles and whispering, and in moments, Tundé found himself being gawked at by all his peers. Some even turned their chairs to eyeball him further, adding to the pressure.

"Errr, let me see," Tundé said nervously. "So, boom. Reptiles shed their skin because theirs doesn't really stretch like ours. They need to get rid of the old stuff to make room for the new skin that fits better as they grow. Kinda like having to get rid of old garms before you can get new ones."

An awkward silence followed as Miss Stephens regarded Tundé, very surprised to receive a comprehensive answer from a pupil who seemed disinterested.

"I bet Tony could do with a trick like that," joked his classmate Eddie. "His face is always bare dry and unmoisturised like a lizard, could probably peel it off right now!"

Laughter erupted throughout the classroom.

"Personally, I wouldn't have it!" Remi shouted.

"Now, we don't need you stirring the pot, Remi," Miss Stephens interjected.

"Eddie. Come say that to my face, pussy'ole!" Tony eventually retorted.

The commotion in the classroom intensified.

"Now, class! And you boys!" Miss Stephens bellowed as she raised her voice, pointing at both Eddie and Tony repeatedly. "Both of you calm down, or I won't hesitate to keep you behind for the most mind-numbing hour of your lives for an after-school detention. Is that understood?"

The tension in the room simmered down as neither of the boys was keen to spend an hour with each other and their biology teacher after school. Especially on a day with such lovely weather.

"Tundé, that was a great answer," Miss Stephens continued. "But please make sure you're paying attention to the lesson. You don't know everything! And you never know what you could learn that will benefit you for school, your exams and life in general."

When the biology lesson finished, Tundé was walking out to the playground when Remi called him.

"Yo, Tunds!" he said whilst running after him in the hallway. Tundé stopped to turn back. "What you been saying man? You've been ghosting recently."

"Yeah bro, I've just been doing my ting, init."

"Alright, lone ranger, calm down! Just wondered what's been gwanin' for you."

"Allow me, man! The last couple of weeks have been a madness, so I'm trying not to be too active."

"Well, you know that can't last for long. Jerry needs that debt worked off, remember?"

"Yo, don't say that too loud, fam!"

I'd slyly forgotten about that as well. Shit man.

"Bruddah, why you moving so anti?" Remi frowned. "We need to work together on this, you know."

"Sorry bro, man's just bare stressed right now. Listen, me and my cousin are still down, so tell Jerry he don't need to worry. I'm just prepping myself for everything, including exams init."

"I hear that. Imagine, my mumsy said if I get less than a B in any subject, she's gonna shift me to my cousin's school in Peterborough for A-Levels."

"Rah, allow living in them next ends!"

At that moment, Tundé spotted Mr Athlima, the head of the PE, leaving the main entrance of the Stebon High Sports Centre with his satchel over his shoulder while typing on his miCell.

Perfect, he's probably heading home early, Tundé thought, whilst Remi's chatter remained in the background. He decided to keep talking to Remi for a bit longer just to be sure Mr Athlima had left.

"...so yeah, after that trip to my other cousin's yard in Stoke-on-Trent, I dunno if I EVER wanna leave London. Wait, were you even listening to what I said, bruv?"

"Yeah, moving out to the sticks sounds like a mission for us, I can't lie," Tundé gestured by rubbing the skin on the back of his hand. "Listen, man forgot something in the Sports Centre. I'm gonna go grab it, so I'll just link you later, yeah?"

"Alright, say nothing, bro. Bless."

They bumped fists and went their separate ways, with Tundé heading for the school's Sports Centre. When he arrived, it was quiet as expected. With the exam period approaching, barely any of the after-school clubs were operating as usual. He walked through the Centre to the old sports hall, which had been shut a few weeks ago for refurbishments scheduled to start once the school year had ended. The large, antiquated doors had been double-locked with reinforced chains. Ensuring that no one was around, Tundé used his superhuman strength to pull the chains apart. He slowly creaked open the doors and walked into the hall. His face scrunched up in disgust. The musty smell of body odour, lingering chalk dust and damp wood filled his nose.

That is nasty, man, Tundé thought with annoyance as he used his shirt to cover his nose.

The old sports hall had only been used sporadically in the months before its closure, and as such, it hadn't been very well maintained. It was extremely dusty, the hardwood flooring was damaged in patches and some of the metal apparatus showed signs of rusting. But inspecting it further, Tundé's optimism was restored. There were complex climbing frames spanning the perimeter, blue gym mats stacked in one corner, a makeshift vault in another corner, and a balance beam and pommel horse resting against the opposite wall.

Not the best training spot, but I've got enough here to practise with, still.

As Uncle Blessing placed huge importance on training, Tundé thought he could benefit if he practised complicated body movements in a safe space before taking it out onto the streets. He set up the equipment, placing the blue mats strategically around the hall so he could safely break any unorthodox or untimely falls. After changing out of his school uniform and into his sports attire, Tundé eagerly got started.

He charged up the climbing frames with determination, strategically taking different routes with each attempt to improve his agility and strength. Next, he worked on perfecting his acrobatic techniques by launching himself over the makeshift vault with precision. Finally, Tundé focused his efforts on the beam, where he tested his coordination and balance with each careful step across it. Sweat glistened from his brow as the lactic acid created a progressively dull ache throughout his body after each set, but he was determined to continue developing his skills.

Fam, I'm gonna be running tings out here at this rate!

Pleased with his progress after an hour, Tundé packed up the equipment, wrapped the chains around the sports hall's doors and headed back home. Despite taking the initiative, he was wary that Uncle Blessing would be waiting for him at home to undertake another training session.

"Hello, son, how was school today?" asked Uncle Blessing with upbeat energy.

"Yeah, it was fine thanks, Uncks. How are you?"

"We thank Olodumare. Why did you take so long to come back home?"

"Just been doing some stuff with my friends. I'm not a little kid, you know."

Tundé was feisty. He didn't like that Uncle Blessing was so involved in his business. It was beginning to irritate him.

"Ah, Babatundé, relax. Remember, it's your uncle you're speaking to, now!"

"I just hate being treated like I'm some helpless baby. I'm gonna be a big man soon."

"Heyyy! You youngsters and your audacity. Life will eventually teach you how young you are!"

Tundé huffed petulantly. He didn't appreciate Uncle Blessing's condescending tone.

"Anyway, yesterday's session was very tough. Tonight, we will do something very basic for today."

Tundé couldn't hide his displeasure. While he understood his uncle's concerns about the threat related to Nigeria, Tundé didn't feel like that was his problem to deal with right now.

This mentoring isn't gonna help me make P's or change our lifestyle here. I can just do all this shit myself.

"Uncle," Tundé finally spoke. "Let's allow this training for now. I've got other important things I wanna do. Plus, I can do my own ting without you always getting on to me."

"Ohhh, you think this is me getting *onto* you? Remember, I'm not one of your age mates, you know. Or maybe a conk on your head will remind you?"

"Uncle, with all due respect, you just turned up randomly like two weeks ago. Thanks for saving my life, but you're taking over it now. And along with all your stories about magic, seaweed and evil spirits, it's getting jarring. You haven't even told Mum about my obligations, so why should I listen to you about them?"

"Yes, but you must understand..."

"Allow it, please. I'm tired after a long day at school so I'm going to my room. I'll see you whenever, init."

"Okay, Babatundé. You may leave. But I'm sure you will come to regret these immature decisions you're making, sha."

Tundé ignored Uncle Blessing and stormed into his bedroom, slamming the door shut behind him. He flopped himself onto his bed. Even though he was exhausted, his mind was buzzing after opposing an authority figure—an uncommon occurrence in Nigerian households. But deep down, Tundé felt compelled by his actions.

I might get in trouble, but fuck it. I'm doing my own ting for now. I just need to get some sleep before facing up to the adults in the morning.

Suddenly, a loud buzzing sound disturbed Tundé's gradual descent into the dream world. He slowly stretched his arm out and opened the draw on his bedside table, picking out the brick phone that Jerry had given him. He had received a message:

'Get ready. 2 key BRF. Pick up @ E1 2QF. 11pm sharp.'

"Oh my days! Not now, for fuck's sake!"

Chapter 25

Disgruntled by the text message, Tundé had no choice but to follow orders since he owed Jerry. He rolled sorrily out of bed, shook the drowsiness off and changed into his usual all-black tracksuit. The signs of damage were visible, with tears and rips scattered across his clothing.

Hopefully, I get paid soon cos man needs new garms ASAP!

Without a smartphone to navigate the streets in real-time, he had to rely on his superhuman memory. Searching on the family computer, Tundé confirmed that the postcode was located near Shadwell Underground Station.

Sliding on his backpack, Tundé examined himself in the mirror. Checking whether Uncle Blessing was awake, he could hear faint breathing sounds from the sofa. Tundé assumed that he probably wasn't asleep, and even so, his mum could return from work at any moment and scupper his plans. He turned to his bedroom window. The clouds were blocking the moonlight from shining over his Equiano House.

It's probably dark enough for me to climb out of my window unnoticed.

Opening the window carefully, Tundé slowly manoeuvred onto the concrete walls of Equiano House, wary not to attract any attention. He carefully closed his window and proceeded to scuttle up a few stories to the top of the building. He looked out to the city landscape as the wind blustered on the roof. The flashiness of Canary Wharf was front and centre, accompanied by the popular landmarks of Tower Bridge and Big Ben in the far distance.

Fam, seeing stuff like this is never gonna get old!

The teenager soon soared down from the Equiano House rooftop onto an adjacent, smaller building as he made his way to Shadwell. As he leapt across the buildings on the Isle of Dogs, Tundé's eyes vividly captured the sight of an old Victorian building with a distinct bell tower on its roof.

Tophall Primary. We always used to play like we had superpowers in that playground. Never thought it would happen like this, though!

While using his polished parkour skills to run and vault over the roof railings, Tundé put his gymnastics practice to good use, adding a front flip to his sequence when he jumped from one building across the street to another.

"WHOO! Man's got it!" he shouted as he landed the jump cleanly with both feet.

Adding more flair to his style, Tundé executed more grand flips and somersaults to his jump, smoothly transitioning into a handstand finish when he landed on a rooftop. He used his auntie's retro MP3 player to play her classic grime playlist.

"Ayyy, in my city, I am that guy! And it's real talk famalam, I can't lie!" he sang the lyrics aloud.

Doing this while listening to Thundrie slaps man!

As he passed through the Canary Wharf area, Tundé was reminded of its stark contrast with the Isle of Dogs. Below him, a buzz emanated from the bars, restaurants and shops as he now scaled huge commercial skyscrapers. His supernatural activity was soon spotted by the finance professionals working late into the night. Some of their voices could be heard as he passed by.

"Hey, look out the window! Who the fuck is that?"

"Kwame, can you see that guy jumping around?"

"Yeah mate, I think he's got a death wish!"

Rah, I hope Kwame doesn't realise it's me!

But Tundé smiled to himself. It was rare that he was heralded for his talents. As he moved away from the bustling business district, he found himself in the Limehouse area, where the ambience closely resembled his residence on the Isle of Dogs. It had overflowing bins, deteriorating buildings and countless dishevelled people roaming the streets.

It's actually mad how dem rich dons enjoy a nice lifestyle right next to all these bummy CCA ends.

A waft of spicy meat and oily chips seeped through Tundé's balaclava while he took a breather above Lahore Kebab House. A group of boys walking in caught his attention.

"Bossman's charging a £12 for just doner and chips, you know!"

"He's taking the piss, bruv!"

"Yo akh, who's that up there? What you saying, fam?"

That's probably my cue to bounce!

Before the boys could continue grilling him, Tundé rushed to his feet and leapt majestically in the air as he resumed his journey to Shadwell.

"Did you man just see that?"

"Yeah, that's a madness!"

Hearing the sounds of amazement from the group gave Tundé's ego a huge boost as they faded into the distance.

"Thank you to the ancestors for making me THAT GUY!"

In due time, Tundé arrived at the meet-up postcode. He stealthily perched himself on top of a retail building next to the Shadwell Underground Station, which was in desperate need of repair. He used his enhanced vision to scan the adjoining streets for any suspicious activity, as his sensitivity to danger had heightened since his experience with the PMD crew.

Anything can turn ugly in a flash.

Like the other CCA areas of the city, Shadwell housed a large working-class population, who were generally in their sixties or above. Some residents had been there for decades. Others were forcibly moved to the area after the government's policy change. The vibe here was gloomy and the streets were lifeless as the wind whistled in the sky. It was the perfect cloak for criminal activity. But while he had to remain vigilant, the sheer darkness of the evening worked in Tundé's favour.

A few minutes later, he saw an old man on the adjacent street. He was walking leisurely while pushing a large trolley basket with a basic red and white fabric design. Tundé suspected that it was a resident.

Hope the old guy gets home alright. It's not safe out here.

With no warning, the light from an old-school, VR billboard across the road shut off, shrouding the area in more darkness. Tundé adjusted his eyeballs to the new conditions. Then, he sensed a car driving closer from a couple of streets away. Before he could explore any further, Jerry's brick phone buzzed.

"Showtime," Tundé whispered as he opened the text message.

'Now. Corner, yellow sign block. Tell him JBS87.'

Tundé was confused. No one other than the old man was present in the area, unless...

'Wheels. Jenkins. Slow.'

The realisation soon hit him.

Wait, the old man? Rah, Jerry's working with schoolkids AND pensioners. Clearly tryna avoid the stereotypes!

Turning around, Tundé quickly discovered that he was standing in front of another VR billboard that had scrolled to a Roco Pops cereal advertisement. It featured their custom yellow branding in the background, with their mascot Betty the Chocolate Bunny in the foreground accompanied by the musician Ray Hus.

That's an odd pairing, still...

Tundé crawled down the wall of the building under the cloak of the night. As he approached the ground, the old man entered the junction between the underground station and an alleyway.

"JBS 87," he said as he slowly approached the old man.

No sooner had the words left Tundé's mouth than the old man drew a long blade swiftly from his trolley basket. He placed it precariously against Tundé's neck.

"Show me where your phone is before I cut ya," the old man said sternly.

Tundé didn't want to screw up another of Jerry's deals, so he thought it best to comply. As he hesitantly reached to his waist, the old man drew another small knife and pricked it against Tundé's hand, preventing it from going into the pocket.

"I'll be fetching that, mate. I don't know who you are under that mask yet."

Contrary to his first impression, Tundé was surprised at how sharp and nimble the old man was as he reached into the teenager's pocket.

"Ah, a Pony Erikson. Great old throwback, this."

To Tundé's amazement, he unlocked it easily despite its passcode and then read through the messages from Jerry.

"Where's the kid? Wasn't he supposed to have this phone?" the old man asked as he pressed the blade more firmly onto Tundé's neck.

"He gave it to me because it's a late-night job," Tundé answered with a deep voice to avoid being identified as said kid. "And I couldn't have him out with me now. It's not safe."

The old man took a long pause, glancing at the phone and then back at Tundé.

"Well then..."

He removed the blade from the neck and raised it above his head as if he were about to axe Tundé down. But instead of striking him, the old man used it to skilfully open the trolley basket. He used the tip of his blade to lift a black drawstring bag from inside and drop it in Tundé's hands.

"There you go, mate. You seem like an honest sport considering. Just remember, you will have a lot of problems if this pack isn't delivered as agreed."

Tundé opened the bag to check its contents. Two large blocks of wrapped-up foil with a bright purple tinge poking through the cracks. It represented the hope that a more prosperous financial future lay ahead while relieving the pressure from Jerry in the short term. Tundé put the drawstring bag in his backpack, then the old man threw his brick phone back to him.

"Good luck out there, kiddo."

"Erm, thanks, Mr Seniorman," Tundé said, unsure how to address someone several decades older than him.

He felt somewhat fond of the old man since his demeanour reminded him of his own grandparents. The old man left the alleyway onto the main road, adopting the slow walking pace that made him seem so unassuming initially.

Tundé climbed up to the roof with the Roco Pops advert. He noticed a red saloon car from the 1990s driving by on the road below.

I've only seen those cars in old pictures of my parents!

His phone then buzzed repeatedly, breaking him out of his nostalgia. Tundé had two text messages:

'Sewell Church. E13. Midnight.'
'Joey Badman. YT WW. Collect 40 bags.'

Tundé's eyes widened with disbelief.

£40,000!!! Am I bugging or did I really just read that?

He couldn't help but picture all the things he could do with even a fraction of the amount. Calling upon his memorisation of the East London area, Tundé headed hastily to the next location. As he hurdled over the numerous buildings on his way, he pondered over all the bizarre recent events that had led him to this moment. His extraordinary powers. His mysterious uncle. The surreal dreams. It still hadn't sunk in.

And I still have no idea what's going on.

He soon arrived in Plaistow and positioned himself on a rooftop a few doors down the road from Sewell Church. He flashed open the Pony Erikson to check the time.

23:58.

Perfect, I'm just in time.

Examining the street down below, he kept his eye out for the white Wilwo car that Jerry mentioned would be driven by an associate called Joey Badman. And there he waited. And waited. And waited. As the minutes ticked by, Tundé's initial enthusiasm was fading as he started to tire.

00:32.

What the fuck? These man are taking the piss, fam.

Still no sign of anyone. At this point, all he wanted to do was finish the job, pay off some of his debt and get some sleep now.

00:57.

Tundé was slouched down on the roof with his legs laid flat and his back resting against the building's ventilation pipe. He was forced to pinch himself to remain awake as he fantasised about his bed. What frustrated him most was that he had to stay put. He was committed to this now, for better or for worse. Suddenly, a car pulled up on the street below. Tundé straightened his body and stood alert. A white Wilwo had parked up opposite Sewell Church.

"Finally, jheeze!"

Tundé hopped across a few buildings to reach the pointed roof of the church. The intoxicated homeless man further down the street was in awe of Tundé's stunning acrobatics. The teenager now stood defiantly, as the moonlight bounced off the Christ symbol at the apex and shone brightly onto him.

"I've just seen God!" cried out the homeless man as he ran down a nearby alleyway, prompting a wry smile from under the woolly balaclava.

The night clouds soon blocked the moonlight and cloaked Tundé under the darkness again. Out of the blue, another car approached. It was the same red saloon model he'd seen in Shadwell earlier that night.

Hmm, that's kinda booky, still.

As he slid down the church to ground level, the red saloon car parked a few dozen yards down the road. Something didn't feel right.

"Woah!"

Tundé was tense as the phone buzzed in his pocket again.

'Here now. Knock on car boot. 3 times. 2 times. Then 1 time.'

Despite his concerns, Tundé thought it was better to meet Joey Badman now and get the deal done as soon as possible. He just needed to remain cautious about the unidentified vehicle.

His heart thumped rapidly as he approached the white Wilwo car boot, nervous about what could unfold. He knocked three times. He took a quick scan for any threats. Nothing. He knocked twice, leaving a pause before he knocked a final time. The silence that followed echoed throughout this side road. Tundé's neck jolted tensely as the driver's side window slid down.

"It's JB. Get in now, bruv."

Tundé scrambled into the car and, for a split second, he saw a flicker of light flash from the red car down the road. He geared himself up for anything to kick off.

"Why you still wearing a mask for, fam?" Joey asked as he pulled out his handgun. But Tundé was more concerned with the possible danger from outside.

"Bro, I promise you. It don't matter. I've got exactly what you need. You got Jerry's money?"

"Fam, why you moving so shifty?" Joey said while waving the handgun casually. "Relax your hype, man. We got time."

"I got the purp you need, init. Let's move."

"Bruv, who you telling to– YO!"

Bullets rained down on the Wilwo in a flash! Shards of glass and metal fragments dispersed inside the car. But both Tundé and Joey had hit the deck after hearing the first shot from what must have been a silencer gun.

"Is this you?" Joey hissed with terror as the bullets continued pinging off the car.

Tundé ignored him. Joey probably wouldn't trust what he said, anyway. Plus, he was of no help now, even with his gun. All his boisterous energy had dissipated.

This don is definitely one of them selective badboys. Maybe we all are to a degree.

Tundé observed that three lamp posts were lighting the street around the white Wilwo. He grabbed a few random items spread on the car floor and thrust them at each lamppost bulb. The lights went out and the street became pitch-black, causing the onslaught of bullets to come to a halt.

Now you're in my playground.

Tundé slowly crawled out of the car and onto the ground. Scoping the scene from under Joey's vehicle, four boys were standing in various positions on the street. All of them were armed. He had to move carefully.

Tundé inhaled and exhaled deeply as he called upon his sessions with Uncle Blessing to channel his energy. Feeling an elevated sense of power, Tundé sneakily scuttled over one of the red car assailants, and before he could react, knocked him out cold with a devastating uppercut to the chin.

"Yo, Frankie, you okay?" one of the assailants asked, as they all took a few timid steps back in the darkness. Tundé concealed himself behind a blue car as he calculated his next move.

I should take the biggest guy out next.

Tundé leapt over the blue car and directly into the next red car assailant, who was completely unaware. Tundé grounded him with a kick to the throat and struck a nerve in his neck so that he passed out immediately. The assailant's croaking gasp for air prompted shouts from the remaining assailants.

"Benny, is that you?"

"Make sure you shoot this yute on sight!"

Alright. Two down. Two to go.

A few bullets were fired Tundé's way, but he managed to duck behind the blue car again. There was an empty skip in the parking bay just behind him. Tundé glanced through the gap under the car as he caught his breath. The last two assailants were now standing together in confusion. That was all the encouragement Tundé needed.

"Come out and fight, you pussy," said one of the assailants tentatively as he pointed his gun around aimlessly.

"If you say so!"

Using his super-strength, Tundé lifted the skip high above his head and threw it at the last two assailants, who were crushed into the pavement under its weight. A colossal set of noises emerged onto the street as the debris from the skip scattered across the road. Tundé was sure he heard bones fracturing amidst the commotion. He stormed back to the now-damaged white Wilwo and was met with hostility.

"Yo, what the fuck, fam!" Joey exclaimed while aiming his gun aggressively at Tundé.

"You got the money, yeah?" Tundé asked nonchalantly. It was hard to feel sympathetic towards a man who had a gun pointed at his face.

Keeping his eyes fixed on the masked man, Joey used his phone's flashlight to assess the damage.

"You coulda set this whole thing up, still. I swear your–"

Suddenly, an unexpected assailant came out from the shadows and put Joey in a headlock. The assailant then pressed the barrel of a pistol onto his temple, causing Joey to drop his firearm.

"Yo, mask yute. Give us all the fucking drugs and P's now. Or I'll blow his head top off. Just like I did to your other boy."

"What other boy?" Tundé didn't understand.

"Oh, I shoulda said *older* boy—the don from Shadwell," the assailant said smugly while pushing the barrel of the gun harder into Joey's head. "How do you think we found you lot?"

Tundé got angrier as the information dawned on him. While not knowing the old man personally, he had taken a liking to him.

"What... what did you lot do?"

"We smoked him after he tried a likkle sword trick. He was old, so his time was coming soon anyway. You best not move, pussy'ole. Cos I really will buss my gun again!"

Tundé couldn't comprehend the senseless nature of murdering an elderly person.

Why the FUCK would they duppy an old man? Who gave them the right?

A powerful rage built up within Tundé. So much so that he was unaware that he was becoming vulnerable to the animal psyches that lay dormant within him. His enhanced eyesight pierced through the darkness to observe that the assailant had lost a very slight grip on his gun as Joey struggled with him. Spotting an opportunity, Tundé pounced.

"Ay, yooo!"

Shouts could be heard under the stray gunshots, as Tundé smashed the assailant's wrist and knocked the gun out of his hand, releasing Joey in the process. Tundé then grabbed the assailant's head and smashed it against his knee. The assailant, now entirely discombobulated, dropped helplessly to the ground. But Tundé wasn't finished.

"How dare you mugs think you could kill that old man? Who gave you the right? You must be fucking mad!"

Seething with anger, Tundé heard the deafening screech of an eagle invade his mind. He blacked out for a few seconds. When his senses returned, Tundé was frozen into shock by what he saw. While in the uncontrolled state, Tundé jumped onto the assailant and punched him repeatedly in the head, progressively crushing his skull. The assailant's head was now drenched in blood, his face was indistinguishable and his body was eerily still. Fortunately for Tundé, the assailant was still drawing breath. Just.

Woah, how did lose control like that? Uncle Blessing warned me about this.

"Okay, bro..." said Joey Badman nervously. "I think you made your point, still..."

Without saying a word, Tundé stretched out the bag of bairaff to Joey solemnly. With no hesitation, Joey handed him the cash in a backpack made of reinforced steel. Tundé almost dropped it because his hands were shaking like branches in a storm. The experience of losing control of his mind and body to the animal psyches frightened him.

"In a bit," Tundé said to Joey abruptly as he ran off into the shadows while blaring sirens grew prominent in the background. A few minutes later, Jerry's brick phone buzzed.

'Drop bread at All Saints Churchyard. Black Machini. 2 am.'

He made his way to meet Jerry while rationalising his actions.

That prick deserved it anyway for killing the old man. I shouldn't be worried.

When he arrived to meet Jerry, he was parked in a blacked-out Machini GLE. A different, equally menacing accomplice occupied the passenger seat.

"Yes, Tanks. That's what I'm fucking talking about!" Jerry ecstatically addressed Tundé's third cousin as he handed over the reinforced steel backpack.

"...298... 299... 300..." Jerry counted his way through the huge stacks of ten and twenty-pound notes.

"I'm actually gassed for you, fam. I thought I was gonna have to pick up the strap and start bussing shots at all of you myself!" Jerry laughed.

Tundé snickered lightly, but the imagery was far from amusing.

"I just got off the phone with Joey. He said the Blue Man Crew ambushed you. I can't believe them man came all the way from Deptford to try a ting. They must be low on P's. Scumbags."

"Yeah, it was a bit mad," Tundé said with his fake deep voice.

"I'm just glad you were there to punch them up, Tanks. Man's defo been eating his pounded yam! Don't worry, though. I'm sending some goons to their spot to make sure they fully learn their lesson."

Jerry then took a deep sigh. "Especially after what they did to Peter. The old guy you met. His missus belled me earlier bawling her eyes out. It sounded so peak man, they didn't need to do an old man like that."

Tundé winced, remembering how violently he reacted to the news.

"Fuck it though. The game is the game. I'll sort her out with some extra P's. Most importantly, you man got the job done. I just had a yute recently, so every penny counts."

Jerry started counting again.

"I wasn't gonna pay you yet after the PMD fuck-up. But since you protected this deal from getting botched, I'll give you man this to share, init."

Jerry handed the cash over to Tundé, who tried to show restraint.

Rah, man got £300? Just for tonight?

"Remember, some of that is for Tunds as well. I'll be checking with him. And I've got bare movements happening in the next few weeks. My connect will have another shipment of purp coming to the UK soon too. And because the fiends love it, this shit's gonna fly off the shelves!"

While Jerry's accomplice started rolling a joint, Jerry then pointed at Tundé.

"Seems like you're a good asset to have too, Tanks. So, once you and Tunds have fully paid off the debt, keep that Pony Erikson alive for more work. You lot are down, yeah?"

"Fully down. I... *we* are fully down."

Chapter 26

THE COLD WIND SLAPPED Tundé in the face as he ran for the D7 bus. The sky was grey and overcast. And he was late to school yet again after another busy night of working for Jerry.

If only Uncle Blessing was young enough to keep changing the weather. It would still be hot!

When he turned the corner, his bus was parked up at the Manchester Road stop letting people on. Tundé upped his speed to a certain level, careful not to run so fast that it made people question whether he was human or not. It was a tough balancing act not to use powers too publicly. After finally catching the bus and finding his seat, Tundé whipped out the brand new miCell that he bought recently. He looked at its screen in shock.

I can't believe it's the last day of April already. The past few weeks have just flown by, boy!

His mind wandered back to that pivotal day in Stratford during London's heatwave, a moment from which his life had transformed significantly. Jerry had employed him for several bairaff deals in that time. Operating under the alias of Tanks—his distant cousin—Tundé played a key role in several bairaff deals, orchestrated by the well-oiled machine that was Jerry's operation. He used his street connections to generate big wholesale deals all over East London. £8,000 in Whitechapel. £17,000 in Canning Town. £22,000 in Barking. £12,000 in Stratford. £57,000 in Shoreditch. So many kilograms were moving that it was hard for Tundé to keep up with. Despite the anxiety that came with every transaction, Tundé's financial gain made it easier to subdue those feelings. Initially, his share was used to cover the goodwill payments to the PMD after the police involvement and ensured Jerry's credibility in the criminal underworld remained intact.

"In this game, your rep is everything," Jerry would tell Tundé frequently. "Can't have people thinking I'm in bed with them pigs. That could put us out of business and in a lot of trouble."

Once the debt was settled with the PMD boss, Zaid, Jerry made full profits from the bairaff deals, and fortunately for Tundé, he believed in paying his workers well.

"I wanna make sure everyone's compensated well so they keep doing good work for me. The most important asset is people after all," Jerry mentioned when paying the teenager his first lump sum. Tundé rather admired his style of leadership, and most certainly appreciated the extra money.

Jerry is patterning me hard, I can't lie!

The gig didn't come without its challenges though. Tundé was always stressed about his identity being revealed or having to fight off random ambushes from other gangs, which would create more enemies. Some local drug addicts eventually banded together to try and steal their coveted bairaff directly from Jerry's transporters. Tundé usually resolved these threats with relative ease, thanks to his superpowers and continuous study of various fighting techniques.

"You better give that shit to us now, boy!" Tundé remembers one of the seven-man strong army of junkies yelling during a wholesale deal in an alleyway on Fish Island, Hackney. He proceeded to bash up the main ringleader with a series of punches.

"Come on then! Who else wants it?" Tundé shouted as he floored another of them with a flying kick, prompting the rest of the clique to flee.

Interestingly, the tales of high-security personnel escorting large quantities of bairaff made their way around the London underworld scene. The surprise attacks became much less frequent.

Tundé's school life had drastically changed too. His enhanced memory allowed him to learn the syllabus exponentially faster. So, despite the lack of sleep from his late-night work, Tundé was emerging as a top performer amongst his peers based on the mock GCSE exam results. A change that pleased his teachers.

"Lianne, great improvement, you just need to sharpen up on showing your workings..." Mr Panther said during a practice exam review in his morning Physics lesson. "...and Tundé, here's your paper. Fantastic effort from you once again. You've really turned the corner!"

There was a large note on the top of Tundé's exam paper with '96% - A*' in large, red letters written on it. Although he was exhausted, he fought off his droopy eyes and acknowledged Mr Panter with a beaming smile.

It wasn't just Tundé's teachers who noticed a visible difference in his aura. The girls in his year group had started to pay a lot more attention to him too.

"Tundsy, please can help me study for our Lit exam?" Omi asked flirtatiously during their afternoon English lesson. "You scored so highly in that coursework we had for the D. Edun novel and I wanna know what techniques you're using to hit *all* the right points."

"No, he's gonna help me because I *actually* need it," said Bella, one of Omi's closest friends. "Besides, I know him more than you do. Isn't that right Tunds?"

"Why don't you help us *both* study?" said Omi, causing her and Bella to giggle uncontrollably.

"Calm down, girls," Laura interjected sharply. "I'm sure you can just spend your time learning everything you need from WeView, instead of scrolling through LyFilter all night like you probably do."

"Jheeeze, man like Tunds, yeah," Remi cheered as he nudged Tundé on the way into the classroom. "Gyaldem sugar!"

Tundé smirked. He was new to receiving all this female attention, so he just revelled in it. Especially witnessing that his crush was jealous!

"Ladies, ladies. There's no need for all this. How about we settle this gladiator-style? Last one standing wins private tutoring from me."

The girls sighed with playful exasperation.

After leaving his final lesson of the day, Tundé bumped into a trio of boys in the school corridor.

"Jheeze, man like Tunds you know," Asif said while he fist bumped Tundé.

"Yeah, little hat-trick hero, 'int ya," said Ross excitedly. "Taking us to a cup final like that, mate."

"Light work man," Tundé joked as he lightly jabbed Ross's shoulder. "We had to beat St Rocs eventually. I'm just gassed I could bang some goals in too!"

Earlier that month, Stebon High's Year 11 football team defeated their East London rivals, St Rocadventures, in the London Cup semi-final, where Tundé scored three goals.

"Maybe Mr Athlima was right. We might need to drug test my man!" joked Kwaku, another football teammate. "But we can do it after beating those Upton Cross boys in the final."

"Haha, nah man. I just developed late on, that's all."

"Believe, Kwaku. He's clearly on stuff!" Asif said in jest. "Anyway, man like Tunds, catch you in a bit bro."

They each fist-bumped Tundé, who was beaming with joy at how much his fortunes had changed. He even had the popular guys in the football team giving him praise and respect now.

Bruv, man's loving these new perks, I can't lie!

But on his way back to the estate after school, Tundé reflected on some of the challenges he faced because of the changes. The late nights with little sleep. The perpetual anxiety that Jerry could betray him and his family at any moment. He never knew what threats lurked, forcing him to be alert constantly. While heading into Equiano House, he bumped into a familiar face.

"Yo, man like Kwame!"

"Yes, Tunds! What are you saying these days?"

"Things are blessed man, how are you?"

"Still working man. It's tough, but while Dad's still sick, this is what I've gotta do."

"I feel you, bro. I pray he recovers soon man. I started working in a restaurant in South too, by the way."

"Oh, that's sick. Must feel nice to have your own money as a yute, right?"

"Yeah it's decent, but I'm tryna help out with the fam like you init."

"Swear down? Haha, remember man's older than you though. You're still a kid, bro! But I guess as long as you ain't hurting anyone, that's the most important thing for you right now."

"I hear you, man."

Tundé couldn't help but reflect on those words, especially since he was constantly spinning excuses and lies to keep his mum from becoming a neurotic wreck. But it rarely worked. Over the past few weeks, he had earned a few thousand pounds through his work for Jerry. Tundé would leave random hundred-pound bundles for her in the kitchen and living room. While he believed he was doing the right thing, his mum's suspicions were a growing concern.

"Don't watch, Mum. Like I've been telling you for weeks, I'm just doing long shifts at Jerry's restaurant," Tundé voiced with frustration after his mum stormed into his bedroom to confront him about his extra-curricular activities. This was standard procedure.

"NONSENSE! I don't know any fifteen-year-old who collects this kind of money from cleaning plates and sweeping floors. And one of your teasha's called me to say that you're always falling asleep at school. Ah ah, kil'ódé?"

Tundé became increasingly irritated by all this questioning.

Rah man, why isn't she grateful? Does she not understand that I'm using this money to help US out?

"Mum, I'm getting top marks at school. Literally bare A*s in my trial exams. Maybe the teachers are jealous cos I can do it without listening to their dead chat. And you know they don't like seeing people like us winning. Jerry's business is also quite popular in South, so that's why the money's good and I'm working long hours."

She kissed her teeth.

"Is it because Brodah Blessing isn't here anymore that you're behaving so recklessly now?"

Tundé looked away guiltily. A few weeks prior, Uncle Blessing had moved into a guesthouse in another part of East London. It was supposedly the plan from the start of his trip because he wanted to give the family their space. But, of course, his mum was unaware of their spat regarding her son's impending obligations. And Tundé couldn't help but feel that was the major reason his uncle left.

"I will let you have your space now, Babatundé. But as the orishas have ordained it, you will eventually realise that you need my help," Uncle Blessing warned Tundé before he moved out.

Tundé took a deep breath while he reached into his bag.

"Mum, don't worry, I'm fine. And remember, before Uncle left, he told you that you need to let me grow into being a man, so just lemme do that. You can enjoy this instead."

He pulled out a bundle of notes and offered it to his mum. His mum's eyes fixated on the bundle with deep concern. Sensing her angst, Tundé gave her a warm, reassuring hug. Her tenseness gradually faded, and once she thought about all the bills and other necessities that needed taking care of, she begrudgingly took the money from Tundé's hands. Even though it went in his favour, Tundé felt guilty deep down for triggering his mum's anxiety. He questioned whether the whole thing was worth it.

But I'm making too much bread to stop now. We're working too hard to make life work. I need... WE need to be getting something out of it!

As the evening wore on, Tundé was consumed by his thoughts and became increasingly anxious. He wanted everything to be perfect and in balance, whether that came to mastery over his powers, how much money he could provide for the family and having the ability to keep all his loved ones happy. He thought back to Uncle Blessing's key guiding principles about the need for patience.

But I just wanna do it my own way.

The circumstances of his customers were also weighing on his conscience. The economic benefits Tundé received were gradually being overshadowed by his shame for contributing to the suffering of addicts. It was hard to ignore the devastation their lives led to. Watching them rummage through rubbish, beg on the streets or commit petty crimes just to scrape together enough money for their fix. It slowly etched away at Tundé's spirit. While he knew that people led these lives anyway, there was a big difference between awareness and being a direct beneficiary of the devastation.

But I'm not forcing them to take the drugs. If I'm not making this money, someone else will.

Tundé entered a profoundly distorted state as his overthinking intensified. He became unaware of his surroundings and the passage of time, as his mind continuously swirled with heavy thoughts. Reflecting on his upbringing, he spent his entire adolescence being raised by his mum, who worked tirelessly to take care of their small unit. And yet, they had little to show for it. He felt responsible for bearing some fruits for the hardships they faced. As much as it pained him to see the misery his line of work brought, Tundé was ready to bottle up his guilt.

None of those people are my problem. We've had it hard too, so lemme just keep making this bread for my fam. It's not affecting me...

"I'm guessing you're gonna stop then, Tunds?"

Violently broken out of his disorientated state, Tundé was stunned. He had been absorbed by a whirlwind of thoughts. He found himself sitting on a bench behind the bushes at his school's playground. It was an infamous courting location for senior pupils.

"Huh, what do you mean about stop?" he asked cautiously.

"Were you even listening to me?" Laura was disgruntled at his intermittent attention. "You zone out a lot, don't you? I guess that's what happens when you get bare smart, bare quickly."

She started to giggle, bringing Tundé a sense of ease. For a moment, he was worried that she really could read his mind.

"Rah, why you gassing?" Tundé playfully nudged her. He quickly glanced at the time on Laura's phone. It was almost one in the afternoon, meaning they were on lunch break.

I can't believe the time just passed by like that, damn.

"Tunds, you're doing it again!" Laura shrieked. "I just wanted to know if you'll still come to school for the revision classes when the exam period starts in a few weeks."

Despite their school's mediocrity, Laura had become somewhat of a high academic achiever based on recent exam results. Even with grades adequate for most top-performing institutions, she was very humble about her book smarts and remained a humble Bow girl at heart. Tundé genuinely liked that about her.

"I dunno. I might come in. But I think I could do everything from yard, to be honest. Are you gonna be here? Cos you're proper about your books, init?"

"Wellll, my dad always puts bare pressure on me and my bro to focus on school—especially me cos he doesn't want me to ever rely on next man. But anyway, it would be nice to see you at school, Tunds."

Tundé perked up as the words entered his ears. Butterflies fluttered away in his stomach. A drop of water landed on his head, signalling that rain was due. But it felt too soon to end this moment.

"I guess you'll be too busy *'doing everything at yard'* though, won't you?" she scoffed, using her fingers to make exaggerated quotation marks. Tundé laughed.

"You're bare cheeky, you know! If I'm about, I'll be about init. Then, maybe we can hang together more."

Tundé was swimming in a sea of bliss as he locked eyes with Laura. He didn't need superpowers to feel the magnetic attraction between them. Laura's eyes were dilating as she subtly bit her lips. While Tundé had limited experience with the opposite sex, he was desperate to change that. He composed himself, and just as he was about to lean in...

"Oh, no!" Laura blurted out under the crackling sound of thunder. A heavy downpour of rain abruptly followed. "Let's go, Tunds. I don't wanna get soaked!"

Tundé was gutted. He plucked up so much courage to even try and make a move on his crush. The opportunity felt lost though as they headed towards the main school building.

"I know we follow each other on LyFilter, but you wanna take my number too?" Laura asked shyly as they walked under an outdoor shelter. "Just in case you wanna VizChat me."

Tundé tried to keep his cool. However, he couldn't hide his wide grin as he shakily brought his fresh miCell phone out.

"Yeah, that's calm. Just put it in here."

"...2-6-1. Okay, I've gotta go to my Geography lesson now. See you later, Tunds!"

Laura joyfully waved goodbye. Throughout the day, Tundé constantly stared at Laura's VizChat profile on his phone. The 15-year-old felt like he had overcome a massive hurdle, previously having little luck with the girls he crushed on.

"I saw you walking out with Laura earlier," Remi asked cheekily during their History lesson. "Is that yooou, yeah?"

"Ay, don't watch, bro! We're just getting to know each other, init."

"Look at the way man's cheesing. You're defo simping for her! The fact you're making P's now will help though. You can thank me for connecting you and Tanks with Jerry."

While that statement was in light jest, it yanked Tundé back into a pensive state. All the same ruminations about morality and consequences resurfaced.

"Erm, yeah... safe... you brought us man in, still."

After the final bell, Tundé was crossing the road outside his school grounds when a metallic grey Scheep sped by. It almost clattered into the schoolboy, who had stepped back instinctively just as the vehicle flew past him and parked down the road. Screwing his face angrily at the car, Tundé's demeanour soon changed when Laura came charging by.

"Hey, Laura. You alright, yeah?"

"Tunds! Sorry, I can't stay and chat. I'm getting picked up today," Laura pointed at the Scheep that just raced past him.

"Oh really?"

"Come on Lozza, my darling!" the driver exclaimed. "I know you wanna chinwag with your mates, but I've got important things to do today."

"Argh, Dad! Please don't embarrass me here," Laura shrieked like a little girl, to Tundé's surprise. "I'm coming!"

She turned to Tundé and lightly stroked his arm. "See you later, Tunds."

Tundé watched her step into the Scheep and it sped off around the corner.

Phew. Thank god I didn't meet her dad then. I would have been far from ready!

When Tundé eventually arrived at the bus stop, he was caught off guard by a familiar face. Judging from her response, she had been waiting for him.

"Wagwan Auntie Abs, you good?" Tundé asked, clearly taken aback. It was unusual that she would turn up unannounced at his school bus stop.

"Oh... I-I-I just wanted to see you, Tunds," Auntie Abi said quiveringly, as her hands fidgeted excessively.

"Well, you know where our yard is. Why did you come all the way here?" Tundé laughed awkwardly.

"Ha... ha... well, I don't see why it's so bad f-f-for me to see my own family wherever, whenever."

"Aren't you supposed to be at work anyway? How's that going? Marketing don't just stop in summer, does it?"

"Oh yeah, work. Yeah, I'm still there. I've just got today off init. It's calm though. It's calm. Everything is fine."

"Okay. Let's cut to the chase. What's up?"

"Well, lemme not lie, Tunds. Things have been a bit on top of me recently, you know. The industry's struggling a lot right now, so m-m-my hours have been cut in half."

Tundé sensed Auntie Abi's profound sorrow. He affectionately patted her arm.

"I'm sorry, Abs. What do you need?"

"I need some P's to just g-g-get back up on my feet. Things have been bare difficult recently."

Tundé wasn't surprised by the request. He had gifted her a few hundred pounds over the past few weeks, so she knew he had money. He thought back to a conversation Jerry had with a business associate on the phone during one of his rare visits to the restaurant.

"People change bares when they realise you got money, ya kna. You've gotta be careful how much you let them know."

I wonder what she's been spending the P's on.

Since Auntie Abi was visibly upset, Tundé chose not to probe. For now.

"Yeah, I can sort you out," Tundé said, as he guided Auntie Abi to a discreet side road away from the bus stop.

There, he reached into his crotch area and brought out a healthy batch of £5 and £10 notes. He kept more spare cash on him these days since he knew he could defend himself from any muggers if he needed to.

"Here's £100 now, Abs. I'll swing by yours later today if you need more."

She responded with a strained smile as tears built up in her eyes.

"I would very much appreciate more. You're such a b-b-blessing, you know."

Auntie Abi then kissed Tundé's hand profusely, as he stared at her with bewilderment. This level of desperation was entirely out of character.

I guess money really DOES change people.

"Actually, l-l-let me come to your y-y-yard with you now, yeah?" Auntie Abi suggested frantically.

Tundé tentatively nodded, and they jumped on the D7 bus back to the Samuda Estate. Onboard, his aunt's strange behaviour continued.

"Ah, it's too hot on this bus," she complained.

In an instant, she quickly got a notepad out of her bag and scribbled down random notes and drawings of the top deck. Then, she got up and opened certain windows at different angles before sitting back down.

"Mmmm, 17.3 degrees Celcius never felt so good," Auntie Abi said proudly. Much to Tundé's shock, his superhuman awareness registered the temperature drop to that exact number too.

How did she possibly work that out?

Things got more bizarre when she started discussing the scientific concepts of Isaac Newton and Nikolai Tesla, explaining why their theories were the basis of modern technologies.

"...and that's how those Niko self-driving cars were made. Have you noticed them around more recently?"

"Not really, no. Since when has physics or cars or any of this shit been your ting?"

Auntie Abi carried herself with a lot more confidence and surety now, as opposed to the jitters she had earlier.

"I have other interests too, Tunds. I decided to arm myself with as much knowledge as possible recently. So here we are!"

When they arrived back at Equiano House, Tundé handed his auntie an extra £150.

"Thank you SO much!" she said, snatching it out of his hands as if it were a bottle of water in a vast desert. She stared devilishly at the money, then gave her nephew a glowing grin. Tundé's suspicions grew.

"Abs, big man ting, are you sure you're okay?"

"I'm fine, Tunds. Truss me. Anyway, I need to dip. Got a few errands to run."

"That reminds me! I need to bring over the Aso Oke fabric that Mum got from those Kent relatives. I would give it to you now, but I don't have a clue where it is, and you know how Mum doesn't like me messing around with her stuff."

"Oh yeah, I need to get it made for Tolani's wedding in August. Can you bring it over later? Maybe like eleven?"

Tundé raised his eyebrows. Auntie Abi didn't know about his superpowers, so it was a surprise that she would suggest he trek through the streets of East London in those late hours.

"Rah, you sure? That late?"

"I mean if not, you can do it tomorrow morning. I swear you're off from school now?" Auntie Abi asked as she began sniffing profusely.

"You know what, I'll let you know," Tundé said while sorting out more cash in his hand. Auntie Abi's eyes were glued.

"Swear down, Jerry's paying you bares for this restaurant job yeah?"

"Come on, g! Man just *sweeps* it up!" Tundé laughed.

But Auntie Abi barely registered his joke. She was too preoccupied with the money. Suddenly, she started glitching back into the unsettled, fidgety state in which Tundé had found her earlier.

"Gotta shoot off Tunds, see you la-la-later," she said, giving him a loose hug before rushing out of the flat.

Before Tundé could even decipher what was happening to his auntie, his pocket started buzzing incessantly. He pulled out his treasured Pony Erikson and read the series of texts that were just received from Jerry.

'10pm 2nite.'
'PU: Bygrove Street E14.'
'DL: Giraud Street E14.'

"Yes, this job is in my ends!"

Tundé punched the air with joy, relieved that he wouldn't have to travel far on a school night. Since it was close to Auntie Abi's house, he decided to check in on her afterwards. Another buzz from the phone grabbed Tundé's attention.

'£10k from I.C.P by end of the night.'

Tundé chuckled to himself about the client's street alias. He wondered what name he would choose if he gave himself one. He didn't rate 'Tanks' all that much, but that was probably for the best so he could act the role of his third cousin effectively. Jerry had fortunately kept his word thus far in keeping Tanks' identity as 'Tundé's distant cousin' a secret. Even though it was a lie anyway, it was close enough to home that the information could put Tundé and his family at significant risk.

Gotta make sure I stay on Jerry's good side and keep his trust.

As he got himself ready to leave the flat, Tundé heard his mum come through the front door, prompting him to greet her.

"Good evening, Mum," he bowed down as usual.

"Good evening, dear," his mum said as she wearily flopped onto the sofa.

"Quickly, where's the Aso Oke fabric that Auntie Abs needs for that August wedding?"

"It's in the red suitcase in my wardrobe. Why do you need it now, sha?"

"I'm going to her yard later. But I need to do a few hours at Jerry's restaurant," Tundé lied as he retrieved the fabric from his mum's room. "But he's gonna drop me back here afterwards, so it's calm."

"Ah, Babatundé. Please be very careful, o. The Holy Spirit tells me that there is danger out there. I can feel the h'energy brewing."

"Don't worry, Mum. I can take care of myself. And like I said, I'll be with Jerry, who's an adult. So, it will be fine."

"I will pray for you, dear," her voice carried a clear undercurrent of stress. "May God bless you and keep you safe, in Jesos name!"

"Amen, mum. Amen," he said indifferently.

Leaving the flat wearing a casual jacket, jeans and some black trainers, Tundé sneakily walked through the indoor access stairs to the Equiano House rooftop, where he waited until it was time to work the job. Outside, it was a chilly, windy evening. Nonetheless, he opened his backpack to pull out the standard all-black attire. Tundé had since purchased three sets of the same tracksuits and gloves to reduce the wear and tear on each set.

He slipped on his balaclava and quickly changed before starting his journey to the pick-up spot on Bygrove Street. As he leapt from building to building effortlessly, Tundé couldn't shake the feelings of guilt that reemerged.

I need to allow all these dark thoughts man. Just gotta keep making bread for the fam, keep the gyaldem loving me and keep the mandem admiring me.

When he arrived on the gloomy Bygrove Street, he sat atop an old maroon building, which bordered onto a narrow alleyway. Using his night vision, he caught sight of a junkie having a considerable fit in the alleyway.

"P-p-p-please help me!" the junkie howled as he fell to the garbage-filled ground. "S-s-s-something is e-e-e-eating me alive from inside! Arrgghh! Help!"

Tundé thought about jumping down to assist him. But he was there to do a job that he didn't want to jeopardise, so he tried his best to ignore the pain-induced noises.

"P-p-please! P-p-p-please! Help!"

The junkie continued screaming as he ran chaotically back and forth through the alleyway, bashing into one of the council bins.

"Asgfhhgd! Ggsghhsfgsh!"

Zooming in closer, Tundé noticed that the junkie was foaming profusely from the mouth while he was laid out on the floor. The sound coming from the junkie's blocked airways was particularly horrifying. Despite feeling pressure to help out, Tundé's pocket vibrated again. It was another text from Jerry.

'Metal Grey Niko car. Now. 3-2-2.'

Tundé's attention was drawn to the junkie again, who was still choking out.

Damn, I can't save my man now. But he shouldn't have been messing with these drugs.

The metal grey Niko car then pulled up on Bygrove Street. Tundé swiftly slid down the maroon building under the shadows and strolled over. He tapped on the car window using a pattern that had served as the signal in his past deals. Three taps. Two taps. Then two taps. A few seconds of quiet followed, giving Tundé a short jolt of concern. Eventually, the driver, a light-skinned man in his twenties signalled to him to get in the vehicle. They barely exchanged a word, as the driver placed a couple of small, purple-tinted packs in Tundé's hands immediately. The passenger's seat was occupied by another young, pale-skinned, slightly overweight male. He addressed Tundé directly.

"Jerry didn't text it, but you're joining us out on the field tonight for extra backup, Tanks. Me and Femz have a lot to push. And cos the prices are going up too, we're expecting a likkle backlash."

"Bruv, what do you mean?" Tundé deepened his voice in the tone of his alias. "I've got shit to do, init."

"Until we sell these packs, you ain't seeing any P's, my yute," the pale-skinned boy said crudely.

"Nah, you're giving me that to me now!"

"Fam, I beg you listen to I.C.P," Femz said, tapping his fingers on his gun. "He's still buying the purp from us, but he's lined up a spot to shot all of it tonight."

Tundé eyeballed him furiously. "Listen, I don't know what you man have heard, but your guns can't intimidate me. I need the P's now."

The two men quickly glanced at each other, then at Tundé, and then back at each other.

"Man's about it too, you know," Femz held his gun firmly. "But man's more about his money. If we sell up quick, we can be done in a couple of hours. Do you wanna be the reason why Jerry doesn't get his P's by tomorrow?"

Tundé scowled at them both. But he knew he had to be careful with his choice of response. After the PMD incident, he wanted to avoid disrupting Jerry's operation again.

"Alright, fine. This time I'll back it. But only this one time. And if you man ever pull a gun on me again, I'm not holding back."

I.C.P and Femz smirked at each other while the latter started the engine for the car. "Whatever you say, boss man."

The metal grey Niko drove for a few minutes before parking on the corner of Giraud Street, where the drop-off was intended. The dead-end street was drowned in darkness. Tundé soon understood the importance of being present. If the disgruntled customers caused a ruckus it might alert the police of their activities. And he could get away with the stash at pace. I.C.P and Femz set up in a discreet patch, while Tundé was posted next to a set of bushes on the other side of the road. The bairaff addicts magically appeared from the darkness, like a group of zombies hunting for brains. As they approached, Tundé observed the usual behaviour—appalling physical health, erratic behaviour and a collective longing to numb their deep-seated pain. It triggered his conscience.

Fucking hell, I can't believe I let that guy in the alleyway earlier potentially die...

But the teenager suppressed his feelings, convincing himself that the addicts were different from him. That they weren't his responsibility. Casting blame on them eased his internal distress.

They should've been more careful with their lives.

"Alright, get your money ready," I.C.P announced to the customers as he pointed to a random spot a few yards away. "Line up there and get ready init. It's half a bill for a gram today."

"What? 50 fucking quid? Why's it so much?" one of the punters asked, his eyes wide open in dismay.

"That's the market we're in. Cost of living crisis and all that. Do you want the purp or not, bruv?"

With no arguments, the punters began handing their cash to I.C.P, who then directed them to a nearby tree to pick up their bairaff from a young boy that he had hired from their estate. As the minutes ticked by, more and more junkies emerged like flies to a piece of flesh. Femz and I.C.P became increasingly delighted with the prospect of selling out completely. Even though it meant Tundé would get paid the agreed amount, he was more concerned about the time.

It's almost twenty past eleven. I need to get moving soon.

Keen to get to Auntie Abi's house before it got too late, he walked away from the bushes and across the road to the two sellers.

"Bruv, what the fuck are you doing?" I.C.P shouted.

"Relax fam. When are we finishing up?" Tundé retorted. "Like I said, I've got things I need to do."

"Can you not see we're busy?" Femz said, taking a hundred pounds from another junkie. "You're supposed to be watching out for any trouble. Do you still wanna get paid tonight, bruv?"

Tundé kissed his teeth irritably. Just as he was about to retaliate, he was interrupted by the muffled voice of the next customer.

"Yeah yeah, lemme grab a two g from you man quickly," the woman had a scarf covering her face, trying to avoid eye contact with the dealers. But strangely, her voice sounded familiar.

"Yo b, I beg you speak up," Femz demanded.

As the woman removed her scarf slightly, Tundé was startled with pure disbelief. He knew that face. It was the face that helped him organise his 5th birthday party when he dropped his cake on the carpet, and she helped him clean it up. The face helped him first learn how to ride his second-hand bike around the Samuda Estate. The face that convinced his mum to stop giving him beatings for his misbehaviour. The face he'd known ever since he could remember anything.

"Oh, you're dat Abi ting, init?" Femz asked.

"Erm, why?"

"Cos I remember your ex, he was bare safe. Man like Dayo!" Femz said excitedly, as he turned to I.C.P. "Yo, just do her two g for 80 quid, init."

Tundé was in a state of physical and mental shock as he tried to process what was happening.

I... I... I can't... believe it...

"Thank you. Appreciate it," she said, fetching cash from her pocket. Cash that Tundé had gifted her earlier that day, devastating him even more.

"Oi, you're kinda peng you know," I.C.P interjected. "Can get yourself a nice discount if you play your cards right. What you saying?"

"I ain't sayin' *nuffin'* to you," Auntie Abi said, side-eyeing I.C.P with disgust.

"Haha!" Femz laughed out loud. "You gotta up your game, fam!"

Tundé was still wrestling with his emotions, which weren't helped by I.C.P's courting attempts. His mind was going berserk.

Auntie Abi? What? This doesn't make any sense? I'm making enough money so the whole fam can thrive. Why is she using bairaff? Have I done something wrong?

What made it unbearably challenging for Tundé was that he couldn't even speak to her. He couldn't afford for his identity to be revealed. But he still projected an uncomfortable energy. One that Auntie Abi picked up on. She stared at Tundé curiously.

"Do I know you?" she asked, wondering who the masked man was.

"Oi! Go round the corner and get your shit, you dumb nitty!" I.C.P shouted, proceeding to spit on the floor right by her feet. He was still feeling bitter about being rejected. Tundé was incensed.

Bruv, I would smack this prick up right now! But I can't blow my cover. Fuck.

Auntie Abi went into the concealed area to collect her two grams of bairaff from the young corner boy, then disappeared into the distance.

What the actual fuck, fam? I didn't just see that. Tell me that I'm hallucinating again, I beg.

Tundé was having an internal crisis. But he didn't want to be seen reacting emotionally to Auntie Abi's presence. Given that he had already beaten down revolting junkies and rival gangs, any sniff of his true identity could be extremely dangerous for his loved ones. As Femz and I.C.P kept selling, Tundé grew increasingly restless. Checking the time on his phone, half an hour had passed since Auntie Abi's appearance. He needed to go to her house now.

"Ite, you man, I'm gonna duck out," said Tundé. "You guys have more than made your money tonight. Give me the P's for Jerry."

"Oi, fam, we're not finished you know!" I.C.P. hissed.

"Forget about me, do you man wanna have to deal with beef from Jerry if I tell him you refused to give me the P's?"

"Just give this dickhead the 10 g's man," Femz snapped. "We're more than good for tonight."

I.C.P quickly counted some bundles that he took from the inner pocket of his puffer jacket and handed the money to Tundé.

"Alright, in a bit. You fucking pricks!" Tundé yelled as he sprinted down Giraud Street as the two dealers barked profanities at him.

Once he disappeared out of sight, the teenager quickly climbed up a nearby estate and desperately hurdled the buildings of Poplar. His auntie's actions were weighing heavy on his mind. He was still so confused.

It's not fair. I'm just tryna do my best for everyone!

While Tunde acrobatically navigated the rooftops, he thought about the circumstances of his customers. Most of them would do obscene acts just to find a short-lived fix.

All these junkies have fucked up, horrible lives. So, why does Abs feel like she has to be on the same ting?

As Tundé approached his auntie's home, he saw the sign for her residence from high above. Malorie Road. He slid down the wall of a 40-foot building, then paced down the street towards her place. She lived in an old Victorian house that had been converted into self-contained units a decade ago. Tundé had visited numerous times when she used to babysit him.

Tundé hid in some bushes to remove his balaclava and change into his everyday clothes. Emerging from the bushes, he observed how the moonlight shone favourably on the CCA-governed cul-de-sac. As picturesque as these converted Victorian flats were, there was a dreadful smell due to the antiquated sewerage system. He fretfully approached Auntie Abi's door. After letting out a huge sigh, he knocked on it three times. There was no answer. He knocked another three times. Still no response.

Strange.

Tundé knew Auntie Abi was in because she always left her main hallway light on when she went to bed. But he couldn't peer through her bedroom window as the blinds were drawn. He reached into a plant pot beside the door to retrieve a spare key. Tundé slowly unlocked the front door. It creaked open. He thought it would alarm her. But he sensed no movement. He shut the door gently and then walked through the narrow hallway to his auntie's room. He knocked on her door.

"Abs, please don't worry. It's just me, Tunds. Just wanna make sure you're okay."

There was no response.

"Sorry if I scared you. Can I come in?"

He waited for a brief moment. The silence lingered. His heart started pounding intensely.

"Fuck it, I'm coming in!"

Tundé opened the door. He stopped dead in his tracks. He was frozen by the painful sight that awaited him. He stood there in sheer despair. He flung himself to his knees. Auntie Abi lay motionless before him in a pool of blood with purple foam oozing out from her mouth and her right nostril.

"Auntie? Please wake up?" Tundé begged, tears streaming down his face as he tried to shake her awake. "Please wake up! You can't... you can't be... you can't be gone?"

Chapter 27

"Yes... mmhmm... we're at 42 Writers House on Malorie Road. Yes, the one in Poplar. Flat number 2. Just don't send too many of your people here though, Chris..."

Tundé sobbed relentlessly as he sat by the curb just outside Auntie Abi's flat. He was distraught. When the emergency services arrived, they found the devastated teenager laid out on the doorstep. Any initial suspicions that he was a suspect dissolved when they inspected Auntie Abi's body and made the early conclusion that she died from a drug overdose. Tundé was so benumbed that he hadn't even bothered to hide his backpack, which contained £10,000 and a balaclava that would ring alarm bells if the authorities found them. But none of that mattered right now. He was broken.

"I'm really sorry, mate," said one of the paramedics, stopping to put his arm on Tundé's shoulder. "If you need a quick chat, I can help."

Tundé stared at him blankly, then shook his head. The paramedic gave him a consoling look and re-entered the flat to join the other ambulance staff. The commotion on this otherwise quiet residential street attracted the attention of some neighbours, with a few peeking through their blinds and others coming out of their homes to satisfy their curiosity. But Tundé couldn't care less. He was too shell-shocked. Mindlessly checking his pockets, he felt a bundle of notes wrapped in a rubber band. A feeling that would normally bring joy instead made his stomach turn.

If I hadn't been working so hard to move this shit around, maybe she would still be alive.

"But it's too late now and it's all my fault!" Tundé cried into his sleeve.

A few minutes later, the doors of the Wilwo car that Tundé heard chatter from earlier flung open. Out stepped three men—two in police uniform and one in a slick, slim-fit suit. He was dressed more like a Hollywood movie star than a Metropolitan Police officer.

"Alright gentlemen, what's the situation here?" one of the uniformed officers said to the ambulance crew in the hallway as they walked in.

The suited and booted man noticed Tundé crying on the side of the road and strolled over.

"Hey kid, is this someone you know?"

"Yeah... it is," Tundé could barely speak over his tears. "I-i-it-it's my auntie."

"Don't worry, we're gunna sort this out for you. I'm Inspector Harry Archibald. I work across both Newham and Tower Hamlets for the Met. We're gunna do a full investigation on what's happened here. Alright?"

Tundé nodded faintly. He didn't need any help finding out what happened, he already knew the sequence of events and who was to blame. Harry gave him a sympathetic gesture, then walked into the house. Twenty minutes later, the forensics team started to leave as the police officers cordoned off the flat. They carried several items as evidence, but what gave Tundé the most gut-wrenching feeling was the bright, white bag they carried out on a stretcher and placed inside the ambulance van.

I can't believe that's her. Just gone, like that.

Tundé stared at the sky with sorrow.

What happens when people die? Where did she go? Why did she have to die now?

He started smacking the side of his head, trying to shut his brain off from the pain.

"Hey kid, don't beat yourself up," Harry said as he overlooked the other officers cordoning off the flat. "This isn't on you, I promise. Come with me, I'll make sure you get home okay."

But there was something Tundé didn't trust about Harry. He couldn't put his finger on it, but the officer seemed insincere. Since the youngster was also involved in the bairaff trade, he didn't want to interact with the police anyway.

"Nah, it's calm," Tundé wiped away the tears from his face. "I'll find my own way home, init."

"You sure, kid?" Harry asked with a sterner tone.

"Yeah, I'm good."

"Okay, fair enough. If you need us, here's our number for non-urgent calls," Harry handed Tundé a police card. "All Abiola's next of kin will be notified ASAP. Take it easy, kid."

Harry hopped into the Wilwo car again and drove away from Malorie Road. While the last forensics specialists and police officers scoured the flat, Tundé stayed glued to the curb, remonstrating with himself, when he heard loud footsteps further down the road. A woman soon appeared. She wore a pair of short black heels, a black pencil skirt and a white blouse that complimented her navy blue blazer. She strode elegantly over to Tundé. For a split second, he was completely absorbed by her aura.

"Hello, are you a relative of this unfortunate woman?" she inquired with a great deal of warmth.

"Yeah, she is..." Tundé sniffled helplessly. He couldn't bear going home just yet. He needed to get a grip before he could face his mum with the tragic news.

"I'm really sorry for your loss. I truly am," the elegant woman said as she gently caressed Tundé's arm. "And I'm here to possibly help you too."

"What, are you from the council or suttin'? Man's not going into care, you know. I've got a mum, so I'm good."

"Oh no, far from it! My name's Lizzie, and I work for *Popular in Poplar*."

"Nah, fuck all that. Man's not doing any interviews with you lot for nuffin'!"

Tundé knew about the *Popular in Poplar* media outlet. They had written a feature piece in their newspaper about the Samuda Estate a few years back. It included a picture of Kwame's mum carrying a young relative in a Kente cloth wrapper, alongside a story about the area's loss of English Cockney culture over the decades. He was well aware of how out of touch the media was and how harmful their narratives could be for his community.

"Again, that's not really why I'm here," Lizzie reiterated. "I'm on your side. I recently lost a close friend, so I understand what you're going through."

"I'm sorry you lost someone. But you don't know shit about me or my family, so you won't understand."

"Honestly, I get why you might hate us journalists and the media. I really do. All I want you to know is I'm taking a big risk by being here, knowing all the information I do."

Tundé looked Lizzie right in the eye, questioning her genuineness. She held her gaze strongly and didn't waver. Perhaps he could trust her, but he still had his doubts. Lizzie then glanced over to the sergeants manning the property, who had just acknowledged her presence. She smiled and waved to them, and they reciprocated, her attractiveness pleasantly surprising the policemen.

"Listen, we can't speak much about this here. But let's just say I want to get justice for your family and my friend," Lizzie produced a card and handed it over to Tundé. "Reach out to me when you're ready to talk."

Tundé hesitantly took the card, which read:

Lizzie Armen
Senior Journalist at Popular in Poplar
Phone: 07353895658
Chirp: @lizzie_armen

"Cool. I'm gonna bounce now, anyway. I need to get out of here. I can't deal with this shit anymore."

"Of course, do what you need to do. But remember, I'm here for you if you need me. Again, please accept my commiserations to you and your family."

After changing back into his all-black street attire, Tundé hopped through the East London rooftops to return to his estate. Once there, he chose to lie aimlessly in the same gardens outside his flat, where the kids usually played. Like the day Remi recruited him for his first deal with Jerry. The whole thing seemed so much more appealing back then. He had his eyes set on chasing the opulence of Canary Wharf, where he and his family were sure to be happy. But Tundé's desire for that dream had almost entirely diminished. Instead, he desired liberation.

Liberation from the constant, burning sensation of guilt cast onto his chest. It was his decisions that led his beloved Auntie Abi to her demise.

As he took off his balaclava, a bolt of lightning flashed in the distance and a loud thunderclap roared through the skies. Rain followed, and the downpour trickled profusely off Tundé's face as he lay there. The smell of the wet grass and mud was pungent. He didn't even budge as his clothes got soaked in the cold, damp conditions. He was still thinking. Still processing. Still trying to understand. Suddenly, he was overcome with an uncontrollable rage. Tundé rose to his feet, bent his knees, and then used all the power he could muster to leap explosively into the air. He clenched his fists and unleashed a fierce cry.

"CAWGH!"

The screech of an eagle was summoned from Tundé's vocal cords, harmonising perfectly with the sound of thunder as another bolt of lightning rumbled the ground. His mouth stretched so widely that its corners split open, and the crimson red blood mixed with his salty tears as the raindrops continued beating down on him. It was a majestic sight for the very few Isle of Dogs residents who happened to be at their windows. Near-total darkness in the intense rain, and then a flash of lightning illuminated the sky to reveal the boy hanging impossibly in mid-air.

Tundé then dropped helplessly to the ground, landing brutally in one of the thorn bushes in the estate's gardens. But instead of freeing himself from its painful stings, he just stayed there, bawling. Auntie Abi was dead.

What am I gonna do now?

Chapter 28

"WAIT... SHE... SHE... SHE's gone?"

"I'm sorry, Sister Fola. I'm sorry," Uncle Blessing consoled Tundé's mum.

"No, you're lying," she cried aloud. "The devil is a liar, sha! Her soul is not gone. I rebuke it!"

In her shell-shocked state, she accidentally dropped one of the new, fancy glasses that Tundé had gifted her. It smashed onto the floor. Like the glass, Tundé was also in pieces. He was numb. He hadn't slept or eaten anything since last night. Auntie Abi's death hit him with a searing anguish because he felt so responsible for it.

"Son, please, go easy on yourself," Uncle Blessing now comforted Tundé, who was sitting inconsolably on the sofa. "There's nothing you could have done, sha."

"I should have done more to protect her, Uncle."

He got a sudden wave of flashbacks of the countless bairaff deals he worked on over the past few weeks. He was struck with a surge of grief so strong that he smashed his hands through the new, glass coffee table. Whilst his mum gasped loudly, Tundé hid his bloody, cut-up hands underneath one of the sofa throws. He couldn't let her witness his healing powers in action. Sensing the intensity of the emotions in the room, Uncle Blessing spread his arms wide to initiate a family hug. Eventually, Tundé and his mum reciprocated.

Later that day, the family were paid a visit by two Metropolitan Police officers, who were there to officially announce the death of Auntie Abi and inform them of the investigations due to take place. In Tundé's mind, though, it was pointless.

There's nothing to investigate, they might as well cuff me here and now.

"Initial forensic examinations of the deceased," the leading policewoman said gravely, "suggest that the cause of death is asphyxiation after the consumption of contaminated food. A very unfortunate accident."

Tundé was outraged. He knew what he saw. Purple-coloured foam guzzled slowly out of his poor auntie's mouth. He fought to resist the urge to blow up.

"Are you sure?" Tundé asked in disbelief. "Cos that sounds like bullshit to me, bruv."

"Ah ah, Babatundé!" his mum pleaded. "Please, stop with the swearing!"

"Sorry, Mum. But none of that choking on food business is what killed Abs!" Tundé raised his voice as he tried to hold back his angry tears.

The policewoman looked solemnly at Tundé.

"Again, we're sorry for what your family is experiencing. We understand that these are truly tragic circumstances. But these are the outcomes of our investigation so far. We'll be in touch when we hear more information from the forensic team or the coroners."

The two police officers excused themselves and left the flat. Tundé was still reeling. He couldn't fathom what he had just witnessed over the past

24 hours. While Uncle Blessing consoled Mrs Adeyemi, Tundé trudged to his bedroom. The distrust he had for the police had magnified.

Why would they come up here while we're still mourning and feed us absolute fucking lies? I need to figure out wagwan.

Looking at his bedside table, he saw his miCell phone lying next to the business card he received from Lizzie the journalist the previous night.

Should I call her? I don't even know if I can trust her.

Tundé stared at his phone for an ungodly amount of time. He couldn't decide whether he was in the right frame of mind. But peering over to his bed, he could foresee another, long night of mental torture.

"Hello...?"

"Hi, this is Lizzie Armen from *Popular in Poplar*. Speaking?"

"Yo, it's Tundé. The boy from last night."

"Oh, hey Tundé, how are you getting on? Again, I'm truly sorry about your auntie."

"Thank you, it's cool," Tundé sniffled as he tried to push away the pain. "Listen, I wanna meet up with you soon and understand what you were speaking about last night."

"Oh, so soon? Are you sure you're comfortable with that?"

"Yeah, I think so. The feds came to my yard earlier, chatting shit about what happened to my auntie. They said that she choked on some food. Bunch of fucking liars."

"Hmm, that does seem quite odd."

"I just don't believe that happened. I know deep down there's more to this story. I wanna know why they would lie like that."

Tundé was cautious to remain vague about what he knew, as he didn't fully trust this journalist yet.

"Yes, of course... I understand," Lizzie could only give a non-committal response.

"That's my fucking auntie, you know!" Tundé raged passionately down the phone.

A click registered in his brain, responding to the frustration and shock that had just reached a boiling point. Inspecting his left arm, Tundé noticed his skin was shedding again. While he was no stranger to the bizarre things his body was capable of, it still startled him. Tundé took a deep breath for a few seconds to calm himself down.

If I don't get a handle on my stress, the animal psyches will take over again!

"Aww, don't worry, Tundé," Lizzie responded softly to the heavy breathing. "I'm going to do my best to help you."

Tundé continued taking deep breaths, feeling his mind and body gradually relax. The skin-shedding process was brought to a steady halt.

"Let's meet at that Roasters Café in Poplar," Lizzie continued. "Let's say 6 p.m. tomorrow?"

"To do what?"

"I want to show you some of my investigative work. And how using this information, we can get justice for you, your family and my friend. Hopefully."

Tundé's curiosity was piqued. "Alright then, 6 should be calm."

"Sorry, what do you mean?"

"See you tomorrow at 6, init."

The next evening, Tundé was wrestling with nervousness when he arrived at Roasters Café and walked towards the entrance.

I'm not sure what to expect here. Can I really trust this random ting?

But he needed answers after witnessing first-hand how the police tried to cover up the cause of Auntie Abi's death. The customary bell on the café door signalled Tundé's arrival as he walked in. He realised quite quickly that this was, in fact, a very old-school East End coffee shop; a common hangout for the working class, white English residents of the area—which consisted of those who had lived in Poplar for generations, and those forcibly relocated here after *The Council Care Act 2015*. As such, the energy in the establishment was less than welcoming.

Rah, I didn't expect this to be one of dem 'we hate foreigners' spots. Oh well, these pussies can't do shit to me.

"Hey, over here," Lizzie waved at Tundé. She was sitting at a table by the window to Tundé's left, away from most of the punters inside. Tundé walked over cautiously and sat down opposite her.

"Yo, how you doing?"

"Good, and you?"

"I'm calm, init."

Lizzie paused as she observed Tundé's body language. "You don't seem it. You look rather uncomfortable, actually."

"Nah, it's just this ain't the friendliest place for people who look like me to come to," Tundé gestured around the café, receiving a few unpleasant stares from the regulars in return.

"Oh, I'm sorry," Lizzie said realising what she had been oblivious to. "We can go somewhere else if you want?"

Tundé examined his hands and then sized up the punters. "You know what? I'll be good. I can handle myself."

"Okay, as long as you're sure. By the way, I just ordered a macchiato. Did you want anything?"

"Erm, I'm good for now," Tundé didn't want to order any drinks here, especially with a woman he was still uncertain about. "Anyway, let's hear what you've gotta say then."

"Well then, where would *you* like to start, Tundé?"

"Ite, boom. So, the pigs rocked up to my yard gassing about some random munch blocking up Auntie Abi's airwaves. And I know dem man are snakes so..."

"Erm, sorry? I don't really understand," Lizzie was mystified as she scrunched up her face.

"Oh, yeah. Lemme start again. So, the police came to my house, with a bullshit excuse that my auntie choked on some food. Now, I know they're not to be trusted."

"Okay, I get you now," Lizzie nervously laughed. "Well, I have to say it's hard for me to disagree with you, especially with some of the events I've witnessed recently."

"Why's that?"

"Well, to give you some context," Lizzie said with a hushed voice as she leaned closer to Tundé. "My former manager, Annabel Campbell, was a Head Journalist at PiP for three years. She was very forward-thinking with her journalism and wanted to change the narrative of the newspaper. A lot of her work was geared towards highlighting the impact that government policies—like *The Council Care Act 2015* for example—had on the everyday lives of the diverse Tower Hamlets community. Initially, our senior stakeholders were resistant to her style. However, when she presented a compelling business case for how her approach had increased advertising sales with her previous establishments, they gradually gave her more freedom."

Lizzie stared out of the window sorrowfully as she rubbed the corner of her teary eyelid. "God bless her soul."

"Wait, your old manager's dead?" Tundé was taken aback.

"Unfortunately, tragically, yes. A few months ago, she was doing classified research on the Department of Health's database, when she stumbled upon a report about a series of experiments called 'Materials of Concern'. One of the standout compounds was called Odabozite Trioxide. It was cultivated from a specific Nigerian seaweed by so-called witch doctors."

Tundé was careful to maintain a neutral expression.

Rah, so they know about the seaweed that Uncle used to heal me already...

"Okay, sounds interesting," he said nonchalantly.

"It's also documented that several unnamed Department of Health officials made regular visits to the West African region, in search of new materials that could be used for medical purposes. During one of their routine trips a few years ago, the officials were informed about the Odabozite Trioxide by the political leaders of a place called Kuroko, located near the Niger River. Their notes claim that the substance was understood to have unimaginable, enhancing effects on the human beings who consumed it."

Tundé couldn't stop himself from leaning forward with curiosity. Lizzie's words were touching too close to home.

"Alright, so what does that mean?"

"Well, once the Department of Health located a small batch of the Odabozite Trioxide for testing—which is found in scarce quantities along the bank of the Niger River—they used it to conduct experiments on standard lab rats. Their findings showed that half an hour after consumption, the rats moved ten times quicker, processed information to solve problems ten times faster and their muscle mass increased by ten times. These developments would seemingly occur with no distinct side effects."

"One macchiato," interrupted the Roasters Café barista, as she placed the drink in front of Lizzie.

"Thank you. You sure you don't want anything, Tundé?"

"Yeah, I'm good," Tundé waved his arms to decline, waiting for the barista to get out of earshot. "So, you were chatting about the experiments?"

"Right, so they *thought* there were no side effects from their initial testing. But after frequent, long-term experiments, the research teams soon discovered that there was a 95% chance that the Odabozite Trioxide slowly degenerated the rats' bodies, causing their internal organs to gradually shrink and enlarge at severe magnitudes, hampering internal body processes until it ultimately... you know..."

"Kills you."

"Yes, exactly. The report claims that this is due to the existence of three, unbonded molecule ends in the compound's structure. They eventually become volatile and rupture the host's DNA."

"Wow."

Tundé then recalled his uncle explaining that his family's lineage had been blessed by Oduduwa with DNA that prevented the breakdown of his body, and in fact, gave him the capacity to use the chemical compound as the foundation for his superpowers.

And the three animal body parts might be the key to those unbonded ends. That's mad.

"What's interesting though is that The Department of Health, while struggling to understand how to prevent this volatility, still chose to invest significant resources into the best methods for processing the seaweed into a powder substance, dating back to 2019."

"Since 2019?" Tundé was shocked at how long ago it was.

"Yes. And this, essentially, led to the formation of the street drug known as bairaff."

Tundé stared at her silently in disbelief. It should have been obvious to him how connected the Yorùbá chemical compound and the drug that he helped distribute were. His guilt intensified.

"So, that's what killed my auntie?"

Lizzie nodded regretfully. "I'm sorry, it's so unfortunate. And I'm afraid to say, the situation could become even more precarious."

Tundé screwed his face up. "What do you mean, Lizzie? How could it be any worse than this?"

"Well, Anna, my mentor, eventually hacked into the Department of Health's security portal, where the most classified documentation for overseas activities is kept. She found an agreement for several PILA 395 underwater digging excavators to be delivered to Lokoja, Nigeria dated in 2024. This coincided with a census on the number of CCA residents a few months prior. When she dug further, Anna found documents revealing that large sums of money were exchanged between the Traditionalist Party, the Strive Party, a few large multinational corporations and some high-net-worth individuals. The most notable payment was made by the TP to an international shipping company in late 2026."

Wait, did she just call her old manager Anna? I swear that was the name of the woman I saved from those thugs in Millwall Park.

While Lizzie took a sip of her macchiato, Tundé asked for clarification.

"Is Anna the name of your old manager, by the way?"

"Yes, that's her name. Why do you ask?"

"Oh, just checking cos you called her something different earlier. But what were you saying before?"

"Yeah, her full name was Annabel. Regardless, being the great journalist she was, Anna worked on putting the puzzle together for why the government would invest substantial sums into the procurement of Odabozite Trioxide when a solution for its side effects hadn't been created yet. That was until one of her informants shared underground stories about families like yours across the city who had lost loved ones to bairaff overdoses, only for the cause of death to be assigned to other circumstances."

Lizzie took another sip of her macchiato before proceeding. "With all the evidence she had gathered, Anna concluded that there was a deliberate attempt by the government to carry out a full-scale genocide, using bairaff as its main tool."

Tundé was wide-eyed with astonishment.

"So, they want to kill everyone?" Tundé had notably increased his volume, triggering the other punters in Roasters Café to stare at him and Lizzie questionably.

"Are they trying to kill everyone?" Tundé whispered more silently. Lizzie sighed.

"Well, not exactly. The Council Care Act was a significant turning point for the government because it allowed them to gather a larger number of citizens that they deemed 'undesirable' into the same areas. It makes it easier to exterminate them. All while being viewed as a responsible project in the eyes of the general public."

Tundé clenched his fist, incensed that his own flesh and blood could fall victim to such a dehumanising agenda. And that despite all his superpowers, he was helpless to save her from it. While the government's malicious behaviour wasn't entirely surprising, he was more unsettled by the lack of awareness about an operation this grand.

"These crazy, drugged-up dons always run around my ends screaming 'they're trying to kill us' and I always air them. Maybe they're more clued up than the rest of us!"

Lizzie laughed mutedly. "Perhaps they are."

"But for real though, why don't more people know about this? Isn't there a way to get the word out?"

"That's exactly what Anna and I were collaborating on actually," Lizzie explained dejectedly. "She was putting together a landmark piece that would expose this genocidal plan, and probably send our newspaper into the stratosphere internationally. It was scheduled to be released in a few weeks, but..."

Lizzie's eyes began filling with tears. She slowly wiped them away, as she took a moment to process her emotions. Tundé offered a compassionate expression.

"I feel so guilty," Lizzie echoed his internal dialogue, making him feel worse. "Anna was adamant to remain the only person with access to the classified servers so that no one else was at risk. She eventually received threatening messages about the ramifications of whistleblowing."

Lizzie took a large gulp of her macchiato.

"About a month ago, Anna's paranoia grew as unusual people began tailing her from outside the office. It got so bad that one evening, a gang of men ambushed her after she worked a late shift. Somewhere on the Isle of Dogs. They wanted to torture her so severely that she would be too traumatised to continue investigating. Luckily, a brave man intervened and saved her, just before I picked her up in my car. That was mental."

So it WAS the same Anna that I saved! This is insane, what are the chances?

"Rah, that's mad."

Maybe if I used that same energy to save Auntie Abi, she'd still be here...

"Yeah, it was mad. Unfortunately, on the morning of April 16th, I received a phone call from a major PiP shareholder informing me that Anna was in a fatal car accident. Just before she was due to visit her grandmother in Barbados. Allegedly, there was an engine failure. Even though Anna's car was serviced by a top-rated London repair service three months prior. She was an excellent journalist, a great mentor and a close friend. And then snap. Gone, just like that."

Tundé was sombre. He watched the traffic slowly build up outside the window, with a great sadness weighing on his chest. He took a deep breath.

"I hate that I'm saying this, but I know the feeling. Be real with me, though. Is there any way this genocide can be stopped?"

"Right now? I don't know how it can be stopped, to be honest. Rumours spread in the industry that Anna was playing with fire. After hearing what happened to her, most journalists are terrified of continuing her efforts. The social media companies are also complicit, using advanced AI tech to shut down anyone sharing this information on their platforms."

"So, why the fuck are you telling *me* all this then?" Tundé projected his feelings of helplessness onto Lizzie.

"Because *I* still feel compelled to get this shit out there. I believe in honest, raw journalism, and I'm not going to let some fat cats upstairs prevent the truth from getting out there when people are DYING. Especially people that I care about!"

Tundé was amazed. He didn't expect such a gutsy response from her.

"I feel you, Lizzie. But I still don't get why you explained all this to me now."

"After the tragedy that struck your family, I did some research of my own. An informant told me that you're well acquainted with a family that is connected to a suspected criminal kingpin."

Tundé was dumbfounded. He didn't know what to say, but he didn't want to give her any confirmation either. His ultimate secret could be on the line. He tried to give off a confused expression.

"Your silence is admirable. That's how I know they can trust you, and that I can trust you too."

Tundé remained unmoved. Lizzie smirked wryly as she reached into her bag to fetch a small, grey item, holding it before him.

"I'm taking a big risk here. This contains access to confidential files that provide context on the current situation. People with powerful networks away from the mainstream—like a criminal kingpin—might have more scope to spread this information. Because who knows where the government will draw the line on human cleansing if they are successful."

She carefully placed the item in Tundé's hands. "Make sure you disconnect from the internet completely before you ever open anything on this USB stick."

Tundé held it with uncertainty. "How would I even use this thing? I've never seen anything like it before."

"Oh dear, you Gen Alphs are so funny! Just use Showall to search for how to use a USB."

Tundé kissed his teeth petulantly as he put the crucial item into his trouser pocket.

"I'll see what I can do with this," Tundé said as he rose from his seat. "No promises though. Man's only a teenager, after all."

Lizzie smiled. "I trust that you'll do your best."

"Alright, thanks for the chat. Catch you in a bit."

Tundé nodded farewell to Lizzie and headed for the café exit, paying little mind to the punters glaring at him on his way out.

Fuck me, I don't even know where to start. But I have to find a way. For Auntie Abi. And for the rest of us...

Chapter 29

"EHEN, IT'S DI OGA, man!"

"Yo, Remi, what are you saying?" Tundé was surprised to bump into his best friend on the way home from Roasters Café.

"Rah, man like Tunds!" said the other boy who accompanied Remi.

"Oh, Dom, what's up man?" Tundé said with a hint of reluctance. He didn't have the bandwidth to deal with their over-the-top acquaintance.

"What's this Oga ting mean anyway, my g's dem?" Dom continued, much to Tundé's annoyance. "We got *kumpel* in Polish slang. It means buddy, but that's all I know, still."

"That sounds like something you'd call your ting!" Remi laughed. "Tunds, tell my man what Oga means."

Tundé barely acknowledged either of them. His eyes were clouded with thoughts. Remi sensed that he was troubled.

"So, it's basically the Yorùbá way of calling someone a boss, init," Remi eventually shared with Dom after the awkward silence. "Not like bossman at the corner shop, but someone running tings. Like Jerry."

"Remi, lemme chat to *you* for a bit, please," Tundé demanded, completely ignoring the cultural exchange.

"Yo, Dom, let's link up later. I need to chat to Tunds in private for a bit, init."

"Alright, I'm going yard," Dom replied as he jumped on a bike perched up against a wall nearby. "Just bell me later, or I'll link you at school. In a bit, my guys!"

"Wagwan for you, bro?" Remi asked once Dom had ridden out of earshot. "I haven't seen you at school for a couple days."

"It's hard for me to say this, but we lost Auntie Abi two nights ago," Tundé collapsed to the ground and burst into tears. Remi froze up and stared into the distance amidst Tundé's muffled crying.

"Are you being fucking serious, bro?" Remi refused to believe the news.

He knew how important Auntie Abi was in Tundé's life, and she had become somewhat of an adopted auntie for him too.

"Bro, it's all my fault," Tundé wept as he faced the ground hopelessly.

"Oh shit, you're being for real? Fuck, man. I'm so so sorry my bro."

Remi was hysterical, as tears started rolling down his face too.

"I should have known. I should have protected her."

"It's not your fault, Tunds. How could it be?"

"Fam, it looked like she was hooked on bairaff. Heavily. I should've stopped her. She overdosed. And I could've saved her if I wasn't moving this shit!"

"Ah, bro. I dunno what to say... I know you're blaming yourself, but it's still not your fault. You didn't force her to take it."

"Fuck all that, bruv. I'm responsible for pushing that shit. I feel bare fucking guilty."

"Honestly, my brother. Think about it this way. The reason you were shotting the food in the first place wasn't to dead people off. You were making P's to support your fam. You weren't tryna hurt no one."

"I guess you're right, but what about everyone else? All those disabled people? All those orphans? All those mentally ill people? Are all those people just like her? Am I destroying another family just like mine has been?"

"I dunno man. These nitties will do *anything* to get their fix. But Auntie Abi wasn't like that. Don't even compare her!"

Tundé acknowledged the words, but deep down, he wasn't convinced.

"My bad, I didn't mean to get us this emotional in public," Tundé said, conscious of the judgement they could face if they were seen crying in public.

"Don't worry about that," Remi said while using his sleeve to wipe the tears from his face. "It gets like this when it's serious shit. Death in the family is no joke, bruv."

Tundé responded solemnly. "I feel you, bro. I feel you..."

A long-winded pause ensued, giving both boys a moment to come to terms with their intense emotions.

"By the way bro, I know it might not be the best time," Remi eventually broke the silence. "But you should speak to Jerry soon. Even just to keep him updated. He's still waiting for his cut from Femz and I.C.P's deal."

Tundé was perplexed. "Really? Now? Allow it fam!"

"I know, bro. I know. But I just don't want Jerry to make life more difficult for you, especially right now. Just chat to him, please."

"Alright, fine. I'll ask Tanks to sort it out soon since he's got the P's."

"How's he taking everything?"

Tundé felt his pulse speed up.

"Erm, to be honest, his bloodline wasn't on that side of the family. And he's a bit of a madman, anyway. Some emotionless bruddah. So he's probably alright. We haven't spoken much since it happened, though."

"It's weird cos I've met most of your family, but never this don. Why is that?"

"Well, he's *really* about this street life, so he don't mingle with many people. Kinda like a masked drill rapper, except that he's actually living his truth."

The boys briefly chuckled.

"Yeah, that makes sense, bro."

"Anyway, Remz, can you drop me back to my yard? I'll just jump on the back of your BMX, init."

"I can't be arsed to be in your ends this late, Tunds," Remi said, noticing the sky as dusk began to settle.

"Come on, bruv! It's only a calm 10-minute ride away."

"Fine, fine, come we go then!"

Tundé hopped on the peg bars of Remi's back wheel and they rode off to the Samuda Estate. As the teenagers cycled down the road, a Niko car aggressively blitzed past them, almost running them over.

"Oi, watch where you're going you fucking prick!" Tundé shouted.

"Pussy'ole!" Remi yelled. "Dem Niko drivers are such pricks. It's like they're just on road to wipe us all out!"

Chapter 30

THE NIKO CONTINUED DRIVING en route to Limehouse. The car was matte black, with a shiny body and fully tinted windows. The diamond-encrusted logo protruding from the bonnet added to its prestige. A conversation was afoot in the vehicle.

"Yes, Russell, I understand matters have been unsettling recently. But we've addressed the issues and we're moving forward with astuteness. We would appreciate your patience in allowing us to execute the plan effectively."

"I told you before, Chris. The DSU stakeholders expected the completion of the final phase before May. Any delays are going to put *all directors* under intense scrutiny. So, spare me the bullshit. Are we going to finish by then or not?"

"I can assure you that because of the unforeseen circumstances, we will complete the project within four weeks of the ideal date, taking us to the end of May at worst."

"That's far from ideal. But I guess that's where your project leadership has brought us. Anyway, we also need to discuss the validity of Michael's exterminat–"

"Listen, Russell, we're arriving at an important meeting for Project Pareto. Let's reconvene later. Goodbye."

After hanging up the phone, Chris glanced to his right at Steve, who was steering the Niko.

"That sounded intense, boss."

"Honestly," Chris was seething. "I look forward to the day that I dethrone that overbearing prick as Director-General. It will be a moment to savour."

The car eventually arrived at Blount Street, a quiet side road in Limehouse, and parked just behind a white Cyrellis car in front of an abandoned retail unit. When Chris slipped out of the Niko car, the driver of the Cyrellis became extremely agitated, like a defendant preparing for their criminal court hearing. Chris jumped into the back seat of the Cyrellis.

"Hello, Red Rob. How are things?"

"Alright, Chris?" said Rob, who had dark red hair and a pinkish face, like it had been exposed to the sun for an unhealthy amount of time. "Hope you're comfortable in the back there?"

"Yes, seeing everything from this position is quite pleasant, actually," Chris laughed mockingly. "Now, I've got a lot to do today, so let's proceed. What's the update on our little East London surveillance project?"

"Well... erm... what we've seen on the streets aligns with our predictions for the strain of bairaff currently in circulation. Seven hundred and eighty-four people have died in the past two weeks, after moderate consumption of this highly addictive version. That covers this community, as well as Bethnal Green, Newham and Barking."

Rob briefly paused while readjusting his rear-view mirror, where he could see a tiny smirk emerging on Chris's face.

"What's helping the bairaff consumption increase is the belief that snorting it exclusively through one nostril gives the user unique enhancements with no downsides. In addition, our undercover forensic team citing unrelated causes of death in their autopsy reports has made it easier for us to control that narrative. And our agreements with the major publications and social media platforms to suppress leaks are still very much intact. No reputable figures outside of our influence are making the connection between bairaff and the deaths."

"Well, money and coercion go a long way I guess. But this is excellent news, Rob. I'm sure our stakeholders will be pleased to hear how smoothly things are moving. It's a useful acid test before we launch the next phase of our plan."

"Chris, I know you're vying for the top job. But are you sure you want to see Project Pareto through to completion? If the public ever discovered our secrets, this whole country could descend into chaos..."

"Robbie, I'm shocked. I thought you knew how much confidence I have in this project and the DSU's mission for national prosperity. Getting rid of the unproductive heathens while increasing our economic output by tenfold makes perfect sense to me."

"I didn't mean to doubt your confidence, my friend. I've known you for far too long. But I just think–"

"It sounds like *you* are doubting our mission, Red Rob," Chris interjected sharply. "Considering we started here together over 12 years ago, that's disappointing. But if you would rather lose all your hard work, prestige and security to show contempt for the Unit's mission, go right ahead. It would be worth it, right?"

"Come on, Chris. I'm just asking the question."

"No, you're making a statement. Let me ask you a question. Do you still want to be a DSU agent?"

Rob was stunned into silence.

"I'm going to take your silence as a confirmation that you'd like to remain an agent, Robbie. Would I be correct?"

Rob nodded meekly, barely able to look Chris in the eye through his rear-view mirror. "Sure."

"Good. Now that we're on the same page, where are we with our preparation for the next phase?"

"The governors for the London Water Council have been paid off accordingly, and we have received detailed blueprints for one of their facilities."

"Brilliant," Chris said with a tone of finality. "I will inform the procurement team of your progress. Please remain on standby for confirmation. I'll be in touch. Take care, old friend."

Chapter 31

After Remi dropped him back home, Tundé collapsed on his bed and tried to calm down his overly active mind. It constantly replayed harrowing flashbacks of his mum descending into despair when she learnt the news of her baby sister. Tundé was still processing the loss of someone so important in his life, amidst the other stresses piling up. Like the revelation that the government were plotting a genocide that would wipe out his loved ones. And he was grappling with the fact he was complicit in their agenda, ultimately devastating his family with grief.

What am I gonna do?

Feeling overwhelmed, Tundé took a deep breath. It triggered memories of his sessions with Uncle Blessing before they fell out. He recalled the elder's forewarning.

"You will realise eventually that you *need* my help."

While admitting he was wrong would crush his ego, Tundé was desperate to reconnect with Uncle Blessing and receive his valued mentorship. He picked up his miCell.

"Hello. Who is this, now?"

"Hey, Uncle. It's me, Tundé. This is my new phone, so save this number please."

"Ah, my son. How are you?"

"I'm fine... actually, no. I'm not doing great, to be honest. I guess it's probably obvious why."

"Ah, pẹ̀lẹ́ now. The mourning process is hard, especially because you are young. Even as adults, it can be very crippling. But you can only try, sha."

"Thanks, Uncks. By the way, I'm sorry about what happened the other day. I think I do actually need your help."

"Well, despite the unfortunate timing, I'm happy you finally used your brain to understand me!"

Tundé rolled his eyes as Uncle Blessing chuckled down the phone.

"So, can we catch up soon, Uncks?"

"H'of course. In fact, let us meet this evening on that Saunders Road at nine. It's very close to your house."

"Err, okay Uncks. I'll see you there."

Seeking a chance to get some air and clear his head, Tundé made the 20-minute stroll until he reached Saunders Road. It was moderately busy, as some cars and buses drove through the area, but not many pedestrians were on foot. Uncle Blessing was standing at a junction, donning a thin, grey jacket and red Yorùbá fila cap.

"Good to see you, Uncks."

"Likewise, Babatundé. How far now?"

"I'm doing alright, I guess. So, why did you want us to come out here now?"

"That's a good question. Come, follow me, jor."

Tundé trailed behind Uncle Blessing as he walked to a less visible section of the road, shadowed by the trees. After a few minutes, his uncle abruptly stopped outside what appeared to be a deserted leisure unit with two distinct shutters and a huge 'For Sale' sign hanging above.

"Oya, cover my back," Uncle Blessing instructed Tundé.

As he scanned the area for any prying eyes, the teenager could hear a few rattles and clinks in the background before peering over his shoulder. Uncle Blessing was lifting one of the shutters to reveal a door.

"Come on, let's go inside."

As they walked in, the unified smell of sweat, rusty iron and aged leather hit Tundé's nose instantly. It reminded him of his school's old sports hall. They were in a garage space containing worn-out punch bags, decrepit training mats and odd pieces of gym equipment.

"Welcome to our new training facility!" Uncle Blessing announced. "It's wonderful, abi?"

"Uncle, this place is mashed up I'm not gonna lie. Are you sure it's even healthy to train in here?"

"Of course, now! This is child's play. If you saw the places in the forest I trained in, chai!"

"How did you even find this place?"

"One person at my B&B informed me about an old garage gym that he used to train at. He was complaining that they closed two months ago to convert it into new apartments next year. So, I knew it could be a useful place for us to continue your training."

Tundé smiled with the knowledge that he was in good hands with his mentor.

"Just make sure you don't doubt me again, sha! Anyway, let's start with our first exercise."

Uncle Blessing pointed to a training mat, and Tundé obediently sat cross-legged on it. He could feel the rough, coarse surface of the mat prick through his jogging bottoms. He jittered uncomfortably as it sent a shiver down his spine.

"Follow my instructions for how long to inhale and exhale," Uncle Blessing said, gesturing to his torso. He then made a sign with his fingers, adding, "I will also introduce signals for when you should hold your breath, to improve your attention to detail, focus and emotional regulation."

Tundé studiously followed his uncle's instructions, adjusting to the signals when he received them. As they proceeded through the session, Uncle Blessing incorporated odd vocal noises, banging weight plates together and throwing foam rollers at his nephew to further test his resolve.

"You must learn to remain focused on the task at hand with additional variables. If you do not complete a cycle, we will start again until you reach a sufficient duration."

"Oh my days!" Tundé blurted out after he was splashed with water. "Surely that's too much, Uncks?"

"On the battlefield, your environment will never be nice and peaceful. It will be random, disturbing and chaotic. You must learn how to breathe effectively during these unexpected conditions to access your true power and gain an advantage against your enemies."

Despite his irritation, Tundé reflected on when he had lost control of himself in frantic battles.

"Alright Uncle, I do hear you. Let's go again."

"Ehen, we shall!"

Uncle Blessing threw everything could at his nephew. He hit his neck with an old towel, rubbed his head repeatedly and flung shoes at his body. But Tundé managed to sustain his concentration and complete the breathing cycles, not allowing himself to be unsettled.

"Okay, son, we are finished today," Uncle Blessing said proudly. "You started with some wahala, but you did very well!"

"Thanks, I guess," Tundé said with a hint of sarcasm. He felt like he was pushed to the limit, but he wasn't sure if it would help him in the long run.

"Just remember this: in the end, you can only trust yourself. I can guide you, but you have all the answers within. You just need to let them emerge, Babatundé!"

Tundé hummed in agreement as he stood to his feet. Then Uncle Blessing checked the time on his phone.

"Chai! It's almost half ten. You should go home and get some rest. I will call you on Sunday and we will discuss our training plan."

"Sounds good, Uncks. I'll chat to you then. Get home safe!"

"You too, my son. You too."

When Tundé left the training garage, instead of heading straight back to his estate, he sent a text to Jerry on the Pony Erikson brick phone:

'Tanks wants to give you the P's. Can you meet him at All Saints Yard tonight?'

Very soon, he received a reply from Jerry:

'Okay. I'm local. Can meet him there at half 11.'

After changing into his black tracksuit and hurdling over rooftops to arrive at the meeting point in Limehouse, Tundé waited impatiently in the bushes, irritated by the pricks of the leaves alongside the uncomfortably cold breeze in the air. A white Scheep soon parked in the same spot they met a few weeks prior. Jerry wound down the window marginally as the car's interior light was switched on by his familar accomplice, Yusuf, in the driver's seat.

"Yo, it's Tanks," Tundé said in his disguised deep voice as he approached the car. "What you saying?"

"Yes, bro," Jerry responded. "You got the P's for me yeah?"

Tundé zipped open his bag and pulled out the bundles of cash from the I.C.P deal.

"Here you go, bro."

After collecting the money, Jerry split off a small portion and handed it to Tundé.

"Sorry to hear about Abi by the way. Send my condolences to my young g, Tunds."

"Erm, yeah... for sure... I will do."

"But I guess the game is the game, init. And we all gotta go someday."

The truth of Jerry's words struck the teenager like a knife slicing through his heart.

"Yeah, I guess so," Tundé's voice cracked as he desperately tried to suppress his tears. "By the way, me and Tunds are gonna take a break from all this."

"Rah, swear down? But we're making bare money. Why stop now?"

"I know, I know. It's not burning me like that. But it doesn't feel right while Tunds' family are grieving, you get me?"

"I get you. But best believe, when it comes down to it, money runs this world. You're gonna be missing out big time."

"I understand. But out of respect, that's what we need to do. Tunds will holla at Remi if we wanna get back on it."

"Alright, say nothing. Keep hold of that Pony Erikson and hit me up if you man wanna jump in again."

Jerry nodded at Yusuf, who promptly started the Scheep's engine.

"In a bit, Tanks."

"Bless."

When Tundé returned home, he lay awake in bed, his thoughts racing uncontrollably. His teenage mind was still working through the life-changing events of the past few weeks. While the pain of Auntie Abi's loss weighed heavy, he was proud of himself for ending the business relationship with Jerry.

Let's hope I have enough P's to keep me and mum going while I work out what the fuck I'm gonna do from here.

One of Uncle Blessing's teachings echoed in his consciousness: "In the end, you can only trust yourself. You have all the answers."

Tundé was grateful that he had some valuable support. And that Lizzie was able to shine some light on the scale of the injustice surrounding his auntie's death.

Thank Olodumare that it's Saturday tomorrow! Gotta read into them classified files first thing.

***

When Tundé woke up the next morning, he fetched Lizzie's USB stick from his jacket. While he appreciated her willingness to trust him, he still thought it was best to remain sceptical. Checking the insertion end of the device again, Tundé chuckled to himself.

Can't believe Lizzie's using this ancient technology for serious stuff like this!

Following Lizzie's instructions, Tundé disconnected from the internet and used an adaptor to connect the USB to his computer. Accessing a folder called 'Materials of Concern Docs', he scrolled through the variety of file names related to his ancestral homeland:

'Odabozite Trioxide: Uncovering a New Frontier in Nigeria'

'The Road to Extraction: Developing Infrastructure for Sustainable Mining in Nigeria'

'From Theory to Practice: Innovations in Mineral Extraction in Nigeria'

'Exploring the Properties of Odabozite Trioxide: A Laboratory Investigation'

'Expediting Extraction: Building the Fastest Routes to Resource Transport'

Tundé's attention was caught by a file named 'Project Pareto: The West African Compound Od_2O_3'. It seemed ominous. Opening the PDF, he was presented with hundreds of pages. He tried to use the search function to find the keywords 'genocide' and 'bairaff', but the feature was restricted. He scrolled back up to the introduction of the report to see if it alluded to any crucial details:

'This comprehensive study delves into the unique properties and potential applications of the compound Od_2O_3, also known as Odabozite Trioxide. Our research aims to uncover its diverse properties, shedding light on its possible benefits and implications for various fields...'

Tundé exasperated wearily. "This is gonna be a long day, bruv!"

After a draining hour of scanning through the document, Tundé randomly registered the words 'master plan', and read from the top of the paragraph to understand its full context:

'Crucial to the success of Project Pareto's master plan, strategic distribution channels have been established, allowing seamless movement of the Odabozite Trioxide. These will be managed by a separate, state-endorsed entity. Its integration into select segments of the global network will ensure the realisation of objectives, fostering a web of interconnected entities poised for the next phase of action...'

Tundé knew that the bairaff on London's streets was probably being supplied by people connected to the government's plan. It reminded him of an iconic line from one of his favourite films.

"Infiltrate the seller. Identify the source. Boom!"

Tundé recalled the different areas in London that were hotspots for large bairaff trades, based on the conversations he heard around Jerry in the restaurant.

Camden Town, Walthamstow, Bermondsey and Wanstead, just off the top of my head. Jerry knows more, but I can't risk going through him. I'll have to work this out alone.

He realised that if he wanted to find out who the suppliers were as quickly as possible, he would need to interrogate the dealers. They were very protective of their sources in normal circumstances, let alone Tundé's agenda.

I'm gonna need to use violence to get the info out of these man. It's the only way...

Tundé paced around his room. His stomach was churning. His hands were moist with nervous sweat. Deep down, he understood the enormous risk this route posed. Fighting multiple battles while keeping his identity and family safe was not going to be easy.

But am I gonna let the government just kill off the rest of us? Or am I gonna fight?

He sighed heavily, and mentally accepted the burden.

I've been blessed with these powers, though. Like Uncks always says, Olodumare is on our side.

"You just need to let them emerge, Babatundé."

At that moment, his spiralling thoughts transformed into a burgeoning feeling of optimism. A warm sensation enveloped his body as he became aware of a spiritual presence, drawing inner strength from it. He stared out of the window at the overcast, morning sky, feeling a profound sense of power and responsibility.

"Alright. I'm gonna do this! But first, I need to make sure I'm fully prepared."

Given how much damage his black tracksuits had sustained—alongside his keenness to distance himself from the Tanks character—Tundé decided he would sport a whole new look. With more funds at his disposal, he wanted to invest in better clothing for the tough challenges ahead. Clearing his computer's cache and reconnecting to the internet, he used the Showall search engine to find an article written by *The Transit*. It described the fashion applications of a material that would be perfect for the wear & tear that came from climbing buildings, dodging weapons and knocking out goons.

'Kevlar: A synthetic fibre known for its exceptional strength, heat resistance, and durability; ideal for tracksuits used in extreme conditions for activities like motorcycling and skiing. It's tenacious, flexible and stylish!'

But Tundé couldn't find a retailer that sold Kevlar tracksuits. As he thought about a practical solution, a brain wave hit him.

Maybe I could learn how to make one.

His mum had a sewing machine and a range of different threads stored in her wardrobe. He would just have to time its usage when she was away from the flat. He loaded up a WeView video on how to make a tracksuit, explaining each step in the process and the items required. Tundé wrote a shopping list, which included the Kevlar fabric, silver zippers and some elastic cord. The pleasant, satiating smell of cooking soon entered his nostrils as his mum called out.

"Tundé! Come and eat breakfast before I go to Mama Fulham's house!"

"Yes, mum. Give me two minutes!"

While Tundé enjoyed his delicious fried yam and egg meal, his mum was headed towards the front door to leave for West London.

"This food bangs, Mum. Thanks! What time will you be back?"

"Ehn, I will be there until late. We are planning our dear Abiola's funeral. And we need to buy some tings for Mama Fulham to take Naija for me soon. So, maybe nine or ten."

Tundé shuddered as a flashback of Auntie Abi's lifeless body flickered in his memory. He quickly pushed down the guilt.

"Okay. Stay safe, Mum. I'll see you when you're back."

"Alright dear, goodbye. And God bless."

With breakfast finished and confirmation that he would be alone for the day, Tundé resumed the task of assembling his new outfit. He banked on his superhuman mind to rapidly learn how to use the sewing machine in one afternoon.

But first, he needed to buy the materials. He strode over to Masood's Materials, a fabric shop in Poplar. After rounding up all the items, Tundé was met at the counter by a very confused Mr Masood, the owner.

"Are you sure you can purchase all this, young man?"

"What? You never seen someone buying stuff for their mumsy before?" Tundé questioned the owner's judgement. "How much for it all anyway?"

"I give you good price. £130."

"Let's do £85, or I walk out the door."

"No, I can't do this one."

"Fine, I'm gonna leave."

As soon as the shop door creaked open, Mr Masood called out.

"Okay, okay. I'll give you for £110."

"£85, or I'll keep walking."

"Fine, fine, let's do £95."

Mr Masood was instantly met with a wad of cash from Tundé. He bagged up all the items for the teenager, who then headed for the exit. He was jubilant.

Watching man like Jerry negotiate has defo helped!

Walking back through the Canary Wharf Shops, Tundé took a quick pitstop at Crephouse to purchase a sturdy pair of black Ralisad running trainers. Since he needed more items, he decided to walk back through the Isle of Dogs market. Thick smoke from fried food hung in the air as he approached its various stalls. There was an energetic shift from the hustle and bustle of numerous people buzzing around, while the smell of raw meat and fish wafted into his nasal passage. His ears were bombarded with constant shouts from different merchants desperate to capture attention and make a sale.

"Four pound fish! Four pound fish, I say! I say, four pound fish!"

"Six peppers, three pounds! Six peppers, three pounds!"

"Two T-shirts for a seven quid! Get 'em 'ere now!"

The teenager browsed around until he eventually stopped at a particular stall run by an old, Cockney bloke named Neil. His stall contained a few interesting items. Namely, a leather balaclava with a camouflaged, breathable mesh over the mouth region. Neil had been a seller at the market for decades and was known for his very affordable items. But Tundé rarely bought from him for a reason.

"I dunno why *you* need the mask. No offence mate, but you lot all look the same to me," Neil uttered casually.

"Yeah, yeah, yeah," Tundé said angrily, throwing his money on the ground for Neil to pick up. "Just give me the fucking mask, you old racist bastard!"

When he got home, Tundé rummaged through his mum's wardrobe. The old sewing machine had a rusted black finish and intricate gold scrollwork. Its thick needle looked capable of piercing anything, and a small drawer on the side held bobbins and other small parts. Despite its age, it had a reassuring weight and seemed ready for many more years of usage. Tundé placed the equipment on his bedroom desk while playing sewing videos on WeView at the same time. With his exceptional learning speed, he quickly grasped how to cut the fabric and sew it together. He made some mistakes implementing the zippers, but undeterred, Tundé kept at it, eventually correcting them. Within a few hours, his homemade black Kevlar suit was complete. It wasn't perfect, but it was functional and stylish enough that he was proud to wear it. He tried on his creation in front of the mirror.

"Yooo, this looks cold. I feel like that yute from Queens!"

Tundé put the leather balaclava on to complete the outfit.

Feels like it might be missing something though.

Hit by a surge of inspiration, Tundé fetched the bespoke Adeyemi handkerchief from his backpack. He experimented by placing it on different parts of the mask to see how it looked. Then, he spent a few minutes carefully stitching the yellow and burgundy patterned Aso Oke material onto its forehead area. After completing the final stitch, Tundé slipped the balaclava back on and stood before his reflection.

"Bruv... this look is soooo certi!"

Tundé undressed and stuffed his new outfit into his backpack, wary in case his mum found it lying around and pressed him for answers.

Now, the hard work really starts. I just pray things don't get ugly.

Before embarking on the first step of his monumental mission, Tundé was excited to take his new outfit for a spin around the city. Just as he reached the Equiano House ground floor, Uncle Blessing was pressing on the buzzer outside.

"Good evening, Uncle," Tundé said, as he opened the main door. "What are you doing here now?"

"Kàálẹ́[1] . Your mother asked me to check on you and make sure everything is okay."

"Oh, I'm fine. I've just spent today studying. Gonna go for a walk now, then I might link Remi later."

Uncle Blessing nodded as he acknowledged his nephew's words.

"Uncle, can I ask a favour of you please?"

"Of course, son. What's bothering you, sha?"

Tundé walked Uncle Blessing into the ground floor hallway, lowering his voice to a whisper so he couldn't be heard.

1. Good evening

"I need you to promise me that you can move yourself and Mum as far away from London as possible if anything dangerous or unusual goes down."

"Okay. Why? And what about you?"

"Don't worry. I'll be calm and I can take care of myself. Just promise me you'll do that if things pop off?"

"Tundé, remember, you would be dead without all my guidance, abi? Tell me what's going on!"

"I appreciate that you've been helping me. But I need to sort this out on my own. I just need you to trust me."

"Listen, if this is about Abiola, please don't put such extravagant pressure on yourself. You couldn't have done anything, sha."

"I fucking could have!" Tundé burst out, tears immediately running down his cheeks. He tried to compose himself. "Sorry. I… I could have. And I… I can. I'm gonna make it right, best believe me."

"I believe your intentions, but you must be careful, o. You're not even close to completing your training! And there's still the matter of Naija to discuss, too."

Tundé was struck with terror, recalling his uncle's tales about demons and destiny.

"I thought we still had time before I had to face ALL dem tings you mentioned?"

"We *might* have time. The Orishas are the only entities that truly know when and what will happen in this Universe. So, we need to be prepared."

"Please, let me sort this out first. Then we can talk about Naij later. Just promise you'll get Mum out of here if things get mad?"

"Okay, fine. I will. But you can't keep doing this your galavanting business. Yorùbáland beckons. And we need to protect our people.

Please, don't do anything too dangerous here. You need to save it for what's likely to come."

"Thank you, Uncle. We'll chat about Naija soon, for sure," Tundé said as he walked out of the door. "Catch you in a bit."

Chapter 32

Dusk fell upon London as the sun descended towards the horizon. The subtle breeze and peaceful sound of water gushing made Tundé introspect, as he walked along a pathway by the River Thames.

I'm crazy for thinking I can stop an entire country's plan. I'm just a yute from East! But I can't just sit on the sidelines with all these powers.

He soon arrived on a quiet, residential street with a public booth near a small park. It was a few minutes away from the main Canary Wharf district. In the distance, the lights from the City Loft apartments flickered on as Tundé entered the booth. He grabbed the new costume from his backpack and changed into it. He stepped out with a swagger.

"Ah, One Canada Square!" Tundé uttered to himself, in awe of the towering building.

I've always wanted to see London from the top since I was a kid. I should probably do it now before life gets even more chaotic.

Once he was close by, Tundé climbed up a tall tree to camouflage himself behind its leaves and used his enhanced vision to monitor One Canada Square's security team. There were eight guards and several cameras dotted around the landmark building. After surveying the scene, he noticed the guards moved in four pairs across each designated flank. At each three-minute interval, two pairs would cross paths at the northwest and southeast corners for a few seconds. It was enough time for Tundé to dash to the unmanned southwest corner and climb up from there. Once the security guards were distracted, he darted towards the open southwest corner. Reaching the base of One Canada Square, he gazed at its coveted pinnacle.

That's beautiful. Just beautiful.

Tundé started climbing the stainless-steel skyscraper. The increasing severity of the winds could be felt with each movement as he surged up the building's facade. But he was determined to reach his prize, not allowing the random thrusts to take him off course. While sticking his right palm down on yet another large windowpane, Tundé realised that the panelling above him was coming to an end.

I'm bare close now! But I think there's a platform just over the edge before I can get to the very top.

One Canada Square was an elongated rectangle for most of its 50-storey structure. At the very top, it transformed into a striking pyramid shape, featuring a shining light at its apex that flashed periodically and captivated the entire city with its brilliance. Tundé hopped over the last glass panel and onto the platform, which spanned all four sides of the building. He wasted no time, racing up the pyramid-like roof as if he were back on the Tophall Primary School playground.

"WOO!"

The feeling was exhilarating. Even with the bustling winds drawing water from his eyes and impairing his visibility, he could still make out the flashing light at the summit that drew him closer. Once the teenager reached the top, he slowly swivelled onto his back and placed his feet firmly on the slope, enabling him to stick to the surface and maintain his balance. He wiped his eyes clean. He was blown away.

"Wow."

For a moment, time stood still. All the thoughts and worries swirling around in his mind came to a halt. The sun setting below the horizon gave the sky a beautiful orange tint, with patches of ensuing darkness as the evening approached. The moon made a faint appearance too. The distinct beauty of the lights shining from different areas of London caught his attention. From the buildings of Canary Wharf close by, to the skyline of the City by the River Thames, and in the distance, the glitz and glamour of the West End. Although Tundé was very familiar with these places, seeing them from this new perspective added another dimension to the experience.

"I can't believe it. I *actually* made it here."

Were his face projectable, Tundé's glowing smile would radiate to the entire city. He marvelled at the breathtaking views. He was blissful, centred and at peace as he soaked up the ambience.

"It would be live to bring gyal up here one day, you know!"

Without warning, a huge gust of wind blew in his direction, knocking him off balance and out of his euphoric state. Tundé panicked while regaining his stability.

Woah! That's probably a sign to get moving soon. I've got important shit to figure out, anyway.

The night sky enveloped London further, with several stars piercing through the polluted air to make an appearance for the city's residents. Gazing at the landscape, Tundé adjusted his superhuman eyesight to the east, where he could easily spot the big Wiley's Supermarket in Plaistow and the old Olympic Park in Stratford. He aimlessly scanned across the city, moving his attention to the South Bank, where Tower Bridge came into view. While the monument looked incredible from this viewpoint, it spurred a thought in Tundé's mind.

I remember when Jerry drove us up that way one time. He mentioned that the Bermondsey Boyz base was close to it.

The Bermondsey Boyz were a gang notorious for selling tonnes of cocaine and heroin in South London, and they had been established in various iterations since the early 1960s. From Tundé's memory, Jerry didn't have any business ties with them, and their clientele was mainly the corporate executives working in The City and London Bridge.

Maybe I could sniff around for some leads there.

Out of the blue, his ears picked up some commotion from the platform below.

"The CCTV team said he climbed to the top."

It sounded like a security guard.

"The only way from up here is down," said another security guard. "The cameras didn't catch him going back. That means he's still close by."

The end of that sentence coincided with a resounding click. There was no confusion in Tundé's mind about what the sound was. He peered down anxiously, grasping how far down the ground was.

I need to get the fuck outta here. Now. These man are strapped!

Tundé hurriedly climbed down, avoiding the side of the platform where he heard the guards. Once he reached the platform, still 45 storeys above ground, Tundé nervously leaned over the edge.

Fam, it's a lot easier to climb up than it is to rush down...

"He's got to be round 'ere, I'm telling you."

"Be ready to shoot if he is!"

The voices, alongside the footsteps, were getting closer. Tundé knew he had to move quickly since the security guards seemed hungry for action. He climbed over the platform's metal railing, sticking his hands and feet to the glass panels. He scurried down against the aggravating winds, eager to escape. Just over halfway, Tundé noticed hordes of people in high-vis jackets on the ground, forming a perimeter around One Canada Square.

Fuck me! I can't be arsed to fight all these man now. Is there another way out?

"Man in black. You have illegally trespassed on this building. Please prepare to surrender yourself to the authorities!"

The blaring call from the megaphone below raised the teenager's sense of urgency. Glancing around quickly, Tundé calculated his chances of successfully landing on the roof of a nearby, smaller building. If he could gather enough momentum, it was possible. Positioning his feet firmly onto the surface, he released his hands so he stood at a 90-degree angle to the building. Facing the ground directly, he lifted his feet a few centimetres from the glass panels and began descending rapidly towards the ground. A second later, Tundé put his toes against the surface of One Canada Square to slide down at an extreme pace. He extended his right hand to maintain his balance and steer himself downward like a skateboarder.

"WOOO!"

Tundé's adrenaline pumped fiercely, and the oppressive air resistance smacked against his face through the balaclava. As he plummeted, Tundé knew he needed to time this right.

"Everyone on the ground, brace yourselves!" the warning from the megaphone boomed.

Gotta jump in three, two, one...

In that instant, Tundé bent his knees to generate force, using his legs to thrust himself off the building and powerfully into the air.

"Oh my fucking god, he's gonna die!" yelled one of the security personnel below, her voice filled with disbelief as she and dozens of her colleagues gawked at Tundé's silhouette leap through the night sky.

But with a combination of luck and skill, Tundé landed in a heap on the nearby building rooftop, scraping against the rough surface. Miraculously, his new Kevlar suit remained pretty unscathed. Underneath his mask, Tundé was ecstatic, raising his arms to the sky gratefully.

"Man's really about this parkour ting! Thank you to the ancestors!"

After revelling in the bewilderment of security guards, Tundé proceeded to hop from rooftop to rooftop, with Tower Bridge locked in his sights. Arriving twenty minutes later, Tundé gracefully navigated the bridge's blue beams, enjoying his newfound athletic prowess. He sprinted across them with blistering speed to generate momentum and execute thrilling acrobatic moves.

"JHEEEEZE! This is so liiiive!"

Tundé was roaring with excitement as he front-flipped onto the next beam. While the moonlight shone brightly upon Tower Bridge, his incredible stunts captured the attention of astonished tourists lounging around and befuddled passengers on the riverboats.

"Look, Dad! Look! Up there!"

"Who's doing those crazy stunts?"

"I've never seen anything like it!"

With the furore escalating below, Tundé didn't want to risk attracting more attention. In a matter of moments, he vaulted onto the skyscrapers and high-rise commercial buildings nearby, gradually distancing himself from the growing public frenzy back at Tower Bridge. Soon, he found himself in a quieter residential area perched on top of a tower block.

Ahead of him, the shiny glass exterior of the Shard shone magnificently in the backdrop above the dull estate.

Man's not here to sightsee though.

Scanning the area to work out where he was, Tundé found a sign confirming his location:

The St Saviours Estate — owned & operated by the London Borough of Southwark, C.C.A. division

Ite boom, so I'm in Bermondsey now then.

The streets of Bermondsey were bleak and near lifeless—bar the vermin running through the shadowed bushes and trees. The only substantial light came from the moon and a few dim street lamps. Countless England flags were plastered over the railings of the tower block. It was no surprise since it was a predominantly white, working-class, nationalist area. But Tundé felt uneasy, nonetheless. The demographic differences meant there was much less police surveillance than in other districts, despite the well-known organised crime in the area.

Could work in my favour tonight, though.

Perusing around for signs of a Bermondsey Boyz base, Tundé spotted a courtyard nearby. It was surrounded by residential buildings on three sides, with the open side serving as an entrance from the main road.

Looks like a focal point for the residents here. And maybe the local gang members too. I should check it out.

Eager to avoid getting blindsided, Tundé zoomed in to carefully check for threats. Something in the courtyard piqued his interest. Freshly discarded butts were littered all over the grounds, with minuscule drops of purple powder around them.

Bairaff. I need to see wagwan.

He climbed down from the tower block and stealthily crept towards the courtyard. As he entered, Tundé detected a nanoscopic trail of bairaff powder on the ground, stemming from the butts. He picked one up and sniffed it. The smell of cannabis stung his nostrils. To his knowledge, the homeless drug addicts preferred hard drugs that plunged them into mental oblivion. It was primarily the drug dealers who smoked marijuana instead. And in this estate, that was likely to be a Bermondsey Boy.

Tundé followed the bairaff trail. It took him to West House—one of the blocks bounding the courtyard. He tested the handle of the main door. It was unlocked. He slowly walked in and caught the trail again, leading to the building's lift. The doors were unexpectedly ajar. Inside, it was grimy and unkempt, with a distinct stench of urine. Tundé tentatively walked in, on the lookout for more clues.

Bingo!

He spotted traces of bairaff on the lift button labelled '7'. He cautiously reached his hand out to press the button. The lift jerked violently in response, catching him off guard and making him hyper-alert. He kissed his teeth as the lift sluggishly rose upwards.

I fucking hate council lifts man! Why are they always so booky?

Masked below Tundé's sass was a jittery bundle of nerves, though. He intuitively thought he was following the right path. But perhaps it was a dangerous one. The tension was mounting. Suddenly, the lift came to an abrupt, clanging stop. Tundé watched the doors slide open at an excruciatingly slow rate. Sweat dripped from his forehead and collected under his mask, sticking it to his skin.

I'm not sure what's about to happen here...

Tundé hesitantly poked his head out. He breathed a short sigh of relief. Nothing jumped out. The landing was clear. The lift was placed midway between the residents' flats lined along the seventh floor. The communal passageway resembled the classic brutalist design of concrete and steel found in traditional council buildings. Spotting the continuation of the bairaff trail on the floor, Tundé warily followed it down the passageway until he reached the second to last home on the floor. It had a dark grey door bearing the number 726.

Would it be moist if I just knocked?

Tundé inspected it further, unsure whether to be polite or enter unprompted.

"Oi, put yer 'ands up, ya fackin' cunt!"

The man pressed a cold, hard object into the back of Tundé's head. At gunpoint, Tundé chose to comply and raise his arms—for now. Then another man swiftly flung open the front door for 726.

"Get this fucker in now, Gaz!" he barked.

"Go on, you 'eard Tony," Gaz demanded as he nudged Tundé with his pistol. "Get moving!"

At least I know I'm in the right place now.

As they stepped into the squalid flat, Tundé activated his night vision. The living room was devoid of much furniture and had a foul stench synonymous with somewhere that housed criminal activity. Tundé assessed the presence of five different threats; two carried guns—including Gaz, Tony held a baseball bat and the other two men wielded large knives. Not too long ago, this predicament would have terrified him. But now, Tundé's anxiety was overshadowed by his sheer confidence.

"You tryna mess with the Bermondsey Boyz, mate?" Gaz antagonised Tundé, pressing the pistol firmly against his temple. "You're 'aving a bubble! Bet you're a fackin' darkie too, ain't ya?"

That ignited Tundé with a fiery rage. He knew these were the type of people who gave families like his unwarranted grief over the decades. Keeping his arms raised, the teenager laughed darkly.

"Oh, like that? Now I'm *really* gonna enjoy this."

"Who does this cheeky cunt fink he is?" raged one of Bermondsey Boyz armed with a knife.

"Any last words before I blast your 'ead off, you bastard?" Gaz asked while pushing the gun against Tundé's head.

"Hmm. I wanna say... suck your mum!"

A fraction of a second before Gaz pulled the trigger, Tundé grabbed his arm from behind. It redirected the bullet into the window, smashing the glass loudly. Then Tundé swivelled, rising with his knee to snap Gaz's arm in half, and subsequently punched him to the floor.

"Actually, suck *all* your mums! Who wants it next?"

"Shoot him! Shoot him!" Tony demanded.

Tundé picked up Gaz's gun and dashed it emphatically onto the second gunman's temple, rendering him unconscious. When the two knife-wielding Bermondsey Boyz stormed at him, Tundé dodged both attacks gracefully, proceeding to disarm the men with a skilful one-two kick combination.

"Come on! I thought you English lads only used your fists to fight?" Tundé taunted them.

"Get him!" Tony shouted.

Tundé dished out a roundhouse kick that shattered the cheekbones of the first guy. Then, as the next lad swung his fist, Tundé ducked it effortlessly and unleashed a crushing punch into his chest, hurtling him into the wall with tremendous force. Tony shook like a leaf holding his baseball bat as he stared at Tundé in disbelief. The atmosphere in the room had changed drastically within a matter of seconds. There was blood, broken weapons and unconscious bodies scattered all over.

"Who the fuck *are* you?" Tony asked fearfully, backing into a corner as Tundé closed in on him.

"Well, I'm *definitely* not a cheeky cunt like you, Tony. Call me..."

Tundé coincidentally remembered his conversation with Remi the previous day.

"Call me... Ogaman."

"Well, fuck off, you ogre prick," Tony snarled as he shakily held the baseball bat. "I ain't givin' you shit!"

"Oh, so you *do* have something I want then?" Ogaman said glowingly. "The yute doth protest too much!"

"Fuck you!" Tony bellowed as he took a swing.

Ogaman punched through the bat, breaking it in half. He then dropped to the floor and swiped at Tony's legs, jumping onto the Bermondsey Boy as he fell. Ogaman wrapped his legs around Tony's body like a jiu-jitsu professional and trapped him in a tight, choking headlock with his arms.

"Listen to me now," Ogaman hissed with fury. "You're gonna tell me what I need to know."

"P... p... piss off."

While Tony heaved for oxygen, Ogaman tightened his grip. The Bermondsey Boy's face steadily turned red.

"Tell me which government name is supplying you the purp!"

"N... n... No!"

Ogaman intensified his chokehold. But in his periphery, he noticed two unconscious Bermondsey Boyz stirring awake from their violently enforced slumber. Worried that his interrogation time was running out, he upped the ante.

"You wanna live, don't you?"

Tony's eyes widened in fright as he strained helplessly against Ogaman's strength. But he stayed silent.

"DON'T YOU?!" Ogaman hissed, tensing his muscles. "One last time. Who is selling you bairaff?"

"O... okay, o... okay. H... His... n... name is P... P... Prez... President B."

Ogaman stared firmly into Tony's eyes as he maintained his grip.

"I will finish you off now if you're lying to me."

"I... I...p...pro...promise..."

He saw desperation and anxiety in the Bermondsey Boy's eyes.

He's probably telling the truth.

Ogaman released his grasp on Tony, who spluttered desperately for air. Before he could return to his senses though, Ogaman knocked him out cold with a blow to the nose. Then, he hurriedly escaped from the gang's quarters and away from their estate. Veiled by the night sky, he climbed up to a random tower block roof and began making his way back home. As Ogaman roof-hopped across London, Tundé was entrenched in a mental whirlwind.

How am I gonna find this President B guy? Do I even have what it takes to stop all this? What's gonna happen if I don't? Ah, I need more clues...

Chapter 33

"Babatundé, come here now!"

"Yes, mum. Coming!"

Tundé jumped off his bed and shuffled out to the living room. His mum stared intensely into the distance whilst sitting on the brand-new sofa—a replacement for the one he damaged a couple of months ago.

"What's up?"

She turned to him with disappointment and concern in her eyes.

"Why am I getting phone calls from your school about your behaviour? Kilonshele?"

"Rah, why are they calling you now? We're finishing up soon for exams, you know."

"One of your teashas—that Miss Stevens lady—told me you were excluded recently, and now, you're falling asleep in class! You think you can treat your school just anyhow, abi?"

Tundé rolled his eyes frustratedly.

"Ah, who do you think you're rolling your eyes at? Is it me, your mother? HEYYY! God help you, o!"

"Mum, you've seen my mock papers. I'm getting top marks anyway, so I dunno why you're making this such a BIG deal!"

Mrs Adeyemi raised her hand holding a wooden rolling pin.

"Ọmọ, you want me to flog you? Just because you are 15 now doesn't mean I won't!"

"No, no... I'm sorry, Mum. I'm sorry. But I'm just trying my best."

"Well, you bettah try harder! The way you conduct yourself outside the house is important. What have you been doing for the past few weeks, jor?"

If only she knew.

***

Tundé had been juggling several priorities. He struggled to manage his sleeping pattern with all the late nights trying to learn who President B was. After he infiltrated the Bermondsey Boyz a fortnight ago, his alter ego, Ogaman, continued digging for more information about President B's relationship with the bairaff trade and state-sanctioned genocide. In the time since, he had stormed London's most notorious, bairaff-dealing gangs.

First, he went after the Camden Cronies gang located close to Regent's Park, which had a similar demographic makeup to the Bermondsey Boyz.

"I... I only... see him... once a month f... f... for the b... big packages," said Percy, one of the Camden Cronies.

Ogaman assumed Percy was their operations leader since he occupied the stash room in their trap house. Given that Ogaman had just smashed through nine of his fellow associates, Percy was more than willing to choke up some answers. Even if it required some persuasion from Ogaman's arms wrapped menacingly around his neck.

"A... a... all I know is w... we... got connected... thr... through our Wal... Walthamstow people."

Using this weak lead, Ogaman arrived at the Snaresbrook Estate in Walthamstow a few days later. It was the Treehouse Mafia's HQ. The gang ran many underground operations in the area. When he arrived, Ogaman faced a sizeable challenge of 14 gang members, each armed with zombie knives and swords. It was a tough obstacle, but he combined his superhuman strength with martial arts skills to disable the threats, leaving only the Treehouse Mafia lieutenant, Osman.

"We've *been* expecting your bloodclaat!" Osman shouted while he fired bullets in Ogaman's direction.

Ogaman dived away and subsequently disarmed him. Giving Osman a series of punches and kicks to subdue him, Ogaman put his foot on the Treehouse Mafia lieutenant's neck.

"If you don't want me to crush your spine, then you'll tell me everything you know about President B."

"Okay... okay... he ain't selling us packs anymore cos we fell out, init. But word on the roads is that he's moving a big shipment to a group in the one-four sometime soon."

Ogaman applied more pressure on Osman's neck.

"When?"

"Wallahi! That's all... I know!" Osman pleaded drifting out of consciousness. "I just know... that it's... soon init."

"How do you contact him?"

"He changes... his line... every week... so I don't know now..."

The one-four was a reference for the E14 postcode, which included Tundé's home territory of Canary Wharf and the Isle of Dogs. At the time, he was unsure how to use this new information, considering many of Jerry's business associates were in the area. There was one gang, though, that he could squeeze more info out from about President B.

A-Dubs—real name Adrian Wallace—was a well-known member of the Limehouse Lions gang. When Tundé moved up to Stebon High School, A-Dubs was a Year 11 pupil. He always remembered the gang member being overly excited to share stories on the D7 bus about all the street shenanigans he got up to with his friends.

"Fam, imagine, my boy Esco just ran up and dipped that yute in his chest. Then I ran through and cut his neck. Moral of the story: don't fuck with the Limehouse boys!"

Fortunately, A-Dubs' younger brother, Stanley, was a Year 8 pupil at Stebon High now. Two days after infiltrating The Treehouse Mafia, Tundé followed Stanley home on a cold, rainy day after school. They soon arrived at the Ratcliff Estate in Limehouse, and once Stanley entered his block, Tundé hid in the bushes to suit up. Ogaman then perched himself atop a nearby building to keep watch. After many hours of non-descript activity and unrelenting rainfall, Ogaman was dozing off. That was until some disturbance stirred him awake.

"Mate, we need to jump in the whip quickly. They're waiting for us."

Ogaman recognised A-Dubs' voice. He peered over the ledge and saw his target leaving the block with two associates. Yellow lights flashed as one of the men unlocked a WMB vehicle in the nearby car park. With little time to waste, Ogaman soared down from the building and accosted them. The boys were apprehensive.

"Let me guess," Ogaman said nonchalantly. "You were *expecting* my bloodclaat?"

"Fam, j-j-just allow it man," quivered one of the boys.

"We don't wanna hurt you, bruv..." said the other associate, walking cautiously towards Ogaman as he reached into his crotch to grab a weapon.

"Aww, safe for thinking about me, mandem!" Ogaman teased, barely moving a muscle as he glared at A-Dubs. "But I don't think it's me who should be worried."

"Oi, you man best fuck him up, you know!" A-Dubs commanded.

Ogaman launched into action, unleashing a flying kick that smashed the first associate's jaw, following up with a triple combo of punches to knock out the second boy. He turned to A-Dubs, who agitatedly reached for his own knife. He tried desperately to stab the masked teenager, but Ogaman was too quick, too nimble and too sharp. Ogaman whacked the knife to the ground and smacked A-Dubs around the car park repeatedly. Eventually, he forced his former schoolmate into submission by sitting on top of him while holding his right arm in a vice.

"Listen here, pussy'ole," Ogaman ordered. "You're gonna tell me all about your relationship with President B, right now."

"Oi, you ain't getting nuttin', so move off me fam! If I get my hands back on that shank, it's over for you."

"You sure you wanna make threats like that now, bruv?" Ogaman asked, twisting A-Dubs' arm further as a resounding crack echoed in the car park. "Give me a hand with the info. Or I'll remove yours."

"Yo, yo, listen, I promise you ogre man. I promise that I don't know nuffin'. I swear!"

"It's Ohr-Gah-Man! Say it like you're saying orange. O-ga-man."

"S-s-sorry bro. Let m-m-me think..." A-Dubs stuttered under Ogaman's pressure. "Th-th-the only thing I kn-kn-know is that P-p-president B rolls with s-s-some don called Vince. K-k-kinda like his b-b-bodyguard. Th-th-that's all I know."

"You promise?" Ogaman sneered, twisting A-Dubs' arm to the brink of almost fracturing it. "Because if you're lying, I promise *you* that I only need to add a likkle more force and you're losing this arm, bruv."

"Bruddah, I swear on my little princess! That's the only shit I know," A-Dubs cried as tears emerged from his eyes. "I beg you allow me, man. I'm not on it."

"I know you're not. You're just a beg. But yeah, safe."

For all the insights he gathered, Tundé was still frustrated with his lack of progress in thwarting the genocide. A few days after the Limehouse run-in, Uncle Blessing gave his nephew an endurance drill that required him to weave away from random attacks without retaliation. His uncle set up behind the punching bag and thrust paddles towards Tundé. He was seething below the surface.

I dunno how I can stop this genocide if I don't get my bloody hands on President B and Vince!

The teenager dodged until he received hits to the face, causing his aggression to emerge. Tundé counter-punched, his fist tearing straight through the punching bag with explosive force. The shredded fabric and sand that filled it flew out, and his fist followed through to hit his uncle square on the mouth.

"Ah, Uncle! I'm sorry! I didn't mean it!"

"No, no. It's okay, son," Uncle Blessing said tentatively, gently touching his bust lip. "You're doing a good job. As these òyìnbó people say, you have the right fiyah in your belly!"

"Thanks. I guess. You sure you're good though?"

"I'm fine," Uncle Blessing said, as he doused a tissue in water to wipe his bleeding lip. "My main concern is that you develop control of your temperament. Especially with all that your flamboyant antics."

"What are you talking about, Uncks?"

"Ṣo gbọ́ ẹ? You haven't heard? People are talking about you. A guest at my B&B was telling me the story of a man who is single-handedly beating up local criminals in their homes. Which kind persin be that?"

"Errr… maybe there's another yute in London with superpowers?"

Tundé's paranoia about protecting his identity had worsened since he started raiding gangs. With all the physical and emotional damage he was dishing out, it was only a matter of time before the underworld retaliated.

***

"Hello? Are you deya? Were you even listening to me, sha?"

"Oh, sorry Mum."

Tundé realised he had returned to the present moment after reminiscing about the past two weeks.

"I promise I'll behave better at school until the end of exams."

"Ehen, you bettah," she said while switching on the TV.

"…and welcome back to London Living News! Tonight, our main talking point is the new vigilante running around the city and performing incredible acrobatic stunts."

Tundé's eyes and ears were locked in now.

"Rumours have it that the vigilante has also taken on London's most high-profile gangs. Alone! And he's come out unscathed! But is he an ally or a threat to the public? Join us as we discuss this and more on The Scoop at Six."

"Jesos is lord! Have you heard about this crazy man, dear?"

"Oh yeah, couple people have mentioned him, still. Anyway, I'm going to my room to revise."

"Okay dear, good luck."

Tundé heard an update from the TV just before he closed his bedroom door.

"So, Mr Barnes what's your take on this?"

"Well, I don't trust this masked menace at all," Mr Barnes remonstrated. "But at least he's cleaning our streets of these undesirable people, predominantly in CCA-governed areas. I'm sure the Strive Party will be pleased after all their calls for the Traditionalists to reduce crime in the capital!"

Tundé was triggered. He didn't want an alignment with any of those political parties.

Fam, I feel sick. I'm at war with ALL of those government fuckers!

Ogaman had also attracted unwanted media attention online. He recently configured his miCell to fabricate his usage data—thanks to WeView tutorials and threads on Grapevine—to prevent any tracking from external entities. But Tundé was still exposed to numerous articles posted on Chirp, the social media app, including:

'MASKED MAN MAKES CLOWNS OF THE CAMDEN CRONIES' – THE MOON

'GANGS IN FEAR OF UNIFORM. AND NO, IT'S NOT THE POLICE!' – THE DIRECT MESSAGE

'THE STREET SWEEPER: A GLANCE AT LONDON'S DUBIOUS VIGILANTE' – POPULAR IN POPLAR

It reinforced how crucial it was that he kept his secret intact. More notoriety would bring more danger. He was also increasingly concerned about where his decisions were leading him.

I have to be very careful now.

Later that evening, Tundé stared at Lizzie's phone number on his miCell. He was conflicted. While he knew that sharing information with her could unearth routes to stopping Project Pareto, he still wasn't sure if he could trust her. Especially after her employers published an inflammatory headline about Ogaman! He also feared that her journalistic curiosity may eventually connect the dots about his alter-ego's identity, which would be disastrous. Tundé jumped into bed filled with doubt and trepidation. It was disheartening that his only little intel was two unidentifiable names and a random deal in E14.

I've only got scraps so far. It's looking peak.

But his obligation to enact revenge on the regime was unwavering. For all the pain and suffering it had caused his family. For all the countless tragic circumstances Tundé bore witness to in the city. For all the years of betrayal inflicted upon his community since *The Council Care Act 2015* came into effect. Buried deep beneath his mental spiralling, though, was a harrowing sense of guilt about his cherished auntie. His pillow became soaked as he cried himself to sleep.

I miss when things were so calm a few months ago. When Auntie Abi was still here. If only I didn't get involved, maybe she'd still be alive...

The next day at school, burdened by the weight of the world on his adolescent shoulders, Tundé was so consumed by his thoughts that he was oblivious to the events around him. A familiar, gentle voice snapped him back to reality though.

"You there, bighead?" Laura asked softly.

"Yo, Lozz. Wagwan?" Tundé replied absentmindedly.

He briefly scanned the room to regain his bearings. He was in Mr Panther's Physics lesson. The setup of the equations on the whiteboard suggested that it was a revision class for their upcoming final exams.

"What are we doing now?" he asked.

"Pfffft, do you even listen to anything I say?" Laura whispered playfully.

"Err, yeah I was. I mean I do. Sorry, I've just got bare shit on my mind right now."

"Okay class, I know we've covered a lot today," Mr Panther's voice interjected. "But the school insists on a thorough approach to your GCSEs. They want to ensure your year doesn't underachieve like past groups. Make sure you work on exercises 14.3 and 14.4 before next week's lesson. I will be checking!"

Tundé and Laura filtered out of the classroom together along with their classmates. They had become a lot closer recently. Tundé wasn't entirely sure what to do with their growing chemistry, but his oozing confidence since gaining superpowers was enough to keep Laura intrigued and frequently in his company.

"You alright, Tunds?"

"Yeah, yeah, I'm blessed. Just thinking about a lot of shit, init."

"Don't worry, things must be really hard after what happened recently. I lost my mum a few years ago, so I kinda understand your pain. Me and Lorenzo were lucky that our dad was really there for us. I don't know what I would've done without him, anyway. You're doing great though, and I'm sure your mum's proud of you."

"I guess. But it's fine."

Tundé's body tensed up. He was desperate to close off emotionally to his deeper feelings.

"Why are you even here, anyway? Shouldn't you be taking time off to recover and heal?"

Tundé asked himself the same question. He hadn't given it much thought. Since Auntie Abi's death, his mind had solely been focused on doing right by everyone else. Maybe deep down, he wanted to distract himself from facing the full extent of his grief.

"It's just better to get all this stuff out of the way now. Man's not tryna take a whole extra year to finish my GCSEs."

"I hear you. Let's just say I have male relatives who handle stuff just like you. But I'm sure you'll smash it anyway. You've been acting so smart the past couple of months. Nerd!"

She hit him softly on the arm, prompting Tundé to put her in a friendly brace. They both laughed.

"I've been learning all that nerdy behaviour from you, still!"

Laura rolled her eyes sarcastically, then she smiled warmly.

"I'm looking forward to going cinema with you tonight. You know, if it's still a ting?"

"Yeah, of course it is. Should be fun!"

In reality, though, Tundé had been so lost in his own world that he completely forgot about the date he planned for them. They left through the school gates and continued walking on the pavement.

"Anyway, I gotta go now," Laura said while pulling her bag over her shoulder. "My dad's picking me up today because apparently, it's not safe with that crazy masked man fighting those gangs everywhere. He thinks he might hurt me for some stupid reason!"

"I'm sure he would never."

"I think he's probably a good guy with a genuine reason for doing all that madness. Maybe *he* can take me to the cinema if you forget next time!"

Tundé was left dumbfounded.

Damn, how did she clock that I forgot?

"Haha, very funny. But will you still be allowed out this evening then?"

"Don't worry, Dad's got plans. So I'll find a way to make it," she winked at Tundé.

The same metallic grey Scheep that almost bulldozed him a few weeks ago pulled up further down the road and beeped at Laura.

"Come on Lozza, let's get going. We don't have all day!"

"Coming Dad! Okay, gotta go. See you tonight, Tunds!"

Just as Laura waved goodbye and rushed to her ride, Tundé felt a hard nudge in his back.

"Yo, my g."

"Yo, Remi. What you telling me?"

Tundé fist-bumped his best friend. Remi briskly put his arm over Tundé's shoulders.

"Tunds the gyallis, you know!"

Tundé laughed humbly as he shook Remi off him.

"Ah, allow me, bro! Just helping out a fellow pupil, init."

"This guy, bruv! I see you."

"Anyway, what you been saying, Remi?"

"Not too much. It's been a minute since we linked up, though. How are you man?"

"Doing okay, bro. It's still hard dealing with the Abs situation. But otherwise, I'm just tryna keep my head down for exams, init."

"I hear you man. Hope your mumsy's doing alright."

"Yeah, she's okay. That woman is a trooper, to be fair."

"You know what? Let me not chat shit now."

"Wagwan, Remi?"

"Bro, Jerry is stressed because of this whole masked man situation. Do you know much about what's going on?"

"I dunno much, to be honest," said Tundé blankly. "What's Jerry saying about it?"

"Well, he has a feeling it might be your cousin. But he doesn't understand why Tanks would do that for no bread. Jerry's worried that he might try to come for him soon, init."

"I hear you, bro. Thankfully, none of it applies to my fam since Tanks left London weeks ago. He's on the run from the Home Office. So, you think he would be crazy enough to climb all these skyscrapers and beef with these killers?"

"But he stole from the PMD crew and shot for Jerry?"

"Yeah, and then he stopped. Why do you think he did?"

Tundé held Remi's gaze. His heart was thumping. He needed the alibi to land. Each millisecond notched up the tension while the silence remained.

"Yeah, that would be nuts. Say no more. To be honest, Jerry has more pressing concerns. He wants to move more lowkey now."

"Oh rah, wagwan?"

"Things got a bit mad for him. Remember his guy, Rishi?"

Tundé remembered alright. He couldn't forget the name after what happened to Auntie Abi. But to protect his family, he couldn't pursue the lead directly.

Ogaman will leave Rishi alone. For now.

"Yeah, I remember him. What happened?"

Remi was suddenly acting suspiciously. "Alright, promise to keep this to yourself bruv?"

"Of course, bro."

"Apparently, his cousin was assigned to some top-secret government project init. They had a breach recently, and the bosses got suspicious of the whole team. After investigating Rishi's cousin, they found out that he was selling info and bairaff to non-authorised people, like Jerry. And he framed some colleagues too."

Tundé eyebrows raised curiously. "Rahtid, so what did they do?"

"Ah man, I dunno how to say this. They knew where his... his two daughters and his wife... ah, it's fucked up man."

Tundé held his head in his hands. He was stunned.

"Oh no, they didn't, did they?"

"What makes it even madder is the fact it's government man. You can't even talk to feds about murder! Those pricks will just be like 'sorry mate, nuffin' we can do I'm afraid.' It's so fucked, bruv!"

Tundé was still taken aback. It was a reminder of the consequences if things went wrong in his attempts to stop Project Pareto.

"Bruv, that sounds fucking crazy. So what's Jerry doing now, then?"

"He's stopped dealing purp for a hot minute, still. He's not sure whether to find a new plug detached from these ruthless government dons or just pack it all in. Remember, he just had a daughter himself."

"Argh, those bastards!"

Tundé's rage bubbled up to the surface so fiercely that he felt the inner animal psyches start asserting themselves. His skin was peeling off slightly in the process.

"You alright Tunds?"

Tundé was startled, as he took a deep breath to calm himself down.

"What? Yeah, yeah, I'm fine. That all sounds like a madness though. Send Jerry my good wishes."

"Yeah, I will do."

"Anyway, let's duck bro. I gotta touch yard real quick."

"Oh yeah, aren't you doing a ting with Laura tonight? Man like!"

Remi rubbed Tundé's shoulder. He chuckled as his best friend pushed him off again.

"Oi, relax fam! Man's just taking it slow."

"Do your ting, bro. Just don't forget the rubbers!"

"Bruv, allow jinxing the whole ting. I proper like Laura, you know."

"Bro, I'm on your side. You don't wanna create any unexpected yutes!"

A few minutes before reaching the main road, the pair noticed a group of five boys loitering on the corner. They all wore dark-coloured hoodies on what was a fairly warm May afternoon. Their demeanour turned hostile when they saw Tundé and Remi approach. One of them stepped forward and dropped his hood.

"What you saying, prick?" Lorenzo snarled with boiling anger.

Tundé was surprised by the ambush, but he felt assured that he could defend himself.

"Wagwan?"

"You think you can try box me up, get me kicked out of school and then link my *sister*?" Lorenzo said while tapping his finger against his cranium. "Like say I wouldn't find you."

Lorenzo then turned back and laughed with his entourage.

"And you, Remi. Always been Tundé's likkle bum boy. You *both* need to learn that I run tings over 'ere. It's in the blood."

Remi gulped as he took a few steps back.

"Yo, allow it, you man. There's no problem here. Everything's blessed."

"Shut the fuck up, pussy'ole!" Lorenzo barked.

As he signalled to his boys. One of them promptly drew a knife. He turned back to Tundé and Remi, clapping his hands.

"You. Man. Need. To. Learn."

"Oh, you lot aren't fucking around today, are you?" Tundé said flippantly.

Meanwhile, Remi was already running back towards the school in a panic. "Yo Tunds! Move man! Them man have–"

"It's cool, I got this," Tundé assured Remi.

"But they might kill you, bruv!"

Registering his best friend's fear, Tundé took a few steps back to make it look like he was more afraid than he actually was.

"Oh, man thinks he's a comedian, yeah?" one of Lorenzo's boys said. "I'm gonna find it bare funny when I slice you up, fam."

He lunged at Tundé with the knife. In a swift movement, Tundé kicked it out of his hands with his right foot, then whacked him in the head with his heel. The boy dropped to the ground with no sign of getting up any time soon. Tundé stood defiantly before them.

"Rasssclart!" Remi shouted.

Everyone was stunned. They weren't expecting that from Tundé! While he didn't want to lose to Lorenzo again, Tundé understood that he had to limit himself if he didn't want to raise suspicions. As the fight ensued, Tundé allowed himself to take a couple of hits from the unarmed boys.

"Yeah, mash that prick up!" Lorenzo lauded his boys.

However, Tundé was secretly in full control. Eventually, he subdued the three remaining accomplices with well-placed attacks to their bodies, wearing them down to the point that they backed off Tundé.

"My man's on some serious shit," said one of Lorenzo's boys as he retreated.

"You might need... to do him... on your ones, Renz," panted another, winded from the punches.

Only Lorenzo was left to confront Tundé. As Tundé walked up to him slowly, Lorenzo guardedly withdrew his knife.

"Don't think I won't cut you," Lorenzo shouted, starting to lose his cool.

But Tundé recognised something emanating from Lorenzo's eyes. It was the same feeling that engulfed him when he learnt that the bairaff, meant to alleviate his family from suffering, had instead dismantled it. At that moment, he saw himself in Lorenzo.

A man is only as powerful as his discipline and integrity allow him to be.

With this new perspective, Tundé seamlessly disarmed Lorenzo of the weapon and dragged him to the floor by his collar with his left hand. Tundé raised his right fist above the ambusher's teenage face.

"Listen, bruv. Go home. I'm not gonna end you. But if you come after me again, I can't guarantee that I'll spare you. Understood?"

Lorenzo ignored him.

"Understood?" Tundé said louder as he tightened his grip on Lorenzo's collar while clenching his fist tighter.

"Yeah, yeah. Alright man. I hear you."

"Good," Tundé said, letting go of Lorenzo and signalling Remi over. "In a bit."

Whilst Lorenzo and his boys recomposed themselves after an embarrassing defeat, Tundé and Remi rushed off to the bus stop without saying a word to each other. Luckily, the D7 arrived at the same time.

"Bruddah, what the fuck was that?" Remi asked once they had safely embarked on the bus.

"Oh, man's been learning martial arts on the sly for the last couple months, init," Tundé explained, worried about getting sussed out.

"I mean, yeah, that was mad to watch! But I mean, why didn't you fully fuck him up? After he tried that? You had him right there! Is it cos of Laura?"

Tundé pondered on the question.

"Ermm, not exactly. Just experience, fam. Just experience."

Chapter 34

WHEN TUNDÉ ARRIVED HOME, his mum was sat broodingly on the sofa, still dressed in her nurse's uniform. He greeted her with the usual bow.

"Good afternoon, Mum. Are you okay?"

"My son, please. Sit down."

"Okay," Tundé tensely sat beside her. A palpable feeling of unease was in the air.

"I want to talk to you about your state of mind. I know as a family, we are still coming to terms with losing Abiola."

She choked up tears. Tundé was on the verge of crying himself, but tried to stay strong for his mum. She then composed herself and continued.

"I remember what happened when your fahda left us. And how tough that was for you to accept. It was very challenging for my soul, o."

"Please, Mum. Let's not talk about Dad now."

Tundé started to well up.

"You remember how difficult it was for us to talk about? I'm just grateful we saw God deliver justice when those thugs went to jail."

Through tearful sobs, Tundé's voice trembled as he struggled to articulate, "I-I just wish he... d-d-di-didn't have to... d-d-die like that."

"And you were still so young! That's what makes me even sadder. I wish you got to know him properly. But I hope you think I've done a good job raising you anyway."

"Of course! You've basically been my mum *and* my dad for most of my life."

Tundé scooted over to hug her. She smiled gratefully as she dried her cheeks with her sleeve.

"As you've heard before, he was a very proud African. A very proud Yorùbá man. So proud, that he wanted to help all our people unleash their potential. Even though he had a Master's in Physics, his first job here was as a chauffeur. It took him several months to find it too, but he was so determined to build himself up here after suffering in Lagos back then."

"I bet he was top of *all* his classes, right?"

Mrs Adeyemi chuckled softly before continuing.

"He got interested in politics after chauffeuring for this very welcoming òyìnbó. His name was Corby Jerome. Obafemi was inspired by his authenticity and genuine care for human beings, including him as a driver. It influenced his entry into politics. During the 2010s, your fahda campaigned with the Democratic Progress Party to increase employment opportunities for talented Africans, whether born in the diaspora or at home. He used social media early to have a big impact on the young working people in this area."

Mrs Adeyemi paused to continue sobbing.

"Then... oh dear... son, it's hard for me to tell this part again, o."

"Don't worry, Mum, it's okay. I remember what happened."

Obafemi Adeyemi—Tundé's father and Fola's husband—was building momentum to become the first Nigerian-born councillor for Tower Hamlets in 2020, with a long-term vision to challenge for the

Poplar MP seat and beyond. A few months before the election, on his way back home from a political conference, he was followed by a group of extremist British nationalists. They were angry that their capital city was supposedly being 'invaded by foreigners' and didn't want an African becoming a leader for change in the capital. Obafemi was subsequently murdered in cold blood, right by the Thames in Rotherhithe.

Tundé's mum reached for a tissue on the coffee table and wiped away more of her tears.

"You took on a lot of responsibility for what happened. Since then, you've always put this unnecessary weight on your shoulders. Even when you can barely control certain things, abi?"

"I guess."

"I just want to make sure you're not doing it again now that Abiola has gone. Remember, I'm your mother. Sometimes I get annoyed at you for certain things, but it's because I love you and want the best for you."

Tundé couldn't take it any longer. He put his head in his hands and burst into tears, his whole body shaking with grief.

"It's all my fault! All mine!"

His mum put her arms around him.

"Aww, Tundé. You shouldn't blame yourself. As cruel and unfair as it feels, this is life, o. But *God* has a way, I promise you. God is with us!"

Tundé still wrestled with the reality. In his mind, he was to blame for not being able to protect his dad from trouble. He was to blame for his family not having enough money to live comfortably. He was to blame for his auntie dying. And he needed to compensate for it.

All on my own.

Tundé cleared away the tears with his palms, as his sobbing subsided.

"Mum, it's calm. It's fine. I'm a man, you know. I've gotta do my job and take care of everyone."

"Kilódé?[1] You're a 15-year-old boy, Tundé! Who said you need to be acting like a big big man already?"

"Honestly, I'm okay, Mum. Don't stress about me. I need to just work stuff out."

"I know, I'm just worried about you. That you'll do something stupid, or dangerous, or both. And I can't lose you too!"

Tundé hugged his mum to assuage her fears.

"Don't worry, Mum. I'll be okay."

But deep down, he wasn't so sure. And if Ogaman didn't act soon, things could be far from okay for everyone he knew and loved.

"But if you ever need me for anything, Mum, I'm always here for you. Always."

"My son. My wondahful son. Modupé o!"[2]

Later that evening, Tundé was dressed uncharacteristically smart. He wore a stylish, tight-fit denim shirt, high-quality trousers and a pair of semi-formal men's boots. He bought these with some of the money left over from working for Jerry. At the last minute, he decided to take his backpack along too.

It doesn't go with the outfit, but I'll bring it. Just in case Ogaman needs to come outside. Can't be too careful.

Tundé checked at the time on his phone. It was quarter past seven.

"Shit, I need to bounce!"

Just as he hurried to the front door, Uncle Blessing was in the living room. He was carrying a plastic bag of containers filled with jollof rice and stew. Tundé presumed his mum had made extra for his uncle since he lived reasonably close.

---

1. *Why?*

2. I thank God!

"Where are you ronnin'?" Uncle Blessing joked.

"I'm meeting a friend. And I'm a little bit late."

Uncle Blessing looked at him from top to bottom, then gave him a cheeky smile.

"Ehen, so you're going to meet that girl, abi?"

Tundé's shyness made him avoid eye contact.

"Nah, just a friend, Uncle."

"So, why are you dressed like an Oga?"

"What's wrong with looking good?"

"Just make sure you don't create anything permanent, jor!"

Tundé groaned dismissively. His uncle gestured quietly to his nephew.

"Oya, let me see you to the door."

Once there, Uncle Blessing placed his hand caringly on Tundé's shoulder.

"Sister Fola has told me she's worried about you. Are you okay? Are you taking care of yourself?"

"Yeah, Uncks, I'm good. I've just gotta learn how to deal with it all. Just remember what I said about Mum, yeah. If things get wild, I need you to get her out of here. Please."

"I understand. After tonight, I think it would be a good time for us to talk about returning to Nigeria."

Tundé nodded hurriedly.

"Yeah, cool. Can the Naija ting wait small small, abeg?"

"Ehen, so you're learning Pidgin now? Wetin dey happen?"

"I've been listening to this artist. Icee Igwe. He uses it in his songs, init. Anyway, Uncks, I need to leave."

"Okay. We dey talk again soon. But we still have much work to chop, sha. I didn't come to London for nothing!"

"For sure, we'll talk later."

"Where are you meeting your 'friend' tonight?"

"At the 4OUR arena in North Greenwich."

"Well, be safe. May Olodumare be with you."

Chapter 35

"YEAH FAM, I'M GONNA beat this peng ting. Don't watch!"

Tundé stared outside the window agitatedly. He thought listening to other conversations on the bus would distract him from his date nerves. Only a few months ago, it would have been a pipedream to be spending time with Laura outside of school. Now, it was an equally exciting but daunting reality. His heart was racing. His breath condensed on the window as he tried to calm himself down. He was surprised at how chilly the evening was for late May.

Weather and discomfort aside, Tundé was excited to unwind and have fun with his teenage crush. But as the bus droned onwards, he was dragged back into his obsessive thoughts about his responsibilities.

Still need to prepare for GCSEs in twelve days... still need to find more clues... still need to stop Project Pareto...

Time was slipping away. Since his last encounter with the Limehouse Lions, he had no more leads for President B or Vince. And even that wouldn't guarantee finding a pathway to stop the government's genocidal plans.

Maybe I should get back on Ogaman duties after this date.

His miCell then buzzed. It was a message from Laura.

'Hey, gonna be 10 mins early. Dw I'll wait. See you soon :) x'

Tundé smiled to himself and wrote back.

'Cool, see you in a bit b x'

When the bus came to a halt at a traffic light, he noticed the nearby Blackwall Estate. As he wiped the window to see more clearly, its four familiar tower blocks became more prominent. They competed in stature—but not wealth—with the Canary Wharf buildings standing tall on the other side of the old docks. Tundé sighed as he reflected on life.

"Olodumare, I really hope you're leading me in the right direction."

In an instant, something grabbed Tundé's attention. Driving in the opposite direction was a dark grey Niko car. It had slowed down and flicked on its right indicator, heading for the Blackwall Estate. His superhuman eyes calibrated automatically, meaning he could identify the faces behind the Niko's tinted windscreen. He didn't recognise the driver or the man sitting in the backseat behind him. But he did recognise the person sitting on the passenger's side.

Rah! That's the don who attacked Anna in Millwall Park. The same don chatting about getting everything he needed...

Tundé was spooked by the coincidence. But given the state of affairs, this mysterious man was a plausible route to learn more about Project Pareto. While the Niko car waited for a gap in oncoming traffic to turn into the Blackwall Estate, Tundé looked at his phone longingly. Laura's display picture on the HowRU messaging app stared back at him. Considering that he had dreamt of this moment for a long time, it was a difficult decision to make.

I have to see wagwan with that guy, though. It's my responsibility. Hopefully, I can get what I need quickly and then link Laura later.

Tundé pressed the stop buttons on the bus incessantly. As the sun set on this spring evening, the teenager leapt off at the next stop and ran along the main road. Under the slowly dimming sky, he saw the Niko turn into a more enclosed area of the Blackwall Estate. While he jogged through a concealed walkway, Tundé fetched the balaclava from his bag and slipped it on.

I can't get fully changed now. Don't wanna lose track of the car!

He trailed the vehicle into the heart of the estate, which closely resembled the one in South London where he stomped on the Bermondsey Boyz. When the car stopped, Tundé hid in a set of bushes nearby. A few seconds later, the man from Millwall Park stepped out.

"Be ready for any danger, Vince," a voice came from the Niko. "Tonight's a big deal."

"Course, boss," Vince replied.

"So *that's* Vince?" Tundé whispered to himself. "I've gotta keep following him."

As the Niko car pulled off, Tundé followed Vince stealthily through the walkways of the estate. Soon, he realised that its layout had a significant feature. Tucked away from the prying eyes of the main residence, a secluded area unveiled itself. It was an abandoned building nestled beside a disused car park and playground. The sunset cast shadows that cloaked the surroundings from public view further. As he got closer to the overgrown car park, Tundé sought refuge under an old, battered Wilwo car parked there. Vince entered the deserted playground and sat on a rusty swing, swaying back and forth with apparent aimlessness.

That seems... weird.

He stayed put under the Wilwo to watch what arose from the situation. Scanning his surroundings, Tundé noticed a large, weathered delivery truck a few yards away, with enough space underneath for a makeshift changing room. The teenager snuck under it and changed into his suit. A couple of minutes later, Ogaman heard two cars pull up into the car park. Multiple doors opened, and soon, a conversation ensued.

"Yo, you got our package, yeah?" said one man.

"Yes bruv, we've brought the 5 keys of purp, as agreed," said another man. "But listen here first. This is gonna be our last dealing with you lot for a while. The supply's going dry this week. The border police all along the south coast are being a nightmare right now, init."

It was a bairaff deal taking place. A pang of grief hit Ogaman's chest as he continued to eavesdrop.

"Yo, what the fuck? We need more bumbaclaat food than that you know, Prez!"

"Yeah man, we needed 10 keys at least!" a new voice added.

"Since you lot wanna get rude, you best fucking address me as President B in full."

Ogaman's ears perked up.

Rah, so that's President B? What kinda luck is that!

One of the boys kissed his teeth, prompting President B to respond.

"Don't play with me, bwoy."

Why does his voice sound familiar though? I guess he sounds like the mandem.

As the night sky blanketed the area, Ogaman considered his next move. He could jump out and fight his targets now. But he thought it was best to listen out for more intel before engaging. Ogaman then noticed a half-full lighter on the ground near him. He placed it in his pocket.

This could be handy.

Ogaman then activated his night vision to get a better view of the proceedings. He identified two cars. The Niko model L and a white WMB X4. Both vehicles were parked a few yards away from each other. The conversation was happening between the two cars, where he finally got a glimpse of President B.

He looks bare different to what I expected.

President B—also known as Prez—was rather tall with dark brown skin, donning a sharp, navy two-piece suit with a red tie and polished loafers. He was interacting with the other two men, both of whom were dressed in a standard hoodie and jeans. Ogaman assumed they were the buyers. Standing beside the Niko car was a smartly dressed man supporting Prez. Lounging on the bonnet of the white WMB car was another young man, dressed very casually in a black tracksuit and white Ralisad trainers—clear from the four black stripes.

"Ite bruv, stop running your gums," said one of the boys to Prez. "Just give us the purp you got, init."

"Ed, tell your likkle bombaclaat to shut his mouth," Prez advised sternly, "before he comes to regret it."

"Who's this prick think he's chatting to?" the angered man responded.

"Oi 3Dom, I beg you allow it bruv," said Ed to his overly aggressive associate. "We're tryna do business here. Sorry, President B. Let's move this quickly."

Ed gestured to his associate in the black tracksuit sitting by the WMB car.

"Reezy, you got the P's ready? Make sure it's the right amount for five kilos."

Reezy nodded silently and retrieved a duffel bag from the car, unzipping it to show the cash. Prez, whose eyes stayed glued to Ed and

3Dom, held up three fingers to his man by the Niko. The man pulled out a Pony Erikson phone from his left pocket and put it to his ear to make a call.

"We've got the product in a van parked close by," Prez explained. "Once I count all the money, I'll jump in the car while my associate, SB, will provide the product from the van and take the P's."

As Reezy was passing the duffel bag of cash to Ed, Prez interjected once more.

"By the way, you man know the prices have gone up by ten points since our last deal, right? It's gonna be £45,000 now, and then another £45,000 in 2 weeks."

"What? But I thought we had a concrete rate, bro!" Ed exclaimed. "You can't be moving like that."

"Are you mad fam?" 3Dom snapped. "You're moving like one dickhead right now!"

"I warned you to watch your mouth, likkle boy," Prez addressed 3Dom firmly.

"Don't start piping up like I'm not on tings!" 3Dom said aggressively, injecting more bass into his voice.

Ogaman detected movement in the playground. Vince had left the swing, but he didn't know where to.

"Bruv, I beg you jam your hype for a minute," Ed pleaded to 3Dom.

"Ed, fuck your guy, init," 3Dom barked, while his hand slid into his waist. "And fuck you, too. Some any next Pissy B guy. Suck your m–"

In the blink of an eye, Vince arose from the shadows and sliced a huge chunk of flesh from 3Dom's face using a dagger.

"ARGH!" screamed 3Dom, dropping to the ground as the blood gushed down his cheek.

"Yo, what the fuck?" shouted Ed.

He swiftly pulled out a pistol from his crotch and pointed it at Prez. In response, Prez drew two Magnum guns from his blazer pockets, pointing one at Ed and one just past Ed's left shoulder. Ed, keeping his gun ready, readjusted his body to see where Prez was pointing his second gun. He was livid.

"Oi, let him go you prick!"

Prez was aiming his second Magnum directly at Reezy, who Vince had in a stranglehold with the dagger held against his throat.

"Don't let these man kill me!" Reezy begged.

Alright, this might be my cue...

"I'm gonna get you out!" Ed said shakily, struggling to remain composed as he kept his gun pointed at Prez. "Tell your fucking guy to get off my brother. Now!"

"I thought *you* were the calm one here, Ed?" Prez sneered, maintaining his aim on both brothers. "I guess not. I told you lot to give me the respect I deserve, but since you wanna do this the hard way..."

A resounding smack echoed throughout the abandoned area of the Blackwall Estate.

"Nah bruv. You lot can't get active without bringing me in!"

"Yo, it's that dickhead, Ogaman!" Ed cried in shock. "How the fuck did he find us?"

Ogaman had emerged from the shadows and smashed the gun pointed at Reezy out of Prez's hand using a stick he found near the truck. Before Ed could react, Ogaman flew into him with a kick that knocked the gun out of Ed's hands.

"President B!" Ogaman yelled angrily while marching towards him.

"The masked bandit. I've been waiting for this day," Prez hissed back, "For the chance to finally dead you."

As Prez raised his second Magnum gun towards Ogaman, the Yorùbá warrior punched it out of his hands before he could fire.

"Who do you work for?" Ogaman shouted as he whacked Prez hard in the face.

All the rage and injustice he felt was rushing to the surface. He grabbed his adversary by the collar and lifted him above his head.

"Because you're gonna take me to them today!"

"Are you dumb fam?" Prez spat blood at Ogaman's mask as he tried to break free. "You think I'm gonna talk to you?"

That enraged Ogaman even more, making him lose focus on his surroundings.

"You better think fast, or else I'm gonn–"

From out of nowhere, Ogaman was launched violently across the car park, skidding dangerously across the concrete. Vince had powerfully kicked him in his midriff. Ogaman felt like he'd been smashed into a brick wall, leaving him in significant pain. His ribcage burned as the impact travelled up to his collarbone. Breathing heavily, he tried to gather himself.

Yo... what the fuck? That kick nearly... nearly knocked me completely out. How is that even possible?

With little time to think, Ogaman was forced to defend himself as Vince pounced on him and unleashed a flurry of punches. Ogaman desperately bobbed and weaved as the fists rained downward. Meanwhile, with Reezy freed, Ed decided it was time for him and his boys to leave before things got out of control.

"Yo Reezy, get 3Dom in the car now!"

Reezy picked 3Dom up and hauled him towards the car, whose face was covered in blood after the blow from Vince.

"You alright bro?"

"I'm good... dem man are lucky... I didn't buss... my ting."

Reezy rolled his eyes. "Bro, that chat is what got us in this mess in the first place!"

Watching Ogaman and Vince's tussle from a distance, Prez retrieved one of his Magnum guns that was flung away.

"If Vince doesn't take you out first, Ogaman, then you best be ready for me to do it!"

Ogaman heeded the warning as he strained under Vince's oppressive force. He was in big trouble if he didn't release himself soon.

"Alright, suck out fam," Ogaman grunted, summoning all his strength to haul Vince off his body, sending him tumbling over his head. Gasping for air, Ogaman scanned the area to find Prez.

"President B! I'm not leaving until I get my answers!"

But from his blindside, Vince grabbed hold of Ogaman again. He lifted the vigilante in the air and threw him forcefully to the ground, fighting to restrain him. Ogaman was bemused by the immense strength of his adversary.

"How the fuck do you keep coming back like this?"

"Got a little something up my sleeve," Vince snarked as he flared his nostrils. "Or should I say, up my nose..."

It took a few seconds for the penny to drop.

"Oh shit, it's the–"

"Odabozite Trioxide," Prez interjected as he walked across the asphalt towards them. "Or what your bloodclaat would call bairaff. But Vince is using a refined version."

"I worked for it too. I had to steal it back from a backstreet journalist who wanted to expose us. Even though you came to ruin things, we soon sorted her out."

Vince chuckled callously at Ogaman while they continued scuffling.

"And with this new formula, we're gonna end you quicker than a fiend can snort a line!" Prez announced, gun aimed at Ogaman. "Hold him still, Vince."

A different version of bairaff? You've got to be joking.

Ogaman was struggling to shake Vince off. Prez was having trouble getting a clear shot, but he was prepared to fire anyway...

"AGGGH!" Ogaman's cry pierced the air after two bullets penetrated his abdomen, causing blood to spew.

"I got him!" Ed shouted from the passenger seat of the white WMB as he fired a third shot. "That's what you get for fucking with the mandem on road, Ogaman!"

The car, also carrying 3Dom and Reezy, sped out of the abandoned car park.

"Those pricks still owe me money!" Prez fumed bitterly at the white WMB disappearing from the abandoned car park. "I'll get dem man later. I'm focusing on you now, ogre..."

Ogaman lay writhing in pain after being blindsided by Ed's gunshots. The tiny silver lining was that the third bullet hit Vince, tearing a sizeable piece of flesh from his torso. He was now preoccupied with his own injury. Ogaman used this brief window to crawl through the agony and hide in some overgrown bushes close by. Prez walked briskly through the car park and glanced at his phone.

"Yo, Vince, you good?"

"Yeah, mate. That cunt's bullet grazed me, but the formula is starting to work. The pain is subsiding."

"Excellent. I've got to leave for the big get-together tonight," Prez said while throwing the gun into Vince's hands, "so, make sure you finish him off with this while I'm gone."

They turned their attention to the bushes. Faint sounds of Ogaman's squirming reached their ears, confirmed by the sight of rustling leaves.

"Shouldn't be a problem, Prez."

"I'll get my people to come here and dispose of the body. You just have to get rid of the burner."

"Gotcha. See you later, pal."

Prez jumped into his black Niko vehicle, where his SB had been hiding since the guns were drawn. He was trembling.

"Boss, I thought you said this job... wasn't gonna be that dangerous?"

"Stop being a pussy, bruv! Didn't they give you the heads-up at DSU training? Danger *is* the job!"

In the meantime, Ogaman lay under the shrubs in torturous despair. His chances of avenging Auntie Abi and stopping the genocide were falling by the second. It wouldn't be long before his enemies tried to put the final nail in the coffin. And even if they didn't, the gunshot wounds eventually would. Blood continued gushing out heavily from his guts while his healing powers couldn't activate with the bullets lodged in his system.

I might be done out here.

He gazed up at the moon in the night sky with a deep and desperate yearning.

"Please, give me something, Olodumare. Anything."

There was an eerie silence as a light breeze whistled through the leaves of the bushes. The threatening sound of Vince's footsteps was heard getting closer in the background.

"Hahaha!" an unfamiliar voice cackled from a distance.

In the blink of an eye, Ogaman's vision was warped and distorted. He felt an ethereal pull into the cosmos, and his very essence was stripped away in the process—clothes, body, and all. Time came to a halt. The feeling of lightness was otherworldly. It was reminiscent of his dreamlike experience during Uncle Blessing's ritual. Soon, a reverberating voice filled the vacuum as if he were wearing booming headphones.

"Babatundé, o dabi ẹni pé o wà ninu wahala?"[1]

Tundé was taken aback. Beyond the celestial experience and the presence of the enigmatic voice, he was amazed that he understood every single word of Yorùbá spoken to him.

"Talo n sọ̀rọ̀? Ṣé mo kú ni?"[2] Tundé asked seamlessly, astounding himself even more—apparently, he could speak Yorùbá now too.

"Eniyan naa pè mi ni Èṣù."[3]

"Èṣù? Ṣé o kin ṣe eniyan ni? Ṣé mo ti kú?"[4]

"You humans! Always asking whether you're dead when I appear!" Èṣù laughed in response. "I am the Chief Orisha of pathways and fate, known for my unpredictable nature. Now, I believe you requested some spiritual assistance, abi?"

"Yes, I did, sha. Please, can you do anything?"

"Well, that may be difficult. See, you have reached a significant crossroads in your destiny. And that means you must make some choices now."

"What do you mean?"

"Oduduwa has blessed you, a Yorùbá warrior, with the powers of the elements. And the stakes are high! Oh, so exciting!"

"Why's that funny? I just wanna do what's right, you know."

---

1. *Babatundé, it seems like you're in trouble?*

2. *Who is speaking? Am I dead?*

3. *The humans call me Eshu.*

4. *Eshu? Are you not human? Have I died?*

"Oh, I am very aware. And because what is 'right' encompasses both selfless *and* selfish aspirations, one must be wary of the duality that any decision brings."

"Okay... so, what are my choices, Mr Èṣù?"

"Èṣù is fine. I trust that you respect my presence already, sha. Anyway, here are your choices. I return you to the Earth in your current physical condition, giving you complete control over your destiny. Or, I amplify your powers using cosmic energy to aid you in this current battle. And you accept the *unfavourable consequences* that come with it. Choose wisely."

That didn't feel like a tough decision for Tundé. "Please, just give me the powers!"

Èṣù paused briefly before responding.

"You seem very sure. Are you?"

"Erm, yeah... I mean, what else am I gonna do? Let Auntie Abi's death be in vain? Leave my family and thousands of others to die? Give me the cosmic powers."

"As you wish, Babatundé."

An onslaught of stars suddenly engulfed Tundé, propelling him into a tumultuous whirlwind piercing countless, boundless dimensions.

"A word of guidance, our young incarnate," Èṣù bellowed. "Ojú ẹni máa là, á rí ìyọnu."[5]

As the words hit his consciousness, Tundé reflected on the loss of his auntie.

Damn, I guess that's how it goes.

"Now, you must return. I can't keep you here all millenia! Ó dàbọ̀."

"Duro, duro... wait, wait..." Tundé pleaded.

---

5. *Whoever desires to succeed will experience challenges on the way.*

He transmuted back into his physical body, concealed under the bushes in the Blackwall Estate. The experience of time was back to normal, and under his damaged vigilante costume, the searing pain of his injuries had returned.

Rah, that was baaare trippy...

But something was different. Ogaman felt a fiery latent energy brewing deep within his core. It appeared that Èṣù had fulfilled his promise. He dialled into his meditation practice to connect with the untapped source. Bravely ignoring the presence of Vince closing in, Ogaman remained focused and attentive. Quickly, his muscles relaxed as his body grew weightless. In a flash, the energy started surging through his body. As his essence ascended, astonishing changes took place.

Oh shit, my hands!

Large, sharp talons were slowly bursting out from his right hand's fingertips, mirroring those of an eagle. Becoming more attuned to his inner wellspring of power, Ogaman used his talons to dig into his own guts and remove the bullets, accelerating the self-healing process. He winced at the bodily fluids spilling out.

Agggh, it feels so strange! But it's working already.

Meanwhile, Vince had walked over to the bushes with his loaded gun in tow. He envisioned being lauded as a hero within London's criminal underworld for exterminating their notorious pest. Once he crunched his way through the twigs though, Vince grew defensive. It was tight and his vision was impaired in the darkness. But he needed to shoot Ogaman from close range to ensure his death. Vince then picked up a silhouette of Ogaman's body, covered by branches and leaves a few yards ahead. He slowly crept towards the vigilante, keeping his gun at the ready. Vince jerked to a stop. Upon further scrutiny, the silhouette turned out to be a thick pile of mud, bark and weeds. Vince was befuddled.

"You must be looking for me!"

Ogaman sprung from the shadows and pawed Vince across the face, who frantically pulled the trigger. The bullet missed Ogaman and bounced off a tree. Nearby, Prez, who was delayed by guiding the bairaff van out of the estate, heard the gunshot.

"Ah, the DSU will be glad to hear we got rid of that scummy yute!" Prez said triumphantly to SB as the Niko car departed from Blackwall and drove through the Limehouse Link Tunnel.

"You picked the wrong bruddah to fuck with!" Ogaman roared mightily at Vince as he harnessed his resurgence of power.

Vince, bleeding profusely from his cheekbone, tried to shoot Ogaman a few more times. But the vigilante was too nimble, dodging each bullet with ease. When Vince ran out of ammunition, he threw the gun away in frustration.

"I'm still strong enough to kill you with my bare hands!" Vince cried out as he charged toward Ogaman.

However, Ogaman's superhuman agility made him as fluid as water, anticipating and evading Vince's attacks with impeccable timing. Amidst the chaos of the fight, memories of Auntie Abi began flooding Ogaman's brain, stoking his anger.

How could these bastards take her away? And now they wanna fight ME? How COULD they?

Ogaman used his wrath as fuel, swinging his right fist powerfully into Vince's neck. It forced the aggressor painfully down to his knees. Ogaman then kicked Vince in his chest mercilessly, the gruelling sounds of fracturing echoed with each strike. As he took the beatings, Vince could feel the effects of the refined bairaff wearing off exponentially. In contrast, Ogaman was growing stronger. But he was losing cognitive control. The constant pangs of guilt destabilised him, causing the animal psyches within to rise to the surface.

"Let me go," begged a severely injured Vince, as he tried to crawl away from the abandoned car park.

"You're going NOWHERE!" Ogaman growled, as he soared across the car park and pummelled Vince's head into the ground.

He stomped on Vince's wrists, shattering them to nullify their threat. Ogaman turned Vince around, facing him whilst he strangled his neck with his left hand.

"Does it look like I'm fucking playing?"

While Ogaman's identity remained a secret, Vince could make no mistake about the rage projecting through his eyes behind the mask. This was personal.

"Listen, Vince! You're gonna tell me EVERYTHING you know about this government operation and the bairaff."

Ogaman tightened his grip on Vince's neck.

"Everything."

"Why... why should... I do... that?" Vince spluttered.

In a spate of fury, Ogaman dug his talons into Vince's leg, latching onto his groin muscles. Everything looked red through his eyes—in more ways than one.

"Agggh! AGGGH!"

"Tell me what I wanna know before I rip you to shreds!"

"Aghh I'm... agh... I'm... agh... I'm not... I'm not telling you... shit," Vince struggled to choke out in excruciating agony.

Entirely consumed by his thirst for revenge, the increased presence of the animal psyches intensified the chaos in Ogaman's mind.

"CAWGGH! EEEE-EEEE! GRRRRR!"

Ogaman pulled out Vince's groin muscles and showed the damage to his victim ruthlessly. He then pushed his sharp talons threateningly onto Vince's neck.

"It's gonna be your SPINE next if you don't speak up fam. Bare people have died. More people are gonna die. So, you best talk!"

Vince's eyes widened. Despite trying to remain defiant, the trembling in his voice couldn't mask his fears.

"I'm not... telling you... shit..."

Incensed by the lack of respect, Ogaman pierced through Vince's neck and gradually pulled at his spinal cord. Ogaman's judgement was heavily clouded by volatility, as Vince's condition quickly deteriorated. He was losing consciousness, as the blood oozed uncontrollably out of his left leg and gushed from his neck.

"Tell me NOW!"

"Agggh! Okay... okay... something... tonight..."

"WHERE?" Ogaman demanded furiously, yanking his spinal cord further away from his body. "Because people's lives are on the line. Including yours."

"Okay... tonight... at... tobac... tsaaedn... todabc..."

As his words became incoherent, Vince's head dropped and his eyes rolled back without warning. It was slight, but definitive. Ogaman felt his adversary's body lighten, instantly snapping him out of his ferocious state. As he stared at Vince's body with dread, a deep sense of dismay swept over him.

"Oh no... oh no..."

Ogaman tried to shake Vince awake, but there was no response. Nothing. His anxiety clicked into overdrive.

What have I done? How can I even explain this? Oh no...

Hands and talons covered in blood, Ogaman put his bare palm on various parts of Vince's body to try transferring his healing powers. Still nothing. Before he could fully process what had happened, Ogaman heard sirens blaring from afar and drawing closer. Vince's body was hopelessly still. Ogaman would never forget the sight.

"Fuck, I've gotta bounce."

After picking up his backpack from under the truck, he escaped the scene to a secluded rooftop of a nearby garage in the area. There, Tundé removed his sweaty balaclava from his face and tried to gather his thoughts.

I'm so fucked right now. Something's happening tonight, but can I stop it? Am I even one of the good guys anymore? Did Èṣù trick me?

Before he could follow that train of thought, his miCell buzzed repeatedly. Tundé retrieved it from his pocket.

I swear I turned this damn thing off... ah mate, I REALLY messed up tonight!

His phone showed it was just past nine in the evening. At this point, he was already over an hour late for his date with Laura. However, the caller ID was showing a different name. Tundé took a deep breath and cleared his throat.

"Yo, Lizzie. What's going on?"

"Hi Tundé. Out of the blue, I know. It's pretty urgent though. I was just wondering if you had time to meet me ASAP tonight. I have some important news about events unfolding, but I can't say much on the phone."

Tundé hesitated.

"I don't think I can. But I know someone else who's keen to meet you. And he can help both of us way more."

"Oh, you sure? Isn't it better if you're there too, though?"

"Just trust me, Lizzie. This guy's... legit," Tundé couldn't help but wince as he said that. "He wants justice just as much as we do."

"Well... okay. We can make it happen if your trustworthy friend can meet me in less than an hour. I'll send you the location via encrypted text."

"Sure. I'll let you know when I hear back from him. In a bit."

Chapter 36

"Two minutes to ten. Tundé's guy should be here anytime soon."

Lizzie was muttering as she sat on an aged, wooden bench near the Old Factory at Limehouse Cut. The factory stood as a reminder of the past, overlooking the historic canal that wound through the Limehouse district of East London.

"This area used to be so vibrant when I moved here in 2014. That damned CCA really did shake things up."

Now, the canal was neglected and brimming with various forms of refuse and muck. It had deteriorated to the point where daytime strolls, bars, and picnics—once commonplace—were now discouraged by its sorry state. Lizzie kept anxiously glancing at her phone. She was concerned about the fact she had no idea who was coming. But she trusted Tundé's intentions and felt intuitively that this meeting would be beneficial.

"For Anna."

Still, it wasn't the most pleasant place for an elegant woman to be loitering in. Lizzie was rightfully on edge as she tightly held onto a bottle of pepper spray. Suddenly, a silhouette crossed her eyeline and a loud thump on the ground could be heard.

"Oh dear!" she said in a fluster. "Hello?"

"Hello madam, are you Lizzie?"

"Yes. Yes, I am. And I'm guessing you're *the* Ogaman?"

"It's me, still."

It was imperative to add more bass to his voice and act like he had never spoken to her before.

"Nice to meet you."

"Likewise, Mr Superhero."

"So, that boy Tundé told me you work for that Poplar newspaper. Is that right?"

"Yes, that's correct."

"Before we talk about the government stuff, why did you lot write all those bullshit articles about me being a 'dubious vigilante' when you just called me a superhero yourself?"

Lizzie fidgeted uncomfortably, as she tried to find an adequate answer.

"Erm, yes. I understand your frustration. Unfortunately, I don't have power over what gets published. In fact, it's one of the reasons why we're meeting here tonight."

Ogaman mused on her words while she looked at him with an air of sincerity.

"You might be gassing, but I hear it. Sometimes there's only so much we can do."

"Indeed. I do actually have a question for you first before we dive in. Why do you do this to yourself, Ogaman?"

"What do you mean?"

"Why are you battling with all of these dangerous people? Don't you worry about your friends? Your family? Your life? You must have a serious reason for all this."

"The drug trade and the system have ruined my family. Like many other families in this country. Then, once I understood the deeper reasons behind this bairaff on the streets, I knew it was up to me to stop it."

"So, how did you become so powerful? And how did you and Tundé even connect? Because your whole thing doesn't make much sense to me."

"Without saying too much, I have to thank the Universe for my gifts. And the only reason I'm helping your likkle boy Tundé is cos he's been through the same institutional bullshit as me. Surely *that* makes sense to a smarty-pants like you."

Lizzie rolled her eyes, while Ogaman was confident that he sufficiently distanced himself from Tundé.

"Anyway, is this an undercover interview or what? Let's just get down to business, Lizzie. I want to stop this government operation, and I got some intel that something's going down tonight."

Ogaman froze up. He had a sudden flashback of Vince's body lying lifelessly in the abandoned Blackwall Estate car park. A shudder came over him. He was still coming to terms with the actions of his inner demons.

"Sorry, yeah... something... tonight."

"You okay?" Lizzie said while fluttering her eyelashes at him.

Ogaman allowed himself to be distracted by Lizzie's vivacious presence for a moment. Anything to get away from his own internal turmoil.

"I'm good. So, tell me. What do you know about tonight?"

Lizzie retrieved a Lemon digital e-Pad out of her bag.

"Yes, something is happening tonight. And it looks worrying. Now, I'm sure you're aware of the government's plan to use bairaff as a tool for Proj–"

"Project Pareto. To wipe out a lot of people. Yeah, I know. Let's not waste time. What's the link with tonight then b?"

Lizzie was startled by Ogaman's straightforwardness.

"Well, whatever it is, I'm almost certain that the leading operatives for Project Pareto will be at the London Water Council's Plant in Wapping—near that defunct Tobacco Dock."

Ogaman winced, realising that Vince was trying to tell him that before he displaced his spine.

"Why would they be there?"

"If you allow me to explain, you might understand," Lizzie said with sass. "I thought Tundé would have explained this to you?"

"Alright, my bad. Clearly, even he's hiding things from me! But please, go on."

Lizzie nodded.

"So, the Project Pareto leaders needed to test that the Odabozite Trioxide—the chemical compound that forms bairaff—had an adverse physiological impact on their undesirables, right? Since the turn of the year, the statisticians have estimated a 257% increase in the number of drug-related deaths in 2027 compared to 2026 already!"

"Rah!"

"I know, right? Scary! What's also been concerning is that the mainstream media and well-known political commentators have largely ignored this trend in their narratives because of who is dying."

In unison, Ogaman and Lizzie took deep breaths, remembering their loved ones who were unfortunate victims in this tragic circumstance.

"The project leaders couldn't force the drugs through the healthcare system directly, as that would be deemed too conspicuous. Instead, they decided to put samples on the streets to gauge how addictive and lethal the drugs were for the struggling working-class population. I've read recent classified reports which confirm that even government officials were surprised by the effectiveness of the bairaff and the number of casualties in such a short period."

"Damn, that's a mad ting."

"Absolutely. The most disturbing part is that they sanctioned this project to a specialist operative team whose main goal is to execute the genocide while making the deaths appear self-inflicted. Deep down, they know it's wrong and they are fearful of nationwide panic or anarchy should the public ever learn of their true motives."

"Crazy. Absolutely crazy. How did you find out about all this, Lizzie?"

"Oh, I have my sources. Being a journalist helps. And I learnt from the best in Annabel Campbell. I'm also using her old notes to hack heavily secured government servers and unearth some key pieces of information."

Lizzie continued to navigate through different screens on her e-Pad.

"Do you remember the large public health initiative after the Council Care Act took effect in 2015? It essentially mandated that all residents get medical check-ups to be guaranteed access to a property via the scheme."

Ogaman trudged through his childhood memories. His superhuman mind eventually projected vivid images of numerous visits to Newham General Hospital with his parents when he was still a little boy, which included several tests and injections.

"Maybe, but I'm not completely sure," Ogaman said, pondering the memory. "Why's that important?"

"My research suggests that those check-up sessions were not entirely legitimate. In fact, they were used as an opportunity to insert a dormant, chemical agent into every single CCA resident. The notes explained how a polymer called Novabond was purposely added to those syringes."

"Swear down?"

"Regrettably so, yes. Following that trail of information, numerous payments were made to each of London's local councils with properties reclaimed under the CCA. Suspiciously, large payments were also recently made to The London Water Council via several multi-threaded transactions that I crosschecked separately."

There was a pause, as they both perceived the depth of complexities that this sadistic project contained.

"I made another vital discovery once I gained access to another database through Anna's old laptop. These scientific documents dated about eighteen months ago—stamped with a massive 'DSU' logo—described how government scientists have been developing a co-opted version of bairaff in UK laboratories so that it would become highly reactive with the Novabond injected into the CCA residents."

"Holy shit! I can't believe it. This is insane."

Ogaman was in disbelief. He remembered Prez alluding to a different strain of bairaff that empowered Vince to become a serious threat.

How powerful could these government dons make this lab-made version?

Lizzie subsequently pulled a video up on her e-Pad.

"And *these* videos have confirmed my suspicions of tonight's agenda. This is CCTV footage from the last 72 hours outside the main Water Plant in Wapping. It was hard, but I seduced a sleazy security guard into giving me access to their files. Anyway, watch this."

It was a collage video comprising three screens, each showing a different angle of the same road just outside the Water Plant. Timestamps occupied the top right corner of the video as the footage played at a fast-forwarded rate. A group of Scheep cars of different colour models—from metallic grey to midnight blue—could be seen driving by.

"There doesn't seem to be anything suspicious here, right?"

Ogaman nodded in agreement. Lizzie pinched her fingers on the e-Pad screen to zoom in.

"Now, look closely at these images and you'll notice a particular brand of storage packaging, through the glass panel of the vehicle's boot. Mr Store boxes. It turns out this brand specialises in packaging highly reactive chemical substances. Seems a little odd to be taking these to a Water Plant, doesn't it?"

"Yeah, that's a bit booky, still."

"Take a peek at the footage now. This collage shows when the same cars are leaving several minutes later. As they depart from the premises, the Scheeps are no longer carrying the boxes. So, what could dozens of different cars be transporting in chemical storage containers?"

"Do you know for certain who's driving these cars, though?"

Lizzie paused the video and opened another file on her e-Pad.

"Well, I ran licence plate searches and couldn't verify any of the vehicles. The plate numbers didn't exist! But I can show you records of lump-sum payments made by the same London local councils to the car wholesale company, Cardican PLC. The rental period for most of these vehicles ends in two days, suggesting something important will happen this evening."

Lizzie proceeded to scroll through dozens of invoices to show her evidence to Ogaman.

"Transactions authorised by using stamps from the boroughs of Tower Hamlets, Newham, and Hackney. Usually alongside another 'DSU' logo stamped at a later date too."

"Why would dem man use cars though, and not vans or lorries?"

"My theory is that using cars would make their distribution much more difficult to stop, especially if any entities wanted to sabotage them," Lizzie said, gesturing to Ogaman. "Luckily though, I'm a smarty pants, so it didn't fool me!"

Ogaman couldn't stop himself from chuckling.

"So, do you know what those DSU symbols stand for?"

"I haven't figured that part out yet. But I would guess that it represents the specialist government organisation managing the project."

There was silence as Ogaman came to grips with the scale of the operation. It endured for long enough that the backlight on Lizzie's e-Pad automatically switched off, plunging them both into utter darkness—a symbolic void given the gravity of the situation. He felt scared. He felt uncertain. He felt overwhelmed.

But I'm committed to this now. There's no going back.

Ogaman took a deep breath.

"Thanks for helping me with this, Lizzie. I'm gonna dash over to the Water Plant now to investigate. If I find anything dodgy, I'll let you know and do my best to stop it."

"Are you sure, Ogaman? You could get really hurt. Or worse..."

"I know, but I signed up for this. Besides, what are my alternatives? My au–" he almost slipped up. "My *answer* is that people have died at the hands of these scum, so I need to settle the score. If anyone has the power to stop them, it's me."

Lizzie's arms unexpectedly wrapped him in a warm embrace. To Ogaman's surprise, he felt a great deal of compassion radiating from her as she started crying.

"Thank you too, Ogaman. I appreciate this on a personal level."

"It's okay. What are you saying though?" Ogaman asked while letting go of Lizzie's embrace. "Don't you think they're gonna come after you for accessing their shit?"

"Yes, and that's precisely why I'm leaving the city tonight. And the country very early tomorrow morning. I don't know where I'll settle, but I'll be using an advanced VPN to connect with the right people and continue publishing content wherever I'm hiding."

"Wow, that's proper brave of you."

"Not as brave as you, though! Besides, I'm a journalist who believes in sharing the *real* news for *real* people."

"I feel you, still," Ogaman responded with a nod. "Anyway, I'm gonna rush to the Water Plant now. You stay safe out here."

"And you be safe, too," Lizzie said, as Ogaman vaulted onto a nearby lamppost. "Good luck!"

Chapter 37

As thunder roared and rain poured down upon the streets of London, the lightning illuminated the iconic skyline to the west. On the rooftop of a nondescript building in Limehouse, Tundé removed his mask, revealing his face to the storm as he gazed pensively into the distance and steadied himself.

I just pray that Olodumare is with me...

After a few minutes, Tundé put his balaclava back on and leapt swiftly from building to building, headed straight for the Water Plant in Wapping. The teenager was anticipating the toughest battle of his life. While Ogaman was unsure about what awaited him, he knew that meddling with a government operation carried a potentially fatal risk.

He eventually landed on a concealed rooftop in Shadwell, just two miles from his destination. Ogaman checked the time on his phone. It was twenty minutes past ten. However, his attention was drawn to the notifications that flashed across the screen:

'6 messages from Laura Thompson'
'10 missed calls from Laura Thompson'

"I fucked that right up. Maybe I can get things back on track with her once I take care of this *minor* genocide issue."

Thinking deeply about all the possible ramifications prompted him to send a voice message to his mum.

"I love you, Mum. See you soon."

He switched his phone off and continued his journey.

"Ogaman! We love you!" a junkie declared loudly from an alleyway down below. "Keep sticking it to those drug dealer bastards for ripping us off!"

At his core, though, Ogaman couldn't accept the praise. He didn't feel worthy of the 'hero' title. A heavy weight of guilt pressed down on him for using his powers so irresponsibly. His actions had sent his auntie to an early grave, and now he was grappling with constant flashbacks of Vince's spinal cord being ripped, driven by Ogaman's manic desire for revenge.

You've gotta stay focused, bruv.

Ogaman slowed down a few minutes from the Water Plant, keen to assess the risks from a safe distance before bursting onto the scene. He was on a commercial building about eight storeys high. Laying flat on its rooftop, Ogaman crawled militantly towards the edge to inspect the streets below. There was no foot traffic, but under the light of the streetlamps, he noticed two cars driving by slowly. Using his superhuman eyesight to scrutinise more closely, Ogaman recognised the vehicles.

They're the same model of Scheeps that Lizzie showed me earlier.

He couldn't identify the people in the Scheeps, but both were full of passengers and stocked with Mr Store boxes. Ogaman punched his fist vigorously into his open palm.

I'm putting bare of these man to sleep tonight!

Once the cars drove a comfortable distance away, Ogaman sprinted across the roof, using his momentum to leap onto a taller building ahead. He was only a couple of streets away from the Water Plant. Poking his head over its ledge gave Ogaman a much clearer view of the Water Plant and its surroundings.

A large metal fence with a threatening mesh of barbed wire spanned the entire Plant. His eyes picked up micro-sparks, suggesting it was electrified too. The grounds were filled with clusters of green bushes and overgrown weeds that seemed to have claimed ownership over the ageing facility. Four faintly lit floodlights were evenly spaced around the grounds, piercing the night sky and casting eerie shadows by the overgrowth. The main Water Plant building was in the centre of the grounds. It was dim and grey in colour, with a small amount of intricate pipework surrounding it. Ogaman also spotted a dark garage door on the side of the main building.

That's probably where they took the bairaff through. That might be my best way in.

The lack of activity on the premises was concerning, but he thought the Scheeps driving by were no coincidence. Ogaman headed decisively for the Water Plant. Cloaked by the night sky, he slid down the commercial building's wall and acrobatically leapt onto another low-rise building, then flipped onto the street level to land perfectly on his feet. He quickly took refuge behind a red car parked alongside the street adjacent to the Water Plant.

Jumping over this fence could make me too bait too soon. Or could get me electrocuted.

Examining a section of the fence that would be undetectable by the human eye, Ogaman spotted that its electrical wires were arranged in a particular way. He recalled one of Mr Panther's Physics lessons.

Looks like the electricity is connected through a series circuit. If I cut that middle wire, it should cut off the power to this section of the fence, still.

Ogaman picked up a sharp stone from the ground and crept to the fence. The wire made a faint, metallic hum as he cut through it. The resultant sparks and scents of burning metal tingled his senses. He glanced over his shoulder, wary not to be caught in the act. When he finally managed to cut off the flow of power to this section of the fence, Ogaman saw its sparks instantly cease. He used his superhuman strength to yank open a large gap in the iron fence and slid his body through. He was in!

Now the real fun begins.

This section was almost completely engulfed by overgrown bushes, allowing him to hide and reassess the scene. Peering through the leaves towards the garage door a hundred yards away, Ogaman saw two men appear on the grounds. Upon closer inspection, he was surprised at how much they resembled a pair of junkies.

But they're both carrying huge straps.

Ogaman gulped. He had to be extremely vigilant. Their automatic machine guns could inflict a lot more damage than the pistol he was shot by earlier. He tiptoed through the bushes and towards the garage door. But his presence was soon sensed by the armed men.

"Oi, you hear that?"

"Yeah, I heard something. Go have a look."

"Okay. Cover me."

The first man walked into the bushy area, machine gun at the ready. With little delay, Ogaman smacked his wrist to disarm him, and then he repeatedly boxed the guard into a coma.

"Mate, you alright over there?" his accomplice called out to the bushes after hearing the rustling. He was met with silence. "Alright, I'm coming in."

Ogaman sprung out of the bushes to kick the gun out of the accomplice's hands, following up with a ferocious swipe to the temple that sent the second guard crashing to the ground.

Aaand he's out for the count!

Arriving at the garage door, Ogaman carefully probed it with his palm. Its coarseness scratched against him. The door was made from robust, reinforced metal and bashing through it would create significant noise. Ogaman stared at his hands, trying to make his talons emerge again so he could cut through the door instead. But nothing happened. Out of nowhere, a buzzing sound arose.

Yo, what's that?

Peering over his shoulder, Ogaman was startled by the sight of a man-sized drone hovering above him. Before he could react though, the drone shot out a ropey, webbed material that forcefully encapsulated him, leaving only his head and feet unwrapped. He desperately tried to break free, but the webbed material was remarkably stiff.

"ARRGGHH!" Ogaman shrieked as the drone electrocuted him through the circuitry lined within the mesh of the trap.

The pain was excruciating. It sent tormenting shockwaves through his body, disrupting his cognitive functions and throttling his anxiety. When it stopped and Ogaman's general awareness slowly returned, he realised that he was being suspended high in mid-air by the drone above the main Water Plant building.

"What the fuck man? Who's doing this? AARRGGGHHH!"

A panel in the roof split open and the drone descended through it while repeatedly zapping Ogaman's body, keeping him subdued.

"Aha, our guest of honour has finally arrived!" a posh, smug voice could be heard.

Still writhing in pain, Ogaman squinted his eyes open to take in the new surroundings. The interior of the Water Plant was a complicated maze of industrial units. He felt the warmth of the moist air and the vibrations of the machinery beneath his feet. It created a subtle hum in the background and indicated the wealth of energy this facility held. There was an imposing pump at the centre of the building. An intricate network of tubes extended from its large frame, connecting with four huge, industrial-sized pipes, each located in a designated quadrant of the expansive Plant. These pipes were also covered with chamber doors.

"Welcome, Mr Ogaman," the smug voice continued as the vigilante was being lowered.

Carrying on with his observations, Ogaman noticed staircases going from the ground level up to a raised platform that lined the inner walls of the Plant. It allowed access to the chamber doors for the four pipes. There was also a deep water bath on the ground level. Its bubbling suggested a vital function to the facility, as the sounds mingled rhythmically with the other mechanical noises.

"I'm so pleased you could join us this evening."

Ogaman soon identified the speaker. It was a man dressed in a tailored, three-piece pinstripe suit with a pristine, polka dot pocket square. He was standing by the water bath with two men, both also dressed in smart attire. Glancing around, the vigilante registered that dozens of men were moving frantically around the Plant while loading barrels, pushing carts, and transporting machinery. Most of them switched their attention from their jobs to revel in the sight of Ogaman captured by the high-tech drone.

Why are all these man dressed like junkies too?

"You've arrived at the perfect time," the smug man added. Ogaman assumed that he was the leader of this operation.

"Who the fuck are you, bruv?" Ogaman barked as he tried to wriggle himself out of the webbed trap.

"Ooo, touchy touchy, Mr Ogaman. I thought your mother would have taught you some manners. Maybe you wouldn't find yourself in this situation if she did!"

He looked expectantly at his two sidekicks and the other workers, encouraging them to join in with his laughter. They awkwardly followed suit.

"I'll follow my own advice and offer you some politeness. We already know who you are, Mr Celebrity. You've got yourself plastered all over the media, after all! While I shouldn't be sharing this with people like you, my name is Chris. I'm a Director at the Discreet Services Unit—or DSU for short. We work on specialist government projects to deliver on our mission of national prosperity by–"

"Killing helpless people just tryna survive!" Ogaman raged. "You're a fucking piece of shit!"

"And this, everyone," Chris gestured at the vigilante while addressing his colleagues, "is why our mission is so important. To elevate our society from these less-developed people that we see in front of us today."

The room murmured fervently. Chris turned to the man standing to his left.

"Harry, why don't we teach our guest that there are punishments for misbehaviour?"

Harry, the secret Metropolitan Police informant, gave Chris a nod and pressed some buttons on the radio controller in his hands.

"As you wish, boss."

"ARRGGHH! ARRGGGHHH!" Ogaman's agonising screams pierced the air.

It felt as though a thousand razor-sharp needles were scraping against his skin. The intensity of electric shocks was surging to unbearable levels.

"Have more respect when you're speaking to me, Mr Ogaman," Chris's voice deepened, projecting authority. "Understood?"

"Err, boss. Don't you fink we should be moving on wiv fings?"

"Steve, there's a reason I joined the Footlights during my final year at Cambridge. I'm a showman! This is who I am. Don't take me out of my element again."

"Sorry, boss. Got it."

"Good. As I was saying before you rudely interrupted me, Mr Ogaman. My DSU team are very professional at ensuring our stakeholders in government and major corporations get their objectives met. Which, if necessary, does require violent measures. Harry, again please."

Harry increased the voltage on his radio controller.

"ARRGGGGHHH! ARRRGGGGHHHH!" Ogaman screamed at an even higher pitch.

"Oh, I shouldn't be enjoying my job *this* much!" Chris said, laughing hysterically.

Ogaman couldn't handle the torture for much longer. But finding a way out of his trap had proven virtually impossible. He needed to think of another solution. Fast.

"Orí laá kọ́, kí a tó kọ́ ara,"[1] he remembered a Yorùbá proverb from one of Uncle Blessing's training sessions. Ogaman tried to focus on his breathing to relax his mind amidst the chaos. While it didn't seem like much, it was all he could work with.

---

1. *"The head is corrected before the body,"*

If I can get my claws out again, maybe I can cut through this...

"Mr Celebrity, since you're clearly such a clever lad," Chris uttered sarcastically. "Your little adventures on the streets must have given you a glimpse into our plans, right?"

Ogaman ignored him.

"Well, the good news is that your suspicions were probably correct. The bad news? We've been preparing for your intervention."

Chris waited for a response. Ogaman tried his best to stay concentrated, but his curiosity soon got the better of him.

"How did you know I'd be coming?"

"It was only a matter of time. In this line of business, Mr Ogaman, you either get what you need. Or, you die trying. But I get paid—and revered—for my exceptional tactical acumen. I know what to expect. I know how to strategise. And I'm ready to execute at a moment's notice."

Ogaman redirected his attention inwards. While it was challenging, he knew that once Chris was satisfied with his grandiose monologue, the DSU were going to kill him.

I've just gotta keep going.

"Because you've been such a wonderfully attentive guest, I'll reveal what's happening here tonight before we exterminate you. This Plant was redesigned decades ago for its present purpose of supplying water to CCA areas exclusively. We have 300 tonnes of Odabozite Trioxide ready to pour into the four water pipes servicing these CCA homes across London. And it's been adjusted to seep through their pores and react with the Novabond. The beauty is they won't even have to consume it! Our estimations suggest we have enough bairaff to exterminate close to 90% of that undesirable population within 72 hours."

Suddenly, Ogaman felt sharp tingles on his fingertips.

"And you think you're gonna just cover this whole thing up?" he asked, intending to keep Chris talking and buy himself more time.

"Oh, don't you worry about that, Mr Ogaman. Why do you think my squad are dressed like typical drug addicts? Why do you think we have hitmen tracking the relatives of the top journalists in the country? We are in control of the narrative!"

Chris held his hands high out in front of him.

"I can see the headline now: Addicts Unleash Deadly Horror on London's Poor in Water Plant Chaos. Then we will move on to the next phase of the mission with our main stakeholders, NikoTech Inc. In case you hadn't noticed, they designed that drone just for you!"

Ogaman peered up and saw the company's distinct 'N' logo faintly printed on the drone's underside.

"Let's just say that NikoTech has extensive plans to replace the absence of the undesirables soon, which will launch the dawn of a flourishing era in Britain."

While Ogaman grasped the extent of the situation, he locked eyes with Chris, who gave him a devious smile.

"Yes, I know. I do my fucking job well."

"Nah, you're actually tapped," Ogaman said with disgust. "You bad mind prick!"

"I don't know what all that bastard English means, but thank you! We are very fascinated by you as a specimen, Mr Ogaman. My hunch is that the Yorùbá wizards sent you here after we raided the bairaff, which perhaps you may have used as a power source too. But instead of poisoning you, it has extended your capabilities far beyond any human we've ever studied."

"Suttin' like that," said Ogaman dismissively as the talons slowly broke through the flesh of his fingertips.

Come on, come on... I'm running out time...

"Whatever it is, we will learn how and why. Because when we drain the life out of you, we're going to ravage your corpse like an organ harvesting."

Chris's entire being struck fear into Ogaman's heart. Even with faith in his superpowers, the raging darkness under the DSU director's calculated demeanour sent chills down his spine. Harry then pressed a button on the radio controller again. Despite the severe jolt of electrocution, Ogaman's raspy voice tried to assert himself.

"That's funny... because... I'm gonna... fuck you up... before you... can even... try..."

"Oh, look at him go, everyone! I love the threats, keep them coming!"

Chris was thoroughly entertained, and his squad were quick to join him with inauthentic chuckles this time.

"Boss, not tryna butt in 'ere," Steve said tentatively, "but I thought we need to go for that meeting soon?"

"And I thought I told *you* not to fucking interrupt me when I'm in the middle. Of. My. Speech!"

"You're right. Sorry, boss."

"Last thing, Ogaman. Our scientists have been modifying the Odabozite Trioxide's chemical structure, as you know. With this new refined formula, we can tap into all its benefits, with an extremely delayed onset of the degeneration process. We call it our *Elite Enforcer Elixir*. The initial tests have been promising. But now, we have a liquid version that is ten times more powerful than any batch we've ever created."

Chris presented a bottle filled with reddish-purple liquid up high for the teenage vigilante to see.

"In other words, even if you somehow escape from your contraption, you aren't getting out alive today!"

"Bullshit!" Ogaman said, continuing to stall the conversation.

"Oh, you must not be as smart as I gave you credit for, Mr Ogaman," Chris said disdainfully. "Surely after your little skirmish with our test patient earlier, you would think it was possible?"

Ogaman instantly saw visions of his fight with Vince.

That elixir ting must be what made him so strong!

"We won't make the same mistake with this bloodclaat again, Chris."

"President B!" Ogaman called out angrily.

He recognised the bold figure as he entered the vicinity, walking directly to Chris. They shook hands while having a short embrace.

"I see that you're already well-acquainted with each other, how wonderful," Chris said in jest. "Prez, I'm disappointed that you didn't kill him for me earlier as promised. Please ensure you do everything in your power to stop him from threatening the success of our project. Am I clear?"

"Sure ting, guv," Prez replied.

"The helicopter will be ready soon, boss," Harry interjected, still holding the radio controller while keeping his eyes cruelly locked on Ogaman's trapped body. "You want me to give him the full voltage?"

"Yes, do it," Chris replied, turning his attention back to the vigilante. "Well, Mr Ogaman, it's been a pleasure. Farewell, and I'm sure you'll be meeting plenty of your fellow Isle of Dogs residents wherever you go next. Spiritually, of course."

Those words knocked the wind right out of Ogaman. His heart began throbbing intensely, and he was shaken to the core.

How does this prick know which ends I'm from? That's way too close to home. And mum. And Uncle Blessing.

"You're chatting shit, fam."

"Bingo!" Chris blared with a malicious laugh. He then signalled to Prez. "You're in charge here now. We're leaving in the helicopter to meet that arrogant bastard, Russell. Please ensure the bairaff is ready to load into the water supply."

"Got you, Chris. I'll take care of everything from here," Prez responded, eyeing Ogaman with distaste. "Our teams have got most of the barrels in position now. We'll be ready to turn off the mains and load the water supply in six minutes."

"Marvellous! So, what are you waiting for, Harry? Shock our wonderful guest into oblivion!"

Harry obliged by pushing the voltage modulator again.

"ARRGGHH! ARRGGHH!" Ogaman screamed violently, as the top voltage put him in a state of excruciating paralysis.

The entire DSU squad was watching, bridling with excitement that their most dangerous threat was soon to be terminated. Harry pressed another button, signalling the drone to descend towards the bubbling water bath. Ogaman growled desperately as he tried to make his talons grow faster.

Oh shit, they're gonna fry me in there! I need to get out!

Chris, Harry and Steve began climbing a spiralled stairway on the side of the building that led to the rooftop, where their helicopter was waiting. Halfway up though, Chris stopped in his tracks and turned back.

"On second thoughts, I'd like to witness his last breath from here. Something tells me it could be quite entertaining."

Now or never, Tunds...

Ogaman was now so close to the water that he could feel the splashes from its bubbles. He used every fibre in his body to push past the painful electrocution. With less than a metre between himself and the bath, his talons had finally finished forming!

"Can't you drop that thing any quicker, Harry?" Chris asked uneasily.

"Going as fast as I can!"

"He should be up in 'eaven in no time, boss!" Steve exclaimed.

"BANG!"

A loud explosion reverberated through the Water Plant as the electrified drone trap plunged into the bath, igniting an explosive display of sparks. Water plunged into the air and the building filled with dense clouds of black smoke.

"Well, that should be that!" Harry said gleefully.

"Let's wait for the smoke to clear," Chris said bluntly. "I want to see his floating corpse with my own two eyes."

All the DSU operatives waited with anticipation as the smoke dissipated. A short few seconds later, they could make out the frazzled, webbed trap floating away in the middle of the water bath.

"Where is he?" asked Prez with confusion.

Suddenly, appearing through the smoke that swallowed up the premises, a dark figure stumbled across as the soaked, debris crunched loudly beneath his feet.

"Wagwan."

Ogaman was dangerously close to a fatal end, but just before his toes touched the water, he cut open a large enough gap for his arms, then swiftly launched himself out of the trap and away from the bath. But a stray bolt of electricity struck Ogaman, leaving him significantly hurt.

"For god's sake, Harry!" Chris snapped furiously. "Prez, make sure our men are ready to load the water tanks when the mains are switched off. And make sure our intruder DOESN'T GET AWAY!"

"You heard the boss, lads," demanded Prez. "Go fuck my man up!"

A group of fifteen DSU agents assembled quickly as they approached the weakened Ogaman with their arsenal of weapons: fists, knives and pistols. At a glance, he noticed that the rest of the agents were hastily preparing the last few barrels of bairaff for loading into the water supply. With so many variables to consider, the wounded vigilante faced an immense challenge.

Before he could make a move, the agents opened fire. Ogaman used his sparse energy to narrowly evade the bullets. A group of five agents then broke off and rushed towards him. Surprised by their willingness to engage in hand-to-hand combat, he was soon on the defensive, parrying the punches and kicks that came at him from all directions.

These man proper know how to fight, Ogaman thought while one of the agent's boots came within a nanometre of connecting with his cheek. At that moment, the self-healing process kicked in. Turning the tide, Ogaman used his building advantage to quickly knock out the five agents with martial arts combos, striking the fifth agent's temple with a devastating hook.

Alright, I'm tapped in. Ten more agents here to go...

Based on his timekeeping, Ogaman had three minutes left before the water supply contamination would commence. Six more armed DSU men faced up to him, half with knives and half with pistols. Sprawling into action, he disarmed and took down the knife-wielding DSU agents, then used their weapons like heat-seeking darts to incapacitate the gun-toting agents.

"ARGHHH!"

"FUCK!"

"BLEUURGGHH!"

Loud cries echoed through the Water Plant as the knives found their marks with pinpoint accuracy, piercing each agent's face in a gory fashion.

"Jheeeze!" Ogaman shouted with excitement at his progress. "I told you man already. I'm not playing any games tonight!"

He was instantly surrounded by the last four agents of this set. But something felt different. They approached him in a calm but intimidating manner. Ogaman was curious. Going on the offensive, he threw a punch at the nearest agent. To his astonishment, the agent blocked his punch and then swiftly countered with a blow to his jaw. Ogaman was rattled and struggled to connect any of his swings, owing to the agile movement of these specific agents. They stepped forward and launched an onslaught of powerful punches and kicks that sent Ogaman tumbling. He backed off, carefully analysing his opponents.

Rah, I think these guys are using Krav Maga techniques.

"We don't invest in premium training facilities for you to dance around with our enemies," Chris blasted from the staircase. "Just kill him already!"

Ogaman had to change his approach, as the few blows he took to the head were already impairing his mental function.

"Almost ready to switch off the mains and get loading, boss!" an agent by the main water pump called out.

A pair of DSU personnel were posted at each chamber door for the four industrial-sized pipes. They were preparing machinery to help them lift the heavy barrels of bairaff.

"Make sure it's done quickly!" Chris commanded.

Ogaman heard the calls and knew that he needed to move quickly too. As he faced up against the Krav Maga-trained DSU agents, he thought of an unusual tactic. In a flash—and to the agents' surprise—Ogaman darted off in the opposite direction, away from the central water pump.

"He's running away," shouted Prez mightily. "Make sure you dead that shook yute!"

Chris was silent, given that the vigilante had proven a difficult task so far. And by no means was Ogaman deserting the battle.

If I trick them into chasing me, their defences may become scattered.

The four Krav Maga-trained agents followed Prez's orders and sprinted after him like cheetahs closing in on a defenceless gazelle. Ogaman briefly glanced over his shoulder at them drawing nearer as he reached a dead end.

I need to get this on point now...

Reaching the wall, Ogaman continued to run dynamically up it using his superhuman reptilian powers. As the agents looked up in confusion, it gave Ogaman just enough time to perform a wall spin down towards the ground. He used the momentum of his leap to claw through the faces of the four agents with his talons, feeling their flesh tear with each swipe of his hand. Blood-curdling screams were heard as the agents dropped to the floor. One by one.

"Jheeeeze!" Ogaman hollered triumphantly, as he navigated the inner workings of the Plant to run to the first industrial-sized pipe a few dozen yards away.

"Prez, you better get a handle on this," Chris ordered sternly. "You know what's at stake here with your child's guaranteed Cambridge admission, after all..."

Prez looked at Chris with a burdened expression. He understood the weight of responsibility to protect the health of their project and their mutual agreement.

"Ogaman!" Prez said loudly. "Have you no respect for your superiors?"

"Fuck you," Ogaman shouted back as he closed in on the first pipe. "I'm not letting you devils get away with this!"

"You won't have a choice!" Prez bellowed.

He gestured to Chris, who held the bottle containing the *Elite Enforcer Elixir*. Chris threw it into his hands.

"As Chris told you earlier, this is the most advanced, refined version of Odabozite Trioxide that has ever been formulated. And I'm ready to test it here, today, on your godforsaken soul. Respect is the last life lesson you're ever gonna learn."

While Ogaman leapt past him and onto the platform, Prez unscrewed the lid, took a deep breath and gulped down the reddish-purple substance. His face instantly grimaced with disgust at its bitter taste, forcing Prez to collapse on his knees.

In the meantime, Ogaman used skilful punch combos to subdue the two agents manning the first set of pipes. Rummaging into his pockets, he pulled out the lighter that he found in the Blackwall Estate car park earlier.

Isn't that fortunate?!

Ogaman set the first batch of ten bairaff barrels on fire. He saw the initial 'W' was engraved on this pipe's chamber doors, presuming that it signified the West London water supply. With three pipes still to go, the East London one was firmly on his mind.

"ARGDHDSFGDGHHDGDHSGH!"

The loud, booming roar engulfed the entire Water Plant, bringing everyone to an immediate halt as they watched the *Elite Enforcer Elixir* aggressively alter Prez's physical makeup. His skin began to ripple and shift, turning into a surreal hue of African Violet. As his frame elongated,

Prez shot up to a towering height of eight feet, causing the grounds of Water Plant to tremble violently. The muscles under his skin swelled to four times their size, eventually tearing through the fabric of his clothes like a force of nature. Caught in a spell of bewilderment, Ogaman stared with terror at the transformation unfolding before his eyes. For the onlooking DSU agents, it was a moment that shattered their understanding of reality.

"AAGGHH! AAGGHH!" Prez continued to scream.

Ogaman's pulse spiked. His chest tightened with each shallow breath. Bearing witness to the birth of the DSU's first official Elite Enforcer had sparked a profound sense of fear.

And I have to fight this thing? Allow it, man...

Many of the DSU agents backed off, doubtful of their own safety around Prez in his unrecognisable form. Chris, on the other hand, bore a smug expression.

"I'm rather impressed with our scientists' work!"

As his violet-hued form continued to evolve, Prez felt the raw power coursing through his veins. The screams that accompanied his metamorphosis fell silent, and he rose to his feet with defiance. An air of terror hung heavily in the Water Plant. Before them stood a towering, muscular behemoth, with fists like large boulders and limbs that resembled mighty oak tree trunks. His facial features had also morphed into something menacing. It was a truly terrifying sight.

"I'm gonna rip you TO PIECES!" Prez roared with spine-tingling intensity as he pointed directly at Ogaman.

"Let's go to our helicopter," Chris advised Steve and Harry. "I think Prez can deal with Ogaman from here, and it's probably going to get rather messy."

They followed him to the top of the spiralled staircase and through its walkway to the rooftop helipad.

Meanwhile, Ogaman's heart was hammering relentlessly against his ribcage. The nerves were overwhelming. But he knew he didn't have time to dwell. Swallowing the lump in his throat, he dashed frantically along the platform to the next set of pipes, feeling dizzy by the prospect that Prez was in hot pursuit. Arriving at the second quadrant, the vigilante swiftly took down the two stationed DSU agents with firm head jabs. Ogaman noticed the 'N' initial etched onto the industrial pipe as he set the bairaff barrels alight.

North London is red... and saved! Two more to go.

A wooshing sound then rumbled throughout the Water Plant, raising his stress levels again.

"The water supply is now off. Teams two and four, initiate the bairaff loading process!" announced a DSU agent.

At both stations, the electric tipper machines hummed to life. They smoothly lifted two barrels at a time. The agents at the remaining stations started pouring the bairaff through the chamber doors and into the water supply. Ogaman charged towards the next quadrant when...

"YOU'RE NOT GOING ANYWHERE!"

A resounding clang reverberated in the air. Ogaman had been flung thunderously to the platform floor. His head was spinning and his vision was blurry. Squinting his eyes to focus, he saw Prez looming over him dauntingly. The purple monster stared barbarously into his eyes with a predatory aura.

"YOU THINK I'm gonna let you get away with YOUR BULLSHIT?" Prez yelled with emphatic force.

"You're gonna have to," Ogaman wobbled as he tried to recompose himself, "cos I ain't backing down, fam."

But he still had goosebumps due to the deep-seated rage emanating from Prez. While the vigilante understood that he wasn't the main catalyst for his anger, it didn't matter because his life was on the line. With no warning, Prez swung his brick-sized fist down at Ogaman. He dodged it at the last second, and Prez's fist smashed straight through the platform's steel floor.

Rah! I'm not tryna get hit by that ANYTIME soon, Ogaman thought in panic, as he backflipped into a standing position and faced his adversary head-on.

"Why are you doing this, Prez? I swear you're from ends too?"

Maybe I can chat to him on a level. Or just buy some extra time to burn the rest of the barrels and get the fuck outta here.

"Because people from the ends only love you when you're the boss," Prez said bitterly. "I used to be a top boy back in the East End."

He pulled his gigantic hand out of the platform floor while Ogaman took an apprehensive step back.

"Cocaine? Weed? Heroin? You name it. I had that shit popping from Brick Lane to Dagenham Heathway."

Prez started walking towards Ogaman with sinister intent.

"The hood boys? Worked for me. Overseas plug? Always picked up my line. Assassins? Did the needful for me. But when you get banged up for a long enough time, the people you thought had your back eventually forget you. And then, you realise you mean absolutely nothing to anyone. I lost my wife while I was in prison, and *nobody* was there for me or my family. They left my kids to fend for themselves, for god's sake! When the DSU said they could end my sentence early to work for them, it was easy to say yes. So why should I give a *FUCK* about anyone from the ends?"

Prez sparked into action and pounced violently at Ogaman, hurling a barrage of punches at him. Ogaman marginally dodged the onslaught from the mammoth fists. The intensity was bubbling as Prez advanced with more venom. Just as one punch was about to land on the vigilante's chin, Ogaman blocked it with his left arm at the last second. An ear-shattering crash rang through the Water Plant. He was in no denial about the raw strength that Prez possessed now.

"I told you... you're not getting rid... of me... easily..." Ogaman strained as he pushed back against the punch.

"Because you're a dumb likkle yute!" Prez bellowed. "How are you gonna stop me in my PRIME?"

He swung his left fist at Ogaman, who blocked it firmly with his right forearm, then retaliated with a swivelling, low roundhouse kick.

"Like that!" Ogaman roared as he popped Prez's left kneecap out of place.

"FUCK!" Prez shot down onto his right knee.

With his adversary temporarily disabled, Ogaman vaulted acrobatically to the adjacent side of the platform, where the third water supply quadrant was located. Using a flurry of jabs, Ogaman effortlessly despatched both DSU agents before they loaded a new set of barrels onto the lifter. Just as he flicked the lighter on though, Prez grappled him from behind before he could set the bairaff barrels on fire.

"You GET back here, Ogaman!"

Meanwhile, the fire from the first two quadrants had slowly inched across the Water Plant's tube network, creating an eerie, orange glow inside. This fiery backdrop set the stage for this intense battle, as its heat and chaos mirrored the turmoil within the building. Prez viciously pinned Ogaman down by the chest, as he roared demands at the DSU agents posted by the fourth quadrant.

"One of you get over here and make sure those barrels are poured into this pipe!"

An agent obeyed and ran over to the third set of pipes, cautiously navigating the growing fire to make his way around the platform. He used the lifter to tip the bairaff into the water supply.

Ah, I'm praying that's not the East London one, Ogaman thought helplessly while trying to survive his relentless grapple with Prez.

Being so close to his nemesis, Ogaman smelt chemical wafts of the elixir radiate from his body. His breath grew fainter by the second from being crushed under the weight of Prez's monstrous physique.

"Are you READY TO DIE?" Prez snarled.

"I'm not... backing down bruv..." Ogaman wheezed.

He closed his eyes and wrestled back vigorously, causing Prez's grip to loosen. That spurred Ogaman to hurl him into the DSU agent operating the barrel lifter nearby. The barrels dropped and rolled along the platform floor towards Ogaman, leaving a trail of purple bairaff powder in its wake. Before he could get his lighter, a flaming piece of metal fell abruptly from the roof truss, instantly setting the barrels alight.

"Oh shit!" Ogaman voiced after realising the true extent of the fire's damage.

It had swallowed up the intricate pipes on the inner walls throughout the building and consumed half of the entire platform. The flames had also engulfed the area by the garage door. Some agents were escaping in panic, as a sweltering wave of heat overcame him.

"This is not good."

In a state of frenzy, Ogaman rushed over to the fourth and final quadrant. He decked the two stationed agents with little resistance. Fortuitously, another large part of the truss fell onto the agents, trapping them under the flaming hot metal. With rips, stains, and wounds exposed through his blood-spattered clothing, Ogaman looked up to the roof with a feeling of gratitude.

"Safe for that."

Burning the final batch of bairaff barrels with his lighter, he saw the initial 'E' scribed at the bottom of the final quadrant's pipe.

"Yeah boy, I did it! I fucking did it!" Ogaman declared triumphantly, barely able to contain his joy.

Now I gotta find Chris. He knows about the Isle of–

Suddenly, Prez thunderously slammed the vigilante out of his thoughts and pummeled him viciously.

"I'M GONNA MAKE YOU REGRET THIS!"

Ogaman's healing powers couldn't keep pace with the devastating punches. It felt like a blizzard of concrete slabs were being launched at him. Each strike resonated loudly like a thunderclap. He tried to hit back, but Prez blocked Ogaman's weak punches with ease and continued attacking him. Eventually, the teenage superhuman collapsed faintly to his knees. Battered and bruised with no time to heal his injuries, Ogaman was almost entirely defenceless. The Elite Enforcer Elixir was amplifying Prez's power as he gained momentum. In contrast, Ogaman was weary and in shock as he desperately tried to endure the savage drubbing.

I... might not... make it... out...

Glancing around hopelessly, Ogaman spotted the water bath still bubbling. His superhuman vision kicked in, allowing him to see the microscopic sparks buzzing in the water.

It's... still... electrified...

While the flames continued spreading, Prez whacked him resoundingly on the temple, propelling Ogaman through the air while blood and sweat oozed out of the rips in his balaclava.

"Aww, is the hero too pussy to fight now?"

Firmly in the ascendancy, the hideous purple monster waltzed casually over to Ogaman. He kicked the vigilante brutally in the midriff, sending shockwaves of pain throughout his entire body. Ogaman coughed up blood, mixed with the taste of smoke that was taking over his respiratory system. He struggled to keep himself from collapsing flat on the floor, as his hands shakily held his body up on the platform floor.

"I'm gonna TEAR you into such TINY pieces," Prez thundered gleefully as he stood over the vulnerable teenager, "that you'll look JUST like the bairaff powder you're so EAGER to destroy!"

Prez bent down and squeezed his enormous, purple right hand around Ogaman's throat while using his left hand to tug Ogaman's right arm forcefully away from his body.

"AAGGHH!" screamed Ogaman breathlessly.

His right arm was separating from his shoulder socket. With the oxygen being cut off from his body, Ogaman glanced down at the electrified water bath again as the fire emblazoned throughout the building. He was in the face of imminent defeat.

"Your àṣẹ is your spiritual power... you have the power within!"

Uncle Blessing's words rang with timeliness in his psyche, as though he were speaking to him in the present. He was in survival mode. It was a fight for his life. He shut his eyes tightly, blocking out the chaos that had captured him. Ogaman delved deep into his soul.

I need to channel my àṣẹ. Inhale as much as I possibly can...

Like a lightning bolt summoning thunder, Ogaman's body began to harness his inner power. Talons emerged from his free left hand. Before Prez realised the danger, it was too late. Ogaman guided a tremendous amount of his dwindling energy to his left arm and slashed Prez across the face. His right eyeball was sliced open.

"AGGGH!"

Prez held his blood-soaked eye, forcing him to release his grip. Now that he had wriggled free of his disorientated enemy, Ogaman stumbled to his feet. With as much force as his weak body could generate, he spun on his tiptoes to build momentum, creating a seismic circular gust that radiated outwards. Then, Ogaman dished out a colossal roundhouse kick directly into Prez's guts. The force of the impact was so intense that the remaining DSU agents felt a strong breeze propagate throughout the Water Plant. His powerful attack launched Prez into mid-air and plunged him uncontrollably into the electrified water bath.

"HELPPP! ARRGGHH! ARGSSGH... ASGH..."

Prez's skin sizzled in the searing temperatures of the water, like a piece of meat in a frying pan filled with oil. The voltage in the bath shook his body violently. Prez's screams were gradually muffled by the water entering his lungs as he dropped further and further below the surface. Before long, the colour of the bath became reddish. Purple chunks of flesh burst up and landed on the surface of the bath, quickly turning the layer into a thick, brownish gunk.

Ogaman panted heavily on his knees as he watched the gruesome display from the burning platform. He was relieved that luck had kept him alive. Just. Despite that, it was hard to feel any joy after witnessing yet another human life lost before his eyes. The flashbacks from the last few weeks came flooding back, making Ogaman taste the bile in his stomach.

"This shit's not easy, man."

While in his state of deep reflection, the flames continued to engulf the building, and its severity soon hauled Ogaman back into the present.

Bruv, I need to bounce quick time.

As he desperately searched for a way out of the Water Plant, a fiery piece of metal dropped onto the platform by his feet, illuminating a stained sheet of glossy paper a few inches away. It caught Ogaman's attention. Still very much injured, he strained to pick it up. It was a photo. Turning it over, his eyes soon widened with distress.

"Oh no... oh, fuck no. No, no, no..."

Ogaman was incredulous. The photo was in a living room with three people cuddled up together on a tanned brown sofa. He instantly recognised Prez, the father who sat between two gleeful children. But it was the twins that sent him into delirium.

"Lorenzo and... and Laura? Oh fuck... oh fuck... ohhh fuck!"

Ogaman was in a state of shock. His head was boiling as the feelings of dread and anxiety intensified.

"Surely not? This can't be right, bruv? What have I done?"

The father of the girl he cared about was dead. Reduced to bits of meat. And it was all down to his choices. Ogaman felt the familiar weight of guilt cast its shadow over him. He remembered how meaningful it was for Laura to open up to him about her family's grief since the loss of her mother. And now, his decisions had made her life even more unbearable. It didn't even matter to him that her father was ready to commit genocide. The teenager had just let down yet another person he cared about.

Laura's an orphan now, and it's all because of me...

While he wrestled with his conscience, the noise of the helicopter's engine came whizzing through to the Water Plant.

"What? They're still here! That bastard Chris is still here!"

Ogaman was seething with anger. His adrenaline levels rose so much that it numbed him to the true extent of his injuries. Peering through the heavy smoke, Ogaman spotted the doorway to access the rooftop helipad. He used his super-strength to launch himself from the platform and jumped straight through the door tumultuously, taking it off its hinges. Now on the rooftop, Ogaman watched as the helicopter slowly ascended above the Water Plant, reaching heights of ten feet. Fifteen feet. Twenty feet. His enhanced hearing tuned into the sound of the pilot speaking on the intercom system.

"We had some difficulties lifting off because of the smoke obstructing our vision, but we're safely airborne now."

Ogaman's eyes were firmly fixed on the flying vehicle as the tears gathered under his mask.

I NEED to catch that helicopter, whatever it takes. For everyone I love!

Consumed by rage, the vigilante used it to push past his body's limits and sprinted powerfully across the rooftop. The cold outdoor air made the hairs on his neck stand up. Just as his toes hit the edge, Ogaman bent his knees and propelled himself up in the air, straining every single muscle fibre in his body to reach his target.

Come on, I'm almost there...

Just as Ogaman stretched his hand out to grab the skid of the helicopter, the door opened.

"Get him!"

Without warning, a double-barrelled shotgun propped out and fired rounds at Ogaman. He acrobatically dodged past the first two bullet clusters in mid-air. But the third round hit him firmly in the stomach and sent Ogaman freefalling back down to the Water Plant.

"Good fucking riddance!" Steve said as he slammed the helicopter door shut.

"Thanks, Steve," Chris said bluntly, face like thunder. "But look at that absolute bloody shitshow down there. It's going to take a lot to explain this all to Russell."

Meanwhile, Ogaman plummeted straight through the roof, crashing onto the hard floor of the Water Plant. The building had transformed into a gigantic fireplace. He was in excruciating pain and sapped of all his energy. While he was rooted to the spot, a few DSU agents fleeing had noticed him.

"Hey, look. It's Ogaman!"

"I know, but we need to get out. This place is gonna blow anyway!"

"But we can make sure he's dead first though."

"Imagine it, we'd be heroes..."

It was like his encounter with the Plaistow Man Dem crew all over again. But this time, the stakes were much higher. As the agents stepped closer though, a loud, whistling disruption entered the building. An imposing cloud had burst through the gap in the roof and unleashed an unorthodox combination of rain, snow and hail—alongside howling winds—to quickly douse the flames. Football-sized hail stones pummelled the DSU agents who remained in the building, rendering them unconscious. The viciousness of the storm drowned out their cries.

A chunk of the cloud dropped down to Ogaman and lifted his depleted body up and out of the building. He felt the cold night air seep beneath his clothing as this mysterious cloud soared through the late night skies of East London. Glancing back towards the Water Plant, Ogaman witnessed the glow of the flames diminishing rapidly with each passing second.

"Who are you? Where are you taking me?" he called out weakly to the cloud, his voice feeble from the injuries.

There was no response. But he decided to trust it since it had just rescued him. Within a few minutes, the cloud had transported him miles away from Wapping and landed in a quiet, residential backstreet. He grimaced with pain while dismounting the cloud and dropped uncertainly onto the pavement.

"Thank you, I guess," Ogaman said hesitantly.

The cloud disappeared into nothingness, as the humming noise of a distant night bus murmured under the otherwise silent evening. It was dark, but there was one street lamp on the road that shone its light on a sign that read:

London Borough of Tower Hamlets: Victoria Park, 100m.

Hidden by the cover of darkness, he stumbled painfully over to the park and locked himself into a disused portaloo cabin just outside the main grounds. The tight space was littered with toilet paper, the bowl was filled with human waste and the stench was dire. But Ogaman didn't care. He was just relieved to find somewhere safe to regroup after such a harrowing evening. Soldiering through pain, Ogaman dug his talons through his bloody intestines to remove the shotgun pellets. His body rattled like a snake's tail, but it did speed up the healing process.

He took his hot, sweaty balaclava off to cool down. It was torn and ripped in several places. But to his surprise, the precious Adeyemi family fabric was still intact. Tundé racked his brain, trying to connect the dots and make sense of everything.

What am I gonna do now? Why did President B have to be Laura's dad? Can I even keep up with the DSU's plans from here?

"Oh shit!" Tundé's voice was dripping with terror. "Chris knows where I live!"

In a state of hysteria, Tundé shot up, slid his balaclava back on and limped out of the toilet. He could never forget the snarky, threatening tone with which the DSU director mentioned the Isle of Dogs. Even though he hadn't fully recovered, Ogaman tried to rush home to defend it. He couldn't bear to imagine what would happen to his family if he didn't. He climbed disjointedly up a residential building on the Old Ford Road. It took him three times longer than usual, but once Ogaman got to the roof, he was presented with a spectacular view of the London skyline. Tapping into his advanced eyesight, he estimated the number of rooftops he would need to jump across to get back to his hometown. It didn't fill him with excitement, especially in his current physical condition.

But it's my responsibility. I have to make the sacrifice.

Ogaman noticed the distinct set of luxury City Lofts apartments illuminating the sky after recognising its beautiful rooftop garden area.

Damn, it only feels like a few days ago that me and Remi were preeing those flats from my living room window...

At the time, their youthful naivety seduced them into believing that bairaff was a route towards the promised land of the wealth and happiness they craved. Whilst it brought some financial rewards, the trade-off was laced with a great deal of misery, grief and burden. It had even forced him to take another human's life. As the sun poked out from beneath the horizon and subtly lightened the surroundings, Ogaman contrastingly felt a deep sense of anguish within.

When he tried to step forward to rush back to the Samuda Estate, a blustery breeze drove him backwards. He tried to forge ahead once more, but another blast of wind returned like an insurmountable wall. With another firm push, the wind put Ogaman on his bum and encircled him.

"Stay... right... here... Baba... Tundé... your... mum... is... safe... I... am... safe..." it whispered. Ogaman breathed a huge sigh of relief, recognising Uncle Blessing's voice instantly.

"But it... is... NOT... safe... to... go... home... now... as... you... may... be... watched..." the wind continued to blow into Ogaman's ears. "Go... to... your... friend's... house... I... will... fetch... you... from... there..."

As the wind subsided, a peaceful ambience was restored to the city's early summer morning. Taking off his mask, Tundé shed tears as he gazed mournfully at the Isle of Dogs. The scent of dew from Victoria Park mingled with the city's dense aura. While it was difficult to accept, life was never going to be the same again.

Chapter 38

"OYA, FIX YOUR TIE, son. It's too short."

"But Uncle, this is how I always wear my tie."

"And so? You want to disrespect your auntie on this very day? Ọmọ, just fix it properly for her sake."

Tundé scowled as he jerked down his tie, adjusting it to align with his belly button.

"Má binu, Babatundé. I'm sorry, I know today is difficult. But by Olodumare's grace, all will be well for our family."

"It's cool, I know you wanna do things the right way. I'm still getting used to how much has changed."

A radio broadcast interrupted their conversation.

"No arrests have been made yet in the Metropolitan Police's investigation into the unexpected arson attack and the murder of Mr Derrick Brian Thompson at the Wapping Water Plant on Friday 21st May."

"Uncle, I beg you turn this off," Tundé said irritably, dialling down the volume on the car radio's centre console.

"Stop Tundé, abeg," Uncle Blessing said, stretching his left hand out to turn the volume up again. "I want to hear what they know, sha."

He was using his right hand to steer the 90s edition Machini Cavalier, which sported an unmistakably vintage design with traditional features such as manual roll-up windows and a boxy frame. The radio continued playing.

"Reports suggest a break-in by rogue drug addicts, led by the street vigilante known as Ogaman. Police are asking witnesses to come forward with any information about the incident or to identify the suspects. The main suspect, Ogaman, is believed to be in his early twenties, between five feet ten and six feet two inches tall and is a frequent visitor to the Isle of Dogs and Canary Wharf areas. The police are also connecting him with the assault of Sean Vincent McCarthy on the same evening, which has left him severely paralysed. It is speculated that Ogaman may have died in the Water Plant fire, but the authorities are still on the lookout."

"See, it's important we heard that, abi? At least they only know small small details. We can be patient and diligent until their search quietens down."

Tundé turned away petulantly and peered out of the passenger window. His gaze was met by endless, bright green trees flanking the narrow country road. The forestry shadowed the road with small spots of the sun's rays slipping through the leaves to add some glow. The warm sunlight reflected off the car's window, giving Tundé's skin a pleasant, tingly sensation. The radio broadcast continued playing.

"A spokesperson for the Home Office said they are investigating the Water Plant fire as a matter of urgency. Amongst the wreckage, detectives uncovered large quantities of burnt Odabozite Trioxide—also known as bairaff—on the scene. The reason for its presence is yet to be understood, but an answer to that question is a large focus of the ongoing investigation. The London Water Council could not be reached for comment. That's all for the news. It's the weather next on MBD—Managing Britain's Dialogue."

Tundé kissed his teeth.

"These politicians are always gassing man. They've *been* knowing why the bairaff was there!"

"It seems so."

"Anyway, I've been struggling a lot with all these changes, Uncks."

"I understand, o. But change is a constant in this life. It wasn't easy for us to leave London as we did, but it wasn't safe for us to stay either. At least for now. How are you finding the new place?"

"It's alright. I don't *love* the countryside, but it's better than sleeping on the streets. Just wish more people like us lived here so I wouldn't feel as isolated."

"I know. But for now, we must be extremely cautious and keep our current residence hidden from everyone."

"Pardon my French, Uncks. But it all just feels shit."

Uncle Blessing shook his head, as he clicked the car's indicator and turned onto another country road.

"Pardin you! Listen, I know it's not easy. But we have to lay low. We're staying near that airport just in case. My weakening powers won't take us far enough. Speaking of airports, we will sort out your Nigerian passport soon. I know someone official at the High Commission who can fast-track us. It's in that Enbanking place, abi?"

"You mean Embankment, Uncle?"

"Ehen, that's it. Embankment. I will arrange that soon, sha."

Tundé stared out of the passenger window again to reflect. He had become more accustomed to the growing steeliness in his heart, fuelled by all the traumatic events of the past few months.

"What for that friend, Oremidé? Is he coming today?"

"Yeah, Remi should be coming. But things will be awkward since that whole thing at his yard."

“I wish I collected you from your friend’s house before you ran to Barking.”

“I know. I was just bare paranoid. Since I left his house, our friendship has drifted apart. It’s mad though cos we’ve been boys for so long.”

“Well, as we say in Naija. Twenty friends cannot play together for twenty years. I’m just happy we found you out there eventually, sha.”

“Same, Uncks. Being out on them streets alone was harder than I could’ve imagined. I saw some dreadful things. Things I’d rather forget.”

“It’s a shame that happened to you, Babatundé. But maybe it was a valuable lesson in patience. Did you hear from that newspaper woman?”

“Nah, I haven’t heard from Lizzie since that night. But they were hunting her down. I hope she’s still alive.”

The car started to slow down as it approached a T-junction further ahead.

“And what about your girlfriend? What was her name, Lauren?”

“Laura.”

Tundé corrected Uncle Blessing with so little emotion that it even caught him by surprise.

“I called her on VizChat with a random SIM after we left London. She was so angry that I went AWOL after missing our date. But she’s completely devastated about her dad. To make it even worse, she despises Ogaman with all her soul. She thinks that he mercilessly killed her dad. But she doesn’t know how prepared Prez was to wipe innocent people! It’s such a messed-up situation.”

“That one is far from easy, o.”

Uncle Blessing turned the car right at the T-junction as they continued the journey to their destination in a nearby market town. However, the traffic had slowed down. Further ahead, numerous police vehicles were parked up as officers patrolled the side of the road. They were performing random vehicle searches.

"Shit!" Uncle Blessing blurted out, shocking his nephew in the passenger seat. "Sorry, I wasn't expecting them to be here. Please tell me you didn't bring your suit with you, Oga?"

"Erm, Uncks, I may have screwed up..." Tundé uttered with a quiver as he gestured to the boot.

"Olodumare help us! Oh dear. Okay, just don't do anything sudden, jor! Let me deal with this."

Their fearfulness skyrocketed. The tension in the car heightened as the wheels bumped along the road and approached the police checkpoint. An officer used a handheld device to scan the vehicle from afar. He glared at the car and then turned to a supervisor. The supervisor paused to assess the device screen and scrutinised the Machini Cavalier.

Oh no, this could be it.

After a few seconds, the supervisor pulled a disinterested face. He shook his head, prompting the initial officer to waive their car through. Uncle Blessing breathed a sigh of relief as they drove past the busy checkpoint.

"Phew! I was on my edge with that one, sha!"

Tundé's heart was still pounding incessantly as he tried to calm himself down.

"You're telling me, Uncks."

A heavy silence settled in the car as they continued driving through the winding country streets into the town, while the revelation of their new lifestyle hung in the air like an unspoken truth.

***

"Let's all look back and wonder, HOW I GOT THROOOUGH THIS! How I got THROOOUGH THIS, how, I, got, throoough this. Let's all look back and wonder, how I got throoough this!"

The choir sang beautifully in the background as the guests arrived for Abiola Ọṣun's funeral. The magnificent, old Victorian church was located in the affluent town of Crowborough, far from the capital.

"Auntie Abi always had this weird fondness for the countryside, Uncks," Tundé explained while the guests filtered into the main congregation area. "I never understood why, but Mum and Mama Fulham said this would be the best place to give her a final send-off."

Tundé was dressed in a black two-piece suit, crisp white shirt and a satin black tie, while most of the adults at the service donned traditional Nigerian attire. Still grappling with the circumstances of the occasion, the teenager's face filled with tears as he processed the altar was carrying his auntie's coffin. Uncle Blessing consoled him.

"Pẹ̀lẹ́," he said, taking his nephew aside, "I know this isn't easy."

Tundé nodded as he sobbed uncontrollably. He tried his hardest to avenge Auntie Abi, but still didn't feel he had done enough to redeem himself.

"Babatundé, don't worry about the speech. We will understand if you would prefer not to do it."

Tundé shook his head sideways as he wiped his tears.

"It's okay. I would never forgive myself if I shied away from honouring her now, as promised. I got this one."

Uncle Blessing put a supportive hand on his nephew's shoulder.

"Do whatever you need to do. I'm proud of you anyhow. You are becoming a true Yorùbá warrior. Some might say a king in the making."

Tundé gave him a trying smile. He really appreciated having an incredible mentor and emotional ally by his side.

"Thank you, Uncle. For everything. I mean it. I'm gonna speak to Auntie Abi for a bit before I start my speech."

Uncle Blessing gave him an affirming nod. As Tundé walked down the aisle past the various sorrowful faces of the funeral assembly, a familiar voice called out to him.

"Yo, Tunds."

"Man like Remi," Tundé embraced Remi, who wore an all-black suit, shirt and tie. "Thanks for being here, bro."

"My condolences again. I still can't believe all this. It's just a mad one to deep."

"I know, man. I know. But I'm trying my best to be strong. What you been saying anyway?"

"Bro, can't lie, now that GCSE exams have started, my mind's just proper focused on that. By the way, how comes you missed the English exam last Thursday?"

"Oh yeah," Tundé remarked, remembering that he rested his head against a Barking & Dagenham council bin to catch up on sleep that day. "I had some stuff I needed to do man."

"Oh swear down?" Remi said with a hint of judgment. "Fair enough, bro."

"By the way, I'm sorry I left your yard silently like that. When I greet your mum later, I'll apologise to her too."

"It's cool now, I guess. My parents just found it bare disrespectful. And we were proper worried about you considering you were hurt. Glad you're safe now, though."

I wish I felt safe.

"What's Jerry been saying anyway?"

"He's good, man. Still laying low though. Especially now there's a bairaff drought on the ends."

"Yeah, that makes sense. Say wagwan to him for me. Anyway, I need to go up and prepare for my speech. I'll chat to you in a bit."

"Ite, good luck with the speech, my guy. You've got this."

The teenagers fist-bumped before parting ways. As he walked to the altar, Tundé saw Kwame arrive with his mother. He waved at them earnestly as they took their seats in the congregation.

It's good to see people from ends here.

Moments later, Tundé was called upon again.

"Ah, my son!" His mum said, wasting no time giving him a massive hug, getting her tears all over his blazer as her Yorùbá gèlè headpiece smacked against his face.

"Good afternoon, Mum. Inú mi dun lati rí yin![1] How are you?"

"Ah, so Uncle Blessing has been teaching you some Yorùbá? You need to work on your accent, but I'm glad you are trying, sha!"

"Thank you."

"How are you now that you're staying with your uncle?"

"It's good, Mum. Sorry, I know it must be stressful. Pardon the pun, but having him around has been a blessing. I feel like he's preparing me to become a proper man. Anyway, how are you doing?"

"I'm alright, now. It feels very strange that you are away, though. But I must thank God that Brodah Blessing has been here to guide you and be a voice of reason. He's your Olubawi."[2]

"Amen to that."

"And Tundé, I'm proud of you for taking the stage today. I would love to but... th-th-this hurts me so much!"

---

1. *I'm happy to see you!*

2. Yoruba expression for "a teacher" or "one who guides"

As his mum started bawling, Tundé felt his eyes welling up again. But he fought them back and hugged his mum tightly, then gently rubbed her arm.

"It's going to be okay, Mum. I promise."

Deep down though, Tundé couldn't guarantee it. Despite thwarting Project Pareto, he was now battling with an underlying anxiety from being uncertain about the DSU's next move.

The teenager ascended the small set of stairs up to the altar where Auntie Abi's coffin rested. Its surface gleamed with a sheen of light brown paint, reflecting the glow of the chapel's lights. The woodwork had intricate carvings of delicate flowers and vines, a testament to the craftsmanship. The family chose to keep the casket closed during the ceremony, anticipating that the emotional toll of confronting her lifeless body would be too much for their family and friends to bear. As he stood beside the coffin, Tundé took a deep sigh.

"Auntie Abs, how you doing my g?" Tundé asked softly, as if he were expecting a response. There was silence. "I know you're still kinda with us. I feel you with me every single day. And I'm never gonna stop until I get you proper justice. I just want you to know that I'm sorry. I'm sorry for chasing the fast money. I'm sorry for selling bairaff. I'm sorry for putting you in danger. This is all my fault, and I just hope everything I do now makes it easier for your spirit to rest and be proud. Wherever the afterlife is."

His tears began falling onto the coffin, tracing a path down its side and into a tiny crevice.

"I miss those times when you'd pick me up from primary school and we'd watch UnicHorn all afternoon until mum picked me up. Remember that time you tried to discipline me after I moved up to Stebon? And we just ended up laughing cos I couldn't take your anger seriously anymore? Haha, good times! And when you'd make that banging jollof rice, but I'd tease you and say it would never be as good as Mum's!"

Tundé used his sleeve to wipe his soaked cheeks, feeling the fabric of his blazer brushing against his skin.

"I also want you to know that I love you. You know that, but I want you to hear it from me. I love you so much, and all I want is for you to remember that. Please forgive me for letting you down. I love you forever. Bless up."

Tundé kissed the coffin, feeling the smooth texture of the gloss on his lips. He made his way toward the stage.

"He-he-he... he-he-he..."

Out of the blue, he heard a loud knock from the coffin. He froze in his tracks and he turned back.

Am I bugging?

Tundé walked back guardedly, his eyes glued firmly on the coffin and the surrounding area. A random drop of water fell from the ceiling and splashed onto the coffin. It led Tundé's eyes to Auntie Abi's framed portrait, which was now flat on its face.

"Ah, that was probably it."

Tundé placed it back on the stand and walked solemnly to the pulpit. After the presiding priest gestured at the microphone, he took a deep breath. A huge gulp projected out to the congregation as he spoke.

"Err, good afternoon, everyone. Thank you for being here with our family this afternoon. I want to say a few words about our treasured sister, auntie and friend. She was a true warrior. Miss Abiola Olubunmi Ọṣun..."

About the author

Dami Edun is a London-born Nigerian author with a professional background in sales, marketing and engineering. A lover of psychology and anthropology, he brings a unique perspective to his stories, exploring the complexities of morality and power. His debut novel, ***Ogaman***, follows the journey of a British Nigerian teenager navigating a dystopian London with newfound superpowers. In addition to writing, Dami creates music under the alias 'DMSTR' and hosts creatives on the Garden of Edun podcast. He also enjoys travelling, salsa dancing, attending Arsenal FC matches and learning Yorùbá.

Instagram / TikTok: @damiedun

YouTube: @TheGardenofEdun

Website: www.damiedun.com